# C.M. O'NEILL

# From Lambs to Lions

*Inspired by true events*

*To the nameless millions who were stolen from their homelands, bound in chains, and subjected to the cruelty of slavery. To those who are enslaved today, whose suffering remains hidden from the world's gaze.*
*This dedication stands as a silent prayer that justice and freedom shall one day be allowed to reign.*

# Contents

# From Lambs to Lions

BY

C.M. O'NEILL

*"... once the storm is over you won't remember how you made it through, how you
managed to survive.
You won't even be sure, in fact, whether the storm is really over.
But one thing is certain. When you come out the
storm you won't be the same person who walked in.
That's what this storm's all about."*

- Haruki Murakami, *Kafka on the Shore*

# Prologue

<br>

*October 3, A.D. 1652*

*To Miss Danielle Van Aard, Cape of Good Hope, AFRICA.*
*From Mr. Sebastiaan De Vries*

<br>

*My Darling Danielle,*

*I'm starting this letter in the middle of my thoughts, for they have no beginning or end. Every thought, every moment, every breath is filled with you.*

*Every day I talk to you, asking your opinion and wanting to hear your thoughts. The other day I did it out loud, and Parmar, my father's old butler, noticed. Though the man judged me out of principle, his disdain for my assumed mental decline was vivid and immediate.*

*My father has passed away peacefully in his sleep, and I was privileged enough to hold his hand in his final moments. The last three months we spent together were an unexpected gift. We'd talked about my mother, a topic I had always fervently avoided, but he knew he held the advantage, and I would not turn away. Whenever there was a tense moment, we would, as always, remark upon the weather and then gradually fall back into more serious matters. He explained his business and the empire he has built. It is impressively daunting and challenging in ways I never thought possible. And we talked about you.*

*I am in the process of purchasing two more merchant vessels, which will arrive later next year. They are called "The Twins" in lieu of proper names. I want you to christen them; it will bring good luck.*

*As everything is settled and under control, I have arranged to depart Batavia in the first week of November. With fair weather and the grace of God, we should reach the Cape of Good Hope by late January. I plan to marry you the moment my feet touch dry land and return here as a happily married couple as soon as we can manage it. Please ready yourself and get your affairs in order. I will not allow anything to stand in our way this time.*

*I live in this colossal house, but I fear it will never be my home until you walk through the door, on my arm, as my wife. You are the very breath in my body, and I will not suffocate a moment longer than I need to.*

*I hope this letter reaches you before I do, but it is of little consequence, for the outcome will be the same.*

*Until I can hold you safely in my arms and say these words to you in person, please remember, I love you today, but not as much as tomorrow and far less than I will after that.*

*Your loving fiancé*
*Sebastiaan De Vries*

# Chapter 1

Like an emerald and sapphire jewel adorns the delicate ear of an elegant woman, so too does the Cape of Good Hope decorate the African continent's southern tip. And just like the precious accessory, it is the wearer that defines it. A mountain, a forest, a beach, and a piece of land that curves to form a bay, not so different from a thousand other places—and yet it competes with no equal and suffers no rival.

However, unlike the Dover Cliffs, the continent does not end abruptly. Instead, it seems to have rushed towards the sea and, at the last moment, changed its mind and came to a stop against itself, creating the flat-topped Table Mountain with its cone-shaped companions on either side.

As the mountain stood guard over all the surrounding splendor, the clever southeast wind found its path around the ridges and valleys and discovered a trick to play on the old sentinel. If it blew hard enough for long enough, it could whip up a blanket of fog so dense it covered the top of the mountain for days. When the wind settled, moisture trickled down the rough sides, like sweat dripping from a weather-beaten face, into the lush green forest, where lions roared in the shadows and hippopotamuses muddied the rivers.

As the forest gave way to the shore, the land curved like a thumb and forefinger, straining to touch but forever fixed apart, forming an alluring bay where boisterous waves pounded the soft white beach.

With such boundless beauty and potential, Africa's jewel unwittingly drew the attention of a commercial giant half a world away in Europe's Amsterdam. The world's largest shipping corporation, the VOC, short for *Vereenigde Oost Indische Compagnie*—the Dutch East India Company, recognized the geographical significance of the perfectly shaped natural harbor, named Table Bay, after the mountain that presided over it.

But the wealthy Dutch traders were not the only ones paying attention. The English and Portuguese also noticed the location, for it was conveniently situated halfway between Europe and Asia. Once established, a settlement could provide fresh food and water to passing merchant vessels.

In 1651, determined not to lose the valuable harbor to anyone else, the VOC dispatched three ships, the *Drommedaris*, the *Reijger*, and the *Goede Hoop*, to fulfill that dream. Many more would follow, but those first three signaled the beginning of a new era for the previously untouched part of the world.

No sooner had the weary passengers set foot on land than a small settlement emerged, with tents dotting the beach and a nearby clearing.

At first, the untamed continent rejected its new inhabitants, sending many days of rain, washing away any attempts at fruit and vegetable gardens. Any foundations meant for future permanent structures, were promptly destroyed. With their fair skins and strange habits, the new inhabitants suffered greatly, for the rains made them sick and miserable. When the land saw that they refused to leave, it sent hurricanes and steered the large herds of antelope far away from the coast. But nothing the ancient continent did could dislodge the fledgling settlement from the virgin soil of its southern tip.

Ten months after stepping onto the African soil, the builders had constructed a fort complete with four bastions and a moat. Several wattle-and-daub buildings were scattered as needed, and fruit orchards and vegetable gardens lay well protected behind their freshly built dikes. Still plagued by hunger and disease, Africa's newly adopted children weren't just surviving any longer; they were starting to thrive.

***

*Dutch settlement, Cape of Good Hope 1652*

A twig snapped with the enthusiasm of a musket shot, disturbing the thin air of the cloudless night. John Van Leyen spun around to glare at his friend for his carelessness, but all he could see was a vague shape behind him. The dark moon cast a pitch-black night.

They'd crept from one tent to the next, avoiding settlers and soldiers alike. It was the perfect night for stealth, but with a dog loudly sniffing each pebble and fallen leaf in its path, stealth was turning into a goal rather than a strategy.

"Shut that damn dog up," Van Leyen hissed under his breath.

Jan Blanx reached down and rested a heavy hand on the mutt's scruff. It ceased its investigations and tensed as if recognizing the weight of the moment. Van Leyen gave the dog a surly look, hoping it would sense his displeasure. However, he knew he was being fanciful, for the witless creature was only good for sensing where its next meal was coming from and not much else.

"Watch your step," he said when Blanx was close enough to hear. The edge of the forest, and the promise of freedom, were less than fifty yards away. But first, they would have to cross the open space behind the fort, where only a few tents dotted the recently cleared area. If they could cover that distance quickly and quietly, they would disappear into the forest without a trace.

"Let's go!" Blanx urged from behind, giving Van Leyen a shove between the shoulder blades.

"Wait," Van Leyen said, looking over his shoulder toward the fort where a fresh guard had just taken up his post on the wall. He walked like he was on the deck of a ship battling high seas, with his confidence fighting for dominance over his feet that just couldn't find a stable spot to stand on. The musket, slung at an awkward angle over his shoulder, seemed to serve as a ballast to his uncertain legs. When finally he found a measure of stability, his chin snapped from his chest, and he turned to face the clearing, swaying slightly in the face of his enthusiasm.

*A cup or five too many at the wedding celebrations,* Van Leyen thought. Even so, he hesitated. A drunk guard's word would still hold more weight than a sober settler's. They stood nearly invisible behind the last tent, so there was no need to tempt fate. All they had to do was wait a moment. The guard would soon grow tired and either leave or settle down for a nap. He was still weighing his options when a burst of raucous singing drew his attention.

*"Be merry my heartsh, and call for your quartsh,*
*and let no liquor be lacking!"*
*We have gold in shtore, we purposhe to roare,*
*until we shent care a packing."*

Every muscle in Van Leyen's body tensed, and he heard Blanx blaspheme as three young men stumbled from the forest, heading for the tents, singing loudly, and leaning into each other for support. The lad in the middle lifted his head toward the guard and gave a mock salute while one of his friends slurred a few lewd insults, his soliloquy tapering off as he became distracted by the half-done-up buttons on his breeches.

"That's going to keep him awake," Van Leyen said as he watched the guard straighten and peer into the dark, trying to identify the revelers.

"If he leans any further forward, he might fall off the wall, and our problem will be solved," Blanx whispered back.

"Who goes there?" the guard demanded, injecting as much authority as he could muster into his voice. The three youngsters only laughed, knowing the dark would keep them from any reprimand in the morning.

"Just shpla- shplashing our boots, General," one offered as the other two continued to serenade the night:

*"There'sh many men get shtore of treasure*
*yet they live like very shlaves:*
*In thish world they have no pleasure*
*the more they have, the more they crave."*

Blanx and Van Leyen remained motionless in the deep shadows waiting for the three drunks to find their tents. Once they did, all would quiet down, and the guard would lose interest. The guards were notoriously heavy drinkers. Hopefully, this one had brought along some fortification to keep him company during his watch. But it was Fly, the settlement's only dog, who created the diversion. Having recognized one of the men as an erstwhile friend who had once shared a meal with him, Fly bounded from their hiding place behind the tent and boisterously raced toward the small group. He did not earn the name because he was swift of foot or elegant, like a bird in flight. Instead, he was named after the bothersome insect that knows few boundaries and gets into everybody's meal when they were not paying attention.

"Now!" Blanx said, pushing into Van Leyen's back.

Clutching their swords beneath their dark coats, the two men sprinted across the last stretch of the clearing, covered by darkness and the ruckus Fly was creating.

Entering the forest was like stepping into another world. Gone was the stench of humans living in close quarters with the barest of amenities, barring the scent of fresh urine still clinging to the night air. The clanging of pots and humming of voices were replaced by stillness and the occasional rustling of leaves; even the breeze had died down.

With the glow of the settlement behind them, the two men pushed forward into the thick blackness.

"It's so dark, I swear I can't breathe," Blanx said, and Van Leyen could hear the slight tint of panic in his voice.

Blanx preferred the open ocean and skies as far as the eye could see. The forest made him claustrophobic, and on a night like tonight, it felt like the walls of the world were closing in. He used to serve as boatswain on the *Goede Hoop,* but was relieved of his position after he and the captain came to blows. The captain was young and foolhardy, and Blanx was drunk. Blanx's performance, however much supported by the crew, had earned him fifty lashes and the loss of his position. The only silver lining in that particular storm was that Captain Turver had insisted on delivering the punishment himself. The young fop's arm was weak though and his shoulders narrow, so that by the eighteenth stroke, his shirt was stained with sweat, and the fire had gone from his spirit. He had tried to hand the whip over to the captain of the guard, but his sailors had cheered him on, and so he had persevered. Blanx was a favorite among the men, and they had done their best to protect him, leaving him with nothing more than a few bloody slashes across his back.

Now the *Goede Hoop* was gone. It had sailed for Batavia with the setting sun that evening, and while her captain was enjoying his wedding night having wed the gardener's daughter only that morning, Blanx was blindly searching his way through the dense forest.

"Hold on to me," Van Leyen whispered. He waited until he felt Blanx's hand on his shoulder, and then, with one arm stretched in front of him, they inched their way deeper into the forest. They had set out in an easterly direction, but with nothing to navigate by, he was relying on pure luck to get them to the river's edge.

As far as escapes went, theirs could be deemed a success. Nevertheless, it was not without its initial obstacles. The night Blanx had mentioned his plan to Van Leyen, they were both lying on their straw pallets in the tent they shared with two young soldiers. Judging by the amount of air the pair were sucking into their bodies, and then expelling in short staccato bursts, it was safe to assume that the two soldiers were fast asleep.

Blanx had had enough. Living conditions at the Cape of Good Hope were testing and pushing each man to his limits. The expedition, littered with good intentions, had started innocently enough. The previous Christmas, three ships—the *Goede Hoop* among them—had set sail from Holland destined for the southern tip of Africa, their aim to establish a halfway station—a haven where Dutch trading vessels en route to India and the Far East could stop to replenish their fresh food and water supplies.

However, after arduous months at sea, their grueling mission was far from over and they immediately set upon constructing a fort and productive gardens. A few more ships followed shortly, bringing precious supplies and more helping hands. However, no one was prepared for the hardship that awaited them. The settlers lacked the required skills for the necessary tasks, and whatever progress was made in constructing the fort and shelters was quickly washed away by one hurricane after the next. They were plagued by no less than three severe storms since their arrival, not including the endless days of rain and wind that dropped temperatures close to freezing. Food was scarce, and with almost no meat, the colony was forced to rely on fish and a few greens to survive.

Dysentery was rampant, and of the one hundred and sixty men that set foot on land, only fifty remained healthy enough to work. The settlers were paid a small salary for their efforts but, for the most part, were treated like slaves with long hours of back-breaking work and harsh punishments for rule-breaking.

"No more bowing and scraping to the governor-all-mighty," Blanx had said.

"He's not so bad." Van Leyen was not an arse kisser, but he could understand the pressures the young governor was under.

"No? The man dropped Pieter from the yardarm. Three times! And for what? A rumor?"

"The governor was afraid Pieter would start an uprising."

"Three times, John. Three times."

Governor Jan van Riebeeck had sentenced Pieter Brackenier to be dropped three times from the yardarm, receive a hundred lashes, and then be banished from the settlement after he was overheard speaking out against the conditions at the Cape. According to the eavesdropper, Brackenier had said he would be better off taking his chances in the African wilderness than staying at the settlement. The rumor had spread like wildfire, and by the time it reached the governor, the settlement was buzzing like an angry beehive.

Governor Van Riebeeck was quick to put an end to the dissent. Brackenier was clapped in irons and held in a dark room for weeks, being *encouraged* daily to confirm the rumor. He never did. The governor had finally grown weary of the game he accused Brackenier of playing, and upon reflection had found him guilty; the sentence was confirmed by the *Meesters*—the Masters.

The *Meesters* were a handful of men advising and supporting the governor in governing the new settlement. The administrative hierarchy was simple; at the bottom were the *Meesters,* which included the captain of the guard, the bookkeeper, the governor's aide-de-camp, and the *dominee* or pastor. Then there was the governor and then God. Perhaps others in Holland would claim a spot on the ladder, but to the common man toiling away day after day on this unforgiving tip of Africa, that was the reality.

Blanx had laid out his plan. It would be best to leave on the night following Captain Turver's marriage when everybody was good and drunk from the celebrations. They would head east, searching the coves for English or Portuguese ships that would take them back to Europe. With rivers aplenty, fresh water would not be a problem, and if they stayed close to the shore, they would have a good supply of fish to sustain them.

"We want to come too," one of the soldiers spoke in an alert and clear voice.

"How long have you been awake?" Blanx asked.

"Long enough to know that you would happily let us join you rather than risk us running to the governor with this lovely tale of dare and do," Adriaen Huytjens, the more outspoken of the two soldiers, threatened.

Nobody trusted the soldiers. They were an illiterate, ill-disciplined, ill-mannered, and any other form of ill conceivable bunch of bottom feeders with too much authority and too little integrity to warrant it.

"What is stopping you from going anyway?" Van Leyen asked.

"Dirks and I want out too. We'll be no trouble to you. We can arrange to patrol the perimeter on the night of the wedding, making sure everybody gets clean away, and lest we forget, we also have access to ammunition. Undertaking such a journey would be much easier and safer with the addition of pistols and extra swords."

"Keep your voice down," Van Leyen hissed. "It is precisely *this* that got Pieter in trouble."

After a moment of weighing his options, Blanx spoke in a voice, soft enough to reach no further than the sides of their tent. "Betray us and I will deny everything. I will claim that it was Dirks' idea." Blanx tilted his head in the other soldier's direction. "Remember, Van Leyen is my witness." A shadow of caution shifted across Huytjens' eyes, and for the briefest of moments, his confidence seemed to falter. There was a dangerous rumor that Dirks' and Huytjens' relationship went beyond the boundaries of friendship. Blanx knew that the two young soldiers would do nothing to risk each other's hide.

Van Leyen and Blanx were deep in the forest when a disturbance drew their attention.  Leaves rustled; something was moving through the underbrush with growing speed.  Van Leyen heard it first, and then he felt Blanx tense behind him, his fingers digging into Van Leyen's shoulder.

"Let go," Van Leyen shrugged his shoulder as he pulled his sword free.

"What the hell is that?" There was always the threat of lions, especially at night.

"Could be a hippopotamus," Blanx's voice sounded muted in the thick air as he answered his own question.

"The sword will not work then. Pray for something smaller." Van Leyen searched the blackness in front of him as he pressed his back against a tree.

"Hippos don't climb trees, but if it's a lion, we have a problem." Blanx was moving to a tree a few yards away, the branches were low, and the trunk was thick, which would make for easy climbing when the time came. He drew his sword as well and waited.

"Lions are stealthy. This thing is definitely not." Van Leyen was going to say something more, but a dark shape broke through the underbrush and charged full bore at Blanx. The creature yipped and whined as it pushed both paws on Blanx's chest to better lick his face.

"Jesus, Fly! Down, you mutt." Blanx scolded the dog while he tried to push it down. The excitement of the reunion made Fly's tail and stomach move in contradicting directions, nearly knocking it off its feet.

"This is a bloody disaster. What if someone saw him?" Van Leyen asked, thinking it would not be a terrible idea to run the dog through.

"No," Blanx said as he tried to scratch the dog's head, "he disappears into the forest all the time to hunt. No one would think anything of it."

The dog was a good hunter, and it was perhaps its only redeeming quality. They continued in silence; their pace much improved, with Blanx no longer holding onto Van Leyen's shoulder. Another tick in the dog's favor.

"Speaking of disasters, do you think those two made it to the river?" Blanx had a habit of picking up a conversation from hours earlier, resuming it midstream as if no time had passed. They'd all agreed to rendezvous at the second bend in the river. The earthy smell of wet soil and animal dung was growing more distinct, and they knew the river was not far.

Van Leyen released a sigh and shook his head. "Let's hope a lion finds them before they find the river."

"Now, that is very uncharitable of you," Huytjens spoke from somewhere to their left. "Here we are eagerly awaiting your arrival with pistols and swords as promised, and there you are wishing us to perdition."

"And four loaves of bread," Dirks added, lifting a heavy linen satchel, bulging with the evidence of his words.

* * *

Governor Van Riebeeck was locked in a deep discussion with his secretary and second in command, Elias Coopman, when the captain of the guard stepped into the spacious yet sparsely decorated chamber after a brisk knock on the newly hung door.

"Pardon the interruption, Governor." Glancing in the other man's direction, Captain Helm greeted Coopman with a sharp nod.

Both men stared at Helm with similar looks of anticipation. The morning was still in its infancy, but the day was shaping up to be a problem child and would most likely end as a deeply troubled adult.

"What is it, Helm?" the governor asked, his forehead furrowed. The governor was pale and his cheeks sunken, but his deep brown eyes were alert, though a trifle cold. Deep lines bracketed his harsh mouth. His clothes were hanging loose on his frame; he had lost weight over the last ten months, as they all did. But where everyone else's suffering was underscored with desperation, his was with anger.

"Governor, four men are missing," the captain reported.

Helm watched as the blood slowly left the governor's face as if a tap somewhere lower on his body had opened, and his life force was steadily draining from him.

"What precisely do you mean when you say four men are missing?" the governor's voice was ominously low.

"Two soldiers did not report for duty this morning, sir. Also, the two settlers they shared a tent with, are not with any of the building teams."

10

"Has anyone searched the forest? They might have fallen asleep after overindulging last night." Coopman was calm and reasonable, his mind invariably working off the assumption that all deserved the benefit of the doubt.

"We did." Helm fell silent and finished his statement with a slight shake of his head.

"Who are they?" The unwelcome news had lit a fire in the governor's eyes, and the effect was most startling against his pale skin; he looked feral and ready to do battle.

"Adriaen Huytjens, Gert Dirks, John Van Leyen, and Jan Blanx," Helm swallowed and looked down, "and the dog."

Silent seconds passed as the governor paced the room, his eyes unfocused, his steps measured and deliberate, absorbing the weight of the news. Neither Helm nor Coopman uttered a word.

"Bloody Blanx. Why is it that whenever there is a problem, his name always seems to float to the top? I want them found," Van Riebeeck said and turned to Helm, "Take the horses and three soldiers."

Helm clicked his heels sharply and reached for the door.

"Put the rest of the soldiers on high alert. The anchor is gone, and the chain is sure to follow."

"Governor?" Helm paused, not understanding the meaning of the governor's words.

"We run the risk of more desertions. Blanx and the others have shown them it can be done."

Once alone, Coopman's cool gaze rested heavily on the young governor. "Governor Van Riebeeck, you must act decisively once these men are brought back. You cannot show them any mercy." The governor nodded absentmindedly at the advice.

"Yes," he agreed, "a strong message must be sent to deter any future attempts at escape."

# Chapter 2

Danielle rushed through the gray stone arch of the fort's main gate, the woven basket she carried filled with rosemary and vegetables. She headed for the kitchen where Mrs. Boom was already waiting to prepare the noon meal, even though the sun was only a few hands above the horizon and the morning air was still crisp. Lingering hints of roasted flatbread and fried fish were all that remained of breakfast. Fresh meat was scarce, and the entire settlement had been on a diet of fish and vegetables for almost ten months.

The large square courtyard was empty when she'd left at dawn. Now, piles of stone and stacks of dried grass studded the space, ready to be turned into the soldiers' quarters. Last night was the first time she'd slept on land since leaving Holland more than a year ago. The last of the expedition's ships, which had served as sleeping quarters for all women and children, had set sail the day before. Danielle was not sad to see those sails disappear over the horizon. The *Goede Hoop* held very few pleasant memories for her, and if she *never* set foot on that dratted vessel again, she would not be poorer for it.

"Why does your face look like an old woman's elbow?" Mattheys called from a distance.

Danielle stopped and placed the heavy basket at her feet. She shielded her eyes against the sun as she traced the trajectory of the gnarly body that made its way toward her, dust puffing with each step he took while pointing the walking stick, that was supposed to help him stay upright, at her like a challenge. His body might have been twisted and warped with age, but his eyes and mind were sharp and clear.

"Mattheys, hasn't anyone shown you how to use a walking stick?" she asked when he was close enough for her not to shout.

"It's my stick, and I can point it where I please."

"Ain't that the truth? I heard you walloped one of the builders on the ear yesterday."

"And his hearing is much improved," he said as he looked at a young man carrying a large boulder on his shoulder. Mattheys had been the carpenter on the same ship she'd traveled on from Holland to the Cape of Good Hope. When the ship had set sail shortly after the settlement began back in April of the previous year, Mattheys had asked to stay behind, claiming he was too old for a life at sea and wished to die and be buried peacefully in the dirt. But Mattheys was worth his weight in gold, for he was the settlement's only skilled thatcher and carpenter. The fact that they managed to build most of the fort within the span of ten months was a testament to his skill and the governor's determination.

"I have a gift for you," Danielle said as she bent down to rummage through the basket. Mattheys quietly waited for her to straighten, and when she dropped the fruit in his hand, his face broke into a sunny smile.

"A peach," he breathed with reverence, lifting it to his nose and inhaling deeply. "I cannot remember the last time I had one."

"It's the first one. I picked it this morning. The rest will be ready in a few days. Mrs. Boom will probably turn them all into jam or chutney." Danielle watched him take a deep bite before she burst out laughing.

"Now who's looking like an old woman's elbow?" she said around her giggles.

"That's about all they would be good for if the rest are as tart as this one." Regardless of his grumbles, he finished the peach and tossed the stone aside.

"So, are you going to tell me why you were frowning?" Mattheys pushed, not ready to let her off the hook just yet.

"I don't want to talk about it, Mattheys, not today."

Mattheys contemplated her for a few seconds, his near-silver eyes searching her face, seeing things she wished he didn't, but he nodded, and she was grateful for the reprieve.

"Fine, run along now. You can take me for a walk this evening."

The kitchen was a hive of activity. Scullery maids were busy chopping and peeling vegetables at the long table in the center of the room, while two boys swept out the hearth and piled fresh wood into a tidy triangle.

"Don't forget to stack the bread oven as well," Mrs. Boom called over her shoulder from where she stood by a workbench against the wall, stacking dishes in neat piles. Her plump body swayed to the rhythm of her task.

Danielle hoisted the heavy basket and placed it on the table.

"Child, where have you been? I thought a lion got hold of you," she scolded as she turned, wiping her hands on her apron. "Did you get the cabbage?" she asked, while looking through the basket. "Oh, you forgot the leek. *Tsk*, never mind, we'll do without for today."

"You speak as though I picked these up from a market somewhere."

"Did you not get them from Hendrik's garden?" Mrs. Boom asked.

"Some, but most of it I found in the forest. Herbs and vegetables are popping up everywhere. The flood waters must have spread the seeds. One only needs to know where to look," Danielle said with a triumphant smile.

"Oh, Danielle, you can't run around the African wilderness as if you own it. You are not invincible, and you know full well that recklessness is the other side of that coin. Promise me you will take more care."

"Nothing is going to happen to me." Danielle gave the older woman a tender smile.

"And that is because I spend my nights on my knees praying to God to keep you and the twins safe. Have you spoken to the governor yet?" Mrs. Boom asked, changing the direction of the conversation.

Danielle patiently waited for the scolding to end, but when she did not answer fast enough, the older woman's eyes snapped up, and her lips compressed in irritation. "Well? Have you?"

The Boom's house was the settlement's first dwelling. Hendrik Boom, the head gardener, cultivated sprawling vegetable gardens and fruit orchards wherever he found fertile soil, with no set pattern. The governor deemed it practical to construct the Boom family's home near the center of Hendrik's gardens, making them the first who resided outside the fort's walls. The house was large enough to accommodate their twin daughters and include several storerooms.

"I was hoping to talk to him this morning," Danielle said as she handed the tomatoes to one of the servant girls.

"Make sure he says yes. I'm not living in that big house all by myself."

Danielle moved around the table and wrapped the cook in a tight hug before kissing her apple-pink cheek.

"Surely you've noticed that your husband, Elsje, and now Gijs, are still living with you?" she asked as she looked into Anke Boom's red-rimmed eyes. The omission of Leesa's name had the same effect as if it had been spoken out loud.

Fishing a handkerchief from her apron pocket, Mrs. Boom dotted her eyes as fresh tears welled. "What does she know about being a wife? And last night was her wedding night and all."

The day before, their youngest daughter had married the captain of the *Goede Hoop*. As the ship sailed off in the late afternoon, Mrs. Boom stood on the shore, waving bravely, only to turn and weep bitterly in her husband's arms.

"Leesa will be fine. She and Captain Turver make a good couple, and you know he cares for her deeply."

"Yes, but he is so …" she waved her hand in the air while searching for the right word. "He's so small."

Danielle curled her lips inward in a bid not to laugh and tactfully nodded. Laugh lines usually spidered Mrs. Boom's eyes, but this morning a deep sorrowful groove curved between her brows. She had begged Danielle the day before to come and live with them.

"Elsje will be impossible without Leesa, and I will be off balance with only one child," she had said. It was a good idea. Danielle loved Elsje like a sister, and she could use a little distance from the fort. She spent all her days within the walls, but now to sleep there as well could become too much.

* * *

"The governor does not have time for visitors this morning, Miss Van Aard. Perhaps you can bring your concerns to me this afternoon." Mr. Coopman was already easing the governor's chamber door shut when Danielle reached it. His voice, as ever, carried a cool, refined edge, but Danielle, undaunted, pressed her hand against the door before it could close.

"It is a personal matter, and he is expecting me," she said while sliding closer to push her back against the door. "I won't take much of his time."

She got the feeling her insistence vexed him, but it was hard to tell, for his face was always carefully neutral, almost serene.

"See that you don't." With a muscle working rhythmically in his cheek, Mr. Coopman regarded her for a moment before releasing the door handle, and Danielle watched him walk away. Everything about him was calculated and elegant. His swarthy skin always held a healthy glow. His dark hair, too short to gather in a queue, was thick and shiny with only a few wisps of gray near the temples, and unlike most men in their forties, his tall frame was well-proportioned and tightly woven with long, lean muscles. She wondered how the hardship they all endured did not show on him.

"We've built stairs by the front entrance for a reason, Miss Van Aard," Governor Van Riebeeck spoke with his back turned to her as he stood in front of the window that overlooked the courtyard. He no longer called her by her first name, and the loss stung each time.

Danielle could hear Captain Helm rallying troops in the garrison hall, a stone-walled chamber at the heart of the fort. His voice carried an urgent edge, hinting that something had happened or was happening.

"I prefer the back door." Danielle looked around the chamber. To say it was spartan would overstate the extent of the décor. At the room's center stood a desk, paired with a chair that seemed plucked from the kitchen. Along the wall behind it, stacks of maps, parchments, and books teetered in haphazard piles.

"How is my wife?" he asked, determined to keep his back to her.

"She's fine." Maria Van Riebeeck had been healthy for months after she contracted dysentery and became so violently ill that no one had thought she would survive. Her problem, and Danielle was sure the one the governor was referring to, was not her physical health. The couple had lost their eighteen-month-old baby boy to a fever en route to the Cape of Good Hope. The child was buried at sea. After that, Maria was never the same, and as time went on and especially after her illness, she sank into a deep melancholy, for which there seemed to be no cure.

Many times, during her fevered delirium, she had called to her baby. The ordeal had left deep scars on a once beautiful marriage. First, the governor had to witness his child's death, and then a few months later, he was tossed into a similarly helpless position, watching his wife wither before his eyes as she begged for death to claim her. The once warm and jovial man had become hardened and distant, never forgetting his wife's pleas. Pleas he now viewed as a betrayal.

Even though their apartment was above the garrison hall, husband and wife saw little of each other. The governor spent his time in his chamber or outside, overseeing the building of the compound and gardens. Maria had confided in Danielle that he often slept in the downstairs guest chamber, not wanting to wake her when he came in late.

The silence stretched between them, and when it was clear that the governor had forgotten she was there, Danielle spoke again.

"I want your permission to move in with the Booms. They have plenty of room, and besides, the one I occupy upstairs can be given to somebody more important." He showed no reaction to her words, and she continued. "I would also have room to set up an apothecary."

Finally, he turned to face her. His eyes were cold, and his mouth was drawn in a grim line, his irritation clear for her to see.

"No." He spoke the single word and moved to his chair, his hand already reaching for a piece of parchment.

Danielle could feel her temper stir, but she held it tight.

"Why not?" she persisted.

"I don't need to explain my decisions to you. Now go. I am busy." He dismissed her with an abrupt flick of his hand, much like one would rid oneself of an insect.

"I'm twenty years old and not a child. Surely, I can live where I please?"

She had deliberately gentled her voice. She was not going to beg, nor did she want to rile him any further. Despite her good intentions, the next words flowed over her lips unbidden.

"You've already taken so much from me, don't take my freedom as well." Even though her words were barely above a whisper, the bitterness in them was clear. She closed her eyes in mortification, wishing she could take the statement back.

A frigid silence filled the chamber, and when she looked at him, his face was contorted with fury. To his credit, he remained seated and spoke in an even tone.

"You are acting like a selfish child. It is most disappointing." Staring her down, he continued. "I did not take anything away from you. You resent my decision to remove you as the settlement's healer and instead employ a proper physician. I assure you it was necessary." Danielle inhaled to protest his statement, but he lifted a finger, and she remained mute. "You are my responsibility and under my protection. Until you marry, you will stay where I tell you to."

The statement was telling in so many ways, and Danielle felt her annoyance at his high-handedness fade. Something had happened that made him think he was losing control. The governor shouldered a heavy burden, and it was taking its toll. He wasn't breathing deep enough, and his once healthy, fair skin had a blueish-gray undertone. His eyes were sunken, and his cheekbones stood in stark relief. He wasn't eating enough, but then no one was, and there were dark half-moons under his eyes, telling her he wasn't sleeping either.

There would be no point in belaboring the matter of her accommodation any further. She could well recognize a lost cause when she saw one. Without asking for permission or uttering another word, she turned and left the chamber, softly closing the door behind her.

Heading upstairs to the apartment, she found Maria sitting by her desk, staring at a piece of parchment covered in harsh lines going in all directions. Maria was a talented artist who used to create charcoal drawings so lifelike they looked ready to reach out and touch the viewer. After her baby's death, her sketches became harsh and lifeless, at times nothing more than a few thick black lines. Often when the gray evening light was too dim to do anything by, and Danielle packed the charcoals away, she found nothing but a blank sheet staring back at her.

"Good morning," Danielle sang in a cheerful voice, putting the incident with Maria's husband behind her. Maria was ten years younger than her husband, but the emptiness in her eyes made her look much older than her twenty-three years. Maria's vacant stare searched the room and having found nothing of interest, landed on Danielle's face. It was like she was looking right through her before staring at the drawing on the desk again.

"What are you sketching?" Danielle asked.

"A street."

"Really?" Danielle leaned closer, squinted her eyes, and turned her head slightly sideways to gain a different perspective. Whatever was on the parchment looked nothing like a street scene.

"Yes," Maria replied sharply.

"It needs a tree," Danielle returned, and at the mention of their old joke, a slow, sad smile spread across Maria's face.

"Yes, perhaps."

Danielle wanted to say more. Anything to preserve the slightly elevated mood in the room, for a sad smile was better than a blank expression, but before she could think of a witty remark, a crisp knock fell on the door and then another before the door flew open and bounced off the wall.

"There's a ship coming in!" Elsje bellowed as she rushed into the chamber with her blond hair unbound, her feet bare, and her bright blue dress rumpled. Elsje was the eldest of Mrs. Boom's twins with a vivacious personality that could outshine the morning sun itself, even in her bedraggled state.

It took Danielle all but three steps to reach the window. Her eyes disregarded the courtyard, the moat, the building site where the infirmary would soon be constructed, and the beach. Instead, they strained against the glittering water, urgently searching the bay.

"Are you sure?" she called over her shoulder.

"Yes, come. Mother needs help to prepare the crates." Elsje still treated the world as her playground and belatedly remembered that Danielle was in Maria Van Riebeeck's employ as her companion and that she couldn't be called away on a whim to help in the kitchen.

"Good morning, mistress," Elsje said in a demure tone, "I beg your pardon. I was overly excited and forgot myself."

*Sebastiaan.* The realization struck Danielle like a bolt of lightning; she could feel the hairs on her arms lift. Finally, he'd come for her. The timing was right. He had planned to reach the Cape in late January. Ignoring the two women behind her, Danielle searched the bay, hoping to catch a glimpse of the sails. Once sails appear on the horizon, it could take as long as three days to cross the capricious bay, before the ship reached the settlement.

She closed her eyes and felt a smile creep from deep within her body all the way to her lips.

What would their lives be like? They would get married straight away and perhaps live in a small hut near the fort. Sebastiaan would hunt, and she would spend her days as she did now, tending to Maria and helping wherever she could until they could get passage on the next ship back to Batavia. Then their lives could begin. Breathing a deep sigh of contentment, she touched the place near her heart where she'd tucked Sebastiaan's letter beneath her stays and turned from the window. The day was suddenly bright and beautiful.

The rest of the day passed in a blur of activity. Tasks that would normally be a chore were done with light-hearted efficiency.

It was late afternoon, almost evening, when Danielle removed her boots and hose and stepped onto the crisp white beach. It was close to sunset, and the day's heat lingered in the sand. Turning left, she headed to the fallen log that had washed up a few months ago. The ocean had deposited the stump near the tree where she and Sebastiaan had shared their last moments all those many months ago.

She sat down, dug her feet deep into the warm sand, and searched the bay once more. The ship was closer, and she could almost count the sails, but not quite. The *Goede Hoop* was now completely out of sight. Another day of good weather, and the incoming ship would drop anchor close to the shore. By this time tomorrow, she would be holding Sebastiaan's beautiful face in her hands. Her eyes traced a seagull as it glided over the powder-blue ocean. She watched the fan of its tail feathers as it dipped and plucked a small silver fish from the shallow waters before soaring again, neatly escaping a few opportunists who tried to dispossess it of its supper. She smiled as the other gulls screeched and grunted at their loss.

"I thought I might find you here," Mattheys said, his voice rasping close behind her.

Danielle greeted her old friend with a smile and then returned her attention to the ship growing ever dimmer as the evening haze engulfed it.

"It's the *Leeuwerik*," Mattheys answered her silent question and joined her on the log.

"How do you know?" It was impossible to distinguish any details from this distance, yet he spoke with certainty.

"I've been a sailor for more than forty years. There's not a VOC ship out there whose sails, captain, boatswain, or upper-deck guns I don't know."

"Fair enough," Danielle conceded. "The real question is: Is it coming from or going to Batavia?"

"Coming."

This time, she gave a burst of laughter.

"How on earth can you tell?"

"I can smell the spices on the wind," he said as he closed his eyes and inhaled deeply before turning to her. "Can't you smell it?"

She gave him a shy smile and shook her head.

"Do you think the lad is on it?" Mattheys had served on the ship captained by Sebastiaan's uncle and had watched the boy grow into a formidable man. Affection shone warmly in his eyes as he, too, stared at the black shape of the *Leeuwerik*.

"The timing is right," she said, trying to keep her tone even, but Mattheys had heard the note of tension it carried.

"You are eager to leave?"

"I have nothing keeping me here. Governor Van Riebeeck made sure of that." Bitterness laced her voice once more.

"I would have done the same thing had I been in his shoes." Mattheys' bone-dry statement drew Danielle's attention, and she slowly turned to face him. She could feel the crease between her brows deepen.

"What?" she breathed.

"Don't get your hackles up," Mattheys said soothingly. "Use that oversized brain God accidentally gave you and look at the situation for a moment through someone else's eyes instead of your own."

Not appreciating his patronizing words, she pinched her lips and waited for his explanation.

Rolling his eyes to the heavens, he released an exasperated sigh.

"Very well. I will lay it out for you. You are a beautiful, young, unmarried woman tending and caring for a bunch of rough-hewn sailors and soldiers who hadn't touched a female body in many months." Ignoring the scandalized look on her face while she undoubtedly was gathering a slew of statements to defend her patients, Mattheys continued. "With Sebastiaan not here to guard over you, how long do you think it would have been before one of them took more than what you were offering?" Danielle had thought about that many times, but she had hoped her reputation as a healer would protect her.

"The governor did the best he could to keep you safe. It is much better to have the physician tending to the sick."

"I could have worked alongside him," she persisted.

"And how do you think that man with his narrow shoulders and a fist the size of a late-in-the-season orange would be able to protect you?" He was right, as always, but Danielle was in no mood to accept defeat so easily.

"I don't want to talk about it any longer, Mattheys."

"Aye, you don't have to talk about it, but a little bit of thinking wouldn't hurt." Mattheys nodded at her before breaking eye contact. "You can't keep fighting the world, sweetheart. So, stop poisoning your heart."

Mattheys had the tendency to view the world through its rear end, and so Danielle decided not to respond to his statement. She only dug her toes deeper into the sand and watched how the ocean turned a dark gray as the sun dipped behind the mountain.

# Chapter 3

anielle had returned from the beach, much later than usual, the previous evening. When reaching her room, she'd polished her boots until the candlelight reflected in their tips, then she'd laid out her best clothes, and brushed her hair until it crackled. When everything was ready for her reunion with Sebastiaan in the morning, she'd settled in her narrow bed, but sleep remained as elusive as a well-oiled eel in a very deep pond. Excitement and anticipation were making her restless, and she spent most of the night tossing and turning. At first the bedclothes were lopsided, then her nightdress had somehow got all twisted and tangled, and she had to get out of bed to straighten the bothersome bit of clothing. Just when she thought she was comfortable enough to fall asleep, she discovered her hair was tickling and scratching her neck. Then there was the irksome itch under her foot that forced her to sit up and relieve the annoyance before adjusting her blankets, clothing, and hair again.

The *Leeuwerik* would creep closer during the night, and by dawn, she would drop anchor in the mouth of the Fresh River. The river was small and even smaller now since it had been diverted to flow around the fort, but its mouth was still deep enough for a large vessel to rest in. When calm, the bay was a haven for tired and battered ships, but it could turn into a death trap when the mighty northwester whipped and frothed the water into a deadly cauldron. The previous winter, a violent storm nearly destroyed one of the expedition's cargo ships, lying so close to the shore they could see the desperate sailors waving from the deck. Had it not been for the dogged determination and fearlessness of those ashore who'd rescued the stricken crew and rowed them to safety in sloops, none would have survived.

Danielle knew that the sooner she fell asleep, the sooner morning would come, and she and Sebastiaan would be together at last. But her brain was vindictively restless. It kept conjuring up all manner of what-ifs and misgivings, making her tremble with yearning the one moment and shiver with apprehension the next. Perhaps counting backward from a hundred would give her something to focus on, but each time she reached the mid-eighties, she lost track, and had to start over. Only once the dawn sky turned gray, and it was nearly time to rise, did her tired mind cave, and she fell asleep against her wishes.

The sun was already warming the bustling courtyard, and the shouts from the men building the new section of the fort had fallen into an easy rhythm when Danielle leapt from her bed. Her eyes were scratchy, as if sand had somehow got stuck under the lids, and her mouth was dry. She hurried to the water pitcher and bowl in the corner; the set was a gift from Maria, but this morning there was no time to admire the delicate blue flowers painted on the creamy white porcelain. Mattheys had promised her a washstand as soon as he was free to work on smaller tasks.

She knelt on the wooden floor, lifted the pitcher and tipped water into the bowl. Reaching for the precious rose-scented soap, she brushed it against a rough linen strip. Bringing the cloth to her nose, she inhaled deeply before washing her body. The excitement coursing through her veins made her heart race and her hands shake, and with each splash of cold water, her skin tingled and buzzed to life. Today was the beginning of her new life.

Growing up, she'd never fawned over young men like the other girls in her village back in Holland. In truth, she'd never paid the idea of settling down and starting a family any thought. Her work as an apothecary alongside her father had always taken precedence. But everything had changed when she'd met Sebastiaan. She closed her eyes and felt his warm skin and soft golden hair under her fingertips. He had blown into her life like a warm ocean breeze, claiming her heart and soul with his bright smile and steadfast presence. Sebastiaan had saved her from the hull of his uncle's ship when she'd accidentally become a stowaway and then continued to watch over her like an avenging angel. Soon after, he'd rescued her again when her sharp tongue and quick temper had landed her strapped to a barrel, facing a whipping, and it was Sebastiaan who had pulled her from the depths of despair after little Antoonie Van Riebeeck's death.

Danielle glanced out the window. It was almost mid-morning, and the *Leeuwerik* would have dropped anchor by now. She wouldn't be surprised if they had already unloaded most of the cargo. Knowing Sebastiaan, he would stay aboard to help with the heavy lifting before disembarking, no matter how eager he was to see her. She smiled at the thought as she carefully dampened and then plaited her dark hair. They were opposites in every way. Her skin was creamy white; his was golden brown. Her hair was almost black as night, whereas his was the color of wheat that sparkled in the sunlight. Her build was slight and feminine; he was large and strong. She was often shy and moody, and he was in love with life and all its wonders.

A gentle knock on the door drew Danielle from her daydream, and she turned to see Maria peeking through the small angle.

"My husband wants to see you in his chamber," she said in her signature gentle voice. Danielle greeted her friend with a soft smile as Maria stepped inside and closed the door behind her. She paused and let her fingers glide over Danielle's wide leather belt draped over the foot of the bed.

Danielle had adopted a peculiar sense of fashion, partly because of Elsje's flights of fancy and her own stubbornness in refusing to wear gowns of any nature. Under Elsje's guiding hand, she was now dressed in shirts and skirts accented with a wide leather belt and calf-high boots; and since they were at the bottom of the world, there were no society matrons to scold her for her daring.

"Have you slept well?" Danielle asked, but could already see the answer in her friend's bloodshot eyes. Maria only nodded and turned toward the window, the morning light haloed around her blond hair.

Danielle was itching to get moving, but somehow Maria seemed to have forgotten her husband's summons.

Having straightened her room and running out of small tasks to do,

Danielle asked, "Shall we go downstairs together?"

"No," Maria replied, her voice distant, "you go ahead, my dear."

Flicking her braid over her shoulder, Danielle rushed to the door, but Maria halted her with a soft call and then hugged her with all her strength. Danielle's heart was beating in her throat with anticipation, and she hurriedly returned Maria's embrace, barely registering that it was the first time the other woman had offered such a gesture.

"Go," Maria whispered close to her ear before releasing her.

Danielle grabbed two handfuls of her skirt and lifted it away from her racing feet as she flew down the stone stairs. Her chest was rising and falling sharply by the time she reached the door to the governor's chamber. Sebastiaan could be waiting inside this very minute. Standing still for a moment, she calmed her breathing and wiped her damp palms on her skirt, then with a shaking hand, she rapped three brisk knocks on the door.

"Enter," replied the firm but muffled voice of the governor.

Three stark faces met her as she entered the chamber: Governor Van Riebeeck, Mr. Coopman, and a man she did not know. Looking from one to the other, she swallowed nervously and waited. She was going to greet each with a 'good morning' but decided to keep her excitement bottled up a little longer.

Governor Van Riebeeck acknowledged her with a sharp nod before rearranging a few documents on his desk while Mr. Coopman stood next to two vacant chairs. Danielle briefly wondered if they were carried down from the governor's apartments for the purpose of this meeting. She glanced in Mr. Coopman's direction, but his face was unreadable as always. The man she did not know stood near the window.

"Have a seat, Miss Van Aard," the governor invited. Danielle declined. She was too impatient this morning to be subjected to such demure behavior; instead, she remained standing. Her silent refusal drew the governor's attention, and he regarded her before speaking.

"Allow me to introduce Captain Zeeuw of the *Leeuwerik*," he said, half turning to the man standing off his left shoulder.

Captain Zeeuw was far older than his posture foretold. He executed a bow, and she performed a small curtsy in return. The governor looked in her direction once more and appeared to reach a conclusion of sorts. Danielle's head snapped from one man to the other, refusing to acknowledge the heaviness in the room.

"Captain Zeeuw, please repeat what you've just shared with us," Van Riebeeck said in a low and measured voice.

The captain's gaze settled on Danielle, and after a brief pause, he spoke in a wind-weathered voice. "When we departed Batavia on the second of November last year," he began and Danielle nodded, for Sebastiaan had written to inform her of his intended departure, "there were three ships in our convoy: the *Leeuwerik, Geloof,* and *Spiegel.*" His gaze sharpened. "I believe your betrothed, Mister Sebastiaan De Vries, boarded the *Geloof.* I had insisted that he join me on the *Leeuwerik,* but he had declined."

Danielle nodded, knowing Sebastiaan, he would not have done so without a valid reason.

She'd seen only one ship in the bay the previous evening; the Geloof and Spiegel must still be en route. That meant that in a few weeks, three ships, instead of one, would depart for Holland, and they would need to hurry to prepare the remaining fresh food. Mrs. Boom would be in a frenzy.

Captain Zeeuw's voice drew her from her thoughts.

"Three weeks into our voyage, we fell victim to a pirate attack during which the *Geloof* and *Spiegel* were stripped of their cargo and set ablaze. Both ships were lost with all hands." He shifted his weight on his feet and stared at a spot on the wall somewhere over her shoulder. "The *Leeuwerik* escaped but later returned to search for survivors; we found none."

A deathly silence fell in the room. Danielle patiently waited for the captain to continue his telling, for surely that could not be the end of his tale. She stared at him in anticipation. When it became clear that he had no more to say, she asked: "You said you believed?" Her voice felt hoarse and weak, and she wondered if she had spoken at all, for her ears were ringing as if she'd been underwater too long.

"Pardon?" the captain asked, confusion making both his eyebrows raise and his body leaned slightly toward her.

"You said you believed Sebastiaan De Vries was aboard the *Geloof*. Could you have been mistaken?" Hope flared in her belly. Perhaps Sebastiaan meant to depart with the *Geloof*, but something had delayed his plans and prevented his departure. Perhaps he'd decided to leave Batavia at a later date.

"No, Miss. A week before the attack, all three captains held a meeting on the *Geloof*, and that was when I saw Mister De Vries, as he was the honored guest of Captain Van Dijk. He was most certainly aboard the *Geloof*."

No, life couldn't be this cruel. Unwilling to accept the captain's words, which had ended all too soon, she waited. Then the reality of his words enveloped her like a thick winter fog, and she looked to the governor, hoping he would contradict the captain. But Van Riebeeck couldn't meet her gaze, and then she knew.

Pressure from inside her pushed upward and blocked her ears. That same heaviness was collecting under her skin, straining against it, trying to find a way out, but failing in the attempt. Her skin felt like it was being pricked with thousands of small, sharp, icy needles and then she heard something break in her chest. It was a delicate break, like a thin glass pane neatly snapping in two. A strange ache blossomed when her heart tore away from its moorings and dropped, leaving a hollow emptiness in its wake. Her lips parted, and she felt the cool air rush over her tongue as her lungs drew a deep gulp.

"I am truly sorry for your loss."

Danielle heard the words, but they floated like feathers in the wind, detached and without meaning. She didn't even know who had spoken them.

The emptiness in her chest spread to her head, leaving it feeling too light, as if detached from her body. The captain's face faded from her view, and her gaze settled on the governor. This time, he held her stare. The compassion and sorrow in his brown eyes were the last things she saw before darkness engulfed her.

Danielle woke to the sensation of floating. Strong arms were wrapped around her. "Sebastiaan," she said, but her voice was not cooperating, and the sound came out as a breath.

"Hush now."

She opened her eyes at the unexpected voice. Mr. Coopman was carrying her into her bedroom. He laid her on her bed before bending down to brush the hair from her face.

"Can I get you some water?" he asked, his eyes were dark and troubled. Danielle turned her face away to stare at the white-washed wall. "I will call for Mistress Van Riebeeck." His footsteps retreated, then the door closed softly, and she was alone.

Danielle wished she could crawl into a small dark corner. Her room felt too bright and open. Turning on her side, she drew her knees to her chest, clutched her fists close to her breast, and pinched her eyes. Mercifully, her mind took control, retreating into the refuge of a bottomless sleep where dreams dared not descend and hours felt like days and days passed in a flash.

She drifted aimlessly, and as her consciousness fought its way to the surface, voices became audible.

She recognized Maria's voice. "It's not good for her to be alone."

"Sleep is the best for her now," Mrs. Boom replied.

"How much can such a young soul bear?"

"She's a strong girl, but this is a heavy blow," Mrs. Boom confirmed. "She will need us now more than ever."

Danielle heaved a deep sigh and slowly opened her eyes. It was nighttime. A single candle made ghastly shadows dance on the walls.

Seeing that she was awake, Mrs. Boom came to sit on the bed, and the straw-filled mattress dipped under her weight.

"Drink this," she said as she held a delicate teacup out to Danielle.

Danielle smelled the familiar tang of valerian and chamomile and turned her face away.

"I don't want it," she said and did not try to sit up.

"What you want and what you need are often not the same. Now drink this. It will settle your insides," Mrs. Boom's words held a note of impatience, but when Danielle looked into her eyes, she saw panic, raw and real.

In little more than a year, Danielle had witnessed the brutal murder of her father, which led to her fleeing for her life and leaving the only home she'd ever known behind. Then she'd witnessed the death of Maria's baby, a child she'd loved and cared for deeply, and now she'd lost Sebastiaan. Mrs. Boom was worried, and rightly so, but Danielle had already made the decision to bury this loss deep inside her. It was hers to carry, and she would not share or burden anyone around her with it.

Danielle pushed herself into a sitting position, took the offered cup, and drained the contents. She knew the medicine would have a calming effect, but it mattered little, for she was not upset. Being upset would require emotions, and she had none. Her heart was beating, and the rest of her organs were functioning as they should, but only because they didn't know how not to do so.

She could not dredge up a single sentiment or feeling. Her every hope and dream had sunk to the bottom of the ocean with Sebastiaan. It had bothered her when the governor discharged her as healer of the settlement and had instead appointed an incompetent physician to fill the void. She had always known that her time at the Cape of Good Hope was temporary, and that soon she would leave for Batavia when Sebastiaan came for her. Once settled as the wife of a busy and successful trader, she would continue to work as an apothecary, much like she had before the African expedition interrupted her life. The sole reason she had stayed behind when Sebastiaan set sail the previous year was that there was no one else at the settlement to care for the sick. Now—everything was lost. Death followed her like a shadow, and it was only a matter of time before it would come for her. Closing her eyes, she sent a wordless prayer for that day to be sooner rather than later.

"I will send Elsje to sleep here tonight," Mrs. Boom said as she took the empty cup from Danielle's hands.

"That's not necessary," Danielle rejected the offer, "it won't change anything. The medicine will soon work, and I will most likely sleep until morning. I promise to resume my duties tomorrow." Danielle was Maria's hired companion. It was a loose title that meant she was paid a small monthly salary to be the governor's wife's friend—Maria's idea. Danielle would have been Maria's friend regardless of any arrangements, but at the time, it had kept her safe and secured a place for her at the settlement.

Having found herself with much free time on her hands, she'd started to help Hendrik Boom in his gardens, Mrs. Boom in the kitchen, sneaking healing potions and ointments to the builders and settlers and secretly tending to the women of the settlement. In her mind, an end date always marked her duties, for she knew she would soon leave the Cape, but now … How would she go on? The world was suddenly empty and without meaning. How would she ever look at a sunny day and think it beautiful? Would she be able to one day look at a color again and see its hue?

"It is not good for you to be alone tonight," Mrs. Boom argued.

"Do as you please," Danielle spoke in a vacant tone when the last of her strength seeped from her body as the medicine took effect.

She did not see the concerned look that passed between the two women. Nor did she notice when Elsje crept into her room later that night with her sleeping bundle under her arm, relieving Maria from her silent vigil. Or when her friend quietly left in the early morning, removing all traces of her being there so as not to intrude on Danielle's privacy.

And so began the first day of the rest of her life.

# Chapter 4

*hree months earlier - November 1652*

T He was engulfed in blackness. Instinctively suppressing the need to breathe, Sebastiaan tilted his head back and stared at the faint orange glow of the rising sun rippling far above him on the water's surface.

He was fifteen years old again, and he and Arent were diving off his uncle's ship to see who could go the deepest and stay under the longest. Arent was bigger, stronger, and broader in the shoulders, but Sebastiaan's tenacity could force the burn from his lungs and the pounding of his heart past the point where most men would start to panic and swallow water like whales in a feeding frenzy. Judging by the heaviness of his limbs, he knew he'd pushed it to the limit this time.

Breaking the surface, he took an even, deep breath, not spluttering and gasping like some green lad fresh from the paddock. But instead of meeting the stillness of the ocean and the sweet morning air, he emerged into an inferno. His lungs instantly rebelled against the hot, acrid air and expelled it from his body in a rough cough that left his chest and throat aching. There was a strange but persistent ringing in both ears, and a warm thickness was coating his left eye, forcing it to close under its weight. Shaking his head, he tried to rid himself of the dizzy spell that held his mind in a vise-like grip.

The vigorous movement of his head only worsened the effects of his malfunctioning body; the stickiness found its way into his mouth, leaving behind the unmistakable metallic tang of blood; a sharp pain radiated from

33

the front of his head down his spine.

With one hand, he splashed salt water over his face, washing most of the blood away, but he could feel it dribbling through his hairline again. His boyhood memory ebbed from his mind as the harsh reality of his circumstance set in.

He had emerged in a war zone where nothing was as it should be. What was supposed to be the morning sun was the VOC merchant ship *Geloof*—Faith, ablaze. Orange flames gluttonously licked at the wooden carcass, devouring the elegant vessel with the same ferocity he'd seen a pack of hyenas once do to a small gazelle. Another explosion sent shards of glass and wood raining down from the night sky. Water and fire were supposed to be enemies, but tonight they were working together, with the fire breaking the ship apart into bite-sized pieces that the dark water greedily swallowed.

Sebastiaan did a quick inventory of his body. Everything seemed to be in good working order. His feet and legs tread the water smoothly, and his arms kept him stable without pain or effort. The only injury seemed to be a wound to the head, accounting for his addled thoughts.

Scanning the surrounding waters, he searched for the other two ships that had set sail with them from Batavia three weeks ago.

The ocean was dead calm, allowing him an unobstructed view. Half a league away, another blaze illuminated the dark night. Turning around, he searched for the third, but there was none. If the third captain had any sense, he would not play the hero and race to their rescue but wait until morning.

The ringing in his ears subsided, letting through the sounds of angry shouting. Sebastiaan calmly moved away from the burning ship's glare and further into the night's darkness. The Ottoman pirate galley that had attacked them was lying only fifty feet from where he had emerged. Its oars were close enough for Sebastiaan to see the color of the wood. On board, a dark-skinned man with an even darker beard trimmed to a neat point was mercilessly whipping a man at his feet. Now and then, a few words drifted towards him. The man was shouting in Arabic, clearly deeply unhappy that his loot, which included ship, sailors, and cargo, was now slowly descending to the bottom of the Indian Ocean. Apparently, the luckless creature at his feet was to blame. A few of the beard's shipmates were scurrying about, securing the few barrels and crates they could scavenge from the burning wreck, while others were furiously hacking away at the burning grappling lines.

A hand closed around Sebastiaan's forearm. The hand was attached to a badly burned arm. Most of the skin was charred, and pieces of raw flesh shone through the water; half the man's face suffered the same damage, and most of his hair was gone except for a few singed clumps. Sebastiaan slowly pulled his arm from the surprisingly firm grasp and moved deeper into the shadows, away from the calls and moaning of drowning and dying men.

The pirates would soon begin the search for survivors either to be used as slaves or for ransom, and those too damaged to be used as either would be left for dead. When that time came, he wanted to be as far away from the ship as possible. Hopefully, he could find a piece of debris to cling to and disappear into the night. The morning would reveal its own problems or solutions, depending on the state and welfare of the third ship.

Moving further away from the burning wreck of the *Geloof*, the scent of tar permeated the heaviness of the smoke. The pirates had tarred their sails, making them nearly invisible on a night like this.

For days they had lain dead in the water with no wind to push them onward, and for all that time, Sebastiaan had argued with Captain Van Dijk to be more vigilant, to post men in the lookouts. Still, the captain had argued that the lack of wind would equally affect any enemy. No matter how many times Sebastiaan had pointed out that sails *and* oars powered the Ottoman galleys, the captain had remained steadfast in his opinion that nobody used such archaic sailing methods any longer. The discussions had become so heated that Sebastiaan refused to spend any more time in the idiot's company and had taken to the lookout basket himself. No sooner had his feet touched the platform, than Van Dijk had ordered him to descend with threats of being chained to the walls of the hull if he did not start behaving like a passenger.

"Mister De Vries," the captain had spat. "I understand you spent some time sailing under the guardianship of your uncle, doing various odd jobs while aboard his ship. But this is the *Geloof*. I am her captain, and *you*," he'd emphasized the pronoun with a curl to his upper lip and a sharply pointed finger right in the middle of Sebastiaan's chest, "are here only as a courtesy. And why did I extend that courtesy?" The man was clearly in love with the sound of his own voice, for he had not waited for an answer but opted to solve the riddle himself. "Because you are the money. So let us not confuse our roles, shall we?" His eyebrows rose as his voice took on the tone one might use with a recalcitrant child.

When his soliloquy had run its course, he had extended a narrow hand between them, palm up. A gesture Sebastiaan had answered with a questioning glance.

"Your weapon, sir. If you please." Pointedly looking to the cutlass strapped to Sebastiaan's waist.

That was the final straw. By then, all work on deck had ceased, and every ear in their vicinity was pricked to absorb as much of the conversation as possible. Sebastiaan had taken a menacing step closer and had growled in a low voice meant only for the captain.

"You touch my blade, Captain, and you and I will have a serious misunderstanding." The captain had capitulated, and Sebastiaan had retreated to his cabin. Six hours later, he was trying to out-swim a pirate galley in the dead of night with a significant portion of his fortune lying on the ocean floor, and the only weapon on his person was Danielle's little paring knife tucked in his boot.

Still, the gods were smiling on him, for he had found a piece of wood large enough to wrap his arms over and lay most of his upper body on.

He must have dozed off, for somewhere in what must have been the early morning hours, he was woken by excited shouts followed by strong hands lifting him from the water and onto a dry wooden deck of one of the pirate galleys.

He had never been on a galley before, but there was no time to look around, for as soon as his bottom touched the deck, someone struck him across the shoulders with something that felt like the working end of a bullwhip. It was a vicious weapon made from a stretched and dried bull's penis. Unlike a regular whip, this one didn't break the skin at first. Rather, it sent pain deep into the body, damaging muscles and organs and leaving behind large purple welts, which would eventually burst after receiving a few more blows. His shoulders tensed, bracing for the next assault, but a fist seized a handful of his hair, yanking him backward and up the short companionway.

Once they reached what must serve as the upper deck, the swine who had him by the hair gave him a hearty kick in the ribs. Forced to his feet, Sebastiaan was then shoved toward the group of Europeans huddled together near the center. Amongst them were the captain of the *Spiegel's* young wife, and their month-old baby girl, accompanied by her maid, who stood protectively in front of her mistress, trying to guard her with her wider body. A dozen sailors, three soldiers, and a priest made up the rest. Most were blood splattered except for the two women. It would appear that the *Spiegel* had not gone down without a fight, either. There was no one he recognized from the *Leeuwerik*. Hopefully, she'd managed to escape.

Empty stares followed him as he took his place among the captives. The sailors were tense but quiet; they knew what was coming. The priest was standing in a puddle, the stench of urine heavy in the dense night air. He clutched a coarse woolen blanket around his shaking shoulders, his muted voice alternating between a monotonous Latin prayer and his pusillanimous weeping, marking him as the most dangerous captive, for he would do and say anything to save his hide. Sebastiaan vaguely remembered the florid-faced, pudgy man from his rantings about having to share a vessel with a woman still unclean after giving birth, but that was when the man was still on land, dry and safely wrapped in the shroud of righteousness.

The corsair captain was coming down the companionway from the covered weather deck. Not the same one he saw earlier. This one was older, with a wiry, bushy beard that parted over his shoulders as he walked. Sebastiaan wondered how many galleys were out there. The captain stopped to bark a few orders at the men guarding the captives and then turned to face his loot.

A custom among the rovers was that when capturing a ship that offered resistance, the captain had the choice of the captives to take as his slave. Moving inconspicuously, Sebastiaan inserted himself between the priest and the two women. Mrs. Bouwer was calm, but her eyes were panic-stricken, her shoulders were tense, and a visible tremble wracked her body. The infant in her arms sensed her mother's anxiety and keened in the scratchy way newborns do. The keening quickly grew to full-blown cries as her mother rocked her unevenly.

"Line them up," the captain ordered in Arabic. Even though Sebastiaan had a moderate understanding of the language, he remained rooted to his spot, the same as all the others. Thanks to his uncle's tutelage over the years, who believed one should be fluent in the language of your enemy, Sebastiaan mastered English, French, to a lesser degree Arabic, and Latin. Not that Rome was considered an enemy, but Latin was found to be the language least offensive to God's ears.

The captain shouted his order a second time, jabbing aggressive gestures at the captives as the rovers' bullwhips cracked viciously across the backs of the huddled white men.

"Try to keep her quiet," Sebastiaan murmured to Mrs. Bouwer before he stepped with the others into the circle of light cast by the lanterns placed at intervals along the deck.

The space between the eighteen men pulsed with tension. Many of them had heard the stories of what happened to Europeans captured by Muslims, and many had chosen death by drowning rather than yielding their fates to these barbarians.

They needed to escape, and the sooner, the better. The first rule was not to be captured, but when that failed, escape or die trying was the second. Sebastiaan made a quick calculation. There were eighteen men, seventeen minus the priest, take away another three; he didn't trust the soldiers, leaving him with thirteen sailors and himself. Not bad odds considering they were surrounded by about the same number of pirates. He did a quick inventory of the sailors in the group. Some were very young, scrawny at best. Two had seen at least fifty winters, and the remaining few stood proud and defiant, but they were unarmed. If they should fail, and the chances of them succeeding in an escape were almost non-existent, it would leave the women in a highly vulnerable position. He was not sure what they could do for them as it was, but to leave them behind seemed wrong—cowardly.

On the other hand, from the Ottomans' point of view, this daring raid brought only twenty potential slaves, a few crates of spices, and no ships. Keeping their human merchandise hale and hearty was in their best interests, but then Sebastiaan remembered what a slave hold looked like, and doubt began to corrode his reasoning.

And so, like so many before him, he kept his eyes downcast, and his mouth shut. Better not draw too much attention to himself and let the scenario play out, for he had no idea what to expect. It was a strategy the priest should have adopted too, but he was wailing louder than the infant, with snot streaming over his upper lip and into his mouth.

One of the galley crewmen, a burly brute with a deep scar to his left cheek that seemed to pull his face askew, raised his arm and aimed his whip at the priest while shouting at him to quiet down. The priest dropped to his knees and scrambled backward to shield himself from the impending blow.

A soft, almost gentle word from the captain stilled the sailor in his violence. The captain then proceeded down the line of captives with lazy arrogance, casually taking the measure of each, undoubtedly calculating his profits. Then the black boots broke their languorous rhythm and came to a standstill.

Sebastiaan raised his eyes. The bastard was standing before him, with shrewd black eyes piercing his, daring him to look down. *God help him*, but he couldn't do what he'd never learned. Sebastiaan wiped all expression from his face and returned the man's stare equally cold and hard.

The captain raised his hand and tilted Sebastiaan's chin up with the handle of his whip. A slow breath left Sebastiaan's nose, and his eyelids lowered as he maintained his locked gaze with the captain. After a few drawn-out seconds, the captain removed the whip, allowing a soft smile to curve his wide mouth. He nodded before moving on to the next man in the line.

By the time he reached the end of the line of captives, the priest had reached a dark corner on the deck behind the women and next to a water barrel. With a sharp flick of his fingers, the captain wordlessly ordered two of his men to bring the priest forward.

Somewhere between the water barrel and where the captain stood, the priest's bowels had lost their already fragile grip on his dignity, and the man landed in an untidy and smelly heap in the center of the deck.

The captain instinctively pulled his head back at the offending odors that shrouded the pathetic creature. He ordered the priest to disrobe, but instead, the man knelt at the captain's feet and feverishly tried to kiss it. A swift lick from the bullwhip across his raised backside ceased the attempted adoration. At last a guard stepped forward, grabbed the end of the priest's simple brown robe, and hoisted it over his head, leaving him writhing in nothing but his stained linen braies. The captain lifted his foot and pushed the kneeling man onto his back, then delivered another vicious blow with his whip to the exposed, round belly.

Sebastiaan had seen the *priest* on a few coincidental occasions in Batavia before. The man was no priest at all, but quite a powerful bishop who had a reputation for his brutal enforcement of the church's morals. Not being of the Roman Catholic faith, Sebastiaan had no business with the bishop personally. However, to run a thriving import and export business, it was most advantageous to possess knowledge, secrets by any other name, of those powerful enough to influence the outcome of certain trade agreements, and bishop Antonio's name had floated past him more than once.

Bishop Antonio had a taste for the finer things in life; good food, soft silks, and a private propensity to entertain himself with the young and innocent. The bishop must have donned the simple priest's robes to disguise his identity. The church was known to look after its own. If his captors believed him to be a humble and lowly priest, they might set his ransom price low, securing him a quick release.

It was becoming glaringly apparent that though bishop Antonio was very assertive when doling out punishment to those he deemed worthy of such; he was exceedingly averse to withstanding physical hardship himself.

"I am a mere priest," the bishop lied. "Please show mercy!" he pleaded in Latin. Sebastiaan wondered how often the bishop had heard those exact words and ignored them. The captain must have sensed that there was more to this *mere priest*, for interest lit in his eyes. When he raised his arm again, Antonio's hands immediately closed over his stomach. "I have information," he blurted, "about one of your captives." A nervous giggle escaped him as he saw the captain stay his hand and raise a questioning eyebrow.

"Continue," the captain returned in an accented Latin.

"That man, over there," the priest extended a finger point-blank to Sebastiaan, "he is a wealthy man. I've seen him dressed in expensive clothes as he walked the docks in Batavia. He is worth a fortune if you were to ransom him." Once the man started, he resembled a broken spigot, for words endlessly poured from him.

There was an uncomfortable shuffling of feet around Sebastiaan. None of the men knew him, but they all felt the betrayal of the priest.

The captain slowly turned from the priest and moved to stand before Sebastiaan once more.

"What is your name?" he asked in Latin.

Sebastiaan remained mute as he shifted his eyes over the captain's shoulder and off into the darkness. He was dressed in a simple rough linen shirt and black breeches. That much did not advertise any wealth or status, but his boots, ruined now from spending hours in the salt water, were once of quality, and the captain took note.

The captain repeated the question, and Sebastiaan heard the menace behind the softly spoken words but ignored the request all the same. With snake-like speed, the captain struck out and grabbed Sebastiaan's right hand, pulled it toward him, and turned it over. Then he reached for the left hand. Years of hard labor on his uncle's ship, climbing the shrouds and doing every job imaginable, had hardened and browned his hands. Calluses and scars marred his skin.

The captain studied his newest acquisition. The young man's eyes were defiant, not arrogant.  His shoulders were broad and powerful and his stance firm, not fearful. This was no pampered, rich, easy ransom standing before him.

An instant fury lit in his black eyes as he threw Sebastiaan's hands down.

"You are lying!" he turned and yelled at the priest. "He is nothing but a common man!" With that last statement, he lowered the whip to the priest several times until his victim was lying curled up in a ball.

"Bring the women," the captain ordered in a dark growl.

There was no struggle, no undignified screaming or begging. The two women complied with every brutal command as far as they could deduce its meaning.

The maid was visibly trying to control her emotions for her mistress's benefit, but her lips trembled, and her hands balled into tight fists to hide their shaking.  Captain Bouwer's young wife was alarmingly pale.  Her narrow shoulders were tense, and her eyes large with fright as she bent her head to whisper soothing words to the hysterical infant. She could have soothed the baby by putting it to her breast, but modesty held her back. Still, it likely wouldn't have changed the outcome.

The captain scowled at the tiny child whose face had turned red from the force of her upset. Closing the distance between him and her mother with a minatory stride, he closed his hand around the dainty ankle and lower leg that churned against her mother's belly. Mrs. Bouwer's breath caught as the stranger wrapped his hand around her daughter's leg, and then her mouth opened in a silent scream as he yanked the child from her arms and, with a powerful backward arch, carelessly flung the infant over the railing, toward the black water beneath. The child's screams tore through the air, and then there was only silence.

The maid stared with unseeing eyes at where the baby's body had disappeared, shocked into a catatonic state. Mrs. Bouwer looked down at her empty arms. The heat of her daughter's tiny body still warmed her chest, and then anguish took the strength from her knees, and she sank to the deck with a raw, primal roar. The sounds of her distress were quickly doused as a heavy fist connected with her temple.

Sebastiaan's feet moved before his brain could assess the wisdom of the act, but a firm hand on his forearm stopped him. One of the older sailors stood stoically beside him, looking straight ahead, and barely moved his lips when he spoke. "It's done now. Let it be."

They watched as the guards ripped away the women's clothes. The maid's head jerked with the rough tugs on her body, but her legs held firm beneath her, even as a blade sheared her crown, her long gray hair hacked off and discarded in clumps. Mrs. Bouwer's unconscious state did not last long enough to save her from the pain and humiliation, and when the men were done, the women stood before them dressed only in their thin cotton shifts, stained by the blood dripping from their scalps.

"I am Captain Yavuz," the captain's voice carried across the deck as he spoke in Latin. Men were fastening iron bands around the priest's and the women's wrists and ankles. "You are now *my* slaves, *my* property, to do with as *I* please."

His rage had not yet subsided, and each phrase sent spittle flying from his mouth. Heavy chains were woven through the iron bands, and the priest, Mrs. Bouwer, and the maid were tied together.

"You have no name," Yavuz's voice raised. "You are infidels, filthy pigs, godless children of whores, and a stain on this land Allah has gifted us." Religious fervor flared in his black eyes, and his cheeks were flushed.

A guard brought a knotted whip down on the backs of the three slaves, where they stood on unsteady legs.

"Take them below."

The chains rattled as their uncoordinated steps strained to find the way forward.

# Chapter 5

Still bleak in its infancy, the breaking dawn marked Sebastiaan's second day at the oars. A warm breeze touched his face, bald scalp, and bare shoulders as his body moved rhythmically; leaning back, his arms straightened, then bent as he pulled through the water, pressing down, lifting the oar, pushing forward, and again. The weight of the oar increased as another man on the bench lost his rhythm.

Sebastiaan spoke in a low voice, "Up, heave! Down, push. Up, heave! Down, push."

The mantra was repeated without pause, and the weight of the oar evened out. They had been rowing with no rest, food, or the chance to relieve themselves, but with nothing to drink, the latter was not a concern—yet.

Six Ottoman galleys attacked the three Dutch merchant ships that night, and only four remained. Soon after, the wind had picked up, and Yavuz and the other captains wanted to put as much distance between them and the third Dutch ship, which had slipped their trap.

Sebastiaan and the four men beside him on the bench were exhausted. He focused on the oar's steady cadence, his hands burning with each pull. A missed rhythm meant the oar dipped too slow or too fast, drawing blistering blows from the whip of the guard patrolling the center aisle. All twenty-four oars had to move as one, and the only way to ensure it was to beat it out of the rowers.

Many welts were pushing against the sunburned skin on Sebastiaan's back. He glanced at the rowers ahead, their shirtless backs peeling in large patches under the harsh sun, exposing tender pink flesh to their keeper's brutality. Their "uniform" consisted of only a pair of short linen breeches, issued the night of their capture.

"Don't piss yourselves," the guard had laughed, "this is your only pair. Now thank *Re'is* Yavuz for his generosity."

When nobody had reacted to the ludicrous demand, they received several blows with a cane to the back of the knees until all were kneeling before the captain.

Sebastiaan didn't want to think about that night. Self-loathing burned in him as that one image kept haunting him. He should have mourned the baby girl's death, but he knew in the depths of his heart that her death, though barbaric and cruel, was probably a blessing—at least it was quick. It was the moment the guard had discovered Danielle's paring knife in his boot that had forced his heart to beat faster and the cold fingers of fury clawing at his insides. When his boots were pulled from his feet, the knife had fallen to the deck. The guard had blinked in confusion, then picked it up, lifted it to the light, and instantly saw the uselessness of the utensil.

Though small and of little worth, the knife was Sebastiaan's most prized possession. It was his link to Danielle, and when the guard carelessly tossed it over the rail, Sebastiaan had to close his eyes to hide the anguish surging through him. A link had been severed; a cord cut. To his eternal shame, he had felt his throat tighten and tears prick his eyes.

The manacles around his ankles and wrists were chafing, and the pain pulled his mind back to the present. There was little relief for it as his feet were bolted to the ship's ribbing, and his wrists were chained to the oar. A chain linked the five men on the bench, binding them together. Sebastiaan occupied the first space, next to the center aisle. Floris, the older sailor who had stood next to him on the deck that night, was chained to his right. The other three had already been there when they were pushed to their seats. They were skeleton-thin, with leathery brown skin, filthy breeches, and dead eyes. They didn't speak or acknowledge the newcomers, but when Sebastiaan called the rhythm, they listened and followed.

When the guard called for a rest, the galley slowly drifted to a halt, and their food rations were distributed. "I've given you my name, yet you withhold yours," Floris said, breaking off small bites from the hard, black biscuit that, with a mug of stale water, formed their entire meal.

Sebastiaan had downed his mug as soon as the slave had given it to him and was now regretting his shortsightedness for the biscuit tenaciously stuck to the sides of his throat. He swallowed a couple more times, using it as an excuse to evade the question. He did not want his real name known. At first, he'd followed his gut and kept his mouth shut. In hindsight, the decision was a prudent one. If anyone were to know his true identity, the price of his ransom would be astronomical.

Floris was an anchor in this maelstrom; closing himself off from him would be a mistake.

"Arent Van Jeveren." He gave the first name to pop into his head and stuck out his hand. The chains rattled as their hands met.

"Well, Arent, finish your food and try to get some sleep. They won't give us more than an hour."

"You seem to know how this works," Sebastiaan spoke around the food in his mouth, trying not to spill a crumb.

"I was captured as a young man off the coast of Sicily. Spent five years as a slave."

A shadow passed Floris' face at the mention of his past, and although Sebastiaan wanted to know more, he was too exhausted to continue their conversation.

They slept, sitting on the floor with their heads resting on the bench. It reminded Sebastiaan of chickens roosting for the night. To accommodate the chain, they all had to lower their bodies simultaneously and face the same direction with their knees tucked close to their chests.

Floris was not wrong. After what felt like only a few moments of sleep, the bullwhip cracked across his back, and this time, the skin parted. Sebastiaan felt the trickle of blood between the grooves of his shoulders.

"Up!" the guards shouted and lowered the whip over the backs of the rowers. Some grunted, others cried out, but none remained on the floor. The chorus of chains was deafening as bodies scampered to take their seats, and then the galley started forward.

Desperation gnawed at the edges of Sebastiaan's mind. He had been in wretched situations before, but never had he been without a plan or the prospect of freedom, no matter how faint. This was different; there was a practiced efficiency about their captivity—this was business, and it had been done many times before. There were no opportunities to seize or blind spots to exploit. He was no longer a person with a name, a past, or a future. He was a piece of merchandise; his only purpose was to line the pockets of his current owner, either in the form of powering the galley or being sold at some point in the future—it mattered little.

By the end of his fifth day, Sebastiaan had consumed four dried black biscuits and five cups of water, slept less than six hours, and watched three men die on their benches from exhaustion, starvation, and abuse. A young man barely past boyhood, who was slow to wake from the seat, was beaten so severely that his kidney ruptured. Floris had determined the cause of death by pointing out the amount and color of the blood spreading toward their feet. Burial was a straightforward procedure. The corpse was unshackled, threaded from the chain, and tossed overboard.

There was no beauty left in a sunrise or sunset; they merely marked the passing of time. Sebastiaan had lost count of how long they'd been at sea. The smell of the African coast pierced the stench of human misery that hung like a thick fog over the galley's deck, prodding his empty mind. Hope rose in his belly at the possibility that they might be unchained and allowed to walk on dry land. The last time he had taken more than two strides in a straight line was when his gaoler had marched him to the bench to which he was chained. The thought that he would spend the rest of his life on this galley was depressing, and there had been times when he'd come close to ending it.

It would be so easy. All he needed to do was not to get up from his moment of rest or give the guard a stare that might be interpreted the wrong way. He could spit at the captain the next time the man deigned to walk the center aisle, though that had happened only once on this voyage. Perhaps not the best option then. Each time he thought of a way to put an end to the hell he was occupying, Danielle's face came to him, and not dim like a dream or a glint of hope, but stark and unyielding.

She stood before him, her almost black hair framing her face, her green eyes alight with fire, and her lips thinned in a stern hyphen, clearly not happy with the direction of his thoughts. He didn't allow any memories to surface any longer. She was the only one that didn't abide by his firm dictate, not that she ever did. Even when he had blamed her for every stroke of the whip, she still returned like clockwork so vivid he was shocked no one else saw her. Each time his thoughts turned to an escape, she stood between him and freedom — he hated her.

Zanzibar glittered like a jewel in the midday sun with a brilliant turquoise ocean pushing toward the powder-white sands. They anchored the galley on the island's lee side, and Sebastiaan watched as lazy palm trees waved from the beach.

He stared at the droplet of land, not sure if it was real or a mirage, a whisper of something glimmering just beyond his reach. The men had received a cup of water before sunrise, but now the heat was oppressive, and their thirst was unbearable. Some, in desperation, began to drink the seawater, only to vomit it back up. All rowers remained chained to the galley, so Sebastiaan sank to the floor, rested his head on the bench, and let sleep soothe his aching muscles and calm his burning thirst.

The galley fired a single shot, announcing their arrival. Soon, it was surrounded by small dhows with colored sails. Traders yelled up at the guards on deck, holding various fruits and vegetables aloft. One man was holding a cage of chickens and pointed to a goat tied to the thin mast. When Yavuz appeared on deck, the cacophony increased as all in the small boats below wanted his attention. He seemed to recognize one man in particular and leaned over the rail to call down to him.

"Get senhor Oliveira," Captain Yavuz called. He reached into his pocket, extracted a small pouch, tossed it down to the dhow, and then waved his hand toward the beach.

By nightfall, a lavish dhow with red sails approached. She moved with the grace of a dancer as her crew drew her close enough to extend a short gangway from the rail to the bottom step of the galley's side stairs that led to the quarterdeck.

Senhor Oliveira was a large man with a past as dark as his polished ebony skin. He was of African descent and a slave from the age of nine. Years had passed, and when his wealthy Portuguese owner had died due to complications from a severed throat, the young slave revealed a letter signed by his former owner, proclaiming him as his son and heir to his fortune.

Draped in a long, dark red silk kaftan, bunched above his round belly and gold jewelry glittering in the lantern light, Oliveira gingerly made his way across the narrow plank and onto the large galley. To keep his balance, the trader had his arms loosely stretched out to the sides, very much resembling a tightrope artist attempting his first crossing.

A few more huffs and a mumbled curse signaled his progress up the short companionway. When he came face to face with Yavuz on the quarterdeck, a member of his entourage delicately patted the thin layer of sweat from his brow. Oliveira reached forward and placed his hands on the captain's shoulders before kissing him on both cheeks.

"As-salamu alaykum," Senhor Oliveira wheezed and leaned in to receive the greeting.

"Wa alaykum as-salam," Yavuz returned, fighting the urge to wipe the clamminess from his face.

Sebastiaan was resting his head on the bench, watching the proceedings on the quarterdeck with disinterest, waiting for sleep to claim him. The two men had exchanged pleasantries for some time, complimenting each other and thanking Allah for all their blessings. He knew that staring would earn him a sound beating, so he was about to close his eyes when one of Yavuz's guards dropped something at Oliveira's feet.

The trader looked down and then at Yavuz with raised eyebrows.

"What did you bring me?" he asked with glittering eyes and a soft chuckle of excitement.

Yavuz bent down and removed the cover from the body.

Mrs. Bouwer lay curled up on her side, her eyes closed, and her hands tightly fisted at her chest. She was shivering and filthy. Her once-white chemise was stained with blood, urine, and feces, and her skin was red from where parasites were attacking it. The bones of her shoulders and hips were visible through the thin fabric.

Oliveira took a step back and squinted at the woman on the floor — confusion and revulsion, vied for dominance over his features.

Yavuz heaved a deep sigh and tilted his head to the heavens, closing his eyes as he foraged about for the last scraps of patience he still possessed. The only claim Oliveira could make to being Portuguese, apart from his last name, was the way he conducted business. Yavuz despised dealing with this swindling picaroon. The man had no regard for the sanctity of fair trade. This raid had been a supreme disaster, and the woman at his feet did not have the mettle to survive until they reached Muscat. Better to get whatever he could for her now while she was still alive. He could have used her as amusement over the last few weeks, but she was so pale and her ice-blue eyes that seemed to look right through him, made his skin crawl.

"What is that?"

Yavuz swallowed his vexation at the unnecessary question.

"It is a Dutch woman."

"No," the trader breathed, "it can't be. It is not like you to let such a specimen of delight fall into this state."

Senhor Oliveira reached for one of his men, grabbed his arm, and lowered himself to one knee with great difficulty. He opened the neck of Mrs. Bouwer's chemise and reached down the front, groping her chest, then pulled back and lifted the hem to search between her thighs. Satisfied with his examination, he wiped his hand on a white square handkerchief before his man helped him back to his feet.

"Well, she's got all the parts, but you know my interests run to those a bit more youthful and," a sly grin scurried across his face, "of a different sex."

Yavuz opened his mouth to speak, but Oliveira beat him to it.

"She's a mess. *If* I take her, I would not be able to sell her. It would take months for her hair to grow back and for her body to take a shape worth looking at."

A look of false pity and hopelessness replaced the smile on the African's face as he looked toward the shoreline, but he was not quick enough to hide the greedy glint in his eye from Yavuz.

"Nonsense," Yavuz countered, "she is young and has already bred successfully. In a month or two, she could be the gem of your harem."

"My harem is for show only, as you well know."

"Yes, but she can be a generous gift to a wealthy benefactor, and we both know you would need one in the near future." Yavuz's cold smile widened when he saw the effect his words were having. Oliveira's shoulders tensed at the mention of his delicate financial situation.

The transaction was concluded with much more speed than it started. Oliveira handed over a leather pouch, which Yavuz expertly weighed in his palm, and at his nod, one of Oliveira's men picked the woman up and slung her over his shoulder. With a few more flowery words, the trader took his leave.

Yavuz waited for the red dhow to be out of sight before he ordered a rowboat to take him to shore.

This would be the first night since his capture that Sebastiaan could sleep until dawn.

* * *

"Captain?" Arent Van Jeveren's voice smoothed through the ill-lit cabin. He placed a tray of food on the heavy desk, ensuring not to touch the open map. "Eat something. Please."

The man behind the desk paid him no attention. His golden head was bent over a map, a sheet of paper with notes and some rough calculations laid under his hand.

The boatswain of the *Drommedaris* waited a few moments before slowly making his retreat.

"You can call me Davit," De Coninck's voice held a note of finality.

Arent paused, confusion pinched between his eyes before he turned back to the desk.

"I beg your pardon?"

"I am not your captain anymore." Davit De Coninck finally raised his head from his studies, leaned back in his chair, stretched his legs in front of him, and laced his fingers where they rested on his flat stomach.

"The VOC no longer employs me—I resigned."

Arent stared into his captain's mercurial blue eyes, now gray with suppressed emotions. The declaration hit him with the force of a wrecking ball. The captain was in his early forties with the air of a lion in his prime; fierce, proud, and powerful. De Coninck was like a father to him, and there was not a sailor in the VOC who did not want to sail under his command.

"When?" he breathed, struggling to put sound to his words.

"This afternoon."

Arent looked around the cabin, trying to picture someone else in it — impossible.

"What now?"

The menacing light in the captain's eyes warned Arent that this was not merely a man with a yearning to end a long and dangerous career in search of peace and quiet.

"I don't believe he's dead," the timber of De Coninck's voice vibrated with conviction, "and neither do you."

The *Drommedaris* had returned from Japan only the day before. The crew had been alive with excitement, bristling to go ashore, eager to part with their hard-earned coin, when they were met with the news of the tragedy that had befallen the *Spiegel* and the *Geloof*. Now, hours later, nobody had left the ship, their enthusiasm extinguished like fire under a wet blanket. They were all waiting as if their silent vigil would bring Sebastiaan back.

Sebastiaan had not sailed with them in months. The voyage from the Cape of Good Hope to Batavia had been his last under his uncle's command, as he had instead taken over his father's lucrative trading business. However, he was still their brother, and Arent suspected that would never change.

Arent inhaled deeply before he spoke, "Look, we know he was supposed to be on the *Leeuwerik*,"

"Yes, but ended up on the *Geloof*," De Coninck interrupted, "and the *Geloof* sank. I know the details." De Coninck's impatience was a relief, and Arent felt a knot began to untangle deep inside him.

"Exploded," Arent interjected.

"It doesn't matter. He is alive, and I am going to find him and bring him home."

"How?"

"The *Annabella* is lying at anchor not a hundred yards from here, ready to set sail."

The trading vessel, named after De Coninck's sister and Sebastiaan's mother, was of a similar size to the *Drommedaris* and the jewel in the De Vries enterprise's crown. She was narrow and fast, and if the wind was in her favor, no ship on the ocean could catch her. With a deadly array of firepower ranging from cannons to small arms, she had beauty and bite.

"You cannot sail that ship by yourself," Arent concentrated on keeping his voice even and on the edge of boredom. His shock was fast dissipating now that a plan was on the horizon.

"I'll find a crew."

Nodding his agreement, Arent looked his captain straight in the eye, "You have a crew."

This time it was De Coninck's turn to frown. "Those are good men earning decent money working for the VOC. I am not asking any of them, including you, to risk your livelihoods to do this with me."

"The hell you aren't," Arent's voice rose in equal measure with his temper.

"Do you think for a second, I would sail under anyone else's command? Do you think I would sit on the side collecting my *decent money* and let you go off searching for my brother on your own?" The words flew from his mouth, and he could feel his upper lip curl with contempt. "Do you think that little of me?" Arent realized that he was shouting and belatedly added, "Captain." But he held De Coninck's stare that had not wavered from his since the beginning of his tirade.

"Fine," De Coninck said, sounding unaffected by Arent's passionate speech, "you can come. But," he said, pointing a finger to what lay beyond the closed cabin door, "you cannot order them to follow."

"I won't have to. Not when you tell them what you have done and the reason for it."

# Chapter 6

Governor Van Riebeeck looked up from the ledger, the warm morning sun assaulting his chamber with slashes of light, and he could feel the heat on his back as Captain Helm pushed four bedraggled and badly sunburned men into the room, followed by four armed soldiers. Shuffling their feet and rustling their weapons, the soldiers arranged themselves to stand ramrod straight in a neat line against the back wall.

When he'd heard the determined knock on his door, he'd known it was Helm, but this fanfare that preceded him was unexpected. As he looked at the four men lining up on the other side of his desk, Van Riebeeck's surprise was quickly replaced by cold, unadulterated fury.

Jan Blanx stood with a downcast mien, broad shoulders hunched, his feet planted a fair distance apart as if he was still on the ship's deck and countering the roll. Next to him, John Van Leyen's tall form was just as weathered, but he attempted to relax his mouth and focus his eyes on the desk that dominated the center of the room. The other two were nothing but boys, soldiers by their dress, but the governor could not recall their names. They stood close to each other, almost touching, as if to draw strength from one another.

Governor Van Riebeeck leaned back in his chair and leveled a pointed but questioning stare at his captain. His anger had not yet cooled, and he did not trust the quality of his voice. Helm filled the extended silence.

"Governor," Helm spoke, but his tone and demeanor suggested that a fire was burning in his belly, and Van Riebeeck could see the sparks of it in his cold blue eyes. "Our deserters have returned."

Helm's words sent a ripple of movement through the deserters. Blanx's hands fisted and then opened. Van Leyen's throat worked as he swallowed, and the other two runaways shared a nervous look. Van Riebeeck took his time studying each man, as he reined in his temper. Unaccustomed to public outbursts or melodramatic displays, he firmly believed that all problems could be resolved, and any obstacle overcome, with an open mind and a level head.

The knowledge that these men were pushing his emotions well past anger and into violence bothered him more than he cared to admit. They had committed an act of treason, and he should punish them accordingly.

The fledgling settlement was responsible for many lives on land and at sea, and their actions had put all at risk. Life at the settlement was hard, but not unbearable. It would be foolish to expect otherwise, for stepping onto a wild and untamed continent would not come without its hardships and challenges. What did these four expect? That they could do better on their own, out in the wilderness? Fools! By doing so, they had set a bad example for others to follow. If more men attempted to flee, the settlement would soon come to a grinding halt.

Van Riebeeck understood the bigger picture. This was not about him or his reputation, nor was it about filling the coffers of the VOC. This was about growth and advancement for all, on all fronts. The establishment at the Cape would benefit those at sea directly by providing a critical halfway haven to replenish supplies, offering repairs, and medical assistance, and by doing so, opening trade routes previously unimaginable. He would not fail, nor would the Cape of Good Hope, all because four idiots sought freedom from their obligations.

"Which one of you instigated this?" Van Riebeeck demanded, his voice deep and even as it rolled across the room.

"Blanx?"

Jan Blanx lifted his head, and the governor was silently taken aback by the defiance in the man's face; a defiance he would soon be rid of.

"I did, Governor," Blanx spoke, and he sounded contrite for all the hatred in his eyes.

"No, it was both of us," John Van Leyen said, and shifted his weight. The man was smart enough to keep his face blank. Van Riebeeck had always liked him. He was a competent builder, and the men respected him, which is why he must be made an example of before he could inspire more with his fanciful ideas.

"Governor, please show mercy. We only ..."

"Enough," Van Riebeeck barked, and Van Leyen swallowed the rest of his words, "you will have plenty of opportunity to speak."

"We only went ..." Adriaen Huytjens began where Van Leyen left off but was abruptly silenced when Captain Helm's open hand landed on his left ear with a slap that sent the young soldier staggering into his friend on his right.

There was not much to be done. It was true — the men had come back of their own accord, but whether they begged for mercy mattered little. Their fates were sealed the minute they had left the settlement nearly two weeks earlier. There would be no interrogations or trials. The only concession Van Riebeeck would make was to interview each before meeting with the *Meesters* that afternoon to discuss their punishment.

Van Riebeeck turned to Helm. "Put them in irons and lock them up separately." With a nod and a dismissive wave of his hand, he returned his focus to the open ledger on his desk.

Blanx knew it was a hare-brained idea to return to the settlement. They had searched every inlet and cove for any trace of a ship that might head back to Europe, finding none. But after two weeks of near starvation and sleeping in the open, vulnerable to all manner of attacks ranging from rhinoceroses to natives, and with little hope of improving their circumstances, they began entertaining the idea of returning to the settlement. The decision had been unanimous after reaching a mountain range too high to cross and too wide to circumnavigate.

Van Leyen firmly believed that once they returned to the settlement, they could appeal to the governor to show mercy, but Blanx had his doubts. The governor was exceedingly heavy-handed regarding any misdeeds against the settlement.

Judging by the glint in the governor's eyes, Blanx doubted if their fate would be any less than that of their friend, Pieter Brackenier. The governor and the *Meesters* were a law unto themselves, and it was becoming patently clear that at the Cape of Good Hope, you toe the line, or you'll find the value of your life drop like a pebble in a pond.

Blanx scanned the courtyard, searching for Fly as they were marched toward a row of newly built storerooms. The dog's face was still raw from an encounter with a porcupine. The previous day, Blanx had painstakingly removed eighteen quills from its head—a small mercy that the luckless creature hadn't lost an eye. A musket butt slammed between his shoulder blades, jarring him from his thoughts. He stumbled into a small, windowless room. As he turned, the heavy wooden door slammed shut, and the lock slid into place.

Blinking hard against the sudden darkness, he fought a wave of panic that threatened to crash over him. He despised small, dark spaces. From the lack of sound and the sudden temperature drop, he knew they'd locked him in one of the future cooling rooms. Blanx dropped to the floor and crawled on his hands and knees until he reached the wall, where he flopped over and pressed his back against the cold stone. Closing his eyes, he focused on taking deep, even breaths while counting from one to ten. He kept repeating the sequence until his heart settled into a steady rhythm.

There was no food or water for the rest of the day, and somewhere in the dark hours, Blanx fell asleep. He woke to the scrape of the door against the stone floor as somebody pulled it open. The unexpected shard of bright light made his eyes smart. He raised his arm and pushed his face into the crook of his elbow.

"Up," came the sharp order from Captain Helm as he and the governor entered the small room. Blanx staggered to his feet, disoriented and unsteady, as he leaned against the back wall.

Helm bent down to place a low three-legged stool on the floor.

They'd left the door open, and fresh morning air filled the small room. Shouts and the sounds of construction told of a world Blanx now wished he'd never given up. Keeping his eyes on the brightly lit courtyard, he noticed three armed guards waiting beyond the door—the governor was not taking any chances.

"Mister Blanx," the governor greeted him and lowered himself onto the stool, "understand that this is not an interrogation." Governor Van Riebeeck shrugged one shoulder before continuing. "This is an opportunity for you to say what's on your mind, air any grievances, or convey any messages you might have."

"Governor," Blanx began, and his voice was rough from thirst and sleep. "I regret my decision to leave and will face the punishment you deem fit but I ask you to show mercy to the others. It was my idea to leave the settlement. I planned it. Van Leyen followed out of loyalty to a friend, and the other two … well, I did not give them much of a choice."

Van Riebeeck stared into the man's eyes as he spoke and could see the truth of his words, but as much as he appreciated the sentiment, he would not allow it to influence the outcome. If he showed mercy or weakness now, it would spell the end of this endeavor.

"Van Leyen told me the same thing, in as many words." The governor's eyes searched the bare room. "It is a pity you were not as honorable and loyal to the settlement as you are to your friends."

"Governor, we were desperate…"

"Everybody is desperate, Blanx." Governor Van Riebeeck's voice rose with frustration, and his mouth hardened in a snarl. "But if we all start running for the hills at any given opportunity, how will we survive?" Blanx was taken aback by the intensity of the governor's words, and ashamed by the truth of it.

"Huytjens said you made a statement, that you would do anything to hurt the colony. Is that so?"

"No, sir. I never said those words." Blanx shook his head as his gaze dropped to his feet. "I swear it."

"Huytjens and Dirks claimed they followed you to determine if you planned to meet with any Portuguese ships and would have returned to the colony as soon as they had evidence of your treachery. They claimed to have acted in the colony's interest."

Since the governor did not pose a question, Blanx decided not to respond. The two soldiers were sniveling little liars with even less honor than Blanx had credited them before.

"Do you have anything to say to that?" Governor Van Riebeeck asked.

"No, sir." His lack of response earned him a few seconds of contemplation from the governor.

"Is there anything else you wish to say?" The governor moved forward, leaning his arms on his knees.

"No, sir." Blanx heard a sharp bark from outside and it brought a wry smile to his face. Fly.

With a nod of acceptance, the governor rose, ducked under the lintel, and stepped into the bright sunlight. Blanx overheard him murmur a few words to someone outside. A guard then entered, carrying a mug of water and a bowl of boiled peas mixed with salted fish. The guard placed an empty bucket in the corner before the heavy door slammed shut and the lock scraped into place once more.

* * *

Governor Jan Van Riebeeck was flanked by the *Meesters,* as they sat in a line at the long main dining table in a hall that was yet to be used for its intended purpose. Thus far, the spacious room had served as a Sunday church, a weekday boardroom, and now a courtroom.

Van Riebeeck barely noticed the smell of the freshly laid oak floor and the newly whitewashed walls. He was exhausted after a day spent debating and deciding the fate of the prisoners. Glancing to his far right, he noted the pastor with his hawklike features relaxing against the back of his chair. The man was inordinately pious and had vigorously argued that the actions of all four were a betrayal against God and the Fatherland and were nothing short of treason.

Next to the pastor sat Elias Coopman. His face was outwardly calm, but Van Riebeeck could see a deep well of emotion roiling behind his eyes. As always, Coopman had been the voice of reason during the long hours of deliberations and in the end, he supported the governor regardless of his own convictions. Van Riebeeck felt a surge of gratitude toward his second in command, without whose counsel he doubted he would have had the fortitude to manage thus far.

At Van Riebeeck's left was Captain Helm and then the bookkeeper, Frederick Verburgh. To his surprise, Helm had argued quite strongly for the release of the two soldiers.

"I know they are two wastrels, but we are short on soldiers, and there is a taste of danger in the air of late. They are scared and will do whatever we desire of them. I suggest we reduce their wages by half and make them understand how deeply in our debt they are for our leniency. I doubt we will have reason to question their loyalty in the future, given that the other two will serve as good examples for how seriously we view this behavior." There was no concrete evidence that the soldiers' testimonies were false. However, Van Riebeeck doubted their actions were as noble as they proclaimed. Blanx had not contradicted their claims, so he had agreed with Helm.

Not surprisingly, Verburgh had earnestly supported the pastor's views and Van Riebeeck wondered if the man could muster an independent thought at all, for when he was not aping Helm, he was parroting the pastor. But what he lacked in the cultivation of a spine, he made up for by being painfully meticulous in the accuracy of his work.

Van Riebeeck nodded to Helm, who rose from his seat and strode from the hall, leaving the echoes of his footsteps to mix with the dust motes that floated in the late afternoon sun. The hall fell silent, each man debating their own conscience or basking in their righteousness. The contemplative mood was disturbed when the prisoners were ushered in, followed by a line of armed guards sufficient to make the odds of any attempts at violence or escape fall heavily in favor of the settlement. Helm closed the doors and walked a measured march back to his chair.

The prisoners stood in the same order as they had in the governor's office the previous morning, except for a slight but noticeable gap between Blanx and Van Leyen on the right and the two soldiers on the left. They all stared at the table, not making eye contact with any of the men sitting behind it.

Governor Van Riebeeck acknowledged the prisoners' presence with a nod and rose from his seat. The line of soldiers snapped to attention and once silence descended on the room again, he spoke in a clear voice.

"By deserting your posts, you have placed the settlement in danger and done so willfully. Your actions are not just against the settlement but also against the VOC and the United Provinces of the Netherlands and you are therefore accused of having committed an act of treason." There was an indrawn breath from one of the young men and Van Leyen and Blanx shared a panicked glance. A dark stain formed on Huytjens' breeches, and he hung his head as his body struggled to contain the shaking of his muscles. The stink of urine and sulfurous sweat filled the room like low fog creeping in from the ocean.

"Adriaen Huytjens, step forward," Van Riebeeck commanded. The chains dragging across the floor punctuated his movements as the young soldier stepped from the line.

"Mister Huytjens, due to a lack of evidence, we found you not guilty of treason." The young man's head snapped up at the governor's words, his features contorted with shock, astonishment, and relief. "However," the governor continued, "you have acted on your own and without the council or an order from your commanding officer. As a result, your salary will be reduced by half, and you will be demoted to the lowest rank and will not be considered for promotion for as long as you are stationed at the Cape of Good Hope. Once your restraints are removed, you are free to go."

Huytjens openly wept as a guard removed the shackles from his ankles. Once freed, he bowed deeply to the assembly at the long table and exited the hall with hurried steps. Only when the door closed behind him did Van Riebeeck proceed.

"Gert Dirks, step forward." Dirks stepped forward, and his face shone with hope when he met the governor's eyes.

"Mister Dirks, due to a lack of evidence, we found you not guilty of treason."

"Thank you, Governor," Dirks blurted, but the governor held a hand to silence him.

"You too, have acted on your own and without the council or an order from your commanding officer. Your salary will be reduced by half, and you will be demoted to the lowest rank and will not be considered for promotion for as long as you are stationed at the Cape of Good Hope. Once your restraints are removed, you are also free to go."

Blanx and Van Leyen remained standing as they were, armed guards at their backs, facing the governor, and the *Meesters*.

"Jan Blanx," the governor said and paused, spreading his legs a little further apart before holding the accused's eyes in an iron lock.

Since the governor did not order him to take a step forward, Blanx remained rooted to the spot on the floor and lifted his head to stare into the cold brown eyes of the man who held his life in his hands.

"You have been found guilty of treason. You are to be keelhauled and receive one hundred and fifty lashes after which, you will remain in irons and work as a slave for the next two years at the Cape of Good Hope." Governor Van Riebeeck watched as the blood leached from the man's face and he noticed the slight adjustment in his stance as he forced himself to remain upright. A brittle silence descended on the room, but Blanx remained mute.

"John Van Leyen." This time, the governor rested his chin on his chest, inhaled deeply, and then went on. "You too, have been found guilty of treason and are hereby sentenced to death by musket shot. Your sentences will be carried out tomorrow, at first light." Nodding at the stunned faces, he said, "You are excused."

The prisoners stood like statues, unable to move, and Helm signaled the soldiers to escort them from the courtroom.

* * *

It was late, and Van Riebeeck, tired to his marrow, did not want to face his thoughts alone in the guest quarters. He needed his wife. He needed to hear her breath and inhale the scent of her skin. Looking into her vacant blue eyes would be better than staring into the void of his own soul.

He stumbled blindly up the stairs and found the door to their apartments unlocked. How often did she sleep with the door unsecured? He wondered as he stepped inside and locked the door behind him. A sliver of light was visible from under the bedroom door. He knocked softly and entered upon her reply.

Inside, Maria was lying on her side, staring at nothing in particular, waiting for sleep to claim her, until the soft knock on the door had focused her eyes.

"Enter," she answered and found herself staring into her husband's troubled face.

"Do you sleep with the candle burning?" he asked, wincing at the harshness of his voice.

"No, I was about to snuff it. I don't like the dark." His heart tightened at the sound of her voice, small and unsure. How many nights had she lain here, waiting for him, alone and afraid?

Maria was held captive by her husband's silent stare. Then he stirred from his trance, and she watched as his hands went to his waistcoat, fingers working absentmindedly to free the buttons, one after another. Once done, he carelessly flung the garment onto the foot of the bed.

"What happened today?" Maria asked, sitting up and swinging her legs from under the blankets. Jan's shoulders were tight, and he was pale, but at the sound of her words, his eyes snapped to hers, and for the briefest of moments, she saw guilt flit across his face. Her gaze dropped to his left hand, where his ring finger tapped against his thigh as he considered her question.

His wife's voice was even and emotionless, much like the woman herself. Her hair was untied and hung around her shoulders like a shield. An air of fragility enveloped her as she sat with her small bare feet dangling from the bed, bathed in the flickering light of the single candle as it valiantly tried to fight off the darkness in the room.

Closing his eyes, he contemplated how much to tell her.

"Just talk to me like you used to," she said in a whisper.

She was always his anchor, but sorrow and misery had robbed him of that and left him adrift. How he wished they could be as they once were.

"I don't know where to start." Even he could hear the hopelessness in his voice.

"Anywhere," she said and the single word reached him like a lifeline.

He began to speak. Some of what he said made no sense, and others did, but he could not stop, and the words flowed from him along with his strength to remain standing. When he finally told her the whole sordid tale, he found himself on his knees before her, staring up into her face, and what he saw shook him to his core.

He watched as her throat worked to keep her tears at bay. Shock, horror, and a depth of sadness no woman should ever feel had widened her eyes and slumped her shoulders. She had retreated from the edge of the bed and was now sitting in the middle of the mattress with her hands trembling in her lap, her legs tucked neatly beneath her nightdress as if she was afraid that he might touch her.

"Husband, what have you done?" she asked, her voice hoarse with agony.

Anger rose like a tide in him, and he pushed from the floor. "It wasn't just me. The *Meesters* decided unanimously on the punishments." He sounded like a petulant child defending himself and blaming others for the mess they'd made.

But she was unmoved by his words. "The *Meesters* answer to you; you have the final say, not them. They are nothing but advisors, and well you know it." For all the fragility surrounding her like morning mist, her voice was soft but strong, and once again, Van Riebeeck reached for something to keep from sinking. But this time, she offered no deliverance.

"By the grace of God, Jan, do not do this. Those are good men. You cannot have their blood on your hands."

"How do you know that?" he snapped at her, wanting to frighten her into silence.

"How do I know what?" she asked without a trace of fear. Instead, her eyes were sparkling with an anger that was slow to ignite but, once lit, could burn fierce and hot for a long time.

"How do you know they are good men? Blanx is a known troublemaker and might survive his punishment tomorrow, and Van Leyen-"

"And Van Leyen will not," she interrupted him. "Van Leyen has never done anything wrong, and everyone respects him. And don't ask me how I know. Do you think that because I keep to myself, it has rendered me blind and deaf? I see, I hear, perhaps better than anyone else." She was still sitting on the bed, but her hands were no longer trembling in her lap. Her husband stood glaring at her, his face darkened by anger and frustration, yet she did not cower before him. He was on the verge of damning his soul, and she would not allow it.

"He deserted the settlement," Van Riebeeck returned point blank.

"Yes, he made a mistake. One mistake!" The passion and fire in Maria's voice took him by surprise. For so long, she'd been a shadow of her former self, but tonight sparks and splinters of who she once was were forcing their way to the surface. "And because of that single misstep, you have deemed it fit to take his life."

He stared at her in silence, her beauty radiant in the soft light, elegant despite her rumpled state, but what struck him most was that she was right.

Seeing the fight drain from his body, Maria slipped back beneath the blankets and turned on her side once more.

"Come to bed, husband," she said softly.

* * *

He waited in the shadows of the storerooms built perpendicular to the fort's main building. The moon, uncooperative, glared brightly in the late-night sky, bathing the structure in a pale blue-white hue, like a long-drowned corpse. When the faint yellow light finally flickered out in the governor's window, he stepped from behind the wall, slid the key into the lock, carefully pushed the latch free, and stepped into the small room.

"It took you long enough." The growl came from somewhere to his left. Pulling the heavy door shut, he stood still for a breath, listening for any sounds of approach from the prisoner. The man would not be able to move quietly with the chains hanging from his wrists and ankles. Satisfied that all was under control, he crouched and fished a candle and flint box from his jacket pockets.

The faint glow of the candle irritated Blanx's eyes as he narrowed them against the light.

Coopman slowly rose to his feet and stepped closer to the prisoner, his booted steps falling quietly on the stone floor.

"You come to kill me?" Blanx asked with resignation, acceptance written in the slant of his shoulders.

Coopman shook his head. "No, your punishment is suitable enough. No need for me to improve on it." Blanx huffed a cynical smile and turned his face away.

"Where are the letters Blanx?" When Blanx turned his lazy eyes back to him, Coopman could see the lies floating behind the plastered-on, blank expression. "Come on now, I know you did not meet with any ships, so don't try to lie to me. You failed in the task I gave you."

"I failed because there were no ships," Blanx growled. "Isn't it ironic that Van Leyen and I are the ones being executed for treason in the morning, while you stand next to the governor, all fancy and polished?"

"Ironic," Coopman smiled, "my, my Blanx, you've learned a new word."

"Good Hope has taught me many new things. Most of all, that there isn't any."

"How positively depressing. Now, tell me where the letters are, and I will leave you to enjoy your maudlin sentiments while you still can."

Coopman flicked his fingers in an irritated gesture when it seemed Blanx would not reply. Blanx might be illiterate, but the man was built like an ox and not altogether stupid. Those were the qualities that drew Coopman's attention in the first place. He knew even if Blanx opened the letters, he would not be able to decipher the content, but if anyone could get them to their destination, it was Blanx, given the right motivation. In his case, his hatred for the settlement and the governor were enough to entice him with the prospect of freedom for the small price of delivering a packet of letters.

"I can't remember what I did with them," Blanx teased as he lifted his eyes to the ceiling and tightened his lips, his hands clasped together near his groin. Coopman was not fool enough to step closer. Even shackled Blanx was lethal, and he had no desire to have his airways cut off by those chains neatly wrapped around his neck. "Perhaps I destroyed them. Perhaps I told somebody about them, or perhaps I hid them somewhere. Anything is possible," he said with a shrug, "and there is nothing you can do about it." Blanx barked a hollow laugh. "I can see how you want to strike me," he nodded at Coopman. "Your lips are all hard, your eyes are sharp, and your hands are curled into tight balls. But how will we explain any damage done to me in the morning? Hmm? Who else has access to that key in your pocket?"

Coopman turned and picked up the candle. The shadows danced in disturbing patterns on his face. Blanx watched with quiet satisfaction as Coopman realized he had nothing to lose and would carry the secret of the letters to his grave, leaving it to haunt him.

"I can still save you from your fate tomorrow, all you have to do is tell me where those letters are." Coopman tried one last time, but Blanx only stared at him, not even drawing a breath to speak. Coopman shook his head in feigned remorse, gave up, and left as quietly as he had come. Blanx waited until he heard the grind of the lock before he sat back down again.

"No, you can't," he murmured.

# Chapter 7

The *Leeuwerik* lay anchored far beyond the crashing waves, where the shore sloped steeply into the deep blue ocean. Laden with spices and silk, she sat so low that her lower gun ports skimmed the waterline. *A pity that,* Blanx thought, *if she was lighter, the time spent in the water would be less—every second was going to count.* He tried to control his thoughts and emotions as he was rowed to the site of his doom.

The worst part of the keelhauling was the anticipation—the agonizing seconds of waiting as others took charge, preparing him for the ordeal ahead. He hoped the governor would skip the ritual of reading a *Bible* passage or muttering a hollow prayer for his soul. Better to just get it over with. His soul was his own concern, and any words spoken on its behalf were merely to ease the orator's conscience.

Today would be his last day on this earth. He watched the sun claw its way up from the horizon; there would be no sunset for him this evening. If he was lucky, this day would be a short one if he could manage to crack his skull against the keel on the way up. At least he'd welcome his old friend Van Leyen to the gates; pearly or fiery was a question that would soon be answered. Van Leyen's execution was postponed to the afternoon due to the *Leeuwerik* wanting to sail with the afternoon tide and so would only be available to accommodate Blanx's keelhauling exhibition for a limited time. Everybody was ordered to gather on the beach to watch the proceedings, not that they would see much from that distance, but, he figured, it's the thought that counted. At least this way, he'd have a few cheers sending him on his way.

He sat in the middle of the sloop with his head bowed and listened to the four rowers grunting and counting their way to the *Leeuwerik*. Closing his eyes, he enjoyed the slight swell of the water beneath the small craft. 'Thank you, God, for letting me die at sea.' He mouthed the silent prayer and allowed himself a faint smile. If the keelhauling by some miracle did not kill him, the hundred and fifty lashes surely would. To that end, he had asked, as a last request, that his whipping be done on the deck of the *Leeuwerik*.

The dull thud against the larger ship's hull announced their arrival, and Blanx opened his eyes and raised his head to look at the rope ladder leading to the upper deck. Black char marks still blemished her sides as a reminder of her near demise at the hands of pirates. *Home.*

Blanx cleared the bulwark and surveyed the scene before him. All the settlers were gathered on the beach, and everybody from the *Leeuwerik* down to the young cabin boys were on deck. In the center, near the mainmast, Captain Zeeuw and Governor Van Riebeeck, with Elias Coopman at his right, stood in waiting.

Captain Zeeuw's feet were shoulder-width apart, and his hands were clasped behind his back. The proceedings were nothing but an irritation to him, an interruption to his busy schedule, and it showed in the set of his mouth and the distortion of his eyebrows as they both lifted at the outer corners.

The governor's expression was difficult to read. If Blanx was still a betting man, he would wager that the governor looked troubled, as though he had something to say, but was waiting for the right moment to do so. And then there was Coopman, cool and calm, standing just behind the governor's right shoulder like some guardian angel watching over his charge. His eyes were heavy-lidded with smugness, and Blanx knew he was biting back a sneer; the bastard was winning, and he knew it. If Satan ever needed a second, Coopman would be a prime candidate.

Blanx bowed to the men. Looking up at the rigging, his eyes followed the line that ran the length of the first yard before it fed through pulleys and down to the deck where two loose ends waited, ready to form a closed loop with his body as the link. The rest of the rope was already threaded under the belly of the ship.

The tense silence on deck shattered when Van Riebeeck's voice rang out.

"We are all gathered here this morning to witness the execution of punishment for Jan Blanx for the crime of treason." Looking to Blanx, he continued, "You will be keelhauled once and then receive one hundred and fifty lashes before you are escorted back to the settlement, where you will live out the rest of your sentence." The governor spoke without intonation in his voice, his face stark and pale as he stared into Blanx's eyes. Blanx returned the stare, foregoing any outward reaction.

Another few brittle seconds passed in the wake of the governor's words, and Blanx counted them by the beats of his heart. If the governor was waiting for him to plead for mercy, they were going to stand here a while.

"Captain," the governor signaled to the captain.

"Boatswain, prepare the prisoner," Captain Zeeuw ordered, and a man similar in build to Blanx stepped from the crowd.

Blanx measured the man standing before him. He used to have the same look on his face and the same strength in the shoulders; perhaps he still did. The boatswain would do his duty and show no weakness, and should Blanx survive the keelhauling, this would be the man that would deliver the rest of his sentence. Judging by the girth of the man's upper arms, he knew he would not be conscious to endure the entire ordeal.

Blanx followed the boatswain's movements as if in a dream, watching him crouch to tie one end of the rope around Blanx's ankles, then rise to wrap the other end neatly around his wrists. His body joined the two ends of the rope looped beneath the ship's breadth. All that remained was for the crew to pull swiftly, ensuring his head struck the keel, knocking him into the hereafter. If they pulled slowly, the rope would sag, sparing him the keel but leaving drowning a real possibility.

For Blanx, the world had contracted to a tight circle. His ears were blocked as if he was already underwater. The only discernible sound was the strong beat of his heart as it pulsed through his veins. His skin felt overly sensitive, and the slight morning breeze licked his face like a cold flame. The bright sunlight made his eyes water, and he closed them before embarrassing himself. He hadn't had anything to drink since last night and emptied his bladder this morning. If he was to meet his maker today, he would do so with his dignity intact.

A steady pull on the rope lifted Blanx onto the bulwark, facing the deck, his arms stretched taut above his head, his feet bound tightly together. The ocean could not have been more beautiful; he noted as he stared across the deck toward the starboard side. She was calm, with not a ripple to mar her oily surface. He felt a tug on his body and glanced down. Two men were securing a cannonball to his ankles. As they stepped back, Blanx filled his lungs with air and shut his eyes.

The shove against his thighs was met, a split second later, with the cold embrace of the water.

Even though he expected it, the cold was still a shock, and Blanx fought the impulse to release the breath he held. Instead, he pressed his lips tight, squeezed his eyes shut, and tucked his face behind his outstretched arms as the rope tightened and drew him toward the barnacle-crusted hull.

The instant the tender flesh of his underarms connected with the ship's side, a scream tore from Blanx's throat as barnacles cut long lines from his armpits to the small bones of his wrists and down the length of his thighs—bubbles of air mixed with his blood made their way to the surface. His body felt as if it was on fire, and he clenched his teeth hard to keep from inhaling.

There was a slight sagging of the line as the crew adjusted their grip, before he was propelled downward again. Blanx knew the cuts on his arms and thighs were deep. He could feel the warmth of his blood in the water as it rushed over his face. Pain was now a visible thing, as it moved in irregular white shapes against the insides of his eyelids. Then another sag, and two seconds later, he moved again, more pain, more blood, another sag, and another forward propulsion that ended abruptly as his head struck the keel with a blunt force.

* * *

72

On deck the boatswain looked up as a hitch disrupted the rhythm of the men pulling the rope. The body was stuck against the keel.

"Easy!" he called, and the line went slack.

"More," he ordered again, watching as more of the rope relaxed until it was loose enough for the body to pass underneath the keel.

"Heave!" he roared, and the line of five men moved forward again, the rope clutched over their left shoulders.

"Steady," he called as he saw their pace increase. Too fast, the man would suffer more damage on his way up. Too slow, and he would drown. He would do this right; controlling the speed and rhythm of the haul could mean the difference between life and death, and he was not prepared to wash the blood of a man he had no quarrel with from his hands.

Twice more, the men adjusted their grips, and on the third haul, Blanx's body broke from the water. They pulled until his feet cleared the bulwark, then the boatswain grasped the line and drew his tattered form back onto the deck.

He looked at the captain, who turned to the governor. The young dark-haired man gave a crisp nod, the gesture then repeated to the boatswain by his captain.

"Cut him loose," the boatswain ordered the nearest sailor.

The boatswain crouched next to the prisoner, searching for any sign of life. But when the body curled unexpectedly and convulsed with involuntary spasms as the prisoner started coughing up seawater, the boatswain snapped his hand away, rose to his feet, and took a quick step backward.

Blanx felt the solid wooden deck boards under his outstretched hands. The rest of his body was numb. He tried to open his eyes and was greeted with bright sunlight and many feet surrounding him. Feeling exposed, he drew his shaking limbs closer to his body, but the action took several seconds as his brain was slow to formulate the order. He tried lifting himself on his hands and knees, but his hands slipped in the blood pooling under his arms, and he collapsed back onto the hard surface.

Orders rang out, but they mingled with the breeze, and Blanx ignored them. He felt firm hands gripping his upper arms, only to slip away as blood washed across his skin. The men readjusted their grip, and Blanx was dragged to a barrel lying on its side near the mainmast. He noticed they did not bother to tie him down, but the thought was cut short when the first whiplash licked across his back, parting the skin from his right shoulder to the left side. The burn from the assault was instant and blinding. Two more followed in close succession, equal in their ferocity. The boatswain's strength shone through every swing of the whip. Darkness enfolded him before he could count the fourth lash.

When the sloop returned to the beach, four sailors carried Blanx on a stretcher through the gathering crowd, drawn to gape at the macabre scene. A second sloop soon followed, transporting the governor and his second-in-command. As soon as the stretcher carriers reached the dry sand, they unceremoniously dumped their grotesque cargo and returned to the waiting vessel.

Blanx's body was damaged beyond recognition. The stretcher with the bloody pulp that used to be his friend passed Van Leyen, where he stood tied to a building post in the center of the clearing between the infirmary and the slave quarters. He watched as four soldiers carried the stretcher into the darkness of the storeroom that served as Blanx's cell, and his mind drifted from the grim present to the day he'd first laid eyes on Blanx—ironically, drenched in blood then too.

* * *

Blanx was nine years old when Van Leyen first saw the stocky lad with curly orange hair. At the time, Blanx had sported a split lip, a bloody nose, and a black eye and was being hauled from a carriage and through the front door of the house he shared with his father, the latter's hand ruthlessly fisted in the white collar of his son's shirt.

That was the day Van Leyen realized that the wealthy have their struggles too. He and the rich boy shared the same age, but that was their only shared thread, for their lives were worlds apart. Van Leyen had to work, but he came to work every day with his father, who watched over him, fed him, and loved him. His clothes were old and work-worn, but there was no blood on them, and his face was sun hardened, not battered. Van Leyen counted his blessings and realized that there were many types of riches, not just those that filled pockets.

The Van Leyen father and son were part of a gang of men in the employ of Abraham Blanx, a wealthy wine merchant. Their days were filled with loading wagons and transporting thousands of crates containing exquisite wines from the Blanx warehouses to the Amsterdam docks, from there they traveled to ports around the world and onto the tables of cultured people with refined palates and expensive tastes. When not hauling crates, the men were tasked to guard and patrol the grounds and house of the Blanx estate—old man Blanx had a penchant for making and hanging on to enemies.

Young Blanx was his father's son in every way but the one that mattered. Same hair, same shape to the face—wide and brawny, and though the boy was still young, his body was already following the same pattern as his sire's. But it was his soul that was different, or rather Blanx junior possessed one. Blanx would regularly sneak food from the kitchens, when his father was not home, to share with Van Leyen.

The boys had become fast friends and had shared a deep bond, one that would see them rescuing each other throughout the course of their lives.

It was a particularly cold winter, and Blanx had just turned eleven when he'd failed to show up for three days. Van Leyen knew the merchant had left for Marseilles and would be gone for weeks, but he usually left his son behind. The child was regularly left in the staff's care, uneducated, unloved, and with more broken bones and bruises than were usual for a boy his age. Van Leyen never knew what had become of Blanx's mother. He only knew that there was no mistress of the house.

At the time Van Leyen had been on guard duty, and his route included the interior of the house and its surrounding gardens. He'd thought it wise to use the opportunity to search for his friend, but the house was empty. There were no servants. The doors to the rooms were closed, and the furniture was covered with rough linens to guard against dust. Even the chandeliers were encased in white linens hanging from the ceiling, making them look like large spider nests. Old man Blanx was apparently gone for more than just a few weeks. Perhaps he had taken his son with him, Van Leyen thought, and the unease around the unknown seemed to loosen a bit.

There was an empty eeriness about the house that made the hairs on the back of his neck rise as he patrolled the dark and empty halls. It was when he reached the wine cellar, a small room dug into the earth below the house, that he heard a faint scratching sound from the inside of the thick wooden door.

In utter disbelief, Van Leyen had lifted the heavy beam securing the door to find a bloody, half-frozen, and starved Blanx lying on the cold stone floor. Blanx shook like a reed in the wind when Van Leyen reached out his hand and pulled him to his feet.

"I thought I was gonna die," Blanx spoke in a thin and shattered voice.

His friend was badly shaken and had clung to him as they'd made their way from the house in search of Van Leyen's father.

That night, Blanx had traveled with the wagon to the harbor and was never seen or heard from again. Not until years later, when a beast of a man had lifted Van Leyen from the gutter behind an Amsterdam tavern and carried him over his wide shoulder to safety.

After finding Blanx in the cellar, Van Leyen could no longer stomach working for the wine merchant and took a job with his uncle, building dockside warehouses. Years later, when he had saved enough money, he married the very shy, but very beautiful butcher's daughter. Van Leyen's life had finally found its rhythm, which inspired him to look to the future with hope and even dreams, indulgences rarely afforded the working class. Those precious hopes and dreams were crushed when his wife gave birth to their first babe. It was a day that started off so bright and hopeful and ended with nothing but emptiness and darkness when his wife didn't stop bleeding and his child wouldn't start breathing. Their deaths had robbed his life of all meaning and purpose and left him alone and broken in one increasingly seedy gambling den after the next. One night he'd gambled more than what he had in his pocket and was left for dead in the gutter, lying in a pool of his own blood and piss, when Blanx had found him.

Neither knew who the other was, and only after Van Leyen was sober enough to introduce himself to his rescuer did the childhood friends reunite.

At the time, Blanx was a boatswain on a vessel called the *Goede Hoop*, and in three months' time, he would depart on an expedition to the Cape of Good Hope at the southern tip of Africa. He had urged Van Leyen to join him. It was a lifeline, a chance to start over, to escape the ghosts that seemed to follow him wherever he went, and so he did.

*****

Van Leyen stood with his hands tied behind the post, the wood pressing sharply between his shoulder blades. His arms trembled, yet for some inexplicable reason, he felt detached from the tension gripping his body. Instead, his gaze fixed on the men across from him. Helm stood resolute, legs firmly planted, musket at his side, his eyes sweeping the crowd for signs of trouble before settling on the two neat rows of soldiers arrayed before the infirmary.

The governor crossed the courtyard with heavy strides and positioned himself between Helm and Coopman near the bridge that crossed the moat surrounding the fort beyond. He was pale and tense, and Van Leyen thought he looked rather blue around the gills. It was one thing to kill a man in anger, but quite another when it was an execution. That was something that could eat at a man's sensibilities. The thought threatened to bring a smile to Van Leyen's face, but he fought the urge. This was no laughing matter. But what did he care? It would be over soon enough, unlike what they'd done to poor Blanx. That was a sin before God. If you mean to kill a man, then kill him; no need to torture him to death. Blanx was an ox—he would have endured far longer than most.

All the spectators from the beach now crowded the generous courtyard, leaving a wide, empty circle around Van Leyen; Helm was an excellent shot, but nobody wanted to take any undue chances.

The morning had passed with incessant slowness. Van Leyen had stood watching the *Leeuwerik* like everybody else. While the others had eagerly chatted amongst themselves, he had stood with his eyes fixed on the ship, not once wavering in his vigil.

Van Leyen was not a praying man; he believed in God all right, but he was not arrogant enough to think that God believed in him. This morning he had wordlessly prayed, not for his soul, but that death would come quickly for Blanx. Judging by the state of the body, God was not in an accommodating mood.

Van Leyen had dropped his gaze, no longer able to look at the three men, but his attention was drawn when a pair of gleaming boots entered his field of vision. He looked up to find Mr. Coopman standing before him with a strip of white linen in his hands.

"No," Van Leyen croaked with a slight shake of his head as Coopman raised his arms to tie the strip over his eyes. Coopman lowered his hands but held his gaze, and Van Leyen watched a slow private smile lift the corners of his mouth.

"As you wish," Coopman said in a low voice, taking a step backward before he pivoted and returned to his place next to the governor, his gait smooth and relaxed.

The crowd was buzzing along with the flies that seemed to be drawn by the midday heat. Movement to his left drew his eye, and Van Leyen slowly turned his head to follow it and watched as a female figure disappeared into the small storeroom.

"We are all gathered here to witness the execution of punishment for John Van Leyen for the crime of treason." The governor's voice silenced the crowd.

Van Leyen thought those words sounded rather rehearsed, and he wondered if the same were spoken to Blanx that morning. The crowd was silent now, and the air crackled with anticipation. Soon, their curiosity would be sated. The spectacle of watching a man shot to death was something not to be missed. They would talk about it tonight around their cooking fires, and tomorrow, the dried blood on the ground would be covered, and life would resume.

Van Leyen kept his eyes on Helm. There was no need to make it easy for him. He would stare him down until his last breath. Helm bent forward slightly when the governor caught his attention and spoke privately to him. It was a brief conversation that left the captain looking confused as he straightened.

Helm took a step forward and raised his rifle. The silence was deafening, and Van Leyen thought if they had any drums at the settlement, now would be a fine time for a crisp tattoo.

And then the shot rang out.

A white cloud of smoke erupted from the rifle and obscured the captain's face. Van Leyen's bowels released. In astonishing slowness, as if time was struggling to move forward, he watched as Helm lowered the musket.

He had missed. Helm never missed.

His brain instantly split in different directions. Half of it went one way while the sheer magnitude of the moment pushed the other half in the opposite direction. The discord was wreaking havoc on his nervous system. He pinched his eyes to force clarity as his muscles spasmed and released. What had just happened?

The crowd was roaring their disappointment. He felt a tugging at his wrists and ankles as the ropes securing him to the post were being cut away. Still, he refused to open his eyes. His knees gave out, and he sank to the ground, lying in the dirt, feeling the warm earth beneath his cheek. Rough hands pulled him to his feet but failed to steady him, dragging him to the slave quarters where he was thrown to the floor and irons were clasped on his wrists and ankles once more.

# Chapter 8

It was the morning of the executions, and Danielle rose from her bed long before the night had released its hold on the dawning day. She crossed the room to her washbowl in the corner, dipped her hands in the water and raised the small puddle to her face. Squeezing her eyes tight, she shivered as the cold water chased the night's ghosts to the quiet part of her mind.

When her ablutions were done and her body dried, she wrapped the long strip of linen around her torso to bind her breasts before donning the loose-fitting shirt. Over the past few days, she had struggled to cope with the emotional demands of those around her. Any tension or upset seemed to push her closer to that dark abyss of oblivion. Even the sound of laughter held a too-sharp ring, causing her to shrink from it. She needed to be alone; others were too taxing, too onerous.

Reaching for her breeches, she pulled them over her undergarments and bent to fasten the buttons near her lower leg and then the four on her left hip. Governor Van Riebeeck had ordered everyone to the beach to witness the executions. The thought of seeing blood spilled made her stomach roil. The sight of it had never bothered her before, but now it was different. She scratched a spot in her hairline below her ear and swallowed the thickness from her throat. Her hair needed washing; she'd do it in the river today.

Mrs. Boom had gifted her a pair of worsted thread stockings. Danielle pulled them through her hands and marveled at their softness. They were dreadfully expensive and a luxury very few could afford, but they were a godsend against footrot. Sitting down on her bed, she pointed her toes and drew the stockings on with care before stepping into her calf-high boots—the only remnant from her life in Texel.

She was not supposed to wear these clothes; she was not supposed to go into the forest unescorted, and she was not supposed to leave the settlement today. Well, life was full of disappointments, and today seemed to be one for the governor. If he were to scold her for disobeying him, he would have to pick from the list, which was already quite significant, and the sun was not even up yet. Swinging her leather satchel across her body, she made for the door. She was short on healing plants and planned to spend the day in the forest foraging near the river where she knew a patch of yarrow grew.

Danielle glided down the stairs, her steps no louder than a whisper on the cold stone. She'd have to slip through the back door. Fortunately, it locked with a sliding bolt from the inside. Anyone trying to get in would quickly learn the futility of the attempt; getting out was no hardship, for the bolt was new and easy to maneuver. Descending the stairs unnoticed at this unholy hour of the morning seemed, however, to be the obstacle she'd not anticipated.

Mr. Coopman was standing at the bottom, patiently waiting for her to clear the last step. His face was serene as usual, his stance relaxed. Danielle felt her lips compress in irritation.

She greeted him with a tight nod. "Where are you off to?" he asked as she passed. At least he had the sense to keep his voice down.

Danielle paused in her tracks, inhaling slowly through her nose before she turned back to face him. Something in the way his eyes were studying her stirred the rage running just below the surface of her civility, making its presence known by the flush that crawled up her neck and onto her face. She'd felt this anger after little Antoonie's death, but then only sporadic bursts had scalded her insides. After her father's death, the anger was there, but shock had laid like a heavy blanket over it, smothering most of the flames. Lately, it was her only awareness, all the time—this blinding white rage.

"I can't be here today," she whispered, surprised at her control over her words and voice. If he was going to deny her, she would fight him. Feeling her fists balled at her sides, she welcomed his resistance, wishing for it, needing an outlet. Instead, his head tipped slightly to the side, and his near-black eyes narrowed as they studied her. Then slowly he nodded as if to have reached a decision.

"I'll make sure there are no questions. Go," Coopman said and gestured to the back door.

She fled on silent feet, rounding the main building at a brisk pace, crossed the inner courtyard and passed through the stone arch and onto the wooden bridge spanning the moat. The bridge led to the large empty outer courtyard, created by the infirmary on the right, and the newly constructed slave quarters on the left.

Thirty-four hasty strides brought her to the low double wooden gates neatly centered between the two hornworks, each studded with a gleaming black demi-culverin pointing out to the bay.

Closing the gate behind her, she instantly averted her eyes, not wanting to see the *Leeuwerik* lying behind the breakwater, with its lights cheerily swinging to the bobbing of the waves. The blasted fort was far too close to the beach. On some full moons, the water pushed almost to the hornworks. What the governor thought when he chose this spot was beyond her. Nonetheless, ten months later, here they were, a fort complete with a surrounding ten-foot wall, bastions, and a moat. God help anyone who tried to attack them, for between the bastions and the hornworks, they sported no less than twelve cannons pointing everywhere but in. Heaving a deep sigh, she took a sharp left turn, crossed the empty clearing where the tent village used to be, and disappeared into the forest, all the while feeling the devil nipping at her heels, and it took everything she had not to break into a dead run.

The forest at predawn was not a safe place. Predators lurked in the shadows, and even though the lions preferred more open spaces to hunt, she had seen their scratch marks on the trees. Also, the chance of running into someone from the settlement was not entirely outside the realm of possibility. Even with the tent village relocated inside the hornworks at the back of the fort, guarded by soldiers on the wall, men still wandered through the forest, and the danger could not be ignored.

Navigating the dark was nerve-wracking, but the thought of turning back hastened her stride. Only when the birds woke, and the sky lost most of its morbidity, did she stop to rest. Slowing her pace, she searched for the Medusa tree. She did not know what species of tree it was, but it reminded her of a picture of the snake-haired Gorgon she'd seen in one of her father's books on Greek mythology.

The tree grew in reckless abandon in all directions, its thick trunk rivaled by branches that, over time, dipped so low they appeared to compete with it. It was hard to distinguish branches from roots, both were equally thick and unruly as they curled and climbed over the forest floor; some growing horizontally and others winding upward. Regardless of its chaotic appearance, it was her favorite hiding place, for the branches were heavy with foliage. Once she sat down between the bulging roots, she became nearly invisible to passers-by; though few ventured into this part of the forest.

The tree grew near a large waterhole with a curious flat-topped boulder at its center. Danielle visited this place as often as she could, swam the length of the pond many times, and lay on the flat stone to dry. Something about this spot made her want to stay. It was so peaceful, and for some inexplicable reason, she always felt close to Sebastiaan here.

She was near the place where the yarrow grew, but it was close to the river and still to dark and therefore too dangerous to approach the water's edge.

The fine hairs on the back of Danielle's neck prickled, and she briefly wondered if she was being watched. Quietly, she rose to her feet, gripped the dagger's handle, and drew it from her belt. The grip was too wide for her hand, but she'd grown used to the size. Standing motionless, she searched the surrounding darkness, listening. She was being silly; nobody was there, just her and her ghosts. Huffing at being such a ninny, she lowered herself to crouch between the bulging roots and pushed her back against the rough trunk of the Medusa tree. Tapping her thumb on the blade, the absentminded act dislodged a memory from the depths of her mind.

"Why does it have this dip?" she'd asked Sebastiaan as she ran her finger down the deep groove in the middle of the dagger's blade. He had let her hold it, but the way he guarded over it like it was a newborn made her laugh.

"The fuller?" he'd asked with eyebrows raised in amusement. "It makes the blade lighter and stiffer." His eyes shone with devilish pleasure when he added, "It's also a nice little cleavage for blood to run down." She had wrinkled her nose at the implication and pulled back when he reached for the weapon.

"Give her back," he'd demanded.

"Her? Is it a girl dagger then?" she had teased whilst tipping it up to look at the bottom of the handle as if to search for evidence of the claimed gender, but stopped when she saw the defensive challenge in his eyes.

"Her name is Mary. Now give her back." She handed the dagger back to him, and he sheathed it protectively, but not before he wiped her fingerprints from the menacing blade.

"Mary?" Danielle could not fathom why he would give such a gentle name to such a wicked thing.

"Yes, Bloody Mary," he said with a wink in that smooth arrogant lilt he knew would melt her insides.

Mary was a thing of simple beauty. Danielle turned her hand, so the dagger balanced perfectly on her pointer finger. The blade was almost as long as her forearm, with a brass pommel and cross-guard weighting down the hilt. The leather on the grip was near black and smooth as silk.

Sebastiaan had placed the dagger in her hand moments before he had kissed her for the last time. She closed her eyes and remembered the pressure of his lips on hers.

Snapping her eyes open and forcing the knot from her throat, she flipped the dagger back into her hand and held it in her lap. There was movement in the forest. Looking up, she saw the sky turning a mild gray. A twig snapped, and she stilled her breathing. Though well concealed, she drew her shoulders in and tightened her hold on Mary.

Danielle was not afraid; she was careful, but not afraid. Mattheys had taught her how to wield the knife and, more importantly, how not to lose it during a fight. A few more slow breaths and a young woman emerged from the undergrowth near Danielle's hiding place. Danielle studied her from the shadows. From the way the girl was looking around, it was clear she did not see Danielle.

The girl sniffed the air, expectation, and excitement lighting her expression.

"I know you're here. I can feel you," she said in a melodic voice. Danielle spent enough time with the Hottentot family living near the fort to understand a few of the words the girl spoke. The young woman seemed carefree, and Danielle could understand why. It was Maheena, Harry's daughter, and she could move through the forest like an invisible breeze. There were few dangers she could not outrun.

The governor had met Maheena's father the first day he'd set foot on land, and since then, the Hottentot family had been under his protection, living near the fort in their grass huts. Harry served as a guide and interpreter when the governor needed to negotiate with local tribes. The negotiations thus far had not been very successful. They mainly comprised Van Riebeeck doling out copper wire and tobacco in exchange for the promise of cattle. Five heads of cattle and a handful of sheep had been secured, but to date, nothing of greater value had materialized.

Maheena's skin glowed a rich honey brown as she stood in the early morning light, her back turned to Danielle. She was wearing a short, animal skin apron that fastened around her waist. The rest of her body was bare except for the seashell necklace around her neck, a length of copper wire twisted around her upper arm, and a few seashells knotted in her hair.

Danielle waited to see if anyone else would emerge from the dense forest, before stepping from the shadows. Maheena snapped around when she detected the movement behind her. Her tranquil demeanor evaporated, and her eyes grew large and round in her heart-shaped face. Danielle shrugged and shook her head, holding one finger in the air, hoping to convey that she was all alone.

It seemed Maheena was expecting someone else; she stood motionless for a while, searching the forest's shadows before her shoulders relaxed, and a slow smile creased her eyes and softened the sharp, high cheekbones.

"Come," she said and waved her hand at Danielle. But Danielle stood her ground and shook her head. Maheena's Dutch was on par with Danielle's KhoeKhoe.

"No," she returned, but curiosity was nagging at her, lighting a tiny spark amidst the darkness she wore like a shroud.

"Come," Maheena repeated, stepping nearer and tentatively taking Danielle's hand, guiding her forward before letting go.

"Where are we going?" Danielle asked as she followed the wraith of a girl. She received only a crisp giggle in response and then had to sprint to keep up with Maheena, whose bare feet seemed to float above the forest floor as she moved between the trees and shrubs.

Language would be a problem if the day were to drag much further beyond this point.

Danielle was by no means unfamiliar with physical exertion, but after a while of following Maheena, her chest was burning, and her legs felt heavy. This part of the forest was utterly unfamiliar to her. She stopped and called to Maheena, then sat down flat on her bottom, pushing her feet out in front of her and tipping her head as she leaned back on her arms. The morning sun teased the forest with golden flashes, shyly flitting about the leaves and dotting their fallen comrades on the ground.

Danielle leveled her gaze and watched the smile fade from Maheena's face as she knelt next to her. There was such compassion and understanding in the wide black eyes that unintended tears rolled down Danielle's face. Good God, why, whenever someone showed her the smallest kindness, did she turn into a watering pot?

Danielle slapped the moisture from her face, but Maheena reached out a small hand and stilled the aggressive movements. The girl shook her head, causing one of the shells woven into her tight curls to dance on her forehead.

"Let them fall," she said in her broken Dutch, and then she moved her hand and laid it over Danielle's heart.

The rush of emotion soon passed, and Danielle inhaled deeply.

"I'm fine now. Thank you. Where are we going?" she asked again, and as before, Maheena jumped to her feet and darted off anew with nary but a single "Come" over her shoulder.

This was madness. Danielle had lost track of where she was, and if Maheena disappeared into the forest, there was no way she could find her way back to the fort. She had no choice but to follow and hope Maheena would not abandon her; she despised relying on others, and serpentine worry curled in her stomach.

After they spent most of the morning dashing through the forest, Maheena suddenly stopped, and Danielle caught her breath. They were standing on the edge of an outcrop overlooking a large clearing. Before them sprawled a bustling village of round animal hide huts. There must have been at least twenty as far as she could see, but soon her attention was shifted by a large herd of cattle. Her breath caught in her throat as she tried to count the heads milling about. The beasts were large and well cared for. Even through the thick dust cloud rising from their stomping hooves, she could see their coats gleaming. Young boys, wielding tall sticks, guided the herd through the opening of an enclosure woven from bramble branches.

"Come." Maheena raised her arm and with a small delicate finger she pointed out the way down the steep slope.

Maheena danced around large boulders and bounded over loose rocks, leaving Danielle once more panting in her wake. Keeping her eyes on her feet, she focused on each step to avoid slipping. One misstep on the loose gravel could send her tumbling down the slope. Not for the first time that day, she questioned the wisdom of following Maheena. But her doubts and silent misgivings promptly fled her mind when she crashed into Maheena from behind. The impact sent Maheena stumbling forward, and then Danielle saw what had stopped her friend in her tracks: three formidable, fierce-looking men blocking their path.

They looked like they'd sprung up from the earth at the foot of the hill. Danielle stepped from behind Maheena to get a better look. Stealing a sideways glance, Danielle noted Maheena did not seem overly worried; instead, she seemed to wait for something. The three men were from a different tribe than the Beach Rangers, from which Maheena and her family hailed. These men were larger in build, much darker in skin color, and they had an arrogant, fearless air about them. Danielle studied the one on the left; he was dressed in a cowhide loincloth and loosely held a spear and a wooden club in one hand. His sparkling eyes held a note of mischief and were fixed on Maheena. She did not return his stare, but a faint blush stained her cheeks. *So that's the way of it*, Danielle thought.

Danielle then looked at the man in the middle. He was a head taller than the other two and wore a large hide mantle flung over one shoulder. She instantly recognized the long, jagged scar on his thigh, the remainder of a vicious wound she had treated shortly after their arrival at the Cape. Her eyes snapped to his face and found herself staring into the calculating black eyes of the Saldanhar chief. Swallowing thickly, she felt sweat running down her arm and disappearing into the sleeve of her shirt. Maheena had deliberately led them to the Saldanhar camp. The Saldanhar was the enemy of the Beach Rangers, and Maheena's family feared them more than anyone else. It was one of the many reasons Harry had sought shelter at the fort. The girl's fearless attitude was something of a concern, and Danielle wondered how many times she had made the journey to the camp and whether her father knew of her defection.

"What—" Danielle was silenced by the slight shake of Maheena's head.

The chief waved them forward with an abrupt gesture, and Danielle followed Maheena at a much more sedated pace. Once they were a few feet from the men, Maheena stopped and fell to her knees before the chief. It looked like the girl was wordlessly begging for her life. Danielle remained rooted to the spot. She felt faint but refused to give in to the sensation, and since the situation was unfortunate but not life-threatening, she decided there was no need for her to beg just yet.

Maheena glanced at Danielle and quickly reached out and grabbed her hand, dragging her down next to her. Danielle went down on bent knees and pressed her forehead to the ground, looking from one side to the other as far as her limited field of vision would allow. Perhaps she had misjudged the situation, and there was every need to start begging.

She was sincerely beginning to regret her decision to follow the girl into the woods this morning. There was no one to protect her, and the Saldanhar was a tribe feared by all the other tribes in the area, including the Dutch at the settlement. Her heart was hammering against her breastbone, and Danielle took several deep breaths through her nose to calm herself. That was a mistake, for inhaling the dust so close to her face resulted in the eruption of a violent sneeze.

As a child, dust and nerves were her nemeses, especially when playing hide-and-seek. As soon as the tension built, so did her need to sneeze. Once she'd hid in an old trunk, and the excitement combined with many years of dust had her release three rapid-fire sneezes, which had her father bowled over with laughter at his easy victory.

The chief barked a few words in an unfamiliar dialect, then reached out a strong hand, wrapped it around her upper arm, and hauled Danielle to her feet. She shrieked sharply at his unexpected touch but smothered the sounds quickly when she noted his frown of displeasure at her outburst. Instead of releasing her, he dragged her toward the huts. Danielle looked back at Maheena, thinking of screaming for help, but Maheena was smiling up at the other young man as they were cozily making their way toward the river. The third warrior was heading in the opposite direction, already waving at a woman standing near one of the round huts.

"Let go of me, you brute!" Danielle hissed as she tried to yank her arm from his grip, only to have her struggles subdued with a few firm shakes. He was speaking to her, but she did not understand the words. His voice was deep and easy, with not a single hint of aggression. Still, her mind refused to make sense of what was happening, and fear was affecting the strength of her legs. When her knees buckled, his firm grip on her arm steadied her, as they continued their trek through the village.

The village was unlike anything she'd ever seen, yet familiar scenes played out everywhere. Families gathered in front of their huts, where men and children sat in the dirt in small circles, eating berries and a type of fruit that looked like a small melon. A bowl of milk was passed among the children, and Danielle watched as a young girl held it steady for one of her siblings to drink. The small boy giggled as the milk dribbled down his chin and over his round belly, before his sister wiped the white streak away with her hand.

Children's laughter filled the air, mothers spoke in soft voices as they served their families, and a few men gathered around a fire, talking loudly with elaborate hand gestures. Danielle's attention was drawn back to the chief when he spoke a few stern words, and she realized it was directed at a group of children running toward them. They looked as shocked and curious as she felt, and Danielle could see they were burning with the desire to touch her. However, their chief's command held them at bay.

They arrived at a hut with a low entrance. The hut was larger than most with smoke curling from a hole in the top. No children were playing outside this hut. The group of children that had followed them through the village was keeping a healthy distance.

The doorway was decorated with many small bones hanging from sinew strings, making hollow clattering noises as they moved in the breeze. The chief pushed these aside and pulled Danielle into the hut after him. He had to almost double over to enter, forcing her to do the same since he still had her arm locked in an iron grip.

In the middle of the hut, an old woman squatted beside a small cooking fire, stirring the contents of a clay pot with what looked like the femur of a small animal. The bone was yellow with age. A sour, smoky charcoal-like smell filled Danielle's nose. It reminded her of the long-forgotten fireplaces in old homes. It was a smell that clung to your skin and crept deep into your memory, never to leave. Beneath the ashy tang, the earthy smells of herbs, both fresh and dried, laced the air.

Danielle stared at the old woman, and for her life, she could not make herself look away, no matter how curious she was to take in the rest of the hut. The woman was sitting between her bony knees, her bare feet ashen with age as they supported her frail frame, two long hide aprons preserved her modesty front and back. She was chanting softly in a deep raspy voice over the brew she stirred. A thin sliver of smoke procrastinated its way to the opening in the ceiling.

Whispering the last of her words, the crone looked up, and only then did the chief release his hold on Danielle's arm. The sensation of his touch dropping away startled her. She had forgotten it was there. The old woman climbed to her feet with alarming alacrity, ignoring the protest of her ancient bones. Every inch of her face was carved with wrinkles, the creases deepening around her beady black eyes as she fixed her gaze on Danielle. This was a woman who had known much laughter and many sorrows.

The chief stood beside Danielle, docile and relaxed, yet she knew he could shift the air from convivial to menacing with a glance—she'd seen it once before. Instinctively, she sensed the old woman held that same power.

A gnarly gray finger reached for Danielle's face, and with a yellow, cracked fingernail, it traced the arch of Danielle's eyebrow, first the one, then the other. Not daring to move, Danielle endured the exploration with short, shallow breaths. Then the bony hand closed around the thick plait that hung between Danielle's shoulder blades, and she pulled it forward over her shoulder. A deep furrow settled between her eyes as she touched the dark ridges of the twisted hair. Danielle slowly reached to untie the ribbon at the end and unwound her hair, only to find her hand impatiently slapped away. The old woman's bony fingers danced eagerly through the strands, letting them fall, then lifting them to her nose, inhaling deeply with closed eyes before her face broke into a wide grin. Most of her teeth were missing, and age had browned the few that remained.

She spoke to the chief in rapid-fire words, to which he nodded. He turned to Danielle and spoke in Maheena's dialect, but so fast that Danielle could only make out a few words. One of them sounded a lot like *tobacco*. The old woman had moved on from Danielle's hair and was now inspecting her clothing, pulling and prodding at the fabric. There was nothing she could do but endure.

"Tobacco?" Danielle asked the chief and was rewarded with a confused look. Then she lifted her thumb and pointer finger to her lips and sucked, a gesture he recognized and nodded vigorously.

She shook her head, turning her hands up to show that she did not have any. He conveyed the message to the old woman, who received the news with obvious disappointment before turning back to the fire and calling to them over her shoulder. The chief nudged Danielle toward the flames, pressing her down into a squat.

Murmuring in a low voice, the old woman resumed her stirring. The chief translated, but his words were too many and too fast, and Danielle gave up trying to understand. Instead, she surveyed the hut's interior. It was a generously sized hut that could easily house a family of four, but it seemed the old woman lived alone, as there was only one sleeping pallet against the wall. On one side, clay bowls with herbs were lined in a neat row. Others contained skulls and bones of small animals, and when Danielle looked over her shoulder to the door at her back, she shuddered. A large baboon's skull hung above the entrance, with menacing fangs exposed and threatening.

The old woman looked up and spoke to the chief in words that sounded urgent and terse. When he made to leave Danielle rose to follow him, but a hand on her knee halted her. Cursing under her breath, she sat back down. *Blasted Maheena.*

The old woman placed the stirring bone next to the fire, then shuffled closer to Danielle. There was a gentle yet determined set to her mouth as she dipped her finger in the bowl and raised it to Danielle's forehead.

Danielle flinched away from the gnarled finger, but the old woman's deep, soothing voice wove lulling words that stilled her. Instead of pursuing Danielle's retreat, she remained rooted in place, waiting as Danielle's body, inexplicably drawn to the strange commands, leaned toward her.

Murmuring soft words the old woman painted the contours of Danielle's face with a gleaming wet finger. The process was repeated several times before the ritual was interrupted by the chief ushering Maheena into the hut. A hard look entered the old woman's eyes when she saw the girl, but then she grunted her approval and pointed to a place next to Danielle. Maheena was tense as she knelt, trying to hide her trembling hands in her lap. The old woman waited until the chief left the hut before speaking in her strange language again, her gaze fixed intently on Danielle.

"Your name," Maheena explained to Danielle.

"What?" Danielle's eyes snapped to Maheena. The girl still looked like a deer caught in a hunter's trap.

"Tell her your name," Maheena insisted and tilted her head in the old woman's direction.

"Danielle," she replied, noting the old woman's head lifted as if catching a sound only she could hear, searching for its source. Her eyes narrowed shrewdly then she frowned and shook her head slowly, making the tight curls on her head move like thick caterpillars before barking a few words to Maheena.

"She will give you a new name," Maheena said reverently, as if it were a matter of great import.

Danielle stared at the old woman in confusion. Whatever was the matter with her name? Perhaps Maheena misunderstood the question.

"'Kaam Gorab," the old woman announced, and her face lit with a brilliance that felt like a sunrise.

"Moon Flower," Maheena said, and bit down on her bottom lip in wonderment, her nervousness temporarily lost in the beauty of the moment.

The old woman took Danielle's hand, placed it against her gaunt chest and said, "Koba."

"Koba," Danielle echoed.

"She's the witch doctor," Maheena added in a whisper, "she heals with magic."

* * *

It was nearly dark when Danielle and Maheena passed by the fruit orchard near the Boom's house. The day had started bright and cloudless, but now she could smell rain on the wind, and the sky was prematurely dark as the storm clouds banked together. The weather suited her mood. Though the day's events were so far from the ordinary, they had required all her attention, and for a moment, she'd not thought about the bleakness that was her life.

This close to the settlement, with the sound of the waves pounding the beach nearby, she felt the heaviness return and resettled beneath her skin. She almost welcomed the gathering storm with all its promise of havoc and destruction. Their journey back to the settlement had been far more heavy-footed than their departure. Maheena had dragged her feet, and Danielle understood the sentiment well. There was something in that Saldanhar village that drew them both. For Maheena, it was the young man. Danielle's reason was still a mystery, but the pull was undeniable.

They stopped when they saw Elsje run toward them at breakneck speed. Maheena whispered a few words and disappeared back into the forest, clearly not wanting to be seen by any of the settlers.

"Danielle!" Elsje shouted and waved her arms. Danielle waited for her friend to reach her before she started walking again.

Elsje panted, her round cheeks flushed as she fought to steady her breathing.

"Danielle, he's alive," she managed between gasps, "You *must* come quickly."

# Chapter 9

"He's alive?" The declaration struck Danielle like a fist to the face; for a moment, white stars ringed the edges of her vision—*he's alive.*

"Yes," Elsje gasped, "he survived the keelhauling and the whipping, and by some miracle, he is still breathing. I know because I slipped into his cell to check."

"Blanx?" Of course. Danielle felt whatever warmth still glowed deep down in the bowels of her heart fade and die like the wick of a candle swallowed by the molten pool of its own wax. She sighed and closed her eyes.

"Danielle, whatever is the matter with you?" Elsje was shaking her by the shoulders but stopped the irritating action to sniff the air around Danielle. "Why are you smelling like an old chimney?"

Danielle pushed the disappointment that threatened to crush her into the ground aside.

"Let's go," she said with resignation.

The infirmary was one long building with a hall housing many straw pallets and a few patients still in the grips of dysentery, but Elsje passed its door.

"He's in the storeroom," she whispered and pushed Danielle toward the last door that led to a small windowless room. Elsje glanced over her shoulder to make sure the dark courtyard was empty.

The door was closed but unlocked. Elsje lifted the door just a fraction, so it didn't scrape too loudly as she pulled it open. Danielle stepped into the thick darkness. Instantly, the metallic smell of blood assaulted her senses, and she lifted the back of her hand against her nose and mouth.

"We need light," she whispered to Elsje.

"What else?" Elsje whispered back.

"Water and clean rags," Danielle said, seeing the whites of Elsje's eyes glint in the dark. "But Elsje, don't let anyone see you." Elsje nodded, her skirts rustling as she vanished into the night.

Danielle couldn't afford to linger at the door. At any moment, the guard on the wall might see her. She pulled at the heavy door, leaving it slightly ajar to let in the salty night air.

"Blanx?" she whispered, but there was no answer. His punishment had been scheduled for just after sunrise, and it was now long past sunset. The odds of him still being alive were minuscule at best. She took a tentative step deeper into the room. When her foot touched something, she crouched to feel what it was. Her hand traced over the sole of a bare foot, then the wide, cold, rough iron around his ankles connected with a chain. Shaking her head at the foolishness of the restraint, she continued to feel her way up his body, finding the backs of his legs bloody but without wounds.

Reaching his buttocks, she discovered his breeches were split horizontally and the fabric heavy with blood. He was lying on his stomach, and she grimaced at the pain the position must cause him, for his stomach would be in no better condition than his back.

"*Please, God, let him be dead,*" she prayed silently, "*don't let him suffer so.*"

Gently, she moved her hands over his back. His shirt was in tatters, most of it sticking to the wet wounds. Reaching his neck, she searched for the throbbing artery, hoping to find none.

Danielle's fingers found the indentation between the thick muscles and the ridges of his windpipe. Closing her eyes against the dark, she focused every ounce of her being on her fingertips. Four slow counts went by without any movement. *Thank you, God.* And then she felt the faint flicker beneath her fingers.

Her movements were more urgent now as she searched for wounds on his head, running her fingers through his hair, finding none, but when she reached his forehead, she found a large wet patch surrounded by a heavy wall of swelling. He must have hit his head against the keel. Many men died during keelhauling, not from drowning but from head injuries. Where was Elsje? Not pausing, she gently touched his face; it was slick with blood from the head wound. There was precious little she could do without light or water, but she had a reasonably clear idea of where to start.

Feeling her way over his arms, she discovered deep lacerations on the undersides, but since his arms were bent near his head, the wounds would remain untreated until she could turn him over.

Danielle returned her fingers to the faint pulse and bent over to whisper close to his ear.

"Blanx, if you want to go, then go in peace. I am here. You'll not die alone." She swallowed against the sorrow that burned her throat. It was wrong to urge another to die, but she knew what he would face if he decided to live. "If you decide to stay in this hellhole, I will help you. I promise. You will not go through this alone." With her free hand, she squeezed his much larger one, the fingers cold, and limp.

The sounds of chains and muted voices from the courtyard interrupted Danielle's soft words, causing her heart to accelerate—Elsje. Had she been discovered?

Elsje was quick-witted and could talk and charm her way out of most disasters, but Blanx would suffer more if the guards noticed her interference. Keeping her hand on Blanx's pulse, she felt the faint thud at regular intervals. His heartbeat was weak but steady—stubborn bastard.

There was a scraping sound at the door, and Danielle rose to peek through the small opening. Seeing Elsje, she opened the door wider.

"Hurry," Elsje hissed.

"What took you so long?" Danielle returned.

"What took me so long?" Elsje sounded exasperated. "Those damn guards on the wall took their sweet time to move so I had to wait. Coming back, Van Leyen offered to cause a ruckus to draw their attention; otherwise, I'd still be in the kitchen waiting." Elsje kept her voice down, but Danielle could hear the annoyance dripping from it as she struggled with the heavy pail of water.

"Van Leyen, is alive?" Danielle frowned in confusion. "I thought he was executed." Heavens, she'd left the settlement for a few hours, and suddenly nothing made sense anymore.

"Yes, well, Helm missed."

"Helm missed? He never misses."

"Today he did," Elsje offered the information as if it was an everyday occurrence and continued to list the things she brought with her, "Tinderbox, candle, and rags are in the bag. There's also a mug if he is able to drink something. Where do you want the water?" she asked as she placed it down without waiting for a reply.

"You are brilliant. Well done, now go home," Danielle said as she hugged her friend. "You've put yourself in enough danger for one night."

"I will do no such thing," Elsje said indignantly and turned to close the door before rummaging through the bag in search of the tinderbox. After striking the flint against the steel a few times, the charred cloth caught fire, and the candle was lit.

Danielle took the candle and crept closer to Blanx, slowly moving the light from the top of his head to his feet. The wound on his forehead was deeper than she'd initially thought. It must have bled profusely but had since slowed. She knew the swelling around the wound was hiding a lot of vital information, but there was nothing to be done save cleaning it and covering it with a vinegar rag, which would reduce the swelling.

She moved the candle farther along his body, taking in the mess they'd made of his back. There was not a single scrap of skin that remained intact. His flesh looked no different from the tattered shirt sticking to him. Deep, gaping wounds stared back at her, where the whip had cut over and over again.

"Danielle, I can't do this," Elsje sounded panicked. "I don't want to leave you, but I fear I am going to be sick."

"We must pull the pieces of fabric from the wounds before we can clean them." Time was not on their side, and as Danielle grasped the full extent of Blanx's injuries, she realized she needed Elsje's help. "You can do this."

She looked up and saw tears streaming down Elsje's slightly green-tinted face, her eyes wide with horror, and her hands shaking. Elsje did not reply, she only stared at the body on the floor and shook her head.

"What is the problem? You saw him earlier, didn't you?"

"Yes, but then it was still light outside, and he'd ..." she gestured to his back, "I didn't see all that much. It was dark inside. He'd made a sound. That's how I knew." The last of her explanation came out as a sob.

"Now you've seen him." Danielle's words were harsh and affectless. This was not the time for coddling. Elsje gave a pathetic nod, desperately trying to keep the contents of her stomach where it belonged.

"I need your help. Blanx needs your help." Danielle did not wait for a reply. They'd wasted enough time. She reached for the first strip of cloth and pulled it from his back; it came away with a wet sound.

Danielle heard a gagging noise from behind her.

"If you are going to spew, do it outside," she spoke without taking her hands or eyes from her work.

With a soft rustle of fabric, Elsje moved to Blanx's other side. Reaching out a trembling hand, she pulled away a blood crusted strip of linen.

They worked in silence and after what must have been hours, they'd peeled Blanx's shirt from his back, and Danielle could start cleaning the wounds.

Elsje was pale and tired as she sat back on her heels. They had worked ceaselessly until deep into the night, and she had not shied away from the task in front of her. *Brave girl*, Danielle thought with no small amount of pride for her friend.

"Go home. You've been a great help," Danielle said. "Tomorrow, we can bandage him." Elsje rose to her feet without protest. The hem of her skirt was soaked in blood. She left without a word.

Danielle and Maheena had stopped by the Medusa tree on their way back from the Saldanhar village, and she had collected the yarrow she'd set out to find this morning. There had been no time to look for more herbs, and she'd stuffed her satchel with as much as possible.

Placing the feather-shaped foliage in a pile on the floor, Danielle crushed the leaves with the earthen mug, then added a bit of water, creating a paste she could pack into the wounds.

She had cleaned and treated the wounds on his back and arms when the four-hour candle spluttered to death. The cuts on his thighs and stomach would remain raw and open until she could find somebody strong enough to hold Blanx's large body steady for her to clean and bandage them. The wound on his head was a concern; but once the swelling subsided, she would have a better understanding of what needed to be done.

Her father had once treated a patient who had been struck on the head by a wooden crate. The man had lived for a few days after the accident, and Danielle could remember the blood oozing from his ears and eyes. Her father believed the blow had dented his skull, damaging the brain behind it.

The swelling around Blanx's wound was too severe to determine if his skull was similarly affected, but the other symptoms were there. Once she had cleaned the blood from his face, she noticed more oozing from his ear, and a thick red tear escaping the corner of his heavily bruised eye.

Sitting down on the wet floor, Danielle rested her back against the wall. There was still much that needed to be done, but that would have to wait until morning. A wave of exhaustion crashed over her, and she closed her eyes.

* * *

"What the devil is going on here?" Helm's thunderous voice filled the small room, and Danielle woke with a start. The storeroom door was flung wide open, and a shard of morning sun hit her full in the face. Raising her forearm over her eyes, she tried to gather her senses. Momentarily confused, she wondered at the kink in her neck and the stickiness under her hands. She found her voice, feet, and senses all at once.

"Keep your voice down, you imbecile," she shouted back, belatedly realizing that she was only adding to the cacophony within the small, crypt-like space.

Not caring much for his intellect being so viciously assaulted, Helm reached forward and clamped a hand around her upper arm. He lifted her away from her patient, out the door, and into the busy courtyard.

Danielle squinted against the bright light, and with her legs and feet still numb from sleeping in a sitting position on the cold floor, she struggled to keep her balance, not noticing the hush that fell around them.

Helm ignored the stunned faces of the builders and propelled his captive over the bridge, through the stone arch, and across the inner courtyard, but before they could reach the stairs leading to the main building's entrance, Mattheys stepped in front of them, effectively halting their march.

"Captain Helm," the old carpenter spoke in a graveled voice as his eyes, round with shock and concern, raked over Danielle's blood-soaked clothes.

"Please, sir, let the girl go. She's injured."

"This is not her blood. She is unharmed. Now, step away, you old fool, or you will find yourself bent over a barrel," Helm spoke between gritted teeth.

Mattheys stubbornly stood his ground, and only when Danielle gave him a small nod did he hesitantly step aside, not taking his eyes off her.

Danielle used the pause Mattheys had created to dig her heels in and tried to pull her arm from Helm's grasp. Helm was unaffected by her protests and dragged her up the steps and into the large square main entrance hall.

The situation was ridiculous. She did not have time for any of this nonsense or the misplaced idea he seemed to labor under that he could haul her about as he saw fit. Blanx desperately needed care because of a state this man had a hand in. What were they planning to do, leave him on that cold stone floor until he miraculously recovered or succumbed to his injuries?

"Captain Helm, I need to gather my supplies. *Please*, cease this lunacy. I do not have time to be dragged hither and yon this morning. Blanx's life is hanging by a thread as it is." Helm appeared deaf to her entire line of reasoning as he turned a blank face toward the governor's chamber door, which seemed to be their destination.

"If you do not unhand me, sir, I swear I will do you violence," she hissed at him, and her voice echoed in the empty space of the garrison hall. Once more, it was as if she was speaking to the wind, for his grasp remained unchanged. His fingers were digging into her flesh as he tried to control her with pain. Thanks to his vice-like grip, she was certain she was already bruised black and blue.

Visions of Blanx's broken body filled her mind, and she knew the time for compliance was up.

"Let go of me," her soft voice contradicted what was to come.

Had he known her better or had he not been so intent on reaching the governor's chamber, he would have paid attention to the note of menace in her whisper. In Danielle's current emotional state, her anger was like an overzealous mother, jumping to her aid in the smallest of instances, let alone when she was cornered or trapped.

Helm held Danielle's upper left arm firmly in his right hand when she swung herself to face him. Belatedly, he registered the blur of her right hand as the small heel slammed into the soft underside of his nose. The effect was instant and blinding. Helm's head snapped back, he growled in pain and let go of her.

She watched in fascination as his head returned to its usual place. Tears were streaming down his face, and blood flowed freely from his nose, over his upper lip, and down his chin, where it landed in fat red splotches on his white shirt. They will flog her for this, and fear pushed gooseflesh to her skin, but she ruthlessly suppressed it. Now was not the time to speculate about the future. She flinched as he raised the back of his hand, ready to strike her face, but the governor's sharp voice stalled him.

"Captain Helm," the governor barked from the open door of his chamber. Helm blinked several times to clear the moisture from his eyes, dropped his hand, and snapped his heels.

"What is the meaning of this?" Van Riebeeck asked, taken aback by the blood streaming from the captain's face, and then his breath caught as he saw Danielle's state as she turned to face him.

"Do you need the physician?" he asked when he noted her blood-soaked breeches and shirt.

"I don't. But he might," she said while pointing a thumb over her shoulder at Helm. Seeing the confusion on the governor's face, she added, "this is not my blood."

"Helm?" Van Riebeeck asked, and from the pitch of his voice, Danielle thought he sounded somewhat panicked.

"I am perfectly fine, sir." His nasal reply gained strength as he continued, "I caught the young lady treating the prisoner."

"Blanx?"

"Yes, sir."

"He is alive?" Van Riebeeck asked, astounded.

"Yes, sir." Helm's voice was tight with anger and pain.

"Miss Van Aard, step into my chamber, please," Governor Van Riebeeck ordered as he cleared the doorway and held out his hand as if she was new to the premises and did not know where to go.

"Is there anything else, Captain Helm?" Van Riebeeck asked, and Danielle waited for him to lay his charge against her for the assault on his person.

"No, sir," Helm replied, punctuating his statement with another crisp click of his heels.

* * *

"How dare you?" Van Riebeeck roared once he firmly closed the door behind him.

She was wearing men's clothing; she'd defied his orders thrice, and she'd struck the captain of his guard. Any of these misdeeds were enough to stir the governor's blood and ire. Her gut was leaning toward the latter, but she could not be sure. He would need to be a touch more specific if he wanted her to respond to the question. But he seemed to think the question spoke for itself and merely glared at her.

"How dare I *what?*" The words burst from Danielle, and for a moment, she was stunned by her own daring, but she rather liked the reckless feeling and opted to indulge herself.

She saw the impact of her words as the governor's body went deadly still before he turned to her with a murderous expression. To his credit, his voice seemed a bit more under control than earlier.

"Do not play games with me, young lady," he threatened. "I specifically told you to stay away from the men."

Usually, the governor preferred the barrier of his desk between him and whomever he was addressing, but not today. He was still standing near the door with his arms crossed over his chest, and Danielle wondered if he was blocking the door on purpose. He looked tired. The grooves on his face were pronounced, and the dark patches beneath his eyes were nearly black. Despite his physical state, he was a dangerous man, and only a fool would cross him.

"What exactly is your meaning, sir?" she asked as she felt her features arranging themselves into something closely resembling the mask of a warrior preparing for battle.

Judging by how his eyes hardened and mouth thinned, Danielle deduced that Van Riebeeck's very shallow puddle of patience had run dry.

"You tended the prisoner!" he shouted.

Danielle released an overdrawn sigh. The governor's anger was fueling her own. She should have a care or a concern for her own welfare, but the warning evaporated as the last of her restraint snapped.

"Oh, thank goodness. For a moment, I thought you had me confused with a whore," she spat, throwing her head back and laughed. The effect of the forgotten act was so liberating that she could not stop and was forced to press her hand to her lips to keep the hysterical sounds from echoing through the room. Van Riebeeck looked at her, horror edged with concern evident in his large brown eyes.

"You have lost your mind," he breathed.

"Oh, sir, I've lost much more than that. My mind was simply the last thing to be thrown onto the wagon as it rattled down the road." She made a sweeping motion as if to farewell her losses.

The governor took a step toward her. He had never raised a hand to a woman before, but she was clearly hysterical, and a good slap might set her to rights again. She must have sensed his intention, for when she looked at him, a savage light lit her vibrant green eyes, giving him pause. She looked feral and dangerous, and it made him rethink his prognosis. He had lost control of the situation and had no idea how to proceed.

Raising his hand in a staying manner, he moved to stand behind his desk, taking several deep breaths to gain a semblance of self-control.

"You will *not* tend the prisoners or anybody else any longer. We have a physician who will see to those tasks. Do I make myself clear?" His voice was deep, and his tone brooked no opposition. His authority was at long last returning to him, and he intended to use it to its fullest.

The woman in front of him was unimpressed.

"Yes, of course, you are right," she conceded, and he felt relief settle over him, but then she continued. "You *do* have a physician; unfortunately, the man is as ill-fitting to his occupation as my left shoe is to my right foot."

"Danielle," he warned, but she ignored him.

"No!" The word cracked like a whip across the room. "If I don't treat Blanx, he will die. He suffered a severe head injury and will need constant care. Your idiot physician is still trying to root out dysentery after ten months of showing little to no success. And I need hardly point out that the man only works from sunrise to high noon, and then he takes himself off to God only knows where." Staring at the governor with her green eyes on fire, she continued, "my guess is he would most likely refuse to treat Blanx."

She was more right than wrong. Van Riebeeck had asked the physician to report to him on Blanx's condition the day before, and he was still waiting. He looked at the enraged young woman standing on the other side of his desk. He had seen that fire in her eyes before. Back then, she had been fighting for a hospital tent to be built for the sick sailors. Now she stood before him, covered in blood, fighting once more for another. He felt his heart soften in the face of her passion.

"Danielle," he spoke in a fatherly tone, "I can't allow you to treat Blanx." She drew a breath to object, but he stopped her. "I cannot make rules and then go back on them when they are inconvenient or hard to follow. Do you understand that?"

"I do understand that. But when one makes a mistake, one should have the fortitude to admit it and do everything possible to remedy it."

Van Riebeeck closed his eyes for the briefest of seconds. Danielle could spit insults in a matter-of-fact way that would hit you only in hindsight. The girl had a razor blade tongue, and she wielded it like a seasoned barber, but he refused to rise to her bait.

"It was not a mistake to remove you as healer. It was for your own safety. You know the potential dangers that the position held."

He watched as her shoulders dropped, and she moved around his desk to stand by the window. Resting her hands on the sill, she stared across the courtyard. When she turned to face him again, the fire in her eyes had died, giving way to a cold hardness, much like lava cooled by the ocean. The effect was startling.

"You owe me a life," she said in a voice so soft he almost missed it.

Van Riebeeck's face contorted with confusion; she must have seen it too.

"I owe you?" he breathed, trying to make sense of the statement that felt more like an accusation.

"You have taken so much from me."

He stilled at her words.

"I could have left here ten months ago with the man I loved, to claim a future we both deserved. But instead, I turned around, and there you were. Standing with your half-dead wife in your arms, begging me to save her. And so, I stayed." She leaned back against the windowsill and pinned him with her cold eyes. "Now, that man is dead, and my future lies in ruins."

Van Riebeeck could not draw a breath or speak a single syllable. The shock of her words was hitting him like bullets from a firing squad.

That dreadful day was vividly etched into his memory. He had thought his wife would not live to see the sun set, and Danielle was the only one he could turn to in his moment of despair. He never thought it would be thrown back in his face in such a callous manner.

Seeing the memories play across his features, she huffed a soft laugh.

"You owe me," she repeated with a cynical smile that reached no further than the corners of her mouth.

"Danielle, you are still young. You will find another to love. You can still have that future you wished for, though slightly altered."

She waited for him to finish speaking.

"Certainly," she replied with a single conceding nod, "and I will say the same to you. You are still young. You will have another child. A chance to have that family you dreamed of, though slightly altered."

Danielle watched the governor's eyes glaze over with a sudden rush of emotion. His throat move as he tried to swallow the lump that was sure to be stuck there, but the man was nothing if not a master of himself.

"Does your insolence know no bounds?" he asked. For all, he sounded old and tired.

"My insolence is no match for your recent bloodlust," she snapped, and when she saw his anger re-ignite, she continued, wanting to push him over the edge. Wanting to hurt him the way she was hurting, wanting to cut him to shreds with her words so that he would bleed the way Blanx had bled.

"Look what you did to make this little dream of yours work—and I am not talking about the fort and the gardens," she said, waving her hand toward the beautiful day outside. "Yet you took my dream of helping others away with a single declaration and a weak excuse, and you expect me to shrug my shoulders and say: 'oh well, as you wish?'"

Van Riebeeck took a menacing step toward her.

"You will hold your tongue or find yourself next to Blanx in the infirmary—*if* you are that fortunate," he growled.

*Finally, we're getting somewhere*, she thought. It was about time the governor got in touch with some of that deeply buried anger of his. She knew him as a reasonable man, but lately, he'd become a hollow shell, cut off from his emotions and allowing others to guide and influence him.

"What do you want to do? Hmm? Keelhaul me for my insolence? Drop me from a yardarm?" Danielle planted her hands on her hips and raised her eyebrows as she mocked him. "I might point out that you are missing the critical component of your favorite pastime, sir. The ship is gone. Unless, of course, you plan to drag me back and forth under the sloop." The image of the small rowboat sprang to mind, and she could not fight the hysterical giggle that skipped over her lips. His mouth opened and closed as he struggled to speak, but she beat him to it.

"Will you at least be there to watch?" she asked. "Because you were not there when Pieter Brackenier received his punishment. You were hiding in here. Safely behind your thick wooden door and your duty laden desk."

"Danielle," the sound of her name quivered with his rage, "the only reason you are still speaking is because I owe you like you so eloquently stated. Because you loved my son and saved my wife. But have a care, my patience, and debt to you have limits."

"I was there," she continued, as if he hadn't spoken at all. "They had put lead weights to his ankles and tied his wrists behind his back, then attached him to a rope hanging from the yardarm. When the boatswain pushed him off, he fell fifty feet toward the ocean. Imagine for a moment, if you can, what that must have felt like." She watched as the governor's lips compressed and his shoulders moved a fraction forward. Anyone who'd not known him so well would have missed the small movements, but she saw them. It was his turn to be punished, and he was handing her the whip. He stared into her eyes but remained silent. Her words were his whiplashes, and she knew he would spend many nights reliving them, imagining the scene, torturing his soul. *Good.*

"The fall stopped when there was no more rope. When they pulled him back up, both his shoulders were dislocated, and his left wrist was broken. They did it twice more. He'd wept like a child before he was bent over a barrel and given a hundred lashes with a whip." Danielle paused to swallow, unaware that tears were streaming down her face. She remembered the raw expanse of Pieter's back that had once belonged to a strong and proud man. She had begged Captain Turver to let her tend him afterward, but he had refused, and Brackenier was locked in the hull of the *Goede Hoop.*

"And you did that to him because you believed the gossip of the bookkeeper's wife. The word of the most vindictive and mean-spirited woman I've ever had the misfortune to know."

"That's enough," Van Riebeeck's voice sounded like coarse gravel crunching beneath a heavy boot. "Leave. Now."

"Give me Blanx," she demanded, "and I will go."

He responded with a tight nod; his face deathly pale as he turned away from her to sit in an untidy heap in his uncomfortable, straight-backed chair.

Danielle walked past him, and as she reached for the door, she said over her shoulder, "By the way. The Saldanhars are back."

# Chapter 10

"Elsje, I do not have time," Mrs. Boom could barely control her annoyance as she hastily pushed her daughter out of her way. "You seem bent on doing nothing today. Can you please do so outside instead of in here?"

"Mother, I am *trying* to help you," Elsje said with hands spread out as if to calm a riotous crowd. "You are the one who moves about the kitchen like a freshly killed chicken searching for its severed head. Nobody can keep up with you. Even if we all stand completely still and mind our tasks, we would still find ourselves under your feet." Several of the kitchen maids tucked their heads and folded their lips inward to stifle the smiles that threatened to reveal their amused agreement.

Mrs. Boom shot her flour-covered daughter a sour look. Given a bolt of fabric, the child was as talented as any Parisian modiste, but in a kitchen, she had two left hands and very little common sense.

"Here, take this to the dining hall." She placed a large tray stacked with bread rolls in Elsje's hands and hoped the girl would live up to her nature and linger there a while.

Harry had shown up this morning with four Saldanhar men, and the governor thought it wise to ply them with food and wine in an effort to persuade them to trade with the settlement. It would be nice to have some red meat again. Apart from the settlement's chicken coop that was coming along steadily, there were only a few goats, but those were treated with more reverence than the *Holy Bible* next to her bed since they were the only source of milk. Their diet depended largely on the daily nets of fish and vegetables from her husband's gardens. Nobody was starving, but everybody was feeling the pinch.

More houses were being built, leaving more settlers to cook for themselves instead of relying on the fort for their meals. There were nevertheless still plenty to feed, for the soldiers were a useless bunch, and many of the young unmarried settler men still lined up every morning for their breakfast and every evening for their dinner. Makeshift tables and stools now dotted the courtyard area outside the kitchen door, and Mrs. Boom felt like her life had finally found meaning — filling hungry bellies.

"Gijs, when Elsje comes back, the two of you take yourselves to Danielle and see if she can use a few extra hands," Mrs. Boom spoke to the kitchen boy without looking up from the stew she was stirring.

Everything about Gijs was too big, his body, his feet, and his heart. The child was only fourteen years old and recently orphaned when both his parents succumbed to dysentery. His parents were bakers in Holland and had planned to set up a bakery inside the fort's walls once they built their house. The settlement had deeply felt the couple's loss. Since the tragedy, Gijs had been living with the Booms.

The day after they'd buried the boy's mother, Anke Boom's heart had neatly broken in two when she'd looked up from her workbench to find her husband standing in their door with his arm around the shaking shoulders of the crying child. Hendrik understood the boy. They both had a shared patience and compassion for living things, resulting in Gijs helping in the kitchen in the mornings, and spending the rest of the day with Hendrik in the gardens.

She had no idea how to raise a boy; she fed him, kept his clothes clean, and ensured his hair did not grow too long, but it was good to have another soul in the house to care for. Over the last few months, she'd noticed the boy's eyes strayed to Elsje more often. Of course, Elsje had also taken note and was ill-impressed with the development. At seventeen, she was young and bold, with a beauty that could be dangerous had her personality been different.

"You might not like him now, but just wait a few years," she had teased her daughter.

"Mother," Elsje spat indignantly, "he is a child."

"Yes, and yet … stranger things have happened."

"There is a difference between strange and deranged. *This* conversation is a prime example of the latter," Elsje had fired back. Anke Boom had just laughed at her daughter's words.

Anke shook her head at the memory and looked up to see Elsje stomping her feet a few times on the step before entering the kitchen. Wiping her hands on her apron, she reached for the next tray to be carried to the dining hall.

"What's happening in there?" Anke asked.

"The governor is soaking them in wine and covering them with tobacco all for the promise that perhaps tomorrow, or the day after, they *might* bring the cattle." Shaking her head in annoyance, Elsje continued, "Harry is strutting about the place as if he owns it, while Helm is nursing what looks like a broken nose, and Mr. Coopman is trying to maintain order by getting the Saldanhar men to trust the chairs." Seeing her mother's confused expression, she explained. "They keep sitting on the floor, which is highly undignified as the governor then feels compelled to do the same."

"The governor is a good man," Anke said. She'd always had a soft spot where he was concerned.

"He's also a desperate man," Elsje commented in her signature dry tone.

* * *

Harry was doing an admirable job ensuring the governor stayed optimistic but unsatisfied. He had brought group after group of Saldanhars to meet with Van Riebeeck with illustrious promises yet to be fulfilled, but yesterday's meeting came perilously close to going against that habit.

Governor Van Riebeeck's generosity and hospitality had nearly swayed the Saldanhars in the settlement's favor, had it not been for the few words of caution Harry had whispered in the older men's ears. The Saldanhars had left the settlement with promises to return soon, bringing with them the much-desired cattle and sheep, a promise they would most likely not keep.

Harry's brother had arrived early this morning with the news that he'd seen a British ship further east, prompting Coopman to leave the settlement with the excuse of scouting for suitable farming land.

Ten hours later his boot heels clipped in sharp strides as he crossed the deck of the British East Indiaman to the companionway that led to the quarterdeck. Reaching the upper level, he spotted a young cabin boy and lowered his head, hiding from the full moon's vulgar attempt to bare all secrets.

"He's not receiving visitors this evening, sir," the young boy said, before it became clear his courage was otherwise occupied. It took only one look into Coopman's dark face to remind him of a long-forgotten task and he hastily scurried away.

Elias Coopman had spent the better part of the day in the saddle. By happenstance, he came upon a group of English sailors hunting for fresh meat and introduced himself as Thomas Bishop. Then, after trudging through the wilderness for hours, enduring their mindless chatter, and feigning interest, he was told by a boy—still young enough to taste the milk from his mother's tit—that the captain, no doubt the third son of some down-on-his-luck baron, was not receiving.

He placed his hand flat on the stateroom door and pushed. If the captain was not receiving, he might wish to invest in a lock, but alas, the door swung open.

Coopman stepped over the sill and paused, keeping his body still, moving only his eyes as he took in the new environment. It was like stepping into a brothel sans the women. The sickly, sweet fecal smell of ambergris hit the back of his nose and trickled down his throat, making his eyes water and his tongue taste bitter. At the back of the opulent cabin, dark green velvet curtains with gold trim framed the windows. Heavy dark wood furniture rested on a deep plush burgundy Turkish rug that covered much of the polished wooden floor. A few candles lent an intimate ambiance, and against the starboard wall on an intricately carved bunk, on a thick brocade counterpane, lay what he presumed must be the captain. The lump on the bed made him think of a large molehill.

"Holsten, sweet boy, I am ready," the lump spoke in a relaxed, high-pitched voice, "you may rub my feet." Ten bean-shaped appendices wriggled in anticipation near the end of the bunk.

"Captain Papley," Coopman's voice held a sharp edge despite his efforts to dull it.

Realizing that the deep, smooth accented voice did not belong to his cabin boy nor any of the crew, the captain leaped from the bunk with a crispness Coopman would not have believed had he not witnessed it firsthand.

"Mister Bishop," Captain Papley bleated; he seemed momentarily out of breath. "You're a bit ahead of schedule. I did not expect you for another week." The man's fingers fumbled to tighten the belt around his barrel shaped torso to secure and control the gaping ends of his robe.

Coopman suppressed the need to roll his eyes. He'd met Captain Papley and a few others over the past year. All believed him to be a spy for the British crown, and that the tint of Dutch freckled across his Westminster English was merely a result of his circumstance.

He had guided them to safe inlets and alcoves along the rugged coastline, where they anchored and refilled their freshwater supplies. He had also secured them a steady supply of fresh red meat straight from the Saldanhar herds. The British captains were indebted to him since the Cape of Good Hope was now under Dutch rule and therefore closed to them, and it was a debt they were willing to repay with their lives, and many had promised to do so—greed, debt, and gratitude was the holy trinity of Coopman's world.

Coopman produced an elegant smile and tilted his head, making a show of regarding the plump little toad before him with affection.

"The Saldanhars have returned to the Cape earlier than expected and are ready to move ten heads of cattle to the Dutch settlement." That got the toad's attention, and his beady eyes narrowed as his chin lifted. Coopman wanted to slap the attempt at cunning and calculation from the fool's face, but instead, he clasped his hands firmly behind his back; better to keep them out of the equation.

"Since you are here, I thought perhaps those cattle would serve *your* needs better."

"Quite right, quite right," Captain Papley agreed, injecting some much-needed authority into his voice. He waddled behind his desk and produced two delicate round-bellied glasses and a bottle of French brandy. The captain took his time pouring the drinks—though why the man was stalling was beyond Coopman.

"And what is in it for you?" the captain asked as he handed Coopman a glass.

"As always, nothing but the knowledge that I have served our passing ships well and perhaps have had a small hand in the welfare of our brave men at sea." The truth was that Coopman could not care one way or the other. Whether they starved or flourished was not his concern. What *was* his concern was how he could use the English ships to starve the Dutch settlement and bring it to its knees.

The governor had eagerly awaited the return of the Saldanhars to the Cape, as they had spent much of the winter higher up the east coast, finding better grazing grounds for their large herd of cattle. Trading cattle with the Saldanhar provided the settlement with its only source of red meat, apart from the small antelope and the occasional rabbit they managed to snare. They had not seen the herds of larger antelope for months.

Van Riebeeck believed that extending the settlers' diet past vegetables and fish would ease much of the illness and discontent at the settlement. The governor relied heavily on Harry's knowledge of the area and the tribes who visited it throughout the year. Once every week, Harry, and the men from his family, went scouting for any tribes that the settlement could trade with, but each time they returned with shaking heads and downcast eyes.

Soon, the settlers and soldiers would lose faith and confidence in their young governor's ability to deliver on his promises to kin, country, and the revered VOC. When that happened, and Coopman suspected the harsh treatment of the deserters had pushed them a little closer to that goal, they would revolt, and Van Riebeeck would either be killed or forced to resign, leaving a power vacuum that only Coopman could fill.

"We are deeply in your debt, sir," Captain Papley's irritating voice drew Coopman from his thoughts, and he clinked his glass against the one already extended across the desk.

The smile had not left his lips, and his cheeks were protesting, but now he coupled it with a humble shake of his head.

"Not at all, Captain. However, this is a favor that will not come cheap." Seeing the question on the little man's face, he explained, "You will have to offer the Saldanhar more than the settlement did. Unfortunately, the settlement is closer to their camp than your ship and, therefore, an easier trading partner. But if you can ply them with tobacco, wine, copper, and ample bread, the odds will swing significantly in your favor."

"How much are we talking about?" Papley sat down in his chair, and Coopman noticed how his sides pushed between the slats of the armrests, much like dough risen beyond the bounds of the bowl.

"At least five lengths of copper, ten loaves of bread, a barrel of wine, and half a bale of tobacco." Coopman was checking the quantities in his head as he spoke, ensuring he outbid the settlement on each account.

"Sir!" the captain exclaimed excessively, and Coopman returned his gaze to the sweat-dotted face.

"It is a king's ransom you are asking." Papley's movements were crisp with indignation as he reached for a delicate linen square to mop the moisture from his brow and bald head before tucking the lace-trimmed sleeves of his robe back into place.

"Things have changed since the Dutch have joined the negotiations. It's now a matter of supply and demand," Coopman shrugged.

"These are savages," the captain's voice, against all odds, rose in pitch as he pointed a pink finger to where the dark African continent rested. "I do not believe for a moment that they have a concept of what you are negotiating for them." A nasty glint entered his eye as a newly formed idea took hold. "I wonder how much of this fortune would actually reach them, and how much of it would end up in your private stores?"

It was a reasonable assumption to make, and Coopman was not in the least offended. If he had the means to skim some of it, he would. But he would be damned if he was to sit here and let this invertebrate think he could insult him.

"Captain Papley," Coopman dripped a little steel into his voice, "savages they might be, but stupid they are not." Then he leveled the other man with a cold black stare that made the captain reach for the linen square again.

"Do not ever question my honor." He held the round captain's stare and let several uncomfortable seconds burn by, during which the man swallowed twice and blinked like a nervous debutante at her first social engagement.

Captain Papley was not one who relied on or cared for physical intimidation; he prided himself on his intellectual prowess, but it was hard to deny that there was something dangerous, almost predator-like, about the man sitting across from him. Bishop had made him nervous from their first meeting nearly six months earlier.

Papley preferred to conduct their meetings sitting down, so he didn't need to tilt his head back to meet the man's gaze. Even now, from behind the safety of his desk, those cold black eyes, which had just hardened like obsidian at his insult, made sweat break out all over his skin. He was suddenly aware of his swollen bare feet beneath the table and felt utterly lacking.

Bishop's wide shoulders were relaxed as he leaned back in the chair, the ankle of one leg resting on the knee of the other, displaying a gleaming black boot. He was dressed only in a white shirt and black breeches, and his skin was sun-browned, but for all that, he looked entirely comfortable and at home in the captain's cabin. Papley felt an unreasonable stab of jealousy. He wanted the man off his ship.

Captain Papley jumped to his feet as fast as his body would allow, momentarily enjoying the feeling of looking down at Bishop.

"You can bring the savages two days from now, and I will have the payment ready," Papley said, then pushed his chest forward and squared his shoulders.

Coopman watched the various emotions played across Papley's glistening face. A flicker of fear flashed through the captain's eyes, but once standing, he puffed his chest and drew back his shoulders, like a young bird, ready to make his first leap from the nest.

Coopman bit down hard on his cheek to stifle a laugh at the thought as he slowly rose from his seat. Papley retreated involuntarily.

"They'll be here on Friday," he said in a voice as smooth as warm honey, "you'll be dealing with a man called Harry. He speaks some English." Coopman waited for any objections from Papley and when none were offered, he reached out his hand. The captain flinched before providing his own soft, damp one for a shake. Coopman instantly gentled his grip lest the man was left with bruises to nurse in the morning.

* * *

Governor Van Riebeeck waved Danielle in with ink-stained fingers and pointed to a chair. He sat behind his desk with his open diary next to a weathered quill and ink pot.

"Take a seat."

"No, thank you, I'll stand," she said as she straightened her back and rolled her neck to ease some of the tension. Her muscles were knotted from spending the day on her knees. She'd cleaned the storeroom floor, bandaged Blanx's broken body, got a few drops of willow bark tea down his ragged throat and cut tall grasses for a sleeping pallet. Blanx was as clean and comfortable as he might be, but it seemed that all the blood and gore had transferred from him to her. She was still dressed in the same clothes from two days before. Rusty brown bloodstains covered everything, hiding her garments' original colors. Thankfully, the stench that emanated from her clothing masked that of her unwashed body.

Van Riebeeck looked at her in earnest. "You need to bathe," he said, "even your face is covered in blood and grime."

"I need to sleep," she countered.

She'd not seen the governor since their last heated conversation and had been trying to sneak up the stairs to her room unnoticed when he'd called her into his chamber. This evening was the first time she felt confident to leave Blanx for a few hours. Every night since Elsje had alerted her to

Blanx's condition, she'd slept on the floor next to him, fearing that each breath would be his last. Her body was aching and filthy.

"How is Blanx?" the governor asked in earnest.

"He'll live—for now," Danielle sighed as she pulled a few sticky strands of hair from her forehead.

Van Riebeeck only nodded. He wanted to say more but wisely concluded that now was probably not the best time. For weeks she had wandered around the fort in a daze, her skin pale, and her eyes dead. She'd looked like somebody wading through thick fog, searching but never finding what she'd lost. But this evening, there was a change. She was a mess and swaying on her feet from fatigue, but there was a light in her tired eyes that he'd not seen in a long time.

"Have you eaten something?" he asked, noting how her shoulder bones showed beneath her coarse linen shirt. She'd lost too much weight.

"Yes, Mistress Boom had sent luncheon and dinner." Seeing his raised eyebrows, she added, "and I ate it all."

"How did you know the Saldanhars were back?"

Taken aback by the unexpected question, Danielle blankly stared at him. Was it only two days ago that she'd visited the tribal village? So much has happened since. Absentmindedly, she raised her hand to touch the place above her heart.

*Koba.* Maheena claimed she was the tribe's witch doctor or healer, a position of veneration and honor, unlike in European cultures. Koba had painted strange markings on Danielle's face and chest. She had said it was for protection.

"Protection against what?" Danielle had asked, but Maheena couldn't answer.

Then Koba had made a minor cut on her hand and a similar incision on Danielle's. She'd collected the blood from their small wounds in an earthen bowl. Koba had spoken a few words over the blood, generously spat into the mixture, before speaking again. Maheena could not translate the words; it was in a dialect she didn't understand. She said they were old words only Koba, and the gods understood.

While still chanting the lilting words, she'd dipped her fingers into the mixture and painted broad, evenly spaced lines across Danielle's chest. Maheena said that she was now marked.

Days later, Danielle still felt the burn of the old woman's fingertips on her skin. She scoffed—it was nothing but her foolish imagination.

"Danielle," the irritation in the governor's voice drew her back to the conversation.

Mistaking her hesitation for stalling, he leaned forward, resting his forearms on his desk. "How did you know?" he asked.

Danielle heard the drop in his tone, but she was too tired to care.

"I saw them the day before yesterday."

"You must be mistaken. Harry scoured the area for weeks and reported the first sightings only this morning."

Harry must not have seen them, or he was lying. Either way, it was of little consequence. The governor had complete faith in Harry and seemed to trust him for whatever reason.

"I'm not mistaken."

"How can you be so sure?" There was a definite tone of agitation in his voice.

"I know, because I've been to their village."

Danielle started as Governor Van Riebeeck shot up, his chair crashing to the floor. His wide eyes burned with shock and anger, nostrils flaring as he breathed heavily.

"You went to their village," Van Riebeeck thundered, and Danielle realized that she might have revealed a little more than she should have, but the proverbial cat was now out of the bag, and there was nothing to be done for it.

"Yes," she admitted point blank.

"Alone?" he sounded more astonished than angry, although his anger was not to be ignored.

"Yes," Danielle lied, not wanting to expose Maheena.

Van Riebeeck exhaled forcefully and closed his eyes. But then his chest deflated, and he pressed his fists on his desk before hanging his head between his arms.

Understanding that she was under his protection and how seriously he took that responsibility, she felt a stab of remorse for her reckless behavior.

"They have a lot of cattle," she offered, hoping the news would mollify him somewhat.

Her words took effect, and he raised his head, eyes gleaming with calculation rather than fury.

"How many?" he asked.

Danielle described the village and the large herd of cattle. The governor sat back down, listening intently to her account. From the tilt of his head and the way he touched his earlobe, she knew he was paying close attention. A deep frown creased his brow as she spoke of the huts, the children, and finally the chief, whom Koba called Kai.

"Harry reported that they had only just arrived," he sounded deep in thought. "Yet, your telling points to them being here for quite some time."

"I would say at least a month, give or take. Judging by how well-trodden the clearing was," Danielle ventured.

Something had shifted during their conversation. Danielle was just not sure exactly what that shift meant. Van Riebeeck was blessed with a sharp mind, fierce ambitions, and determination to see him through challenges that would cripple most, and as she and everybody else at the settlement had learned, the young governor was not to be crossed. He had every right to be furious with her, and yet when she dared a glance at him, he appeared lost in thought, staring across his desk.

"Why don't you find your room?" Distracted, he tapped a gentle rhythm on his diary's page. "You've given me much to think about."

This sudden dismissal couldn't be good, but she would worry over the consequences of her actions in the morning.

# Chapter 11

*The Annabella—five days off the African coast.*

"They would've determined his value fairly quickly. His wealth and intelligence show in the way he dresses and speaks; even just that look in his eyes would have been enough. Nothing about him screams common sailor." Arent reasoned and leaned closer to study De Coninck's notes.

"Chances are they will ransom him unless somebody offers to buy him for more. They won't risk exposing him in the smaller markets. He will stand out, people will remember, and," Arent scratched his jaw, an unconscious gesture that signaled his frustration, "it might also increase the risk of him escaping. I say we skip all these small ports and head straight for Muscat."

The African coast, for the most part, was under Arab control in one form or another, except for Zanzibar, which lingered under Portuguese rule—for how much longer, was an open question. As such, the slave markets teemed with black slaves taken from the continent. Europeans were mostly sold on the Barbary coast in the north or along the Red Sea.

De Coninck stared at the table where several maps were spread out. Knowing that Sebastiaan was missing, presumed dead, but most likely being held as a slave sent a visceral pain through his heart. He crossed his arms over his chest and swayed with the ship's movements. Even with fair winds and a competent and familiar crew, his guess was that they were still a good two weeks behind, pursuing this phantom that had stolen his nephew. He agreed with Arent on one point, Muscat might be the best port of call. If they came up empty in Muscat, Mecca would be their next destination.

"I don't enjoy playing catch-up any more than you do," he said, unfolding his arms to support himself as he leaned over the charts, "but, there are too many unknowns."

"Meaning?" Arent challenged.

De Coninck straightened from the table and audibly exhaled as he stared out the windows of the dayroom. The ocean was choppy. Thank God for it. Presently, he wouldn't mind a full-blown tropical storm—anything to push them faster.

"Meaning, what if he's escaped? What if he's fooled them into thinking he's just a common sailor, and they've made him a galley slave?"

"That would drop his value considerably," Arent said with a pained expression.

"Precisely, so they might decide to sell him earlier while they can still get a half-decent price."

"You're thinking, Zanzibar?" Arent murmured and then nodded as the idea took root.

"I do, and besides," De Coninck paced the length of the room before continuing. "Zanzibar will be the perfect place for us to refit the ship and catch up on gossip. Somebody might know something."

"I have a contact there who could provide information if there's any to be had," Arent said, his eyes drifting as he searched his memory.

"That sounds ominously vague."

"And I would prefer it to stay that way. He's not an acquaintance I am proud of. The man is easily the biggest clump of scum I've ever known—and trust me, that is being generous. But he can be a useful evil." De Coninck nodded his approval.

* * *

Five days later, they dropped anchor off the coast of Zanzibar, close enough to see the island but far enough to not be recognized. The *Annabella* looked nothing like her former self. At the top of her mainmast, the Ottoman

Empire's red flag, with three golden crescent moons on a green square, proudly snapped in the breeze. Gone were the crisp white waterline and the honey-brown hull. Instead, the freshly painted black hull now gleamed menacingly in the morning sun. Her original figurehead, the naked bust of a maiden with long flowing hair, had been carefully removed, wrapped, and stowed below decks. In its place was the head of a feral dog with mean eyes and bared teeth. It was crudely crafted, but her new carpenter showed talent, and the piece would be refined en route.

De Coninck ran his fingers along the gunwale as he watched the carpenter paint the new name on the side in large white letters—*As-Sayf*, Sword of Orion. The name served a dual purpose. They chose the name to honor their little cabin boy, Orion, whom Arent had adopted after rescuing him from a slave market when the child was just two years old. Also, should Sebastiaan see it, the hope was that he would recognize the reference.

Arent had refused to bring Orion on this mission. It was too dangerous, and he couldn't risk the child's safety if things turned south for them. If they were to fall prey to the Ottoman pirates, the horrors that awaited a boy of seven were too vile to consider.

Orion was to stay with Parmar, Sebastiaan's butler, to continue his schooling and general education. Naturally, this decision was met with rebellious and mutinous behavior, for although Orion was well-mannered, the word 'no' held little weight in his vernacular. Not used to having his orders gainsaid, Arent's already stunted supply of patience and parental skill had quickly run dry, and he had resorted to his usual profusion of oaths and blustering threats, all of which had secured the obedience and compliance of the most hardened sailor. Immune to colorful language and volatile tempers, Orion had stood boldly in the face of the storm, firmly sticking to his protests, until De Coninck had stepped in, motivated by the pleading look he received from Arent and the pressing need to set sail.

De Coninck took the boy aside, crouching to meet his gaze, but Orion, defiantly kept his eyes fixed blankly on the bookshelves.

"Orion, look at me," he'd demanded, waiting until the boy relented. "Arent promised your mother that he would take care of you and always keep you safe." Orion inhaled to launch his protest, but De Coninck shook his head, and the child swallowed his retort. "We are deliberately sailing into harm's way. Do you understand?"

"But I belong with you," Orion had argued, his large, brown eyes swimming in tears.

De Coninck realized that he would need a different approach and briefly wondered if obstinacy was something a person was born with or learned from his environment.

"Listen," he said in a conspiratorial tone, dropping his voice to a low hum that reached no further than the two of them. "I don't know how long we will be gone for."

Orion shook his head violently at the words, dislodging the tears and sending them streaming down his round cheeks.

De Coninck gently wiped the tears away with his handkerchief and continued, "I need a man here to take care of things." He waved his hand to encompass the opulent library, and all it entailed. "A man I can trust. I cannot search for Sebastiaan and ensure everybody's safety if I'm worried about the welfare of the business."

"Don't you trust Parmar?" Orion asked.

De Coninck smiled at the child's last but cunning attempt at arguing his case. "Yes, I trust Parmar, but I trust you more."

Orion had conceded, placated by the knowledge that his sacrifice would bring Sebastiaan home. Yet, on the day of their departure, he'd stood on the dock, a forlorn little figure, watched by the stoic but vigilant butler, as the ship sailed from the harbor. His resolute expression ensured the crew felt the sting of guilt for leaving their smallest member behind.

* * *

The guards at the gates parted as Arent stepped into Oliveira's opulent residence. Approaching with open arms, the trader showered him with fervent kisses in a melodramatic display of welcome, leaving Arent to wipe his face and neck with his sleeve. Oliveira pretended not to notice the insult and led his guest deeper into his compound.

Crossing a tiled courtyard with a grand fountain at its center, surrounded by arched doorways, they passed flowing gauze curtains that obscured but did not conceal the figures moving behind. The scent of flowers and incense hung heavily within the walled dwelling. Arent noted more guards discreetly posted. They were docile but alert, and he sensed that the slightest twitch from Oliveira would spur them into action. All were eunuchs, tasked with guarding their master's harem. Yet, in Arent's mind, losing such vital body parts could only make a man more single-minded in his task and, therefore, significantly more lethal.

"How is it that a Dutchman can so confidently walk the streets of a Portuguese territory? Are our countries not at war?" Oliveira asked as they entered a sitting area scattered with plush cushions and large potted palms. Wall sconces cast the room in an intimate orange glow, and thick Turkish rugs covered the cool stone floor.

"Fortunately for me, I don't look Dutch, and even less so at night," Arent replied with a lazy smile. "Besides, I'm not in the employ of the Dutch anymore. I find myself to be a much more reasonable employer."

"Ah, power, and wisdom, what a potent combination," Oliveira said as he allowed himself to indulge in an appraisal of his guest.

Arent Van Jeveren had a wild look about him, which he used to his advantage rather than attempting to tame it. He was a magnificent cross between Malay and Dutch. Black tribal markings were etched into his skin, showing in lines and curves where his rolled-up sleeves exposed his muscular forearms. Oliveira wondered what it would feel like to run his hand over the long, black hair that fell like a waterfall between the overly broad shoulders. No, the Dutchman did not look European at all.

Arent felt the man's gaze smear over him from head to toe, and he forcibly suppressed a shudder.

"Well," Oliveira's eyes took on a sharper glint, "a man of your stature would certainly not be short on wealth."

"A man of my stature is, however, short on able-bodied men to crew his ship," Arent cut him short before the trader carried himself away in a direction that might become exceedingly expensive.

Oliveira snapped his fingers, and three women clad in layers of sheer fabric entered with trays of food. Two of the girls were African and very young—too young, but the third one drew his attention. She was older than the others, with skin as white as marble, accentuated by her delicate Japanese features. For a moment they stared at each other. She showed no fear, shame, or interest. What struck him was the depth of her desolation, the look of a slaughtered soul.

The bag of gold coins felt heavy where it pressed into his side. He could buy her, set her free. Oliveira was speaking somewhere to his left. He could save her from this hell she's living in—take her some place safe. Only when Oliveira laid a heavy hand on Arent's forearm did he force his attention away from the woman.

Noticing, but misunderstanding Arent's interest in the slave, he dismissed the two younger girls.

"You are tired, my friend," Oliveira said, not removing his hand. "Rest for the night, and in the morning, we can discuss the business of your crew."

"No," Arent replied firmly, unsure if he spoke to himself or Oliveira. There would be many more ports and many more slaves, and he could not save them all.

Oliveira dismissed the woman with a tilt of his chin and an exaggerated sigh.

"We will conclude our business tonight. I need men, and don't try to sell me the poor souls you abducted from the mainland. They are mostly farmers and warriors, ill-suited to life at sea. I need European men who know how to handle a ship."

Oliveira's hand tightened on Arent's arm as he searched through his vast array of flowery excuses and beguiling deceits to devise a reply that would serve him best.

"What can I say? It is Ramadan, our holy month of purification. I prefer not to trade during my time of fasting." Oliveira turned his large black eyes to Arent, his face a mask of tranquil piety.

"But," Oliveira continued, eager to maintain control of the conversation,

"I can ask around. Others might know if there are any white slaves available. It will take a little time and, of course, a small investment on your part, but it can be done."

Oliveira plopped a fig dripping with honey into his cavernous mouth.

"Please don't insult me by playing innocent or ignorant." Arent shook his head as his host extended the platter of food to him. "Human flesh is your stock-in-trade, and I don't believe for a moment that you didn't make a single deal in the last month." Arent struggled to keep his annoyance in check as he watched Oliveira waste time by languidly indulging in the offerings and noisily licking his fingers. "I'm going to give you one more chance to come up with a solution to my problem, and this time it had better be impressive."

Arent took a step back, putting a healthier distance between himself and Oliveira. Crossing his arms over his chest, he raised his eyebrows in anticipation of a propitious answer.

Oliveira briefly found a perverse sense of joy in seeing the tension and unease in his guest, but his keen sense of self-preservation warned him that this was not a man to trifle with for too long, if at all. Lifting his bejeweled hands in a calming motion, he switched tactics; the man was a sailor and brute after all.

"Why don't you amuse yourself with the lovely Sakura tonight, and in the morning, you can make a donation to the household to show your gratitude? In return, I will endeavor to find you the men you need."

Without warning, Arent's fist slammed into Oliveira's face, sending the trader staggering backward. Oliveira's knees buckled and he ended up sprawled across three large square cushions on the floor, blood streaming from his nose.

The blow had the salutary effect of clearing Arent's mind from the black rage that had descended on him at the mention of the girl's name. He never wanted to know her name. Now, she was real.

"You will not exit my gates alive!" Oliveira screamed. "Guards!"

"You might want to think twice about that," Arent warned quietly. "Do you honestly believe I would come here alone? My men surrounded your compound as I was led through the gates, ready to set it ablaze should I not return. They have orders to let everybody pass who wishes to flee. All except you. You will burn here with me."

Oliveira's eyes erratically moved from side to side as Arent's relaxed yet portentous words tore his confidence asunder. Three guards rushed through the curtained arches; scimitars drawn. Arent stood his ground, not taking his eyes off Oliveira, but not reaching for his weapons either.

Oliveira's throat moved as he tried to swallow. "Leave us," he ordered the guards before rolling onto his hands and knees, trying to push himself upright, but Arent's boot in his side made him collapse back into the cushions again. Lifting a moist linen square from the low table next to him, he tenderly patted the blood from his face.

"Tell me about the white slaves," Arent demanded as he towered over his quarry.

"I know nothing. I don't trade in white slaves. I swear it on my mother's grave."

"You lying sack of shit! You don't even know who your mother is."

This time Arent made sure not to hit him in the nose again, but aimed the blow to land just below the left eye. The effect was most impressive, for it loosened the African's tongue mere seconds after miraculously refreshing his memory.

"Fine, fine," Oliveira spluttered as he tapped a middle finger to the small cut beneath his already swelling eye. "I bought one slave about a month ago." His hand nervously fluttered as he tried to remember the exact date. Arent narrowed his eyes and tilted his head toward the prone form as he sank to his haunches.

"Tell me more," and although the order was softly delivered, the threat behind the words was clear.

"It was a young Dutch woman; she was in bad shape. I got her for a good price, and you know the Portuguese turn a blind eye when it is a Dutch slave." Oliveira raised his shoulders in a helpless shrug. "How could I not? As you said, it is my stock-in-trade." He swallowed the rest of his justifications when he saw Arent's lips thin. "If," he tried to clear his throat, "if it is the woman you wanted; you are too late. She cut her wrists the second day after her arrival here. She was …"

"Don't tell me her name," Arent growled. He couldn't bear the knowledge of another name. Oliveira seemed quite relieved to be granted the opportunity to shut his mouth.

A Dutch woman, somebody from the *Spiegel* or the *Geloof*, most likely. The timing made sense. Arent regarded the man before him, then hit him again in the same place as before. This time, Oliveira's eyes glazed over for a moment before his mind cleared again.

"Why?" he wailed.

"Lying comes to you like breathing. You do it without thinking, and without it, you cannot live. I have a few more questions and don't want to spend all night convincing you to tell me the truth. This saves time." Arent gave him a moment to absorb the fact and then continued. "Who sold you the woman?"

Oliveira looked at Arent's blood-stained fist where it hung over his taut thigh, ready to deliver another vicious blow. He tried to swallow, but his throat was too dry.

"Yavuz," he whispered.

"Yavuz?" Arent roared. "What is that? It means nothing to me. Every second Arab from here to Constantinople is called Yavuz."

Oliveira might be telling the truth. It was also possible that it was all he knew, but it was not enough. Arent rose to his feet in frustration. "Give me the name of his ship."

"I don't know," Oliveira replied instinctively, as he belatedly remembered the rule against lying just when Arent's boot connected with his side. A searing white pain shot through his body as his ribs caved under the blunt force of the impact.

"*Aqrab*! It was the *Aqrab*," Oliveira quietly sobbed while he clutched his side with both hands, leaving the mucus-mingled blood from his broken nose to stream down his face unhindered.

* * *

Davit De Coninck had been pacing the quarterdeck for the last hour when the call from the lookout sent him down the companionway toward the rope ladder.

"Where the hell have you been? It's almost dawn." De Coninck scolded as he reached out to pull Arent over the bulwark.

"It's a long way to row, Cap," Arent defended himself as if he was twelve years old again.

"I told you to take men with you. Well?" De Coninck asked as they walked toward the stateroom.

"I have a name."

# Chapter 12



**F**ebruary 1653

They were nearing their final destination. The crew was bristling with excitement to see their home and families again after months at sea. The cracks of the bullwhips, as they urged the slaves to row faster, intermingled with their animated chatter. Sebastiaan raised his eyes over the bleeding backs of the rowers to search the horizon. Muscat harbor was but a dusty haze in the distance. Judging by their current speed, they might reach it within the next three to five hours, assuming the overseers didn't beat most of the men to death in the interim.

A welt burst open, and dark red blood dripped over the ebony-black skin of the man sitting in the row in front of him. He was one of the new rowers they had picked up from the African coast.

After Zanzibar, they had headed for Malindi, a small harbor town bustling with eager sellers and buyers. Yavuz had grudgingly parted with a heavy pouch of coins for enough sacks of cloves to fill half of the *Aqrab's* hull. He'd traded Mrs. Bouwer's maid for three large ivory tusks and a bolt of bright blue silk. From there, they had sailed some distance up the coast to the mouth of a large river, where a village was rumored to be. Nearing their quarry, the *Aqrab* had slowed her pace, and by nightfall, the galley had quietly snuck up to the coastline and unleashed her heavily armed crew.

Sebastiaan remembered watching the carnage and horror as the villagers were roused from their beds and rounded up onto the beach like cattle. Whips flicked through the air and landed on virgin skin with sickening wet slaps. Screams rose like flames of fire into the night air. The guards had then ferried men, women, children, and even old folk to the galley. After the guards had stowed and secured the small rowboat, the *Aqrab* had disappeared again, and where once the small thriving fishing village had been, only the carcasses of burnt-out huts remained.

He had felt nothing. His emotions had long ago been shoved deep into a dark hole beneath the weight of emptiness. It was like an air pocket on a sunken ship, a barrier between alive and dead. He no longer felt the blows as they landed on his back, and he doubted he even bled anymore, unlike the young man in front of him, who still bucked and grunted every time the bullwhip split his skin.

Even death was beyond his reach. Each time he'd considered it, Danielle was there guarding that threshold like a venerable archangel, denying him passage.

Sometimes, his father would sit next to him and talk while he rowed. Once, he dreamed he was a young lad playing with his mother, dancing with her in their garden. His daily cup of water chased the dreams away, but as soon as his thirst took hold of his mind, the line between what was real and what was not, faded and often disappeared altogether. Only Danielle would not visit him. He had to conjure her from his memory if he wished to see her face. Then again, he knew exactly where to find her, guarding that line between the living and the dead, glaring at him with her phosphorous green eyes if he dared come too close to her liking.

A private smile tugged at the corners of his mouth. *He loved her.*

Noises from the deck and the harbor beyond brought his mind back to the present. The guards were unchaining the rowers from the benches. They were moving row by row, starting from the back. It would soon be his turn.

Sebastiaan tested the soles of his feet. The skin had knitted nicely over the last two weeks. He hoped it had healed enough for him to take more than a mere stride or two. It had been his own foolishness. During one of his rare moments of clarity, he noticed the guard passing Floris over when he handed out the drinking cup. According to the guard, Floris had looked at him too arrogantly, and therefore was denied water for two days. Floris was already weak from weeks without proper food and days without water. Sebastiaan had given him his cup, but he wasn't careful enough. The guard had seen, and within minutes Sebastiaan had found himself face down on the deck, receiving a hundred lashes to the soles of his feet. He couldn't stand up for days to take a piss, so all his bodily functions were left to run their course where he sat on the bench.

From the moment the Muscat harbor came into view, Yavuz had ordered the cannons to fire a shot every fifteen minutes, alerting buyers and spectators to his return. The woody scent of the cloves and the smell of diarrhea and vomit hung like a cloud around the *Aqrab*. Those ashore could often smell a slave ship long before they saw it. Yavuz should save his powder. The light breeze, blowing toward the coast, would announce their arrival just as effectively as any cannon could.

By noon, the galley slaves and those below decks were chained together and lined up to start their march through the narrow streets, first to the barbers and then on toward the slave market.

As they left the galley, they paused by Yavuz, one by one. Depending on the skin color, he wrote the amount he wished to receive for each slave in charcoal or chalk. For most, the amount ranged between seventy and ninety Venetian ducats. He'd given Sebastiaan a quick study from head to toe before writing *one hundred and fifty* in large black numbers across his chest.

Frowning in disgust at the soiled cotton breeches, Yavuz barked to a guard, "Keep him at the back of the line and hand him to Mustafa. Don't shave the head, just the beard."

Only three years had passed since the sultan had driven the Portuguese from Muscat, and the locals' hatred toward any foreigner was declared in every insult and filth thrown at the new slaves. Squat buildings with small windows lining the narrow streets offered the perfect vantage point for pelting the row of slaves with rocks and rotten food. Children ran along the shuffling procession, mocking and humiliating the newcomers returning from the barbers, who were once more dripping with blood.

The street was nothing but an uneven dirt clearing between the buildings.

Often a slave would stumble, bringing all to a halt. A quick lick from the overseer's whip would get them moving again, and they continued their arduous trudge to the town square. Sebastiaan was grateful for the extended walk. It was a vast improvement from his daily two strides to and from the side of the galley. He was the only one whose head wasn't shaved, and he now wished it was, as clumps of rotten food clung to his hair, dripping down his face and mixing with the grime of his unwashed body.

A guard approached and threaded a leather leash through the ring of the iron band around Sebastiaan's neck before unchaining him from the rest. He was then pulled aside and handed over to an old man who would serve as his auctioneer. Sebastiaan flicked the muck from his face and watched with satisfaction as some landed on the auctioneer. The guard did not leave his side but spoke to the old man, who he called Mustafa, in hushed tones as they held Sebastiaan back, allowing the other slaves and their auctioneers to enter the market square ahead of them.

When Mustafa deemed it time to enter the square, he did so slowly, searching the crowd with his small, shrewd, black eyes, no doubt looking for his favorite buyer.

All the slaves wore the same clothes they did during the voyage. It would be up to their new owners to provide them with clean clothing, if they wished to do so. Sebastiaan felt a wave of embarrassment as he looked down at his soiled breeches, now being the object of much hilarity for the women and children they passed. Turning his head away from the laughter, he saw one of the black girls from the African village being inspected by a potential buyer. She was stripped completely naked and bent over, her head almost pushed to her knees by her auctioneer, while the prospective buyer leaned in to inspect her in the most degrading manner. The girl was crying softly at her humiliation, but her sobs were quieted when the buyer handed the agreed sum to her auctioneer and crisply delivered an openhanded slap to her face.

"Good, the Pasha has made his purchase. Now we can start," Mustafa spoke to himself, knowing the European slave did not understand their language. Sebastiaan understood every word but kept the knowledge to himself.

"What is your name?" Mustafa asked in broken French.

Sebastiaan ignored the question. Only when the old man yanked on the strap around his neck did he turn to look at him. Sebastiaan kept his chin high as he stared down his nose at the old bastard, thinking how easy it would be to pull him close and ram his forehead into the beaked nose, sending it to the back of his skull. But then what? Where would he go, and how far would he get? Quietly staring at the old man, he let the thought go.

"Where are you from?" his auctioneer asked again, and once more, Sebastiaan wordlessly stared him down.

"Tsk," the old man sounded and spat to the side. "Illiterate, stupid, filthy dog. How will I get that enormous amount scratched onto your sorry hide if I don't know what I am selling?" He continued to lament his lot in inaudible grumbles as he pulled Sebastiaan along.

The auctioneers prided themselves on their independence and impartiality, but the world was delightfully imperfect, and opportunity bloomed where it was most harshly suppressed. Scanning the crowd with cunning eyes, the auctioneers knew who the real buyers were and slowed their pace as they neared them.

Shaykh Hassan watched as slave after slave trotted past him. The leather leashes around their necks went taut and slack as they were encouraged to leap and jump with a few deftly placed strikes from the auctioneers' canes. They were all presented to him, but he dismissed each with a slow flick of the three fingers not occupied in stroking his neatly trimmed beard.

The market was a sweltering mixture of noise, color, and smells. Large square, flat-roofed, brown-gray buildings that looked as if they were hewn from the soil they stood upon, spilled onto an all-connected, expansive terrace edged by two long steps leading to the paved, sunken square. Usually, the stalls would fill the square wherever space was free, leaving just enough room for buyers to wander through. Today, they were all pushed side-by-side to line the steps, leaving the center free of clutter.

People milled about; the air quivered with their excited twittering as the auctioneers enthusiastically called out the virtues and aptitudes of their stock. The twangy staccato sounds from an oud lent a steady, monotonous beat to the background. Women pointed, and giddy whispers drifted from behind the veils that covered their faces. Children were jumping up and down like fleas on a dog's back, yipping and squealing as they bet against each other at which slave would sell next. The winner impatiently and triumphantly stretched out a grimy hand for his winnings and the loser reluctantly parted with his sweet treats. Even the noisy stall owners had momentarily forgotten to sell their wares. All attention was on the main attraction of the day.

Hassan despised coming down here. Being surrounded by so many pushing and shoving bodies always made him feel dirty. Beneath his shirt, sweat was already running down his back.

So far, the day had yet to prove fruitful. He'd seen a priest who had been brought in earlier, but the Pasha had first choice and had snagged him and a young black woman before the auctioneers could parade them around the square. Any member of the clergy was always a solid bet, for the Roman Catholic Church was known to take care of its own, and as soon as a ransom was set, it was paid—easy money. Not that Hassan ever bothered setting ransoms. He was just a middleman.

Hassan had recognized the cannon fire earlier as the galley came into port. The *Aqrab* was a gift from the Pasha to his cousin Yavuz, with the condition that the Pasha would get ten percent of the loot, the first pick of the slaves, and ownership of any liberated vessels.

Yavuz was no fool. He always held the slaves he reserved for his cousin back until the Pasha had made his selection. He then handed them off to selected auctioneers, who would lead them past the other buyers and straight to Hassan. For his part, Hassan would go on to sell the stock at the palace auction, sharing the profits with his cousin.

Hassan's eyes were drawn to the wide arch as their auctioneer entered with the slave Yavuz had kept aside for him. The pair was a study in contradiction. Mustafa was rake-thin and weathered with age. The slave on the end of his leash, in contrast, was young and tall, with once-pale skin and yellow hair that glimmered in the midday sun.

"Shaykh Hassan," Mustafa's scratchy voice called to him, touching his mouth and forehead in greeting.

"I've brought you a rare specimen," he said, yanking the slave closer.

"Hmm," Hassan exhaled as he wrinkled his nose before studying the offering. Apart from the obvious undernourishment, the young man was well built and thickly muscled, with broad shoulders, narrow hips, strong legs, and long elegant feet, though slightly swollen; he wondered at the cause. They hadn't shaven his head. A wise decision. Those pale curls would help to drive the price up tonight.

"What is his name?" he asked the auctioneer.

"I don't know," Mustafa said with a resigned sigh, as if he'd asked and had gotten no reply.

"Ask him," Hassan barked at the old man.

Mustafa employed his best but extremely limited French, but his question was met with stony silence and a cold glare from the pale green eyes.

"Answer," Hassan ordered, not bothering to speak the impossible language that made the orator sound as if suffering from nasal congestion. Again, his demand was met with nothing but the sound of the music floating on the thick, dusty air. A quick flick from his hand brought the cane across the slave's face, leaving a red welt and a thin line of blood to coat the bottom lip of the harshly curved mouth.

"Your name," Mustafa's French became more accented with his growing concern. If the slave continued with his obstinacy, it would jeopardize Mustafa's commission.

"Arent Van Jeveren." The slave didn't bother to wipe the blood from his mouth as he spoke.

"Dutch?" Hassan asked, and the slave gave a single nod.

Hassan looked into the man's eyes. They shone with anger, defiance, and intelligence. He needed more information to sell him successfully at the palace tonight, but he got the impression it would take a lot of beatings from the cane, which would only bring the price down. He could see why his cousin kept this one aside for them. Although his body was thin and a bit scarred from his time spent on the oars, he had grit. Hassan liked that, but this was neither the time nor place for such a display.

"He's too thin. Move on," Hassan said dispassionately, knowing Mustafa would play along in their game of keeping up appearances. If others suspected Mustafa was working for the cousins, the Pasha would fine them harshly and forbid the auctioneer to enter the market square again.

"Oh, Shaykh Hassan, don't make a hasty decision. Look at the shoulders," Mustafa said as his hand swept the young man's shoulders. Indeed, impressive. He spun the man around to continue his blandishments. "Look at his strong back and legs. He would be a good worker. Imagine the load those shoulders could carry."

Hassan's face remained impassive as he feigned disinterest. Not one to let a quiet moment linger, Mustafa continued to sing the praises of his charge. Finally, Hassan called an end to the theatrics.

"Very well," he capitulated with an excessive exhale, lifting his cane to wedge it between the slave's lips.

"Open," he ordered in Arabic. The gesture was clear enough, and the slave obeyed. "Wider," he said, and the man responded. The teeth were in good condition. They were intact, and none were broken or missing—excellent.

"Remove his breeches," he ordered.

Mustafa yanked the offending piece of cloth away from the slave's body. Instinctively, the man's hands snapped forward to cover himself, but Hassan gave his knuckles a quick rap with his cane, and the hands retracted.

"See. No disease," Mustafa chimed.

"Does he have gout?" Hassan asked.

"No, Shaykh! I would never— "

"Have him run for about twenty yards and back." Hassan watched as the pair jogged away. The slave's strides were shortened by the chain connecting his ankles. There was a slight unevenness to his gait, and he wondered again at the reason for the swelling in the feet.

Upon their return, Hassan had him jump up and down a few times, keeping a close eye on his face. There was no wincing to show any pain. Tapping his cane to the slave's ankle, he motioned for the man to lift his foot. There was no sign of gout, but blood-soaked dirt caked the sole. On closer inspection, he saw the many scars from recently healed wounds.

Hassan was not overly concerned. With the golden hair and sculpted body, he would make a fortune off him tonight at the palace. All he needed to do was clean him up a bit, nothing a drop of water couldn't fix, and the oncoming infection would be the new owner's problem.

* * *

Six guards, three in front and three at the back, were leading Sebastiaan through the palace gardens to an entrance hidden by date palms and potted plants. Even without the shackles around his ankles and wrists, escape was not an option. The men were fit and well trained, their eyes alert but not frantic, their hands relaxed but well placed next to the weapons in their waistbands.

After the midday auction, Hassan had taken him to his home. It was a lavish but not opulent affair. A guard had led Sebastiaan to a small private courtyard where a platter of food, a bowl of water, soap, and fresh, crisp white breeches awaited him. The guard had retreated to the back wall, blocking the entrance. Sebastiaan had fallen on the food like a starved savage. He couldn't remember what he ate, only that he did. The taste and textures were foreign to him, but he did not care as long as it filled his stomach. Then he had washed, and for the first time in months he felt clean, but the feeling lasted only until two slave girls entered with a jar of sweet-smelling oil.

Torches lit the palace garden, and Sebastiaan watched as the orange glow reflected on his oiled skin. The night air was warm and carried notes of incense and dust. They rounded a water fountain surrounded by beautifully crafted containers with colorful flowers, and an unbidden image of his garden in Batavia flitted through his mind. Loud birds with long, swooping tails drifted through the trees, monkeys rustled in the leaves, and the smell of gardenias filled his memory. He felt a pang of longing he'd never thought he'd feel for his father's home. The mansion was nothing more than the place he'd inherited; it held no meaning and was no anchor. Danielle would have changed that. Once he brought her there, it would become a home. She would bring warmth and noise and happiness. He could see them walking hand in hand through the gardens, laughing and talking. *Enough.* He shoved the unwanted dreams back to where they belonged. They would eventually die if ignored and starved long enough. All that was important was to survive the moment he was in. Breathe, don't think, and wait. He was unsure what he was waiting for, perhaps the moment to escape, fight back, or die. Time would tell.

The six guards stayed with him until it was his turn to pass through the heavy doors. The sickly sweet smell of shisha hung like a cloud in the air, and he suppressed a cough. Sebastiaan entered a room large enough to accommodate at least a hundred guests. It was a sitting room of sorts. Another guard took him by the arm and led him to a round raised dais in the center. Hookah pipes on octagonal tables surrounded by plush cushions were scattered around the dais. Brass cut-out lanterns, suspended from silk ribbons, cast flowery shadows on the walls and floor. Against the outer wall, potted palms filled the spaces between the similarly decorated alcoves, and thick blue and white tiled pillars supported the intricately carved ceiling.

Slave girls dressed in thin gauze-like robes meandered amongst the men serving food and dancing to the hypnotic tunes from the musicians. They all had the same sedated, far-away look in their eyes.

As Sebastiaan stepped onto the dais, the hum of voices quieted. The evening's auctioneer was a well-dressed man with a meticulously curled mustache. The tips extended past the bounds of his face, visible from behind as they bobbed while he announced the next item for sale. With eloquent honey-toned words, the auctioneer introduced Sebastiaan to the room. He spoke in a deep, soothing voice that expertly carried through the crowd, highlighting Sebastiaan's physical prowess, golden hair, and obvious stamina.

When the auctioneer's voice quieted, he spread his arms wide, indicating that the bidding could begin. At once, the room erupted with noise as the buyers shouted and raised their bids.

Sebastiaan searched the room, looking for Hassan, but he could not see his face in the dimly lit space. He had no reason to look for the snake, but he was the only face he knew.

He was standing on a raised dais in the palace auction room, oiled and clad only in braies, surrounded by men eager to bid for him. The brutal reality of his situation struck with overwhelming force. His heart started racing as he realized he was nothing more than livestock; this was the auction where his value and worth were determined. This was to be the moment that would decide and define the rest of his life. He was a slave, the property of another to do with as they pleased. Whether used for pleasure or profit, he had no control over the matter. No longer a human being, he existed without a past or future. His only purpose was to serve. Panic surged from his stomach, threatening to make him retch. The oil coating his skin felt suffocating, the cloying air choking his throat. His vision blurred at the edges, his breaths rapid and shallow.

Sebastiaan closed his eyes and drifted to the bottom of the waterhole, allowing the water to close over his head. Slowly exhaling through his nose, he pushed from the sandy bottom and felt the heat of the African sun on his skin as he swam in easy strokes to where Danielle sat on the large rock in the middle of the pond, her feet swaying gently, sending small waves rippling to the muddy bank. She was so beautiful, so full of life and vitality. Her smile called to him, and he felt his body relax. His breathing evened out. He reached the rock and shook the water from his hair and face, sending it in a brilliant array of drops falling on her white dress, and she squealed with delight as it hit her face.

He opened his eyes. The squeal came not from Danielle, but from one of the girls as a man grabbed her by the arm and hauled her onto his lap.

"Three hundred," a buyer shouted from the back, but was quickly silenced when another raised the bet by fifty more. The two men bid back and forth until the latter won and triumphantly looked at the other.

"Five hundred," another man called, and his rival shook his head and graciously bowed out to find his seat again. The winner looked around the room, daring any to raise their hand. It was a ridiculously high price to spend on a slave. What does a man want or intend when he pays that much for anything? All in attendance were wealthy, judging by their dress and the fact that they were guests of the sultan, but clearly, this bid had crossed some invisible line—a new benchmark was set, and all seemed to honor it.

"One thousand Venetian ducats," a deep voice rose from somewhere in the middle of the room. A stunned silence punctuated with a few gasps followed the bid. A thousand ducats was madness.

Then the room vibrated with a hum of murmurs as the crowd parted to let the bidder through.

He was a man in his fifties. A large white turban, elaborately wrapped to resemble a very large upside-down acorn, obscured most of his hair. He wore a glimmering white silk kaftan with a wide, gold waistband wrapped around his midsection. A long outer kaftan of salmon pink was left to hang over his shoulders, his arms folded in abstention, allowing the empty sleeves of the cloak to sway as he floated toward the dais. Two bejeweled daggers were tucked in the waistband near his left side, and to the right, the ivory grip of a pistol showed. A pair of dark red shoes with upturned tips completed the ensemble.

"Sold to Shaykh Ahmet!" the auctioneer called, his voice breaking the spell that held all enthralled, and the room erupted in cheers and congratulatory exclamations. The shaykh ignored all the commotion his bid had caused. Instead, he kept his gaze steady on Sebastiaan; a predatory gleam sparkled in his dark eyes.

"Bring him to me," he called to the auctioneer.

Two guards pulled Sebastiaan from the dais and brought him face-to-face with his new owner.

Sebastiaan raised his chin and looked the man dead in the eye, knowing he could receive a fierce beating for such insolence. He kept his locked stare, even as a slow smile spread across the man's lips. He would not cower, and if they wanted him to bend a knee, they would have to beat him until he could no longer stand. They might own his body, but his soul was still his, and it was not for sale—not tonight, not ever.

Shaykh Ahmet slowly circled his newest acquisition. When he finally completed his orbit, he came to stand before Sebastiaan with only the distance of an open hand between them. The icy glint in his young slave's eyes betrayed his unease with the closeness.

Ahmet softly laughed as he leaned closer still, speaking so only Sebastiaan could hear.

"I've spent my money well. You please me, slave," he purred and watched as the breath from his words stirred the golden curls near the slave's ear. "I can see the defiance and the anger burning in your eyes."

Sebastiaan swallowed as his owner's eyes bore into his. The man's breath hit him full in the face, and he felt real fear stirring in his belly for the first time since his capture. Keeping all emotion from his face, he remained rooted to the floor, not retreating, nor turning his head away.

In the next instant, shock spewed up Sebastiaan's spine as Ahmet's hand closed in a firm grip around his genitals. The lewd act had gone entirely unnoticed, for the slight twist to Ahmet's shoulder and the sides of the outer kaftan obscured his outstretched hand.

"I intend to harness that energy and passion quite efficiently," Ahmet continued in hushed tones. "And should you fail to rise to the occasion," Ahmet's eyes narrowed, and a sly smile played on his lips, "I will simply remove the source of disappointment and feed it to my dogs. I promise you; they are as hungry for your balls as I am."

The shaykh was about to elaborate when the slimy gob hit his upper lip. Shaykh Ahmet's head snapped back in startlement. His eyes grew large as awareness dawned. Instantly the guards stepped forward, but he lifted his hand to stay their advance as his other hand let go of Sebastiaan to wipe the moisture from his face.

Sebastiaan watched as the curiosity and lust faded from his owner's eyes to be replaced by a fury so intense it turned his black eyes hard as flint.

"I will kill you for this," Ahmet forced the words between his teeth, his lips thin and taut, "I will kill you slowly until you beg for my mercy, until you curse your mother, and cry for your god."

"Fuck you," Sebastiaan whispered back in Arabic. Belatedly, he realized his mistake. He had neatly stepped into the trap laid out for him, tipping his hand and revealing more than he had wanted to.

Ahmet released a laugh that did not reach his cold eyes.

"So, you *do* understand."

# Chapter 13



Danielle hit the wall of the small storeroom with enough force to drive the air from her lungs. Her head hit the wall, sparking stars behind her eyes, her knees buckled, and her body slumped in a rumpled bundle on the floor. Her brain temporarily suspended command of her lower half as it dealt with the unexpected assault on her head. A guttural roar tore from Blanx's throat as he fought his way up from the depths of his mind. As an exclamation of his outrage, a gust of wind slammed the door shut, blocking out the midday sunlight and engulfing them in blackness.

Blanx sounded like a tortured beast, and Danielle heard the ripping of bandages as he clawed at the restrictions around his chest. It was five days since his keelhauling and whipping, and last night the fever from his wounds had taken a more lethal grip that left him shaking, yet still unconscious, on his sleeping pallet.

Danielle had hoped he would battle the worst of the fever while still asleep. That hope was viciously dashed a few minutes ago when he'd breached the surface of his awareness, deliriously thrashing and bellowing, fighting invisible demons lurking in the shadows of his mind. His raw, broken cries of anguish and rage tore at her heart.

Scrambling to her feet, she tripped on the falls of her skirt and, not for the first time, cursed the abominable garment.

As Danielle reached for the heavy wooden door, it flew open, and she found herself staring into the two faces she'd least expected to see.

John Van Leyen, the settlement's newest slave, rushed past her toward

Blanx, leaving the governor's wife round-eyed and clearly shocked, waiting outside.

"Danielle, what happened?" Maria asked.

"Blanx is awake," Danielle said, reaching into her hair to touch the back of her head. She winced as her hand came away bloody.

"Yes, I can hear that. You are bleeding." Maria's voice had regained its normal strength now that blood was drawn.

"Where are your supplies? Come sit down." Maria reached to close the door, but Van Leyen's voice stopped her.

"No," he barked from inside the small room. He'd managed to wrestle Blanx back onto his pallet, and for the most part, Danielle's patient was calming down. Blanx's head was still restlessly turning from side to side, but the movements were not as violent as earlier.

"He is afraid of small, dark places." A shadow passed over Van Leyen's face, and he quickly looked away from the two women gawking at him.

"Danielle, can you please sit down and let me have a look at your head?" Maria sounded stern though a touch brittle.

"It's just a scratch," Danielle soothed, though she felt the blood creeping down her skull and into the folds of her neck. She slumped into the open doorway, leaning against the frame and looked to where Blanx lay. His breathing was easing. A week ago, he was a strong, robust man. Now, he was a broken wreck. Van Leyen knelt beside his friend, his ankles raw from where the shackles chafed the skin. She would tend to him this evening when his chores were done.

"How is it that the governor's wife and slave ended up at the door together?" Danielle asked, not meaning to be cruel but sounding it, nonetheless.

Maria knew the question was asked in an unguarded moment, but the implication stung all the same. She splashed vinegar onto a linen square, pushed Danielle's head forward, and pressed the cloth against the small yet operatic wound.

"I was on my way to have my lunch at the beach when I heard the screaming. Van Leyen and I came from opposite directions and reached the door simultaneously," Maria said, with an edge of warning in her gentle tone.

"There, the bleeding stopped." Maria put the linen square to the side and picked up her lunch basket. "Would you care to join me?" The question was merely a guise to hide the command.

Blanx had fallen asleep again.

"He'll probably not wake for a while yet," Van Leyen said as he shuffled past them, the chains connecting his feet scraped the cement floor.

"Mistress," he greeted Maria, before turning to Danielle. "Perhaps if you could leave the door ajar, it might settle him." Danielle nodded, wondering if he had heard her harsh question earlier, but his face was blank, and his eyes shuttered.

"Thank you, Mister Van Leyen," she spoke to his back since he'd already turned to hobble his way across the courtyard.

Blanx was resting on his side, and Danielle tucked a rolled blanket against his back to bolster his position before she followed Maria to the beach.

* * *

The day was windless, and the occurrence was so out of the ordinary that Danielle wondered if mother nature had forgotten about that annoying detail. Danielle and Maria walked some distance up the beach until they found a shady tree far enough to mute the construction noises that seemed to cling to every minute of daylight.

Maria never ventured far from her apartment and, judging by the feast Mrs. Boom had packed for her, this outing was richly rewarded. They sat in companionable silence as they shared the meal of dried fish, fresh pot bread, apples, and a bladder of wine. Danielle stole a glance at Maria and noted the changes in her friend. Her cheeks had filled out over the last week, and there was a rosy tint to her usually pale complexion. She looked content and at peace.

They shared a friendship born of unusual circumstances. Maria had saved Danielle from her deepest despair after her father's death and had kept her safe during the long months at sea as they'd made their journey from Holland to the Cape. Danielle was there the night Maria's little boy had died and had comforted her in the months following the harrowing incident. The one seemed to be forever pulling the other from some depth of misery as both see-sawed their way through life.

"What I said was unforgivable," Danielle's voice broke on the admission. "Van Leyen is a good man, and neither of you deserved the sharp edge of my tongue." She wanted to add that she had not meant it, but at the time, she did, and she was well past the point of lying to herself or her closest friend.

"Many things are unforgivable, Danielle. That was not one of them." Maria did not look at her as she spoke. Instead, she kept her gaze fixed on the smooth bay. Africa was a place of extremes. It seemed unable to do anything in half measures. The climate was harsh, storms were fierce, and nature's colors were bold and clearly defined. Today the water was a calm, deep blue, contrasting with the crisp white beach, where waves crashed loudly upon the black boulders.

"Your heart is raw, and the hurt comes out in anger." A soft smile pulled at Maria's lips when she continued, "I know. I've lived with that blinding anger for nigh on a year now."

Two gulls were arguing over the possession of a gleaming silver fish, their future meal thrashing vigorously in a bid for freedom, but ultimately in vain as the hunter unceremoniously dropped it on the dry sand to confront the gathering crowd wanting to share in the bounty.

"Will it ever go away?" Danielle wondered aloud. She understood the emptiness that loss brought, but what she felt after Sebastiaan's death was not mere emptiness; it reached far beyond that. It was a bottomless void. The only time she felt a scintilla of meaning to her existence was when she treated Blanx, when her hands and mind focused on mending his broken body.

"The anger fizzles out over time, but the hollowness stays. One simply learns to live around it. The key is to find meaning again and use it to weave a new reality."

"How very poetic," Danielle said dryly as she watched the fish jerk up and down as the victorious gull tore pieces of flesh from its body.

"However, your anger at me is not misplaced."

Danielle's attention snapped to her friend. Maria gave her a fragile smile, guilt clearly written on her soft features.

"What is your meaning?"

"If I wasn't so sick, you would not have stayed, and then this whole," she waved her hand toward the ocean, before wiping the thin layer of sweat from her forehead under the guise to hide her anguish, "this whole tragedy would not have come to pass."

Danielle remained silent long after Maria's words had died away. It was true, in her darkest moments at night, alone in her bed, she had cursed her friendship with Maria. She had riled against the unfairness of the situation. But seeing the pain and guilt on her friend's face soothed the misguided resentment.

"Yes, of course." Danielle took a deep sip from the bladder of wine, then wiped her mouth with the back of her hand. "You are to blame for getting sick, and you are to blame for the infernal pirates who attacked the convoy. Just as I am to blame for not being able to save Antoonie that night." Picking up a small pebble, she hurled it at a nearby boulder, hoping to obliterate the small projectile, but it merely bounced away and landed with an unsatisfying thud in the soft sand.

"You are not to blame for Antoonie's death," Maria said thickly as tears welled in her eyes before she swallowed them down.

"And you are not to blame for Sebastiaan's," Danielle returned. Then she reached over and pulled Maria into a tight embrace. They held each other for long minutes, silently sharing their grief and drawing strength from each other.

"One day, we will sit down, eat and laugh over something silly, I'm sure," Maria said as she packed away the remains of their luncheon.

"I have no doubt. Lift," Danielle said as she pulled the blanket from underneath Maria, who stood to brush sand from her dress.

"We need to get you back to the fort before the sun robs your husband of the claim of putting that blush on your cheeks." Maria's breath hitched, and Danielle adopted an innocent expression. "He's clearly not sleeping in the guest quarters any longer," Danielle stated matter-of-factly as she gave the blanket a firm shake before folding it in a neat square.

Maria's mouth opened and closed several times as she scrambled for something to say, while her blush deepened. "You are impossible, and I am not having this conversation with you," Maria said incredulously, looking like a house cat that had unwittingly stepped into a puddle of dirty water when she saw the triumphant smile on her friend's face.

"Am I right?" Danielle asked with a raised brow.

"Yes," Maria replied, fighting to contain the smile that threatened to lay bare all her secrets.

* * *

To say that Blanx was a handful was an unfair understatement. Unfair in the sense that it was not his fault directly, and to assume that his antics could add up to a mere handful was underplaying it in the extreme.

The day after he'd regained consciousness, Danielle found him clawing and tearing at the bandages that covered the worst lacerations on his chest and shoulders. His eyes were wild and unfocused as he struggled to voice his confusion and frustrations. Danielle's soothing words and gentle touches were brutally rejected. When he discovered he couldn't shape the words he wished to say, his panic multiplied, and the storeroom seemed to shrink in size to where Danielle was forced to call for help.

It had taken the combined efforts of four men and enough laudanum to incapacitate an entire regiment to get Blanx to settle down, after which Danielle spent the rest of the day re-suturing and redressing his wounds. By sundown, Blanx resembled something close to a well-tended patient rather than a mummy set upon by a pack of wolves.

The storm that had brewed all afternoon thickened the air, shrouded the mountain in dense haze, and now unleashed its fury on them. Lightning split the night air with vibrant silver flashes, and thunder shook the ground.

Unable to leave the storeroom door open, Danielle had driven a nail into the far wall on which she'd hooked a sconce with a fresh candle. It was far and high enough from Blanx that he wouldn't accidentally knock it over. She looked around the small space with a contented smile. The room was clean, warm, and dry, and the candle lent an orange glow that made it feel almost homely.

Confident that Blanx was calm enough to be left by himself for a while, she reached for her medicine satchel and headed out the door. Closing it softly, she darted across the muddy courtyard to the slave quarters. By the time she reached Van Leyen's door, she was drenched. She knocked firmly and waited for his voice.

"There's no lock on the door?" Danielle asked by way of greeting. She entered the pitch-black room and fumbled in her satchel for the tinderbox and candle. Van Leyen closed the door behind her and reached for the items in her hand. Soon a candle spluttered to life. They were alone in the large room that could easily house twenty slaves, but his lone pallet was the only bed for now.

"The governor's idea of a show of good faith," he replied. "You're not supposed to be here. If someone catches you, there will be hell to pay, and I'll be the one paying it." He sounded gruff and looked annoyed.

"Yes, I know I'm not supposed to be here but neither are you," she said, before rummaging through her satchel again. "I've come to tend to your wounds and to bring you this." She handed him a copy of the *Bible*. "My name is written in the front. It was a gift, but I hardly get time to read it," she said with a shrug.

"And you think I have the time to read it? In the dark?"

She sighed at his harsh tone.

"You can keep the candle. I'll make sure you always have one." She said and went to sit next to his sleeping pallet, opening the ointment she'd prepared earlier.

"I don't want your medicine. I don't want your candles and don't need you to tend to me." He did not move to the pallet, but remained near the door.

"You're angry about what I said yesterday," she whispered. After speaking to Maria, she'd forgotten about the incident altogether.

"It was a dangerous observation to make. A rumor like that can cost a man his life, and just in case you haven't noticed, our lives hold precious little value here."

"I have noticed," she said and looked away, unable to meet his eye, "and I apologize for my behavior. I was out of line and have no excuse for it." When she finally looked at him, his expression hadn't changed, and his posture was just as rigid as earlier.

She'd come to treat his wounds and to talk about Blanx, but his mood was too foul to achieve any of her goals. They stared at each other in a contest of wills, but it was Van Leyen who broke the silence. "You need to go. Now." And with that, he doused the candle and opened the door.

Danielle gathered her satchel and stood up, leaving the ointment next to the pallet. She walked to the door, but he stopped her before she stepped out into the rain.

"Here, take these back," he said as he held the *Bible* and the candle out to her. She ignored him and moved past him. "How am I supposed to explain these?" he snarled.

Danielle's eyes searched the top of the wall. Only one guard was patrolling the perimeter tonight, and he was not in sight. If she wanted to return to the storeroom unseen, she had to go now.

"Van Leyen," her patience was running thin, and she could not keep the edge from her voice, "it's hardly a crime to read the damn *Bible*."

"I don't want your charity."

"We can talk about that later. Use the ointment," Danielle snapped before pushing past him and into the downpour.

* * *

Two days had passed in which Blanx had woken at intervals, delirious with fever at first, which seemed to finally have run its course. Today, his skin was cool to the touch and his hair was no longer soaked with sweat.

Gijs had sat with Blanx the previous night, allowing Danielle to retreat to the comforts of her bed. She'd barely reached the mattress before falling into a deep, black, dreamless sleep.

This morning, soft clouds obscured the hour. Danielle was sitting cross-legged in the corner of the storeroom, detailing Blanx's condition and treatment in her journal. His head injury was still a mystery. Maria had provided her with notes made by a botanist who had previously visited the Cape. The notes were a godsend, filled with meticulous illustrations and information on the various herbs of the region and their uses.

Blanx was freshly dressed and peacefully resting on a new pallet of cut grass with crisp, clean sheets, and a woolen blanket. Gijs was becoming quite adept at rolling Blanx from one side to the other so Danielle could make his bed, but she could not ask anybody to help her change his clothing.

Throughout his unconsciousness and helpless state, she'd helped him relieve himself, but it was messy and private work. To preserve as much of his dignity as she could, she'd cleaned his body and changed his clothing before calling for help with the bedding.

A sound by the door drew her attention, and she looked up to find the bookkeeper's wife gracing the small step. Mrs. Verburgh wore a muted pink dress with white lace along the edges of the bodice. She had piled her yellow-blond hair high on her head in an intricate tangle of swirls and braids. Her appearance contrasted quite violently with Danielle's boots, breeches, unadorned shirt, and clean hair twisted in a long plait that snaked down her back.

Danielle suppressed a sigh when the petite woman uninvitedly stepped inside. She and her dress absorbed most of the space in the small storeroom. With greedy eyes, she took in the condition of the large man on the floor, and Danielle saw a flash of disappointment at what she saw or, rather, what she could not see. Blanx's head wound was neatly bandaged, and the rest of his body was covered by a white sheet.

"Heavens!" she exclaimed in a falsetto voice as she raised her hand to her heart. "I almost mistook you for a man." Aletta Verburgh's giggle pierced the quiet of the sickroom. Danielle winced at the shrill sound, and her eyes darted to where Blanx slept, but his eyes remained closed, and his shoulders relaxed.

"Good morning, Aletta. What can I do for you?" Everybody called her Lettie, but Danielle refused to use the moniker.

Mrs. Verburgh pinched her thin lips and blinked rapidly, no doubt taken aback by Danielle's brisk tone, before answering.

"I came to fulfill my Christian duty and to see how Mister Blanx is faring, and you, of course."

More blinking. Danielle was not fooled by the woman's thin veil of virtue or her plastered-on serene expression. Aletta Verburgh was the biggest gossip in the settlement and loved to stir up trouble wherever she could with her wicked tongue. It was her reckless gossip and masterful manipulation that had convinced the governor and the *Meesters* of Pieter Brackenier's guilt, even though not a scrap of evidence existed. She was a dangerous woman; the least said in her presence, the better, so Danielle remained mute and waited for her to continue.

"Oh, the poor dear," Aletta said with a sigh and a light sympathetic shake of her head. "I find myself in a rare moment of idleness this morning and thought to offer my assistance. Only for a short while, of course."

*Rare moment of idleness indeed,* the woman was the first to receive slaves for a household. A Javanese girl to clean the two-bedroom dwelling and a young man to tend the vegetable garden. Mrs. Verburgh was a good twenty years younger than her husband and was not at all shy to demand her comforts because of his esteemed position as bookkeeper to the settlement and advisor to the governor. That she was the first woman of the settlement to give birth on African soil also lent fodder to her entitlement.

Nodding thoughtfully, Danielle thought her timing could not have been better. Looking around the clean and tidy room, her eyes fell on the freshly used chamber pot. She was just about to empty it in the pit next to the fort when her visitor called.

"You are a beacon of virtue," Danielle crooned, "and so humble." She wondered if she was laying it on a bit too thick, but Aletta was positively glowing with the praise. "Your timing is, as always, impeccable. I am inundated with work this morning and was praying for someone to offer a kind hand. Here." Danielle removed the cloth that covered the pot and neatly pushed the vessel into Aletta's stomach, forcing her hands to close around it instinctively. "If you can empty that in the pit, it would be much appreciated. You know where it is, right?"

Without waiting for an answer, Danielle turned to sit by her pestle and mortar and started grinding the next batch of healing herbs meant to go on Blanx's back that evening.

The task had proven to be Mrs. Verburgh's undoing. She had carefully lowered the chamber pot and its unappealing contents to the floor, covered her mouth with a dainty hand to stifle either a scream or a gag, and fled the room. When Danielle turned to look at her patient, she saw Blanx's clear, brown eyes fixed on her and the corner of his mouth slightly raised.

It would soon prove to be a bittersweet moment.

"Are you awake?" Danielle whispered. He nodded. She went to his bedside and laid her hand against his cheek. It was cool.

"You've been asleep for almost a week. You hit your head pretty badly and cracked the skull. It's a miracle you survived. There were moments where you had me quite worried." Her relief at seeing him awake and lucid was so overwhelming she could not stop herself from prattling on as she wiped his hair away from his bandaged forehead.

He opened his mouth to say something, and she quieted down to listen. His large brown eyes grew severe and distant as he tried to speak, but no sound came forth.

"Blanx?" she prodded, while holding his gaze.

Again, he separated his lips, his mouth moved as if to speak, again the look of confusion, but no words emerged.

Danielle reached for a mug of willow bark tea and held it to his lips. He swallowed thirstily, draining the contents.

"Try again," she said. A low, meaningless growl was the only sound he could produce.

"Oh, sweet Jesus, no," Danielle prayed, "Blanx, can you say your name?"

He shook his head, and a lone tear crept from the corner of one eye. A look of utter devastation and confusion marred his features.

"No!" she cried and gripped his face between her hands, forcing him to look at her. "Don't you dare look like that. Not after what you've been through." Danielle did not mean to shout, but her voice bounced off the walls. He held still in her grasp, but kept his eyes shut.

"You can hear me, right?" He nodded. "You can understand me?" Again, he nodded, and she felt his beard scrape her palms. "Then soon, you will speak as well." This time, there was no movement.

He opened his eyes, and their gazes clashed. Hers determined, his shattered.

# Chapter 14

"I am at my wit's end." Van Riebeeck's voice drifted down to his plate with its unappealing contents. Pushing away from the table, he went to stand in front of the window looking out over the dark courtyard. Laughter was coming from the soldiers' quarters, where a line of orange light shone from under the closed door. Above, two guards were patrolling the wall.

"Every second week, Harry arrives with scores of men whom he claims are Saldanhars, demanding tobacco, wine, and food in exchange for vague promises of trade—promises yet to be fulfilled," Van Riebeeck muttered bitterly. He charges exorbitant amounts of copper for merely bringing them here and permitting talks, an outright extortion I'm forced to endure, all to secure food for the settlement." In the black window's reflection, he saw a man with thin, hardened lips and eyes cold with exhaustion. As he spoke, his words sharpened, rising to a strained crescendo just shy of a shout.

Helm and Coopman stared at him in silence. The governor losing his composure was not a common occurrence, and when it happened, it was impressive in its intensity.

Coopman pushed his chair back and extended his long legs, crossing them at the ankles.

"Why don't you let me handle the negotiations with the Saldanhars?" he asked. "You shoulder a lot of responsibility. Look how far you've brought this settlement in such a short time and against overwhelming odds." Encouraged by the silence in the room, he continued, "You've built this fort in just over ten months with an unskilled workforce, securing us all against attacks from sea and land. All this while battling sickness, storms, and hunger. Even though your accomplishments are nothing short of a miracle, just remember you are only one man." He looked at Van Riebeeck as he spoke, his voice even and his eyes warm with compassion. This was the moment he'd been hoping for. "Let us carry some of the responsibility. Allow me to deal with Harry and the Saldanhars and use the little free time it affords you to spend with your wife. She needs you."

Van Riebeeck was getting desperate, and much as he despised admitting it, the truth was plain to see. The evidence was glaring at him from his dinner plate. In a desperate bid to supply the colony with meat, he and Helm, with the help of four settlers, had killed six hundred penguins and had harvested three hundred eggs. As they had now discovered, penguin meat was almost inedible. It tasted of beef, duck, and cod liver oil, all deceptively disguised in a beautiful piece of red meat marbled with veins of fat. The eggs tasted better, almost like caviar, but the sight was nauseating. The whites were blue, and no matter how long they were cooked, they remained translucent and runny.

He was failing on all fronts. His harsh treatment of the settlers was near tyrannical, relying on fear to keep them from wandering off into the wilderness in search of a better life. He knew such a life did not exist, but they didn't, and once they left, they would not return. Not after the examples he'd made of Brackenier, Blanx, and Van Leyen. He knew that their only chance of survival, let alone success, was to stay together, but not if he couldn't feed them.

The harsh reality of living at the Cape was so far removed from the hopes and dreams he had for the settlement, as a bad marriage was to a sweet romance. Many of the Dutch sailors who were stranded here before had found trading with the locals easy. Some had even lived among the tribes for a time without incident. Van Riebeeck had expected to face difficulties, but he had not expected trading with the local tribes to be such a trial. Perhaps it was time to take a step back, time to study this from a different angle and come up with a new plan.

Listening to Coopman, Van Riebeeck felt the anger and frustration leave his body. His shoulders relaxed, and he leaned against the windowsill.

"Your wife is young and has endured much. Most of it alone," Coopman continued. "It is not your fault, but it is something you can change."

The governor nodded silently, contemplating the possibility of relinquishing this critical issue to somebody else. Perhaps somebody like Coopman, who was level-headed and even-tempered, would succeed where he, to date, had only failed. The notion held merit.

"Helm, what do you think?" Van Riebeeck asked his captain. Helm was a brute of a man, but far from unintelligent and loyal to his marrow.

"I think it is an idea worth exploring. I would love nothing better than to lighten your load, but I can't do it. Everyone knows the Beach Rangers and the Saldanhars are afraid of me. They seemed to think I would do them harm by simply turning my head in their direction."

That was the truth, if stated somewhat demurely. Helm portentously affected the natives and the settlers as Moses did the Red Sea. His large frame, icy blue eyes which perpetually guarded over a deep ravine of a scowl, and his white hair were the embodiment of evil to local tribes.

"Very well, Mr. Coopman," Van Riebeeck said, "I wish you the best of luck."

* * *

Two weeks later and Blanx was walking. Per Danielle's exact specifications, Mattheys had carved a walking stick for him that suited his size. He was currently leaning on the cane while draping his free arm heavily over her narrow shoulders as his still uncoordinated legs labored with the extra weight of the shackles. Danielle moved the large mixing bowl she'd pilfered from the kitchen to her other side, then adjusted her stride to better accommodate him.

With a low grunt, he pointed to a large boulder.

"I can't, Blanx," Danielle complained, "you are too heavy, and that boulder is too far. Just wait here until I come back." She'd promised Mrs. Boom oysters and mussels for tonight's soup. He ignored her protests and angled toward the too-thick and too-loose beach sand. Why the stubborn man insisted every day on trying to reach the water was beyond her.

The wounds on his arms, torso, and back had healed into thick scars that Danielle massaged each evening with almond oil so they wouldn't pain him during the night. The wound on his brow lingered, healing more slowly than his other scars. A deep hollow now marked the fractured skull, lending a deformed quality to his already rugged features. The injury had affected more than just his looks. He now struggled to walk, and the left side of his body was rendered weak and often uncooperative. There was a time when she'd thought he would never walk again, but Blanx had proved her wrong, and step by step, day after day, he had fought against the restraints of his injuries.

The worst of his impairments, and one causing the most frustration, was his inability to speak. Blanx could not form words. Only raw grunts managed past his lips. The cruelest cut indeed, since his mind was as sharp as ever, only the path to his mouth seemed to be damaged beyond repair.

Sweat was streaming down his face and onto Danielle's shoulder. He'd stumbled twice on their way to the beach. Each time she insisted they turn back he squeezed her shoulder and shook his head. On the bright side, the trial of reaching the beach had given birth to a breakthrough. Blanx had found a way to curse. He released a grunt when he stumbled the second time, trying to raise himself from his knees. The sound was harsh, short, and punctuated, leaving no room for doubt as to its meaning.

"Language, Blanx," Danielle chastised through her giggles, and for the first time since she'd known him, Blanx smiled. The right side of his mouth twisted in something closely resembling a snarl, and his eyes sparkled when he looked at her.

"Next time, put an 'f' to that, and you'll be speaking in no time." Danielle teased as she lowered him onto the boulder to face the ocean. It was a typical day, hot and windy, with sand whipping at their legs. Blanx turned his face into the wind and closed his eyes. He inhaled deeply, drinking in the beloved scent of the ocean, his red hair sparkling like polished copper as it danced in the breeze.

"Stay here, while I see what can be found amongst the rocks."

She was about to walk away when he made a guttural sound, and she paused.  Reaching out, he took one of her hands and flipped it over. Clamping her third, fourth, and fifth fingers together, he showed her the size of the mussels she needed to look for. With a nod and a crooked smile, he studied her to see if she understood.

"Can they be bigger?"

More nodding.

"How about a little smaller?"

Vigorous shaking accompanied by pursed lips followed her question. Definitely not smaller, then. Blanx pointed a blunt finger to the inside of the bowl and then to the water.

"Yes, I know," Danielle replied with mild annoyance. Must he treat her as if she were a child? "I'll fill it with water first. I have done this before, you know."

He waved her away and closed his eyes again, letting the wind and the salty air wash over his upturned face.

Danielle worked swiftly, eager to return with a full bowl before Blanx grew restless. He disliked staying in the same place or doing the same task for too long, only the nearness of the ocean seemed to soothe him.

After finding enough large mussels to fill half the bowl, she searched the undersides of the rocks for oysters. Wrapping each oyster in the fabric of her skirt, she worked the tip of her dagger along the shell's rough edge until it popped free from the rock.

The bowl was filling up fast, every now and again Danielle cast a quick glance over her shoulder at Blanx. He was still frail, and it was a miracle they'd reached the beach today, then again everything about Blanx felt like a miracle. Each day he grew stronger, and each day she learned more of his quiet resilience.

"For you," she said, standing in front of him with her offering displayed on the palm of her outstretched hand. He stared at the oyster with a lopsided smile.

Danielle carefully wedged the dagger's tip along the seam. She worked slowly and carefully as the oyster shells were difficult to separate, and the task required delicate but firm movements. The blade could easily slip and cut into her flesh if she pushed too hard.

Blanx made an impatient sound, gesturing for her to hand the dagger and the oyster over.

"No," she said without pausing in her task, "you know your hand is not strong enough to do this yet."

In the next breath, Blanx gained his feet and lunged at her. He sounded like a wounded bear as he tried to wrench the dagger from her hand. Anger was twisting his face in a scowl, making his features look like they were melting, and a feral glint lit his eyes. 'Twas a good thing Danielle was faster, for she snatched the dagger from his grasp, but the hem of her skirt was waterlogged, and she tripped and fell backward, landing on her bottom in the soft sand; a surprised shriek completed the series of unfortunate events. Keeping the dagger from his reach, she tried to stand up, but Blanx pushed her back down with a heavy hand on her shoulder.

The hardness in his face began to fade, the sharp glint in his eyes giving way to an anguish so overwhelming it robbed her of words.

Blanx was prone to violent outbursts and swift mood changes. According to Van Leyen, he used to be even-natured with a temper reserved only for those who greatly merited it.

Blanx made a staying motion with his hand, dropped to his knees and search for the oyster. Rubbing the sand from his gift, he looked so dejected that Danielle's heart tightened in her chest. She scrambled over to where he sat and knelt in front of him, her knees pressing against his. His head dropped to his chest, and his eyes remained fixed on his hands, where they rested in his lap.

"Blanx, look at me," Danielle said softly. He stubbornly refused to raise his face, but she'd learned his weakness quickly enough. "Please?" He was utterly and helplessly vulnerable to her pleading, a disadvantage Danielle had employed and abused with piratical impenitence.

Slowly, he lifted his head to face her.

"I know you are frustrated." His lips hardened, and his brows tried to draw together as his eyes searched hers. He smacked his lips and pointed to her damp, sand-encrusted skirt.

"It's fine. It's just sand," Danielle smiled and reached for the oyster in his hand. He watched her intently as she pried the morsel open and offered it to him. Blanx ate with obvious delight, but his shoulders were still tight with tension.

"Are you in pain?" she asked, studying his face. He usually suffered a blinding headache after an outburst, and the pallor of his skin told Danielle his head was throbbing. He nodded slowly and touched the place on his chest where his heart was beating.

"You feel bad for scaring me?"

He answered with a single nod.

"Blanx, you are quite a sight when your hackles are up; I'll give you that. But I don't scare that easily; in fact, I was planning to send you arse over next time we pass a bramble bush." She stood to brush the sand from her skirt.

"Do you think you can help me harvest the oysters?" she asked and tried to pull him to his feet. Though his frame wavered under her gentle tug, he rose without the support of his cane.

She watched him walk away from her toward the rocks. His balance was precarious, but he seemed determined to walk the short distance unassisted. Blanx removed the oysters with slow and calculated movements, his face pinched in concentration. Relinquishing the task to him, she climbed onto the rock and stared out over the ocean. Summer was drawing to an end, another season separating her from the time she'd spent with Sebastiaan.

Movement caught her eye, and she squinted in its direction. Mr. Coopman was making his way through the loose, dry sand toward them. With the breeze ruffling his dark hair, he appeared younger, almost carefree. He was a handsome man and she could understand why he was a favorite among the women of the settlement with his easy charm and elegant smile; even Mrs. Boom flashed a blush now and then at his engaging ways. Danielle couldn't remember a single time he'd bestowed that dazzling smile on her, or perhaps he did, and she'd not noticed. She was more familiar with his stern and unyielding expressions. Not that it bothered her. She was likely the only female not to crumble at his feet.

He trudged across the sand, waving and calling to her, but his words were lost in the wind.

Danielle made to jump from the rock, but Blanx stopped her with his hand. His face was contorted with unbridled hatred as he stared at the approaching figure.

"Miss Van Aard. Blanx," Mr. Coopman greeted in his deep, smooth voice. A stare passed between the two men before Coopman gave Blanx a thin smile.

"You look well, Blanx," he said while reaching out to help Danielle from the rock. Blanx did not react but kept his furious eyes trained hard on Coopman's face.

After assisting Danielle onto the sand, Coopman kept his hand on her arm longer than was necessary. Though his grip was warm, her skin chilled beneath it, and she stepped away from his touch.

"Time for you to get back," he commanded.

"Why? Is something wrong?" Danielle bent down to lift the large bowl filled with the day's harvest. She noticed the dagger lying among the oysters. Blanx must have dropped it when Mr. Coopman approached. Then she remembered that slaves were only allowed to handle tools, not weapons.

"You are needed at the fort." Coopman spoke in a clipped tone, reaching for the bowl as she straightened. Some inexplicable but instinctive rebellious streak always dictated her behavior when she was near him and she twisted away, quietly spurning his aid.

"Blanx and I will be there shortly," she said dismissively.

"Danielle." The use of her name so intimately spoken in a voice low with warning drew her attention. Once more, he reached for the bowl, and this time, she let it go.

"But Blanx—" she started.

"Blanx can look after himself. Can't you, Blanx?" he interrupted while giving Blanx a passing glance.

Danielle's eyes darted between Blanx and Coopman. Blanx was looking less resentful and more concerned. Was he concerned for her? Perhaps it was just his mistrust of Coopman. Either way, she had little time to ponder his expression, for Mr. Coopman had his free hand firmly under her elbow and was pulling her away. She spared one quick questioning look at Blanx and he gave her a reassuring nod.

# Chapter 15

lsje, a nervous-looking Maheena, and the governor met Danielle and Coopman at the fort's gate. A Saldanhar man lingered a short distance away, watchful. Maheena, stumbling through broken Dutch laced with KhoeKhoe, shared that the tribe's healer had summoned Danielle to assist with a difficult birth. After absorbing the information about the emergency, Danielle hurried to the kitchen and then to her chamber to collect all she might need for the birth. When she was ready to depart with Maheena and the Saldanhar, Mr. Coopman adamantly stated his intention to join them. To make matters worse, he also insisted on the company of two armed soldiers.

It was a bad idea. The Saldanhars were notoriously skittish around the white settlers and only visited the fort as a group or when accompanied by Harry. That this man had come alone, delivering the healer's message, revealed the desperate urgency and fragile trust of the moment.

Danielle drew the governor aside amidst Mr. Coopman's demands.

"Sir," she said, her voice sharp with haste. "They've never reached out for help before. This is a huge step forward. It will only create consternation if I arrive with so many men. Let me go alone. I've been to the village without an escort before and was treated well." The governor did not interrupt her. Instead, he listened with his head bowed, and an intense, calculating look in his eye.

"I need you to trust me and let me go alone. Besides," she pleaded, "for Koba to send for me, can only mean that the situation is dire. We will most likely have to move fast, and the extra men will only slow us down. This is a chance to build a rapport with the Saldanhars and do something without asking anything in return."

Van Riebeeck was weighing the benefits against the dangers, and by the set of his shoulders and the tilt of his chin, she knew the former outweighed the latter. Time was critical, and she felt each minute as it slipped away. They had, at best, a two-hour fast trek through the forest ahead of them, and most of the morning was already gone.

"Governor," she said as she slung her satchel across her body, her voice holding a regrettable edge that belied her heightened state, "I can't waste any more time debating this."

"How long will you be gone?" Van Riebeeck asked.

"I do not know. It is almost noon already; I might have to spend the night." That brought his eyebrows closer to his hairline, more rapidly than she would have liked.

"I will be safe. Please trust me."

"Fine," Van Riebeeck acquiesced.

She could see there was more he wanted to say, but he held back the words. Instead, he heaved a deep sigh and turned to speak privately with Mr. Coopman.

From the crisp hand movements to the thinning of his lips, it was clear Coopman was not pleased with what the governor was saying. Maheena and the Saldanhar were already leaving. Danielle cast Coopman a final worried glance, then hurried to catch up with them.

Once they were inside the forest and away from the settlement they paused briefly, Maheena introduced the man as Tau. He was tall, and dark, with an open, friendly face that was easy to like. She learned the woman in labor was a young first-time mother. After that, it became an endurance race to reach the village, stopping only once by the river for a quick rest and to fill her water bladder before pressing on through the forest along an unfamiliar route.

They reached the Saldanhar village by mid-afternoon. The woman's agony-filled wails could be heard from a good three huts away, and Danielle sprinted the remaining distance, ignoring those who eagerly tried to show her the way.

Danielle slapped the leather hanging covering the door aside. The sudden darkness of the hut's interior halted her briefly as she waited for her eyes to adjust. Near the back wall, on a cowhide *kaross*, lay the young mother on her side, clutching her large belly. Her skin was ashen and damp with sweat.

Koba was rubbing the woman's back in slow rhythmic circles, murmuring strange words in a soothing voice. White smoke curled from a small fire, and the smell of herbs hung heavily in the air. A few feet away, a young man squatted, he appeared outwardly calm, but his eyes were burning with panic—the husband; his powerful arms and capable hands suddenly rendered useless in the face of his wife's suffering.

Maheena entered and positioned herself as far away from the scene as she could.

Koba reached for Danielle, and when she knelt next to the witch doctor, Koba took her face in both hands and pressed her forehead against Danielle's, a gesture so intimate and welcoming that Danielle fought against a rush of emotion.

"How long has she been like this?" she asked Koba. Maheena interpreted; Koba answered the girl, but kept her tired and worried eyes on Danielle.

"It started around midnight."

Fourteen hours, give or take. Too long, Danielle thought, but nodded without showing her concern. There were bloodstains on the *kaross* and between the woman's thighs. Koba had made the correct decision to call for help, but was it too late?

Danielle knelt next to the patient and placed one hand on the woman's forehead and the other on the side of her belly.

"What is her name?" she asked.

"Xhitha," Koba answered and then pointed to the husband, "Kuhle."

Xhitha briefly opened her eyes and stared at Danielle. A flicker of weariness entered her gaze as she took in the foreign face. Koba spoke soothingly, and her uneasiness ebbed away, leaving only the unmistakable footprints of pain and hopelessness. A tired keening sound escaped the woman as another powerful contraction contorted her body, leaving her quietly sobbing in its aftermath.

"She needs water and something to eat," Danielle spoke to Maheena. After a few extra crisp instructions from Koba, Maheena left the hut.

Too late, Danielle registered her mistake; she'd just sent away her interpreter. There was no time to bemoan her loss, though. The patient needed to be turned on her back, and in broken KhoeKhoe and Dutch, Danielle tried to explain what needed to be done. Koba's sharp mind swiftly grasped the meaning of the only now-and-then familiar words.

At Koba's instruction, Kuhle positioned himself behind his wife. Pushing his arms under hers, he lifted her into a near sitting position, and then leaned her back against his chest. Xhitha screamed as the pressure on her bottom increased, but settled when she heard her husband's calm, raspy voice near her ear.

Before leaving the fort, Danielle had gathered everything she might need for such an emergency and emptied her satchel, placing her oils and sachets of herbs in a neat line on the floor beside the *kaross*. Koba came to squat across from her, listening to the names Danielle attached to each item, trying to mimic the sounds. The old woman's tongue was set in its ways, and after a while, she gave up and opted instead to sniff at everything to familiarize herself with the medicine. Each time she lifted one to her nose, she closed her eyes, inhaled deeply, and gave Danielle an approving nod, but when she reached the almond oil, a wrinkled brow and a questioning look replaced the nod.

Maheena returned with water and food, then retreated to plaster herself against the wall by the hut's entrance. Danielle filled a small *calabash* and raised it to Xhitha's lips. At first, she turned her head away, but Danielle persisted, and once the first few drops of sweet fresh water coated her tongue, she thirstily gulped down the rest.

Koba scraped the thorns off a cactus-like plant then cut it into thick slices, placing one in Xhitha's mouth and another in Danielle's. It tasted wild and foreign, and the acerbic tang made Danielle's jaw muscles contract and squeeze in protest.

"*Xhoba*. The men eat this before they go hunting. It will keep her a long time," Koba explained.

Danielle remembered her father had told her that dehydration and weakness brought on by hunger were often to blame for complications during difficult births. However, he had preferred to administer honey sweetened tea or broth.

While Xhitha was distracted by the food and Koba's soft encouragements, Danielle knelt next to her and gently placed her hands on her round belly. The baby was moving, but the curve of its body felt wrong.

Just when she thought she'd located the small solid rounding of the head, Xhitha was gripped by another strong contraction. Screaming, she lifted herself away from her husband as she instinctively tried to push with the contraction.

"Don't push," Danielle kept her voice steady as she tried not to spook the overwrought mother.

The baby was lying sideways, and she could feel the head just to the left of its mother's pelvic bone. Danielle coated her hands with sweet almond oil as Xhitha pushed instinctively with the contraction.

To Danielle's horror, a tiny arm appeared between Xhitha's legs.

"The baby's head is not where it's supposed to be," Danielle spoke clearly, and Maheena relayed. "I will try to move it." Koba nodded, and Danielle instructed Kuhle to lay Xhitha flat on her back. The position was uncomfortable, and Danielle prayed the baby would cooperate.

Sliding two fingers past the small arm, Danielle located the baby's shoulder and gently pushed upward. The movement was counter to what nature intended and resulted in a harrowing scream, but after a few agonizing seconds, the small arm retreated. Danielle wasted no time and splashed a liberal amount of oil on Xhitha's stomach, moistening the skin enough to massage and knead the little body inside.

Danielle's hands found their rhythm, up around the right side of Xhitha's stomach, down on the left, then up on the right again. With each stroke, Danielle prayed. She prayed for the mother and child to live, for her father to guide her hands, and for God to watch over her.

With each contraction, Xhitha was becoming more worn out as she fought the urge to push, and with each contraction, their time was running out.

Danielle closed her eyes and focused on where her hands moved over the smooth, tight skin. Xhitha's cries had softened to small, keening moans. Danielle's hands moved in predictable patterns over and over without pause. Suddenly, as if it had had enough, the baby slid into place with a force that made Xhitha's breath hitched and then her eyes flew wide and locked with Danielle's. It was the moment a mother never forgot; when she realized the task required a strength that was beyond her, but even if it cost her life, she would deliver her child.

"Xhitha," Danielle spoke, "on the next cramp, I want you to push." Maheena must have sensed the pivotal moment, for her voice rang out clearly as she translated, and Xhitha nodded. Fear and helplessness were smothered by a blind determination as Xhitha gripped her husband's hand.

It took three more contractions and blood-curdling screams before the little boy entered the world.

Through the white wax covering his body, Danielle could see that his skin held an alarming purple tinge, but when she placed her fingers on his chest, the tiny heart was signaling back. Handing the silent, limp newborn to Koba, Danielle focused her attention on the mother. Trusting Koba to force air into his lungs and clean the babe before placing him at his mother's breast.

Xhitha was utterly exhausted and lay back with her eyes closed, and almost instantly drifted off to sleep.

"Xhitha," Danielle called to her, "one last push, and then it is all done."

As the last stage of the birthing process concluded, the little boy gave his first cry, and the sound drew a tired smile from Xhitha's lips. Kuhle's face was wet with tears as Koba placed his son on his wife's chest. Tonight, the placenta would be buried during a special ceremony where the newest member of the tribe would be announced and welcomed.

* * *

A large fire roared in the open space in the center of the village. Flames were licking high into the night sky, casting the huts and the forest beyond in stark relief. It was the site of many gatherings judging by the ring of stones around the sunken fire pit and the well-trodden earth.

The village, its people, and the fabric of belonging enfolding them all, felt a world removed from the Dutch settlement. This far from the ocean and deep inside the forest, the wind was still, the night air crisp and tinged with an earthy scent that told of moss and animals. Danielle spotted the large herd of cattle again as the herd boys brought them into their bramble enclosure for the night. Even now, safely behind the thorny barrier, small fires and young men armed with clubs and spears guarded the perimeter. Lions and other opportunistic predators were a constant threat.

After washing in the river, Danielle found Koba waiting by the fire with an extra *kaross* of soft animal skin which she draped around her shoulders. The nights were turning cool this late in February, and Danielle was grateful for the kindness. She sat between Maheena and Koba. Maheena was in deep conversation with Tau on her left, leaving Danielle and Koba to their charade-like conversation.

Sharing a bowl of berries and nuts, Koba taught Danielle the names of the food, patiently waiting for her tongue to master the clicking sounds that made up much of their speech.

The entire village had gathered around the fire. Everywhere, people were talking and laughing. Children were running and playing under the watchful eyes of their parents and the village elders. Two little girls broke away from the group and cautiously approached Danielle, as if she were a wild animal that might bolt if they got too close too quickly. When they gestured to her hair, Danielle understood their unspoken question and nodded in agreement, receiving bright smiles in return. Danielle felt the tension drain from her shoulders and neck as their delicate fingers untangled her thick braid. Squeals of undiluted delight floated around her as they buried their tiny hands in the thick, loose mass of her hair, giggling at the unfamiliar sensation as the hair fell through their thin fingers.

A small distance away, Kuhle and Xhitha were showing off their newborn baby, who was greedily latched on to his mother's breast, blissfully unaware of the special occasion held in his honor. The warmth of the flames showed in the young mother's tired, but contented face as she rested her head against her husband's shoulder.

A sense of tranquility washed over Danielle as she watched the young family. The feeling so pure and foreign her mind and body grasped it without hesitation. In that moment, her troubled emotions rearranged themselves, allowing just enough space for solace to find a foothold. As if knowing her thoughts, Koba reached out and took hold of her hand. The joining of their hands had the singular effect of a fissure opening in the thick crust of her sorrow, letting a sharp but thin burst of light to shine through. As Danielle tightened her fingers around the old bony hand, her breathing deepened, and her soul found its balance. Peace at last. With the unexpected realization, she opened her eyes and found Koba watching her with a knowing smile. Silence weaved back and forth between them, for neither had the language to express their emotions, but the message was clear: she had found her place—her home.

Danielle searched the many faces; she had not seen the Saldanhar chief all day and had expected him at the gathering to celebrate the little boy's birth, but he was nowhere in sight and she wondered where he was. Her pondering was interrupted when one of the elders, a man thin and gray with age, emerged from a hut clutching a bundle under his arm whilst carrying a large *calabash* with both hands.

"That is the pelt of a baboon under his arm and the *calabash* holds the heart fat of the Eland," Maheena whispered. "The baboon will give the baby strength, and the fat is a gift of honor."

The celebrations started the moment the young mother accepted the gifts and wrapped her baby in the soft black-haired skin. All the men gathered around the fire while the women remained seated, clapping and singing. When the rhythm was set, the men launched into a stomping dance. The lead dancer pressed long eland horns to his head, his slender legs pounding out the tempo. The others followed, bent at the waist with their hands raised to imitate horns. They moved clockwise at first, kicking up small dust clouds that swelled higher when they reversed direction.

"The Eland dance," Maheena explained. The Eland was sacred to all the tribes. Kuhle had shot a large cow the day before, and the tribe believed that the animal's spirit now lived in the new baby. It was a dance reserved for special occasions, such as when a boy entered manhood, a girl womanhood, when the elders needed to talk to the gods, or when a baby was born.

The dancing continued as the men's bodies mimicked the movements of the eland, harnessing its strength and power. With each cycle, the rhythm intensified, and as it peaked, the women raised their voices in a high, ringing warble. The men's feet stomped in time without pause. Their bodies, gleaming with sweat, shone and contorted in the heat of the flames.

Danielle clapped along until she could no longer feel her hands. The beat of the dance was pulsing through her veins, setting the pace for her heart, and pulling her mind into a trance, where she floated on the waves of the music.

The stomping feet, the swaying bodies, and the heat lulled her into a dreamlike state. Swaying from side to side like the pendulum in a grandfather clock, she let the waves rock her deeper. Sebastiaan's face floated from the depths. She raised her hand to touch him, wanting to feel the roughness of his stubbled jaw and the softness of his hair as she brushed it away from his eyes. He was near naked, dressed in nothing but a pair of white linen breeches, as if he was going for a swim in the ocean. Her smile faded when she saw the hard edge in his eyes. He was angry and panicked, and it made her sweat. Her chest felt tight, and an unfamiliar sweet smell coated the inside of her nose. Her hands reached for his face as she tried to draw him closer, but he pulled from her grasp and turned away. She tried to call him back, but he kept retreating, fading into the murky depths of her mind, and then he was gone.

Koba touched her arm and pulled her from her trance. Danielle blinked hard to dispel the tears that welled in her eyes and cleared her throat. Koba handed her a bowl containing a pinkish mixture that was making its way around the circle. Danielle raised the bowl to her nose and inhaled deeply. The smell of soured milk was unmistakable, but she could not identify the rest.

"Sour milk, blood, and honey," Maheena responded to the uncertain look on Danielle's face.

"Drink," Koba encouraged, nodding toward the bowl.

Eland blood and sour milk, the idea was unpleasant in the extreme. Danielle took a deep breath, raised the bowl to her lips, closed her eyes, and drank the lukewarm amalgamation. She swallowed quickly, her body already recoiling at the thought of drinking raw blood but, to her surprise, the taste was rich and earthy, and not at all disagreeable, leaving her mouth tingling in its aftermath.

As soon as the dancing ended, the smell of roasted Eland meat filled the air. Danielle's stomach gave a loud growl and her saliva thinned in anticipation. She didn't realize how hungry she was. Her only meal for the day had been a piece of flatbread and half an oyster, which felt like a distant memory.

There was a hitch in the celebration and a sudden hush before the women's joyful clapping burst forth. The little children jumped with excitement when the chief and five men stepped from the dark forest into the clearing. They moved as quietly as stalkers approaching their prey. Without the villagers' boisterous exultation, Danielle would never have noticed their arrival.

The chief smiled as he lowered the pack from his shoulders, then lifted a small child dancing around his legs high in the air. As if drawn, his eyes landed heavily on Danielle, surprise sketched across his face and his smile faded as he slowly lowered the child.

Maheena tugged on Danielle's hand, urging her to stand.

"We must go," the urgency in the girl's voice was underpinned by the trepidation on her face.

"Why? What is wrong?" Danielle asked as Maheena pulled her to her feet.

"My father cannot know I am here. He will punish me." Tears gathered in her eyes, and the first tipped over the rim and rolled down her cheek.

"Harry is not here," Danielle tried to soothe the distraught girl, but Maheena shook her head.

"He returned with the men. I know he is close by, in the forest."

"Maheena, I don't understand," Danielle was agitated by the girl's unreasonable panic. "How is your father here?"

"He takes the men to trade. They pay him in copper and tobacco. The Saldanhars trade cattle for copper, bread, tobacco, and wine," she sputtered, pointing to the bundles the men had brought with them.

Danielle searched for Harry, but she could not see him. All she saw were men reuniting with their families, laughing, and hugging their wives and children. The chief was making his way to where Koba sat; he looked tired, and his legs were dust-coated.

"Come, we must leave. Tau will take us back," she said, touching the young man's arm where he stood next to her. Tau gave Maheena a reassuring nod.

After Kai greeted Koba, he turned to speak to Maheena in a stern voice, leaving the girl to obediently nod.

"The chief says I must go, but you must stay. He will take you back in the morning."

Danielle started to protest the decision, but Kai's hand clamped onto her shoulder, holding her in place, as he dismissed Maheena and Tau with a sharp flick of his other hand.

It was clear the Saldanhars didn't fully accept Maheena and merely tolerated her. After Tau and Maheena disappeared into the dark forest, other women joined Danielle and Koba. The first attempts at conversation were awkward, consisting of a mixture of hand gestures and broken words. As with most sticky situations, food was the lubricant to smooth over the rough edges, and soon she was wrapped in the warmth of companionship. Portion after portion of warm juicy meat was pushed into her hands, followed by a *calabash* of fresh milk.

Danielle knew she would surely be sick if she took another bite. After months of relying only on fish and vegetables, her stomach had grown unaccustomed to the richness of the food. Next to her, Koba nestled deeper into her *kaross* and dozed off. In the fire's glow, the old woman's face appeared drawn, as if a pain deep inside her was making its presence known by pulling at the unguarded muscles of her face. When awake, the witch doctor was a force of nature, agile, sharp-witted, and fierce, but in repose, there was a hint of vulnerability—a frailty that would not stay hidden.

The children had long since found their sleeping mats, leaving the adults to share the events of the day with muted enthusiasm. All were sleeping around the fire tonight, except for the sentries who were keeping watch, guarding the group. A full stomach, the heat of the fire, and the safety of the many bodies surrounding her were slowly pulling at Danielle's eyelids. Had it not been for her bladder's insistent prodding, she would have curled up and let herself drift off to oblivion, but some things just couldn't be ignored.

Weaving through the sleeping mats, she slipped toward the river, passing the newly acquired pile of goods. Curiosity pricked her like a persistent itch.

She approached the goods that looked as out of place as she did. Frowning, she glided her hand over the bale of tobacco neatly tied with rope. The rope was similar to that used on ships to secure cargo in the hull, not as thick as the lines used for the sails, but strong enough to keep everything in place even amidst the fiercest of storms.

Four skin satchels bulging with many loaves of bread were lying next to the tobacco. Danielle had shared in the pieces of bread passed around the circle tonight and had thought nothing of it other than it tasted different from those which Mrs. Boom baked. Bread was a delicacy to the Saldanhars, something they'd not tasted before visiting the fort. Since they didn't grow wheat, they also didn't bake. Their meals consisted of meat roasted on an open fire, fresh berries, nuts, and the large tubers and bulbs they dug from the ground. This bread did not come from the settlement. She would have known if Mrs. Boom was baking this large a quantity, and besides, they didn't have enough wheat to feed themselves, let alone the neighboring tribes. Maheena had said her father took the Saldanhar to trade and was rewarded for it. Trade with whom? For a tribe whose survival depended on their cattle and what they gathered and hunted from the land, this haul was a veritable fortune.

A small wine cask caught Danielle's eye. The aged barrel bore a faded coat of arms on its side, depicting a creature with a lion's golden body and a blue tail studded with red fins. Squinting, she studied the once-vivid image, now dulled by time. Atop the cask lay three large, flat iron plates and she lightly ran her fingers along the cool metal.

The hardest materials known to the Saldanhars were bone, wood, and stone. They didn't have knives. Instead, they used sharpened pieces of flat stone to carve away meat or scrape flesh from bulbs; the tips of their arrows were crafted from bone or sharpened stone, and their spears were nothing more than sharpened wood. These innocent pieces of iron would change their lives forever. It would allow them to fashion better weapons and tools. Nothing would be the same again. Did the iron have the power to strip them of their innocence? She did not doubt that they were astute enough to know that to survive in this harsh world, they would have to adapt, but were they shrewd enough to survive the white man? Feeling a sudden surge of inexplicable protectiveness, Danielle closed her eyes and wished the wretched things away.

The chief came to stand next to her. He had a curious look on his face, and a smile rolled around his lips, bouncing between sardonic and pleased.

"Where did these come from?" Danielle asked in KhoeKhoe.

"Ships."

Danielle contemplated the answer. All Dutch ships reported to the fort. Were some of them dealing with the Saldanhars directly? It made no sense.

"Which ships?" she asked, but he shrugged and directed her back to her spot by the fire. Danielle needed a moment of privacy, but her grasp on the KhoeKhoe language did not stretch far enough to explain her need. Instead, she shook her head and pointed to a thicket a few yards away, near the river.

Careful to remain on the little footpath, she made her way to a dense shrub. To her dismay, she found Kai trailing behind her. This would not do. He obviously misunderstood her meaning. Turning to face him, she placed one hand on his chest, and with the other, she waved him back toward the fire.

"Go away," she demanded, but her words fell flat as he shook his head and advanced, using her outstretched arm to force her backward. Alarm surged through her, and she yanked her hand away from him. Searching his eyes for any sign of safety, she found only an unreadable mask. She was in his village, and under his rule and law, he could do with her as he pleased, and none would object or come to her defense.

"Please," her voice shook with distress as she begged. The chief paid her little heed, wrapping his hand around her upper arm; he spun her around and propelled her toward her destination. Once they reached the thicket, he let her go and nodded toward the shrub.

"I watch. You go," he said.

How on earth was she supposed to relieve herself with him watching?

"Please leave," she begged again, but he just smiled and shook his head.

Pointing to the campfire, he said, "Meat," and then to the dark shadows beyond, "Lions. I watch, you go."

The smell of meat would attract lions. Understanding his intentions did not make the situation any less humiliating, for her dedicated bodyguard remained, though he had the grace to present her with his back. She accepted the gesture and, with the utmost equanimity, ducked behind the dense shrub and lowered into a squatting position. Never had she relieved herself within earshot of anybody, let alone a man dressed only in a loincloth, guarding over her with a club and spear.

# Chapter 16

"I think Harry is misleading you."

The lone candle cast a harsh shadow over the governor's left cheek as he leaned back in his new chair. His chamber no longer looked like it was furnished with kitchen cast-offs. Mattheys had constructed an intricately carved high-back chair with a cushion luxuriously stuffed with sawdust.

Van Riebeeck's outstretched legs were crossed while his hands lazily hung over the edges of the armrests. As Danielle turned from the small bookcase, she noticed he no longer sat up and scowled at unfavorable reports. Life at the Cape had inured him to the point where he didn't even consider the existence of good news.

"Did you hear me?" she asked when he showed no reaction to her statement.

"Yes, I heard you." He exhaled a weary sigh. "What made you say that?"

"I know you like him and trust him, but …"

"Like and trust are two castles entirely built on sand."

The light caught his eye revealing the glint of steel in them. Danielle settled into one of the two chairs facing the desk and began recounting everything she had witnessed the previous night at the Saldanhar village. Van Riebeeck listened and the more she spoke, the colder his eyes grew.

"With whom are they trading?" he asked in a voice low and graveled with menace and controlled ire.

"I don't know. I asked, but they don't seem to know either or rather, they don't seem to care."

"They are getting handsomely paid. No wonder they don't care," he returned acerbically.

"I don't think they know the difference between the European ships. To them, we are all just white men. Our enemies and allies mean very little to them—if anything at all."

Van Riebeeck had fallen silent as his gaze fixed somewhere between the wall and the desk. He was a fiercely loyal man; betrayal was the Achilles' heel of his spirit, the one act or deed that had the power to knock his equilibrium off kilter and send it careening into chaos.

"I saw an emblem on a wine barrel," Danielle continued. The statement focused his attention and his eyes drew sharp with sudden interest. She described the half-faded image of the golden lion with the blue fishtail.

"The East India Company," he muttered. They sat in silence as he contemplated all she'd revealed.

Harry harbored a deep admiration for the English, which was why he so readily introduced himself by his English name rather than by his native Autshumao. Rumor had it that Harry was booted from his own tribe because of his backstabbing and manipulative ways, which had forced him to seek shelter with the Dutch. Not one to pay any mind to senseless gossip, Van Riebeeck had ignored that particular whiff of smoke, but now it would seem that there might have been a fire after all.

"Why have you not told me this earlier today?"

Danielle did not immediately respond to the question. She could clearly hear the accusation in his voice, but knew it was only his anger searching for a target.

This afternoon when she and four Saldanhar men arrived from the village with her payment, the governor had resembled the young man he had been a year ago with hope and determination emanating from him, filling the air around him and infecting others. For the first time in such a long time, he was happy, and she'd not wanted to ruin it then. But as always, the truth will out.

Before she could answer, a firm knock fell on the door and an instant later, it opened. Elias Coopman entered the dimly lit room with an easy smile creasing his face. His carefree expression stiffened slightly as his eyes flickered over Danielle. The warmth returned to Coopman's expression when Governor Van Riebeeck rose from his seat and gestured for Elias to take the unoccupied chair. The man had a commanding presence with a loose-limbed elegance that reminded her of a large predator, comfortable with its power.

"My apologies, Governor. Am I interrupting? I can come back later if you are busy." His deep voice faded when he half turned toward the door as if to leave, ignoring the proffered chair.

"We were just finishing," Van Riebeeck said and went to the sideboard to pour two glasses of wine.

It was getting late, and Danielle was tired after an eventful couple of days.

"Good evening, gentlemen," she said as she rose from her seat and was surprised to find Coopman's assisting hand firmly supporting her elbow.

She couldn't help but think that she was being escorted from the room. As he walked her to the door, she fought the urge to pull her arm from his grip. The man had developed the habit of late to touch her whenever they were walking somewhere. She had seen him do it with other women, and his handsome gallantry was always rewarded with beaming smiles and delicate blushes. If only his touch did not disturb her so. It was as if she was being caressed by something cold and dangerous.

* * *

*Three cows, four sheep, and two ostriches for the love of all that is holy!* He took his eyes off the woman for a day, and she laid to waste all his carefully constructed plans. Elias could feel his blood simmer through his veins, his irritation pushing to the surface of his skin like bubbles in a glass of champagne. It was a wonder she did not feel the burn when his hand closed under her dainty elbow as he led her to the door. Closing the door slowly but firmly behind her, he took the time to settle himself before turning to the governor.

"She saved us—again," Van Riebeeck said. Every word he spoke gleamed with the gratitude for the meddling and irritating chit.

Coopman remembered well the first time Miss Van Aard had secured five heads of cattle from the Saldanhar. They had only been at the Cape for a few weeks and were in desperate need of red meat. Most of the expedition's ships were eager to continue on their journey to Batavia and needed their fresh meat supplies replenished. Although Coopman had remained onboard the ship that day, to manage the countless administrative demands of the fledgling settlement, he had heard the story at least a dozen times. Of how the young woman had bravely stepped between the governor and the Saldanhar chief and offered to tend the chief's wounded leg. In a show of appreciation, the chief had gifted the requested amount of cattle to the colony without batting an eyelid.

He would have to be stark raving blind not to see that her latest stunt had cemented her in the governor's good graces regardless of the countless misdeeds she perpetrated on a daily basis. From this point hence, the woman's irreverent attitude toward authority and her blatant disregard for propriety and rules would be overlooked and even encouraged. He had to quash this little hellion before she became utterly unmanageable. He would prefer to push her off a cliff, but instantly closed his eyes against the dark thought. No, it would be far more entertaining to have her under his control, and there was only one way to achieve that.

"Yes, she is quite remarkable," he agreed, his voice relaxed and velvety as he rolled the stem of the wineglass between his thumb and forefinger.

"Are you making headway with the Saldanhars?" Van Riebeeck asked and took his seat again.

Coopman nodded slowly while he played with the words before he let any slip past his lips.

"It is a delicate process, as you've experienced yourself. But with Harry's assistance, I am nurturing a mutual trust between us. I am convinced our patience and persistence will serve us well soon."

After a longer-than-expected silence, Coopman glanced up to find the governor staring at him with an expression that made the fine hairs on his forearms quiver to life.

"You rely much on Harry?"

Why would the governor be asking a question he very well knew the answer to? Coopman decided to play along until he could decipher what, if anything, was afoot.

"I do," he replied but removed the certainty from his voice; instead, he leaned forward to rest his elbows on his knees, leaving his hands free to fondle the wineglass. "Is that a mistake?"

Coopman noticed the governor's attention was captured by the glass between his hands and he deliberately rolled the stem, making the light dance and skip along the crystal ridges, like a magician misdirecting the attention of his audience.

"I wonder if Harry is selling us down the river?" Van Riebeeck stared at the spinning glass before he shifted his gaze to Coopman.

A sudden breath left Coopman's nose, and he forcibly brought his heartbeat under control. What had the fool done now? Harry was getting greedier by the day. Coopman had warned him many times to curb his ambitions, but the man was growing more and more arrogant. Elias feared that it was only a matter of time before Harry exposed their partnership.

"Why do you say that?" He kept his voice even, if not a touch bored, despite the turmoil that whirled through him.

"Miss Van Aard witnessed the Saldanhars returning to their village with goods traded from the British." Van Riebeeck's mouth hardened with irritation before continuing. "It is not a secret that Harry harbors a deep admiration for the British and it would seem that he has convinced the Saldanhars to trade with them, rather than with us."

"Does she have evidence of his duplicity?"

The blasted woman was like a wrecking ball, obliterating his life.

"She had not seen him, but his daughter had confessed Harry's involvement to her. I plan to send Helm and Verburgh in the morning to patrol the bays and inlets, searching for ships, especially ones belonging to the Portuguese or the English. If Harry is involved, they might find the evidence we need to act more decisively."

At least there was a silver lining to this calamity. With Verburgh gone for a few days, Coopman could rid himself of much of his frustrations in the arms of the bookkeeper's young and very eager little wife.

Misinterpreting the agitation in Coopman's eyes, Van Riebeeck said: "I understand your disappointment. Harry sat at our table, shared our food, and shook our hands. His betrayal is incomprehensible. Had Miss Van Aard not spent the night at the Saldanhar village, we might never have suspected him."

"She spent the night?" Coopman let his eyebrows climb while entertaining an expression of deep concern.

Van Riebeeck acknowledged the question with a nonchalant shrug. "The birth lasted longer than expected."

"I admire her spirit and her bravery." Coopman's words prompted a smile that warmed the governor's face. He needed to move cautiously where Miss Van Aard was concerned. The governor was her guardian and benefactor and had a disconcertingly blind eye to any of her misdeeds.

"May I alter the course of our conversation?" Coopman leaned back in his chair, crossing one ankle over his knee before taking a sip of wine, notes of plum and a hint of smoke lingering on his tongue.

"Of course," Van Riebeeck invited.

Coopman momentarily found himself in uncharted waters. He was not a man accustomed to asking for what he wanted. Manipulation, artifice and coercion were much more soothing to his soul. Those required intelligence, whereas begging required nothing but indolence and hebetude.

"I … uh."

Van Riebeeck's eyebrows raised seconds before they lowered over narrowed eyes. The corners of his mouth quirked up and his arms crossed over his chest. Coopman on tenterhooks was an anomaly, a refreshing deviation from the ordinary. He had always wondered what it would take to ruffle the man's feathers and it seemed he was about to find out. Not wanting to interrupt the moment or make it any less awkward, he remained mute.

"What I want to discuss is something of a personal nature," Coopman looked almost pleadingly to Van Riebeeck, "if you would indulge me?"

Unwilling to break the spell, Van Riebeeck nodded.

When Coopman's eyes locked with Van Riebeeck's, his features had rearranged themselves once more into the familiar mask of self-control and serenity.

"I am not getting any younger and have come to realize that it might be time to settle down."

The governor was regarding him with a soft smile—eventually we all bent a knee, some to God, some to money and some to a woman, and he was honest enough with himself to admit that he'd done all three.

Coopman cleared his throat, and when he spoke, his voice carried an air of strength and determination. "I wish to ask for Miss Van Aard's hand in marriage. I am well aware that her qualities far outweigh mine, but I vow to keep her safe and give her a comfortable home."

The governor leaned back in his chair, bringing the glass of wine to his lips. He had sensed a shift in the air around Coopman, of late, whenever Danielle entered a room. "She is young, headstrong, and spirited. She would not be a conventional wife," he cautioned.

"That is what I admire most about her. I would never dream of crushing her spirit. Instead, I would treasure it. If I had wished for a conventional wife, I would have married a long time ago," Coopman said with a self-deprecating smile.

Compassion and understanding soften the governor's face.

"You might face an uphill battle," Van Riebeeck said, and Coopman tilted his head in question. "She still mourns the loss of De Vries."

"Young love can be volatile," Coopman intoned, seemingly unconcerned, "I will make no demands of her, but perhaps, one day, the addition of a child might bring her some peace and comfort."

A shadow passed over the governor's face, there and then gone. He understood the power a child held in a marriage. The unbridled joy and boundless love culminating in a small being that held all the hopes and dreams of its parents; and then the never-ending despair when those hopes and dreams were torn from their world when that little flame was extinguished, leaving the parents adrift in a black ocean trying to breathe, to keep their heads above the water, blindly searching for one another or anything to cling to.

"I cannot think of a better husband for her," Van Riebeeck avouched, "but I will not force her. It will be her choice when and whom she marries. Nonetheless, you have my blessing."

A slow, satisfied smile arched Coopman's elegant lips as he stood to shake the governor's hand.

* * *

"You are spending a lot of time with Blanx lately," Maria remarked as they leisurely strolled through the peach orchard.

Blanx had been working on Mr. Coopman's house for the past three weeks. His coordination was improving, but his speech showed no signs of returning. The mood swings he suffered were also not getting any better. In fact, they were getting worse, but Danielle suspected the leg shackles had much to do with the decline of his mental state.

"Blanx is my friend," Danielle responded, her eyes studying the horizon where dark storm clouds were once more bunching together. "In a way, he saved my life by giving me a purpose."

She shifted the heavy lunch basket from one hand to the other as they continued toward the newly constructed house. The structure was a distance from the fort, in a natural clearing at the edge of the forest, lending a secluded and intimate feel to the dwelling. The governor had gifted Mr. Coopman a large portion of land that would, over time, be turned into a profitable farm.

"Shall we rest for a moment?" Danielle asked, noting the thin sheen of sweat on Maria's forehead. For many mornings, Danielle had woken to the sound of Maria's morning sickness. It had taken her friend two weeks before she'd confided in Danielle about her new pregnancy.

"Perhaps just for a bit. At times I feel wonderful and then other times it feels like my life is draining away through my feet." She placed her hand over her still-flat belly and gingerly sank to the ground. "I never felt this frazzled the first time. Is this normal?" she asked as she arranged her skirt.

"The baby is making its presence known. It's a sign of strength," Danielle said reassuringly.

"I am so glad you're here with me. I don't think I could do this without you." Maria squeezed Danielle's hand gently, the softest of smiles adorning her face.

It was late morning by the time they reached the building site. Two men toiled in the scorching sun, while Fly snored in the shade of a nearby tree. Having stripped down to their breeches, their bare torsos gleamed like polished bronze. Van Leyen and Blanx's bodies had undergone a remarkable transformation. Muscles roiled and bunched as they lifted and secured one heavy stone after another to form part of an outer wall.

Van Leyen worked with fatalistic determination, but often stopped to pay attention to the signals and sounds coming from Blanx. There was an easy rhythm between the two men, and Danielle watched as Van Leyen paused to accommodate for the slowness of Blanx's movements.

The house was quite humble by European standards, but here at the Cape of Good Hope, it was extravagant. Once completed, it would feature four rooms, and a thatched roof. Unlike most of the wattle-and-daub houses at the settlement, this one was built with stone from a nearby quarry, and with a generous hearth in the kitchen.

"No outside cooking for this household," Danielle remarked as she lowered the heavy food basket to the ground.

"No, it will be a lucky woman indeed who gets to live here." Maria entertained a secretive smile as she stole a quick glance at Danielle.

"*If* Mister Coopman ever marries it would most certainly not be to anybody from the settlement," Danielle said dryly.

"Why not?"

"I can't think of anyone who would suit his sophisticated taste."

"You can't?" Maria asked and watched as Danielle pursed her lips and shook her head as her eyes took in the spot reserved for the vegetable garden.

"Oh, I don't know about that," Maria continued, "he is quite the favorite among the women." But Danielle seemed uninterested in the conversation and was waving to the two men on the scaffolding.

Upon noticing the women, both reached simultaneously for their shirts.

"No Fly. Sit down," Danielle commanded the large dog, who had begun sniffing her hands the moment the basket touched the ground.

"Let us leave them to enjoy their meal in peace," Danielle said and steered Maria back the way they came.

"You seemed very certain about Mister Coopman not being interested in anyone at the settlement," Maria prodded again as they slowly followed the footpath through the forest, leading back to the orchard.

"I honestly don't care one way or another about Mister Coopman or his marriage prospects. I, for one, would not marry—ever." Maria paused and Danielle looked at her with concern, wondering if something was amiss. Maria turned serious and a deep groove carved itself between her eyes.

"Danielle, you are still young. Your heart will thaw one day. But if you lock it away now, you will deprive yourself of so many beautiful experiences. Having a baby of your own, for one."

"My heart is not frozen," Danielle said with a mien no less serious than her friend's. "It is dead. It died with Sebastiaan."

Maria slowly shook her head in denial, but Danielle ignored her and turned back toward their path.

# Chapter 17

Governor Van Riebeeck swept the bedclothes aside in a smooth, silent motion, tucking them snugly against his wife's warm body. She groaned and rolled toward the comfort of the soft blanket cocoon he'd created. Gathering his clothes, he entered the small sitting room. He dressed in silent efficiency before softly closing the door to their apartment and stepping into the black hallway and down the stone stairway to the ground floor of the fort.

Reaching his chamber, he went to the window and stared out into the darkness. The moon hadn't lost her milkiness and the stars still shone brightly, but he felt, more than saw, the weight of the night lifting.

After lighting the wall sconces and a couple more candles, the room was sufficiently illuminated for him to settle in his chair behind his desk. Enjoying the quiet of the predawn, he closed his eyes in prayer.

"Heavenly Father," he released a breath that imploded his chest. "Guide my feet. Steady my hand and open my eyes to the opportunities You provide."

A nervous rapping sounded on the windowpane behind him.

"Father, grant me wisdom."

More knocking and, by some stretch of incredulity, fiercer than before.

"And patience. Amen."

He rose from his seat and rammed the window outward, meaning to obliterate the offending disturbance.

"What?" he hissed into the darkness. The unexpected interruption of his prayers had left him in a supremely undiplomatic temper.

"Oh! Governor, you're up. Good. Can I come in?"

"Mattheys …" But the sack of bones that was his hallowed carpenter was already scurrying up the stairs that led to the large double front doors. He walked toward the garrison hall's door. Barely a minute had passed since the unsullying of his soul, and here he was trying, and failing, to hold back the colorful curses dancing on his lips.

When the door opened scarcely enough to let a cat in, the old man slipped through like a mouse with a collapsible ribcage. Mattheys' mouth rounded as he primed himself to blurt out the reason for his visit, but the governor cut him short.

"In there," Van Riebeeck's hushed words followed his outstretched hand and the old carpenter scurried toward the governor's chambers.

Once inside, he stared at Van Riebeeck with wide-eyed intensity.

"There are Saldanhars in the forest," Mattheys spoke in a low voice.

"Are you drunk?" Van Riebeeck asked as he closed the door behind them.

"What? No!" Mattheys then paused to consider the question.

"Although, had I been drunk and lost to oblivion, my night would have been a hell of a lot more restful. As it was, I'd been running about in the godforsaken forest chasing a wastrel of a thief when I came across the warriors. I nearly shat my pants when I found them crouching in the underbrush. And I am an old man, Your Grace. The control I exhibited over my bowels at that moment will serve as an immortal source of pride for me."

Van Riebeeck's eyebrows plummeted over the bridge of his nose as he listened to the ceaseless torrent of words.

"How did you know they were Saldanhar warriors?" Van Riebeeck asked.

"Who else would they be?" Mattheys' eyes darted from the desk to the governor's, a look of all-out perplexity clouding his features. "They were dark, big and had weapons," he said as he counted his obvious-to-all deductions on his arthritic fingers.

"What time was this?"

"Around six bells," Mattheys answered, the only way a man who'd spent his entire life on a ship would. "Which is to say, around three o'clock, Your Grace," he clarified.

Having served as a ship's surgeon in his youth, Van Riebeeck was familiar with the vernacular.

Letting the point slide, the governor focused on the other. "I am not a duke nor a bishop, there is no need to call me *Your Grace*," he said.

"I am well aware of what you are, but I can't be calling you *Captain*, and so *Your Grace* is the next most respectful title I know, apart from *My Lord*, but that I reserve for my prayers, no disrespect intended."

"None taken. Now tell me more about this thief you were chasing."

"Well, since Helm and Verburgh are out patrolling the bays and inlets, the watch is spinning out of control."

"That is nonsense. They still answer to me and Mister Coopman," Van Riebeeck defended.

"Yes, that they do, but the respect and fear you and Coopman demand do not extend past the setting of the sun. So, when the night watch takes over from the day, the mimicry of efficiency turns to the downright neglecting of duties. Of the two who are supposed to patrol the wall, usually only one is sober, last night that one happened to be Martinus De Hase." Seeing the frown on the governor's forehead he clarified, "You wouldn't know him, he keeps to himself, talks very little but he has the eyes of a pickpocket on market day. He misses nothing, and if you watch him long enough, you can see the cogs turning in his head and giving him the balls to put his thoughts into action.

"So last night when his partner was well and truly toasting Bacchus and his disciples, Martinus deserted his post, slipped into my house and helped himself to a pair of overalls, pants and four of my five shirts, five copper rings, two knives and a pair of shoes, my church shoes, which I've only worn once, mind you." After listing the inventory of stolen items, Mattheys stared at the cabinet by the wall and the governor bit back a smile. He did, however, rise to pour a glass of red wine, which he held at port arms to his carpenter.

"Thank you, Your Grace, most kind."

Mattheys swallowed the delicate wine in two large gulps, wiped his mouth with the back of his hand and slammed the glass down on the desk like one would an earthen mug. The cut glass vessel endured the abuse without so much as a clink in protest.

"After he outfitted himself from my home, he moved on to Willem Gabrielsz's where he relieved the household of six knives, another pair of shoes and a copper pot. As an encore to his little performance for the night, he lifted a chisel from Frans Hendriksz."

"Where were you, Willem, and Frans at the time of the alleged thefts?" Van Riebeeck interrupted the elaborate telling which had caused the old man's voice to grow in volume as the tale progressed.

"We were out late tying the grass we'd cut earlier for Mister Coopman's roof. There is no need to waste daylight on a task that can easily be done by the glow of a fire down by the beach."

"Then how can you be so sure it was Martinus De Hase, and not others who did the stealing?"

"Well, I had gone back to the workshop to collect more rope and that's when I saw Martinus duck out of Frans' tent. I called out to him but when he heard my voice, he ran for the forest like the devil was nipping at his heels, large bag slung over his shoulder and all."

"Did you get a good look at his face, then?" Van Riebeeck asked.

"Only for a moment when he came out of the tent. For the most part, he had his back turned to me. I went back to the beach to alert the other two and then I went home to discover that someone had gone through my things. The three of us went to the wall to report the incident and that's when we found only Gert Maass, out cold like yesterday's piss, begging your pardon, sir. I searched for Martinus but could not find him anywhere. And then the three of us took to the forest, each in a different direction. I don't know if the other two have returned yet."

"I don't doubt your word, Mattheys but it was dark, and we don't know for certain that it was Martinus who has stolen the items. We cannot make accusations such as these without the firmest sort of proof." Van Riebeeck was deeply disappointed in his soldiers, and he would take the matter up with Helm and Coopman at the earliest opportunity. "We'll start searching for Martinus as soon as daylight arrives, and if we cannot locate him, we can safely assume that he was the thief you saw and suffered from last night."

"Daylight is still an hour or two away and by then, the idiot will be deep in the forest. My guess is he will try to hide among the Saldanhars with his *firmest sort of proof* traded for protection." Mattheys was preparing to release a well-formed ball of spittle and mucus to show his disgust when he, in the eleventh hour of his habit, realized where he was and hastily swallowed it away.

"Let us focus on what we can manage," Van Riebeeck said as he rounded the desk. "Do you think you can lead me to where you've spotted the Saldanhar warriors?"

* * *

Elias Coopman followed the tracks in the sand. Deep pockets dotted the beach where the three cows' hooves had penetrated the moist sand, smaller sheep tracks were scattered around, followed by two sets of large, flat human footprints. Here and there, short scrape marks showed, typical of those made by someone carrying a long stick. Judging by the freshness of the tracks, the theft must have occurred within the last two hours.

It was the interminable headache; the one that made his vertebrae grind together with every breath he took, that had driven him from his bed and to the beach at this unholy hour of the morning. For some unknown reason, walking and breathing in the ocean air seemed to ease the affliction. He could probably ask Miss Van Aard for a remedy, but the idea held little appeal.

The hellion was, more than likely, the cause of his discomfort, for the headaches started soon after she began interfering with his plans. The only source of levity during this trying time was that she would soon be his wife. Once married, he would not permit her any of the liberties she now so thoroughly and extravagantly squandered. No, she will knit, cook and scrub like all the other women at the settlement.

As to how he was going to draw a positive response to his quest from her, was a headache for another morning. His once gushing font of an imagination currently resembled a dried-up desert well, with not even a tumble weed for ambiance.

He followed the tracks until they veered from the beach and disappeared into the shallow waters of one of the many small rivulets that emptied itself into the ocean. With nothing left to follow, Coopman turned and made his way back to the settlement. The incoming tide was filling the indentations left by the cattle. The smaller ones were already wiped from the memory of the beach.

An hour later, he found himself staring at the animal pen where the chickens were still clinging to their roosts as if fearing the thieves would return and abscond with them as well. To the side, the two ostriches were observing the goings on from on high. They seemed unperturbed, safe in the knowledge that anyone who tried to steal an ostrich would need time and a volume of patience most thieves were not, by nature, endowed with.

"Who did this?" Coopman barked at the young soldier who came to a halt behind him, forcing him to turn around to look the boy in the eye.

"We … I mean, I don't know. When we came on duty an hour ago, we found Maass asleep on the wall, sir." The boy snapped his eyes to his shoes and kept them there while Coopman stared at him in silence.

"What are you not telling me?"

"Maass was drunk, sir. It looked like he's been out for most of his shift." The boy raised his eyes but could not face Coopman, so instead he looked at the pen with the condemned expression of the one who got caught stealing fruit while his mates got clean away.

"Gert Maass was not the only one on duty. Who else was guarding the wall and where is he?"

The fuse on Coopman's temper was inversely correlated to the list of problems stretching before him. On his way back to the settlement, he'd stopped by Harry's camp. Of course, Harry was nowhere in sight, and neither was his eldest son. Harry's brother was away hunting, and his father was still asleep. None of the women would look at him, let alone speak to him, all finding fascinating tasks to occupy themselves with inside their empty huts.

"Martinus De Hase," the young soldier replied, "but we can't find him anywhere." The soldier studied his feet once more, only this time they did him the courtesy to move, albeit in an uncomfortable up and down sort of rhythm. There was obviously more to the story, but Elias was not inclined to drag it from the soldier, thread by tedious thread.

"Spit it out," Coopman demanded.

"There are rumors that De Hase had stolen things from some settlers in the middle of the night and had run away."

Coopman spun on his heel and left the bewildered soldier by the animal pen. He needed to scream, curse and blaspheme and he needed to do so in the privacy of his own quarters. Once he had purged himself of the frustrations that were currently scorching his gut, he would seek out the governor and report the events of the morning.

Damn Harry to the deepest pit of hell, and may he rot there until Coopman had the time to strap his worthless hide to a tree and relieve him of his manhood.

His catastrophe of an accomplice was acting on his own, stealing the cattle and sheep Danielle had secured from the Saldanhars to sell to some British ship hiding in one of the coves. Unaware that Helm and Verburgh were scouring the coastline for precisely this act of deceit. Harry's blind avarice was serving them the evidence they were looking for, on a silver platter with a flower to boot. Damn his eyes. The man had the rectitude of a polecat in heat.

After an hour of diligent self-care, which involved releasing a torrent of curses that would have brought down a bolt of lightning, were there even the slightest wisp of a cloud in the sky, and scrubbing his body until his skin felt raw, Elias Coopman stepped from his room in search of Miss Van Aard. He would have to beg a brew of willow bark tea. His headache seemed to have taken up permanent residency between his ears and, by all accounts, had started renovating its new lodgings with chisels and hammers.

"Where is Miss Van Aard?" he asked a young maid as she exited the governor's apartments.

"I don't know sir, she is not at the fort," the maid replied, not entirely in control of the blush that spread over her face.

"Is the governor in his chambers?" he asked.

"No sir, he is not at the fort either," she said before gathering the laundry basket at her feet and making for the stairs.

Coopman suddenly felt like that last Israelite, waking up in Egypt, with a monstrous hangover the morning after everyone had up and gone to follow Moses to the promised land.

Heading into the blinding sunlight, he made his way up the stairs to the top of the wall and was surprised to find the governor's wife.

The bay sparkled as if someone had opened a sack of diamonds on the water, but Maria Van Riebeeck's focus was elsewhere. She was staring intently at the space between the fort and the forest, leaning slightly forward as if the added few inches would somehow enhance her vision. Her face was creased with questioning lines as she stared down at the spectacle swirling through the gate of the hornworks.

"I don't mean to be presumptuous, nor do I enjoy stating the obvious, but is that my husband dancing through the gates of the fort with twenty Saldanhar men at his heels?" she asked, forgoing the usual courtesies of morning greetings.

Her once joyful and insouciant husband, turned staid and stoic under the weight of hardship and responsibility, had ostensibly made a one hundred and eighty degree turn back to his roots. With his arms flying out at rhythmic intervals, his coat panels cheerfully flapping by his sides and his knees lifting high, he twirled through the air. Each twist and leap were interspersed with a few fleet-footed skips. He moved with the grace and elegance of a marionette that got its strings caught in a crosswind. Behind him, the Saldanhar chief and his men followed in a fantastical exhibition of wildly bobbing heads and swaying torsos. Some were clapping while others were stomping their feet, allowing the seed pods around their ankles to rattle and sputter their earthy pulse.

"Yes, ma'am," Coopman replied, his eyes narrowed at the troop that was making their way across the outer courtyard and through the gray stone arch. "Why don't you withdraw to your sitting room and let me see what is amiss?" he suggested with a firm hand to her back.

Coopman felt her muscles tighten under his touch as she straightened her back.

"For once, Mister Coopman, nothing seems to be amiss. All seems to be just as it should be." Maria's voice held the quiver of laughter as she rushed to make her way down the stairs. "Where is Harry?" she called over her shoulder.

*Where is Harry indeed?* After the busy night he had, it was no wonder the miscreant was nowhere to be found.

"I have not seen him this morning," Coopman replied, rushing to keep up with the governor's wife.

"I thought you were handling the dealings with the Saldanhars," she said as he pulled up next to her.

"The situation is very … fluid at the moment," he returned as he bit down on his own confusions. The situation was spinning out of control. Best to let a disaster of this magnitude run its course.

"No wonder things are going well with the Saldanhars, then." Her words drifted toward him and he missed a step, snapping his hand out to the wall to maintain his balance.

"Husband," Maria breathed as she reached her husband near the middle of the inner courtyard, "What on earth is all this?"

"We're going to need an interpreter. Quick," Van Riebeeck held his wife's upper arm in a bruising grip as he spoke near her ear, his out-of-breath whispers pushing warm air over her skin. He was enveloped in a joyous urgency, like a little boy anxiously waiting to receive a long promised present.

"Get Maheena," he added when he saw her eyes lose a little of their focus as she tried to figure out who the best candidate for the task might be. Danielle would be his first choice, but she was not at the fort, for Hendrik had developed a nasty fever, and she'd stayed the night at the Boom's.

"Ask Elsje to go with you. Or better yet, send Elsje by herself, she'll be faster." Seeing the indignation on his wife's face, he added, "She's not with child, woman."

By the time the bewildered and uncertain looking Maheena teetered on the dining hall threshold, the room was already huddling under a malodorous, blue-gray cloud of tobacco smoke.

All were seated on the floor in a circle around a tablecloth supporting offerings of bread and wine. Maheena looked first to Coopman and then to the governor before deciding that retreat was the better part of discretion, but the governor halted her by waving her over. The girl's eyes darted through the room and landed on a young Saldanhar. The warm smile he flashed her seemed to fortify the girl, and she cautiously stepped closer.

Once Maheena settled herself, the stunted conversation started. The governor kept the mood light, but there was an urgency to the Saldanhar chief that could not be ignored.

* * *

"How was your day, my dear?" Maria asked as her husband sat down on their bed, dipping the mattress as he pulled his boots from his feet. Once the task was done, he turned to her and shook his head while huffing a perplexed laugh.

"Long and very insightful," he said, reaching out and tugging a strand of hair behind her ear. "The Saldanhars finally agreed to negotiate without Harry's aid. It has taken us all day and nearly a barrel of wine and a sack of tobacco, but I do believe that for the first time we are getting somewhere."

Van Riebeeck had learned that there were multiple Saldanhar tribes, and all were in various stages of arriving at the Cape. They all got along fine, but each traded and acted independently, according to the wishes of its chief. Kai was worried the Dutch would trade with the other tribes instead, leaving them without the luxuries of bread, tobacco, and copper and, not to mention—wine. Therefore, he'd made the overture to come this morning wishing to speak to the governor man-to-man. But once in sight of the fort, his men grew hesitant and refused to approach, regardless of his assurances.

"I met them at the edge of the trees. They were wary, but friendly. Luckily, I had the foresight to take tobacco with me so we smoked for a while and then I was struck by a streak of inspiration that would have made a priest weep," he said. His wife was practically hanging on his every word, her eyes wide in wonder and her brow slightly creased with anticipation.

"What did you do?" she prodded.

"I asked them to teach me their dance of friendship," he said. His eyes were alight with mischief before he dipped one in a wink.

"And with that, you lured them to the fort?" she asked suspiciously, her bottom lip pushing over her top teeth.

"Well, that, and the promise of more tobacco and wine, of course," he confessed, flashing her a conquering smile.

After a long day of discussions, entreaties, and promises, they have reached an accord. Van Riebeeck had promised that he would only trade with Kai's tribe if they agreed to supply the settlement with cattle and sheep in exchange for copper wire and plates until the settlement could sustain their own herds.

The negotiations had turned into promises of friendship and, as a show of good faith, the chief had offered to show Van Riebeeck a forest thick with large, tall trees, a bay teeming with seals, and a nearby salt pan.

"That is wonderful," his wife exclaimed.

"Soon we will be able to supply ships with masts, as well as fresh food and water," he said, the relief clear on his face. "Finally, things are coming together."

"And Harry was not here today," Maria mused. Her husband nodded, and his face hardened at her words.

"Once I have evidence of his duplicity, I have a good mind to ban him and his entire family to Robben Island. He has been quite diligent in his efforts to poison every well for us with the Saldanhars. I have always offered him the benefit of the doubt, but I find myself with nothing left to give."

# Chapter 18

*M*alindi, *African east coast.*

De Coninck stood with folded arms as he watched the net clear the bulwark. His eyes narrowed at the shape of the contents.

Arent had arrived moments earlier from the small harbor town of Malindi, the next stop after Zanzibar, on their way up the African coast. With the *Annabella* disguised as an Arab trading vessel, they no longer had to wait for the cover of darkness to gather information and inquire about the *Aqrab*.

Despite his dual heritage, Arent's Javanese genes had hectored their Dutch counterparts into submission, and with his newly grown beard bursting out in all directions, most of his non-Arabic facial features were well hidden. His elaborate turban, baggy shirt, pantaloons, waistband, and long vest dispelled any further doubt that he was indeed a wealthy Ottoman *Re'is* or ship's captain.

The crew eased the net down to the deck as Arent's legs swung over the bulwark. They released its sides, and the carpenter stepped closer to lend a hand to the woman they'd hoisted from the rowboat.

De Coninck's gaze shifted from the European woman, slumped in a pitiful heap on the deck to Arent, not bothering to ask the obvious question regarding their unexpected guest.

"I bought her— " Arent started.

"Arent," De Coninck sounded resigned as his chin dropped to his chest. "You cannot buy every slave that tugs at your heartstrings."

The woman was standing a few feet away, dressed only in a shift that used to be white. Her arms, legs, and feet were bare and filthy, her shaven head covered in scabbed lacerations. It was difficult to judge her age, given that her skin was dull and clung to her bones like an empty leather sack. Though her back stood ramrod straight, her breaths came quick and unsteady. Despite the blood-warm, humid night air, shivers shook her body and she wrapped her arms around her chest.

"She's Dutch and was aboard the *Aqrab*," Arent said.

That piqued De Coninck's interest, and his sharp eyes bored into Arent's searching for the rest of that statement.

"They were selling her for less than you would a dog," Arent whispered, pain and disgust pulling at his features.

De Coninck dipped his head before turning to the woman. He noted she didn't lift her chin to face him. Instead, she stared at his booted feet.

"What is your name?" he asked, keeping his voice even so as not to startle the poor creature further.

"Cornelia Stiens," she said, and her voice broke over the words.

"Look at me when you speak," De Coninck's command was softly delivered but no less stern. It took the woman a moment to summon her courage, and when she looked up, her eyes were large in her battered face, and filled with desperation and fear.

"And who are you, Cornelia Stiens?" he asked.

"I was the maid to Mistress Bouwer, wife of Jorn Bouwer, Captain of the *Spiegel*." No sooner had the words left her lips than she sagged to her knees.

De Coninck knew she had used the last of her strength to answer his question. He was burning to extract every bit of information from her, but knew he'd have to wait.

"Take her to a cabin." His voice was thick with emotion, none of it good, as he growled his order to his newly promoted first officer. Arent scooped her from the deck as if she weighed no more than a child.

"Barent," he barked, searching for his cook. "She needs food and extra water for washing." The cook was already moving down the companionway to the galley before he even finished the order.

"What else did you learn while in town?" De Coninck asked the rowers who had accompanied Arent to the small port.

"Nothing, Captain. Once she told Arent everything she knew, he was in a mighty hurry to get her to the *Annabe-* I mean the *As-Sayf*," one of the younger lads answered.

* * *

Mid-morning the next day, De Coninck entered the dayroom and found their newest acquisition already waiting. The woman was sitting at the dining table. Dressed in a large, rough linen shirt, and sailor slops, she almost looked like a man with her bald scalp and shapeless body. A coarse blanket was wrapped around her shoulders and her feet were still bare. On the upside, she was clean and rested. She rose when she noticed his presence, but his staying hand made her sink back into the chair.

Barent followed with a tea tray, set the refreshments on the table, and softly closed the door behind him upon his exit.

"Allow me," De Coninck said and reached for the elegant teapot. Uncertainty flickered across the woman's face. Cornelia was accustomed to being a maid and having the captain serve her tea was making her uncomfortable.

De Coninck studied the woman as she took a sip from the fine porcelain cup. With her downcast eyes and shaking hands, she exuded a fragility that went beyond the circumstances of the moment. Last night in the captain's cabin, Arent had relayed everything he'd learned from Mrs. Stiens, but De Coninck suspected there was more to the sorry tale.

"Mistress Stiens," he began, but she corrected him.

"It's Miss, sir, but Cornelia will do just fine since I am your property now."

"I've never owned another human being in my life and have no desire to do so now. You are my guest and as such are safe and free to come and go as you wish." Tears flooded her eyes and she once more lowered them to study her hands. "I assume your lodgings are to your satisfaction?"

"Yes, very much. Thank you, Captain. What can I do in return?" She lifted her head as she remembered the first words he had spoken to her on deck the day before.

"You can start by telling me everything that happened from the first moment the pirates attacked the convoy." De Coninck's tone was businesslike as he casually leaned a shoulder against the windows lining the room's back wall, keeping an eye on the ocean and his guest.

De Coninck listened with muted patience, not interrupting the flow of the woman's words. She narrated the ship under attack, how pirate galleys with blackened sails had furtively closed in on them during the night; the mayhem and panic that spread like wildfire amongst the passengers and crew when the corsairs had boarded their vessel.

The scenario was familiar. He'd faced half a dozen pirate attacks in his career. Hell, in his youth he'd often wished for them—the rush of battle fever that boiled the blood and focused the mind, the crisp, sharp actions that would decide between life and death. It was exhilarating. As captain of his own ship, he'd made sure his crew was as handy with a rapier and cutlass as they were with the tools of their trade. However, the responsibility of having so many lives depend on his decisions and judgments had calmed the battle fever. Still, he viewed pirate attacks as an occupational hazard, an intense battle where losing was not an option. Never had the aftermath of such an attack been painted with this much detail.

From what he gathered from Miss Stiens, the captain of the *Spiegel* had done all he could to keep his ship, crew, and family safe, and in the end, it was simply not enough. They were caught by surprise and overrun by a greater and more motivated force.

"When it became clear that the battle was lost, the captain had quietly lowered my mistress, the little one, and me into a small rowboat and told us to get as far away from the ship as we could. Mrs. Bouwer and I took to the oars, but having never rowed a boat before we didn't get far before we were captured and pulled onto the galley," Miss Stiens spoke in a monotone voice, her eyes were unfocused as her mind relived the events of that fateful night.

"Do you recall who the captain of the galley was?" he asked.

She swallowed hard and then nodded. "Yes, his name was Yavuz."

The name sent a bolt of lightning through De Coninck and he was grateful for the wall bracing his shoulder. With more control than he believed possible, he listened to her retelling of how they were made to wait on deck while the pirates scoured the area, searching for survivors from both the *Spiegel* and the *Geloof*. As far as he could tell, Yavuz had drawn the short end of the deal, left to scavenge scraps from the aftermath as the other three galleys claimed the valuable cargo.

"The captives were all herded together. There were sailors, one or two soldiers, us, and a priest. We were all scared and unsure as to what would become of us, but we were calm except for the priest. At first, he was giving my mistress nasty stares and later, after the little one wouldn't stop fussing, he'd threatened her with his fists." She reached absentmindedly for her tea, held the cup in both hands, but then continued speaking without raising it to her lips.

"It was shortly before dawn when they fished the last man from the ocean. I remember him well. He seemed different from the others."

De Coninck straightened from the window and came to lean with both fists on the table. The woman had fallen silent; the teacup forgotten in her hands. Tears were streaming down her face. He knew she needed to do the telling in her own time, but his impatience made him want to shake the words from her lips.

"Continue," he said when he could no longer stand the silence. The single word startled her, and she spilled tea on her borrowed shirt. "Continue," he repeated in a gentler tone, offering her a linen square from his pocket.

Miss Stiens returned the cup to the table and blotted her shirt before speaking again.

"I— ," she seemed to search for words, clearly having lost her train of thought.

"You said the man seemed different. How? Can you describe him?" De Coninck pressed. His heart was fluttering in his chest, but he knew that staying calm and patient was the best way forward.

She nodded. "He was young, blond hair, taller than the others," she looked at him. "He was not afraid. I could see anger, courage and even that arrogance some young men have, but no fear; that's what made him different. When he saw my mistress and the babe, he came to stand close to her, as if to protect her."

"Did you hear his name?"

"No sir," she said as she shook her head. It mattered little. He knew she was talking about Sebastiaan. The evidence was thin at best, but it was better than chasing a gut feeling. Her narrative linked Yavuz, the *Aqrab* and possibly Sebastiaan. *Possibly* was better than *maybe*.

He listened as she continued to describe the priest's humiliation.

"I know it is unchristian of me, but I felt no pity for him. He even tried to win favor with our captors by claiming that the gallant young man was wealthy and influential."

"Did they believe him?"

"I don't know, for what happened next brought the world to a standstill and I cannot remember much past that point." Fresh tears were now dripping onto her bosom and this time, her shoulders shook with the force of her misery.

De Coninck left the room, giving her the privacy she needed. Moments later, he returned with a bottle of French brandy and two glasses, poured a generous measure into each, and offered her one.

"Drink," he ordered, and she obeyed. Spluttering and coughing as the liquid burned its way down her throat, she tried to put the glass down, but he shook his head and made her take another sip. After a few fortifying sips, she regained some of her composure, enough to reveal the most execrable series of events that he was certain would haunt him for the rest of his life.

"In the hull, they chained us together and to the shelf we lay on. The shelf was so close to the one above that we could not sit up, we could only raise ourselves on our elbows, but no higher. We had no way to use the necessities, and so had no choice but to relieve ourselves where we were. There were no other slaves in the hull, and that was a blessing. Hunger was a constant torture. Our daily food rations were made up of one biscuit and a cup of water, but often days would go by with nothing to eat or drink, and we feared they had entirely forgotten about us. On those days, the priest took the milk from my mistress's body," she revealed, and this time she sobbed openly. "I could do nothing to stop him," she snarled through her tears. Her eyes burned with the fire of her disgust and hatred.

De Coninck's mouth had gone dry. He swallowed a few times to ease the emotions that threatened to burn through his throat. Remembering the glass in his hand, he savagely downed the entire measure.

Pirates, in his view, were a dark force that struck at night, to be fought with cannon and blade. He understood there was more to it, but for him, the problem ended when the scoundrels laid dead at his feet. Listening to Cornelia Stiens, had torn the veil, and showed him a peek at the hidden, corrupt underbelly of the world and the dirty, soulless cruelty that surrounded slavery, a world his nephew, whom he loved as a son, was now ensnared in.

"You were not to blame," he whispered, feeling wholly inadequate to console the woman.

"I have never wished for anyone's death," she said. "But I prayed every day for the Lord to take my mistress. She was the gentlest of souls, the type of woman who saw only the good in others; too soft for this world…" her voice trailed off and her eyes glazed over as memories flooded her. "They sold her in Zanzibar." Her final words drifted as though Zanzibar were a distant place and the events belonged to a long-forgotten past.

"Miss Stiens," De Coninck called her name twice before her eyes regained their focus and settled on him. "Your mistress," he searched for the best way to deliver the news. There was no good way. Raking his hand through his hair, he drew a deep breath, and said, "Your prayers have been answered."

A stunned silence filled the room as Cornelia settled the words in her mind.

"Do you know how she passed?" she asked, her shoulders so tense he feared they would shatter at the faintest touch.

"She died by her own hand two days after she was sold."

Relief washed over Cornelia's features as the breath she was holding left her body.

"Thank you." She sounded stronger, as if the knowledge had lifted a weight from her shoulders.

Their conversation had come to an end, and De Coninck gave her leave to go, before striding from the room.

She had not named Sebastiaan, but she had given him enough.

"Niklas," De Coninck called to his navigator as he reached the quarterdeck.

With his right hand fused to the whipstaff, the man acknowledged his captain with a crisp nod.

"Set course for Muscat. We're done here."

***

*Muscat*

By the end of his first week as a quarry slave, Sebastiaan had learned two very important lessons:

*One*, his new owner, was just one shade more avaricious than he was sadistic. *Two*, to sleep with his arse pressed against a wall was a privilege.

Sebastiaan's little display of rebellion in the palace's auction room had not brought the result he'd pinned his hopes on. Shaykh Ahmet had not cut Sebastiaan's throat on the spot for humiliating him in public.

Ahmet was renowned for keeping his slaves close at hand. They lived in his compound, some even slept on the floor by his bed. All were well dressed, well fed, and well perfumed. However, Sebastiaan was the exception to this generous rule. Instead of wearing pantaloons and waistbands of the finest silk, he was dressed in a pair of canvas drawers and nothing else, and instead of sleeping on feather filled cushions next to his master's bed, he slept on the dirt floor of the slave prison or bagnio's courtyard. To further show his supreme disappointment in his newest slave, Ahmet rented Sebastiaan to the pasha to work in the city's stone quarry, where he was to receive one cup of water every day and no food.

The night Ahmet's men brought him into the bagnio, a guard stopped them at the tall iron gate.

"Name," the guard barked.

The men by his side remained silent and when Sebastiaan did not answer quickly enough, the cane from the one at the gate came down so fast across his right bicep that he felt the sting before he saw the movement. Same drill then, Sebastiaan thought, speak when spoken to and get caned; shut your mouth when spoken to and get caned.

"Arent Van Jeveren," Sebastiaan answered. Speaking his friend's name brought him peace. It was a nod to his past; gone but not yet forgotten. Sebastiaan De Vries was dead, along with all his colorful dreams and staunch ambitions. His soul was another matter altogether. For some reason beyond his understanding, it was anchored by three stalwart weights: the love of his life, Danielle Van Aard; the man who was more father than uncle, Davit De Coninck; and the true owner of his new name who was more brother than friend, Arent Van Jeveren.

He glanced at the scribbles the guard was scratching on the parchment in his hand. It seemed shorter than the name would necessitate, and he briefly wondered if the fool knew how to spell. He kept his doubts to himself; it was late, and he was tired and in no mood to offer a lesson in spelling that would, as sure as the sun would rise in the morning, lead to another beating.

The chain attached to his collar passed hands, and the new guard led him into the dark courtyard like a dog on a leash, chained him to the back wall, leaving him to negotiate a space between two pungent bodies.

The gray of the new day dragged with it the realities of his situation, and he wished with devout sincerity that it would slither back into the darkness of the night. Filth, suffering, and hopelessness were on copious display all around. Close to a hundred slaves were crammed together in a space not fit to house a third.

A whistle sounded, and all rose from where they'd lain moments before. Sebastiaan could practically hear the rattle of their bones as they lined up behind the gate. These were all once strong and healthy men with wives, children, and sweethearts to give meaning to their lives and purpose to their hearts. He watched as they scurried to form a jagged line, scratching their heads, between their legs and under their arms. Their ragged, lank, and haggard bodies were crawling with lice. Sebastiaan scratched a vicarious itch behind his ear. It was only a matter of time before the need would become real.

A few heads turned his way, the faces furrowed and shriveled with protracted wretchedness. Their eyes were sunken and distorted without a glimmer of the finer impulses of human nature. Pity and concern were to the soul like a decent meal and water for washing were to the body—long forgotten luxuries that belonged to a time and a place where it mattered to be good and honorable. All that mattered here was survival, a useless pursuit none would forsake.

Why he was clinging to survival was an enigma. Sebastiaan knew that being set free was not an option and hopes of being rescued were a fool's dream. His uncle would be searching for him by now but even *if* he managed to find him, he would have to arrive with an armada to break Sebastiaan from his bonds. His only option was escape. Deep inside some dark corner of his mind, the notion held a euphoric allure, but he'd have to do it soon, while he still had the physical strength.

Another sharp shrill from the whistle, and the heads snapped to the iron gates where four guards armed with canes and bull whips were ready to let the slaves out. Working together as a team, the slaves could easily overrun the men on the other side of the iron gate. The guards were overconfident in the power their weapons lent them, their stances were relaxed, and their expressions bored, but the pitiful horde seemed to lack the foresight of cooperation. Sebastiaan sighed and tamped down the fruitless fantasy. Best to focus on the situation at hand, not that he could do much about that either, since he was still chained to the courtyard wall.

Any bagnio slave with strength to speak would describe a life of stealing and scavenging to stay alive. Instead of feeding them, their overseers granted them an hour each morning and evening to scavenge for scraps to fill their bellies. The hour before sunrise, when stall owners set up their stations, was when the slaves could beg or pilfer food. As soon as the sun's first rays touched the calm waters of the bay, the guards would gather them into small groups and sent them off to their respective labors for the day. The same ritual would occur an hour after sunset when the slaves returned from their toils. Afterward, the whistles would sound, and all would line up before the iron gates where their names were called and one by one, they would enter the filthy courtyard to settle down for the night.

After dark, the bagnio descended into a level of hell where the devil played out his most perverse fantasies, from hunger and illness to forced sodomy and every kind of violence. As with any society, there was a hierarchy, and the more depraved the living conditions, the more brutal the pecking order.

At the bottom were the young boys, the ones too old, or not pretty enough to warm the beds of their masters. Next came the new slaves, yet to find their place in the decrepit fraternity. Then came the lot in the middle who excelled at forging alliances and concocting schemes to outsmart the top and exploit the bottom. At the very top stood the boss, last to rise in the mornings yet first in line when leaving the courtyard. He strutted past the guards and always had a little extra to eat at day's end. In their world, he was called Dario.

Dario was an Italian who refused to—and Sebastiaan suspected he could not—speak any language other than his mother tongue. But where Dario's mental horizons refused to expand, his brawn suffered no such impediments. He was built like a battering ram with a preternatural gift for malice.

Sebastiaan's condition was rapidly worsening. Hunger was becoming a problem as he was forbidden to roam the city with the other slaves. In the mornings after the others had gone, a guard escorted him to the quarry, where he worked till after sunset. Then they escorted him back just in time for the roll call outside the gates. There was neither time nor opportunity for him to steal food. Twice he was able to dispossess his fellow quarry workers of the bread rolls they were careless enough to bring with them. Once he had snatched an apple from the side of the street; the guard let him to keep it, but he was later beaten for stealing.

He thought he might be suffering from a cold; he shivered more than the night temperatures demanded, often struggled to catch his breath, and found the walk back to the bagnio at night far harder than before.

The last few nights Sebastiaan had woken to find a small boy pressed up to him. There was not much he could do about it, for his back was already firmly pressed to the wall, leaving him no room to retreat. With few options left, he put his knee to the small of his unwanted companion's back and pushed him away, only to have to do it again after the imp scurried back.

"Jiya, what are you doing?" Sebastiaan whispered in Arabic. The little African boy had been taken as a slave at a very young age and resold countless times since. By day he sold water on the streets of Muscat. All the proceeds of his venture went to his owner, but it left him with ample opportunity to find food.

"I am scared," came the soft reply.

"What are you afraid of?" But Sebastiaan already knew the answer before he felt the shrug from the bony shoulders. Sounds of men giving in to their baser needs drifted to them from a few yards away.

Two body-warm pieces of shortbread filled with dates made their way into Sebastiaan's hand. Saliva flooded his mouth and he had to swallow several times before he tore into the offerings.

"If I bring you food, will you protect me?" The boy edged closer until he was pressed tightly against Sebastiaan's stomach.

"What makes you think you can trust me?" he asked, paying attention to the squirming body. Often, a lie was felt before it was heard. The boy remained relaxed.

"You are a good man. It shows in your eyes. You are strong, I can see it in your legs when you walk." There was a pause and then the boy continued, "And you are not afraid of anything. You are not afraid of Dario; it shows in the way he looks at you. Like he's angry, but he's also careful. Because there is nothing he or his cronies can do, you are not to be touched."

"What do you mean, I'm not to be touched?"

"Everybody knows your master has forbidden it. The guards can beat you, but they can't kill you, and so they told Dario to mind his step. If he killed you, they would get into a lot of trouble. So, would you do it?"

"Do what?"

"Watch over me at night?"

"You bring me food every day for as long as I'm chained to this wall, and

I'll watch over you. You have my word. Now go to sleep."

* * *

Sebastiaan woke somewhere in the early morning hours to sounds of muffled cries. The side of his body where Jiya usually lay was cold and empty. Instinct warned him to stay quiet and still. Without moving his head, he opened his eyes and searched the space where the boy was supposed to be. A noticeable tang of angst hung in the air.

In the darkness, about a foot away, he saw Jiya lying prone on the ground. A large form was straddling him, one hand pressing down firmly over the child's mouth, while the other feverishly tried to disrobe the writhing body.

"Shut up or I'll cut your throat."

Sebastiaan recognized Dario's voice beneath the whispered threat followed by Jiya's muffled mewling.

Sebastiaan's position was less than stellar. The chain around his neck allowed just enough length to lie on the ground and not much more. His hands were free, but the distance between them and Dario was too great. His legs were shackled with a chain running between them, long enough to take a comfortable stride, and long enough to wrap around the bastard's neck. Decision made.

Sebastiaan's hands shot to the chain tethering him to the wall. Drawing on his arms, chest, and stomach muscles, he lifted his hips and legs off the ground, wrapping the chain around Dario's neck in one smooth, near-soundless motion, and pulled.

Dario toppled sideways off the child and onto Sebastiaan. His hands reflexively snapped to the chain around his neck—a mistake. In moments like these, where every second counted, he was wasting valuable time trying to tear iron from skin. Sebastiaan used every fraction of time the idiot gave him to twist his legs and tighten the chain some more. Dario's eyes were bulging, the whites shining like alabaster in the dark.

Time was not on his side for the principal keeper and most of the guards kept rooms on the second level above the courtyard, and Dario was gurgling and groaning his demise to all and sundry. Death by uncontrolled strangulation was never quiet.

*"Two hundred counts—you have to hold him for two hundred counts,"* came Arent's voice from the depths of his memory, *"and then two hundred more after the body goes slack."*

Two hundred counts might as well have been written in the stars, for Sebastiaan had forgotten to start the count when he'd launched his attack. It was pointless to guess, as Dario, like any true predator, fought death with savage ferocity. His large hand darted beneath his burnous, pulling out a small dagger. He wielded it frantically, slashing at Sebastiaan's naked abdomen and legs.

The first of the slashes hit home and Sebastiaan felt a warm pain burning into his right side just above the waistband of his smalls.

*"As long as you can feel them, it's still good. It's the ones you don't feel that take your life."* Not wanting to test his uncle's theory on knife and sword wounds, he pulled harder on the chain by the wall and extended his legs, pushing Dario a few inches from his body while increasing the pressure on the cur's windpipe. The adjustment to his position had a minor effect, for Dario had the arms, and luckily also the brain capacity, of a gorilla.

Instead of small, precise strikes, Dario wasted his fading strength, swinging his arms in broad, frantic arcs. His dagger inflicted shallow cuts across Sebastiaan's thighs and stomach, merely scratching the thick muscle beneath and little else.

As the seconds passed, Dario's movements became more labored. Each lift and swing took enormous effort and then the big man gave up. His body went slack and collapsed on top of Sebastiaan's legs.

Twisting his hips to the side, Sebastiaan let Dario's heavy, lifeless carcass slide off him. Keeping the chain tightly locked around Dario's neck, he started to count.

"He's dead Effendi." Two small hands were clasping both sides of his face. Jiya's tear-filled eyes were staring into his. "You can let go. You saved me."

Sebastiaan wrapped his arm around the child's small shaking shoulders and pulled him to his chest. His side was on fire and his thighs were protesting loudly, but he did not have the strength to untangle his legs from around Dario's neck.

"You saved me," Jiya repeated reverently.

"I know, hush now before you wake the others," Sebastiaan was exhausted beyond comprehension. Starvation had robbed him of his strength.

"Nobody has ever saved me before." A skinny arm crept over Sebastiaan's chest and held him tight. "And the others are already awake."

By the time the morning sun was high enough to streak the courtyard, all that remained was one bloody slave chained to the wall after receiving fifty cane lashes for the murder of another.

# Chapter 19

*The previous evening.*

Since they hadn't entered the Muscat harbor with the desire to trade, the *As-Sayf* arrived without fanfare. No calling-all-traders shots were fired, no banners were flying from her masts. She slid elegantly and silently between the two Portuguese fortresses that guarded the entrance to the harbor, just as the sun was melting into the desert to the west, leaving the sand to ripple like molten lava and stain the sky inferno red.

Davit De Coninck stood at the quarterdeck railing, staring out over the unfolding landscape. The tactician in him noted the city's location. Muscat nestled between tall mountains. To the south and north, ridges rose high like the back teeth of a dog—sharp and uneven. The northern range ended with a curved headland forming one side of the bay, while the other side was shaped by three large rock islands, curving similarly, as if the southern range had mirrored its northern sister before breaking apart upon touching the water. Nonetheless, the mountains' remnants formed a perfect harbor, especially after the Portuguese improved on God's design by adding two large fortresses studded with long-range cannons.

A wide wall spanned the harbor, further protecting the city from nefarious visitors. The city itself was an unremarkable collection of squat brown dwellings. Not a single building stood out for its uniqueness in color or design. All were built in the same style, and apparently with the same material. It looked like some desert djinn had risen from the soil and sneezed a large cloud of dust over the city, coating everything to resemble the earth it stood upon. The only discernible difference between the structures was their height.

They had been debating the wisdom of their decision for weeks. De Coninck was convinced that Muscat was going to be another dead-end, while Arent was equally convinced that it would not. In the end, it was the *'what if you are wrong'* from Arent that had swayed the argument in his favor.

De Coninck was prepared to spend the rest of his life searching for his nephew, and if that meant raising every stone on land and disturbing every droplet in the ocean, then so be it. But one reality always thrashed its way to the surface of every consideration or vow: time was not on their side. A European slave under a Muslim master, especially one like Sebastiaan, faced a short, brutal life. De Coninck knew Sebastiaan would not easily bend a knee. They would beat, abuse, and torture him every day, until his eyes lost their light, and his broad shoulders, which he carried with pride and ease, became slumped and broken. The thought was like a burr in his heart. His nights were filled with images of Sebastiaan's bloodied body. His days were a living hell ruled by the need to move faster, all the while knowing he was chasing ghosts and gut feelings, but also knowing it was all he had.

Arent's heavy footfalls signaled his approach, and De Coninck turned to lean his back against the wooden fortification. Anger and frustration were twisting his gut, making the acid in his stomach rise and lighting the fuse to his tortured temper.

"Are you happy now?" he gritted the words through his teeth. Arent did not respond. "We are here," De Coninck said, arcing his arm toward the dusty city. "Wasting time, we do not have."

When no defense was presented by the younger man, he continued. "This does not make sense! Why would anybody sail from Batavia to Africa, and up that treacherous coast, only to head east again? Past Yemen! Past Oman! And around the horn to dock at Muscat? Look at it," he shouted. "It is small!"

It was far from a small settlement, but Arent thought it prudent to keep his mouth shut. Instead, he clasped his hands behind his back and squared his shoulders, readying himself for the next onslaught. He had boarded De Coninck's ship as a lad of eleven and had looked up to the man who was part god, part father and fully the master and commander of his universe.

Davit De Coninck was a man who had weathered every storm the ocean had tossed at them, who could keep a near drowned and exhausted crew focused and on their feet with nothing more than a word of encouragement and a slap on the shoulder. Who had faced a freak wave head on and smiled. Who had stared death in the eye and winked.

What depth of emotion was so strong that it had the power to drive this giant of a man to his knees; so powerful that it obliterated his judgment and shattered his senses?  For the first time in his life, Arent saw raw, unconcealed fear burning like cold fire in De Coninck's eyes as they bore into his.

"It makes much more sense to sail for Mecca, rather than this," De Coninck's lip curled and his hand snapped out as if to slap the city in its face.

"Oh, this is fantastic," he continued, spitting the words at his first officer after yet another pause, "now you decide to shut up, while you've been henpecking me for the last three weeks about the wisdom of this decision!"

Arent glanced sideways at Niklas, but the navigator was heavily engaged in steering the ship through the harbor traffic, to which there seemed to be no rules or order.

"He is here. I can feel it," Arent said in a quiet voice, knowing full well his argument held less water than a fork.

"Good. You have two days to prove me wrong, but do not— ,"

Whatever Arent was not supposed to do died in De Coninck's throat as his eyes sharpened and fixed on something off their starboard side.

"The *Aqrab*," De Coninck breathed.

"What?" Arent said as he turned around to follow the direction of De Coninck's words.  And there she was, a phantom coming to life as they sailed past the galley.

"Cap, we have to get you off this deck," Arent said urgently but his words bounced off the captain's back, who was already marching across the deck as though it were a field of battle, and his nemesis was standing a mere forty feet away. De Coninck's right hand was curled around the grip of his rapier, his index finger already looped inside the forward arm of the hilt.

Arent had seen that walk many times before. It was the smooth and calculating stride of the lethal savage De Coninck devolved into when pirates boarded his ship. It usually went along with a lot of screaming, the sound of steel meeting steel and the clashing of blades, followed by the smell of blood and a death grunt.

For an instant, Arent was distracted by the memories which that walk triggered. His hand reached instinctively for the cutlass by his side and his nostrils flared, but instead of blood he smelled the amalgamation of refuse and lamb fat drifting in from the city, and instead of a heathenish horde boarding their ship, there was only the *Aqrab*.

Rushing to De Coninck's side, Arent took a quick inventory of his captain's features. It was as if a stone mask had slid over his face. It was devoid of emotion, pale and hard except for the eyes. The pale blue orbs were filled with hatred and murderous intent, seeing only his enemy. Arent understood the transformation his captain was experiencing. This serene state of focus caused confidence to surge and doubt to evaporate. Sounds sharpened, smells intensified, and vision cleared as the body braced for a mortal duel where defeat was not an option.

Arent shot a quick glance over his shoulder at Niklas, who was still clutching the whipstaff as if they were battling heavy seas, even though the deck beneath their feet had stopped moving minutes earlier. The usually unflappable and stoic navigator looked confused and slightly panicked and Arent knew that if De Coninck did not soon meet a formidable obstacle he would walk right off the ship.

His mind and his feet found their working relationship, and he sprinted across the deck, reaching the opposite railing and inserting himself between it and his advancing captain.

De Coninck's mouth twisted with rage, and his eyes turned almost translucent with fury when he saw Arent blocking his path. The man had clearly no plan of stopping until his enemy lay dead at his feet.

"Cap, listen to me. We must get you off this deck," Arent repeated as he slapped one hand on De Coninck's shoulder and the other on top of his sword hand, pinning it to the weapon and stopping him from drawing the blade.

"It is a damn blessing that the sun is already down, and nobody can see how white you are. Please," Arent pleaded, but his words had no effect. "Look, Sebastiaan is not on the galley. They would have taken him ashore weeks ago. If we make a ruckus now, we will alert the entire city and every guard in it, and then we will lose any advantage we've ever had."

Arent had never been the voice of reason and found the current state of affairs disconcerting. He had to stay calm and therefore resisted the urge to shake some of the fury out and a little sense into De Coninck, an action that would ensure a fist to his mouth with enough force to convince his teeth to surrender their position and exit his body in single file through his arse.

De Coninck stopped advancing, but his body was still bristling with unspent violence.

"I want that bastard Yavuz bleeding at my feet, screaming for his mother as he dies like the rabid dog he is," De Coninck spoke in a voice low with menace and his breath hot against Arent's face.

"Yes, and you shall have that, but not tonight," Arent vowed.

Even though De Coninck had stopped advancing toward the *Aqrab*, Arent did not feel confident enough to disengage. However, De Coninck made the decision for him when he snaked his hand inside Arent's arm and smacked the offending restraint away from his shoulder.

Sidestepping Arent, De Coninck moved to the center railing to ordered the rowboat to be lowered, only to find his first officer's large body once again in his way.

"Move," De Coninck barked, and his fingers curled on their own accord into a tight fist.

The lone lantern near the companionway cast a faint yellow glow, and the light did strange things to the lines on the captain's face. His eyes were burning with battle fever, and in that moment De Coninck resembled something Arent had never seen before, something feral and the sight stirred the hairs on the back of his neck.

"Arent," De Coninck growled, his threatening tone cold and ruthless. "Get out of my way!"

De Coninck inhaled deeply and prepared himself to address the crew on the lower deck. Arent knew that once the order was given, no one could gainsay it and his chances of keeping De Coninck safe and aboard the ship would vanish like scruples in a whorehouse.

"Cap, let's talk inside," Arent said as he kept himself between De Coninck and his crew.  Noting the slight movement of his captain's hand, he instinctively tucked his chin and bit down on his teeth.

He did not have to wait long.  The blow landed on the side of his face with a jarring force that would have laid a lesser man out cold. His head almost snapped past his shoulder, and he had to blink hard several times to clear the stars from his vision. The captain might be twice his age, but that did not lessen the power in his arm. Ignoring the metallic tang of blood that was fast filling his mouth, Arent's hands snapped out, latched on to De Coninck's upper arms, and then he pushed. Keeping his head down so his forehead was near the captain's nose, protecting most of his face. The pair started backward toward the stateroom door in something that resembled a stilted dance.

Arent closed the cabin door behind them and watched as De Coninck stalked into his private quarters, drawing to a halt by the bank of windows lining the back wall. Niklas had positioned the ship so that the stern was facing the city, the maneuver done to assist their planning and aid their departure, should the need arise to do so swiftly. Being the tactical genius that the navigator was, nothing was ever done without consideration and near clairvoyant forethought.

A dense silence hung in the cabin while De Coninck stared out into the night. Somebody must have prepared the cabin, for a single candle stood to attention on the desk, bravely trying to hold its own against the increasing darkness of the room.

"Cap, why don't you—," Arent started but didn't get any further.

"Don't patronize me," De Coninck roared as he turned away from the window to sit behind his desk, where he dropped his chin to his chest as he tried to rake together the shreds of his self-control.

Arent walked to the liquor cabinet next to the bookshelf. It was well stocked, from the exotic to the expensive and every craving in between. Their usual refined French brandy would not do. Tonight called for something more robust, something with balls. His eyes landed on the unlabeled bottle of barrel proof whiskey. It was a drink brewed by the gods themselves and was to be taken with extreme care and in the greatest of moderation.

Arent filled a third of the glass and pushed the drink into De Coninck's hand.

"Drink," he commanded and moved to the other side of the desk to appease his sense of self preservation.

De Coninck raised the glass to his lips and the amber liquid rippled with the shaking of his hand, but the ill-fated liquor never made it to its intended destination. Instead of taking a sip, he lowered the glass, placing it on the desk with delicate precision, before slowly raising his eyes to Arent.

"What are you doing here?" he asked so softly that Arent had to lean forward, then he remembered the old trick and snapped his back straight again. He was not about to be lured in for a second drubbing. The captain was a force to be reckoned with when he was loud and bellowing, but he became chillingly dangerous when he turned quiet.

Seeing the confusion on his first officer's face, De Coninck continued. "It is dark outside. Yes?"

"Yes, sir," Arent answered.

"Then I will ask again, and this time don't look at me like you've never seen me before. Give me an answer. What are you still doing here?"

"You want me to—,"

"It is dark. Surely, you've noticed!" His tone rose again, "I want you out there, searching for Sebastiaan," he thundered as he swiped his hand in the direction of the dark city behind him.

The unfortunate crystal glass, with its precious content, was sadly in the wrong place at the worst of times and the force of the captain's gesture sent the tumbler flying off the desk, missing the thick carpet, and landing on the polished wooden floor. A wet slap marked the moment of impact as the liquor was unexpectedly set free from its confines when the glass shattered.

The violence of the simple accident seemed to have the opposite effect on the room's occupants. Arent immediately moved to rectify the travesty by pouring another. De Coninck stood transfixed as he stared at the shattered glass on the floor.

"I despise being tucked away in this cabin like a coward," De Coninck's words pierced the pregnant silence as he accepted another drink from Arent.

Closing his hand around the glass, he downed the whiskey in one swift gulp and rose from his seat to step around the desk. But days of meager meals and fragmented sleep had worn him thin. The combined effects of hunger, exhaustion, and alcohol sent the room spinning violently, forcing him to grip the desk for stability.

Exhaling through his nose, he reached for his chair and sat down once more. Leaning his head back, he closed his eyes and allowed the whiskey's fiery path to burn itself out.

"There is nothing we can do tonight," Arent said in a voice heavy with sympathy. "The streets will be quiet. If I go, I will draw too much attention, and besides, all the slaves will be locked away," he reasoned. "But Cap, you must stay out of sight, with your looks…" shaking his head, he continued. "You are an abduction waiting for a dark alley."

De Coninck raised his head and opened his eyes. Although he seemed calm, he had yet to firmly pursue sound judgment. Not trusting his voice, he gave Arent a single nod.

* * *

"Lads, remember you are slaves," Arent spoke to the four men at the oars of the rowboat, "act like it. Heads down, don't look at anyone, be as shy and timid as a country girl on her wedding night."

"That's not going to be hard. I've never rowed through a busy harbor in nothing but a scrap of cloth barely long enough to cover my pissing poker," one sailor grumbled as his sinewy arms pulled on the oar.

Arent had chosen the four scrawniest men from the crew and dressed them in the manner of slaves, wearing a rough linen wrap that only covered their loins. The men's skins were naturally sun browned, but they were clearly European. He stood in the center of the rowboat, legs planted wide, his right hand resting on his scimitar.

For all the world, Arent was dressed to resemble a wealthy merchant, if not downright nobility. His beard had been hacked back and now protested the tight confines of a sharp goatee. He was dressed in dark blue pantaloons, neatly tucked into his polished black leather boots, accentuating his narrow hips but hiding the bulging muscles of his legs. A high collared shirt of the same dark blue wrapped tightly around his shoulders and did an admirable job of concealing the black ink swirls on his chest and biceps. A wide waistband of emerald green silk separated the shirt and pantaloons. The waistband was adorned with various weapons, sporting a twin set of gold-inlaid, ivory-handled pistols tucked neatly together precisely midway between his navel and his left hip. On the other side of that indented center point glimmered the bejeweled handle of a short dagger. His actual weapons were carefully concealed. At his back, hidden beneath the ankle length ox-blood red overcoat, his dagger was tucked into the waistband at a slight angle, waiting for its master's right hand. Between his shoulder blades, underneath his shirt, and close to his skin was his almost torso length custom made dussack, resting peacefully in its scabbard secured around Arent's chest and waist. It was a simple matter of dropping his hand inside his collar at the back of his neck and pulling the menacing weapon free should the need arise. Hopefully it would not, but he'd never ventured anywhere off a ship without it. To complete the dazzling ensemble, he'd hidden his nearly waist long black hair beneath an elaborately folded green turban.

The morning sun was just streaking through the twin heads of the harbor and already sweat was running down his sides.

"Most men seem to wear white shirts," one sailor grumbled under his breath as they rowed deeper into the city.

"They are all used to this goddamned heat. If I wore a white shirt, you'd be able to count my nipples by the time I set foot on the riverbank." Arent held his head high and spoke down his nose to the man at his feet. "Also," he continued, "this color hides bloodstains better, should it come to that."

"Aye, good thinking, good thinking," another chimed.

They were nearing the riverbank, and the sailors positioned the rowboat so that Arent could disembark without getting so much as a spittle of water on his boots.

"Come back for me at sunset," he instructed, before stepping from the craft. "If I'm not here, wait. Should I find Sebastiaan, I might need a hand. Now, quick as you please; back to the *As-Sayf*."

"Godspeed, brother," the men whispered. With a barely perceptible nod, he stepped onto the soft sand and strode away without a backward glance.

A row of date palms lined the river and beyond that, the city was coming to life. Women with large empty baskets and children screaming with excitement all seemed to head in the same direction. Arent followed at a distance, hoping they were going to the marketplace and not the bathhouse.

He needed information, and the best place to find it would be at the heart of commerce and trade. His eyes took in the unfamiliar surroundings. The city was quite beautiful, at least near the river. The streets snaking through the throngs of domestic dwellings would be different. As with all cities, waste was often dumped from the windows onto the street below.

The farther he walked, the stronger the scent of lamb fat grew. Every city had its own distinct smell: Tokyo carried the tang of raw fish, Bombay the spice of curry, and Singapore a blend of both, laced with musky orchids. In Muscat, the signature aroma appeared to be cooked lamb fat. It slithered through the dusty streets like a serpent, coiling around Arent's ankles, seeping into every fiber of his clothing, and clinging to his skin, where it lingered.

Easing his jaw, Arent breathed through his mouth to escape the lamb fat's cloying stench. He wasn't squeamish by nature, and his years as a sailor had cured him of picky eating. The list of things he had eaten was extensive, ranging from dried and salted tarantula—a drunken dare that had gone the wrong way—to live fish that closely resembled fat, spotted tape worms swimming in a shot glass of soy sauce. The Japanese delicacy left the gourmand with a most unsettling tickling sensation right at the entry to the stomach. That particular treat had not been ingested as the result of a drunken dare but rather to impress a singularly beautiful woman and by the grace of the saints, he'd managed to not embarrass himself. After tossing the entire colony down his throat the little devils had reached his stomach without incident and stayed put. But lamb he could not abide, neither the taste nor the smell. It was something that seemed incapable of remaining inside him for more than a mere few seconds before it fought its way to freedom the same way it lost it.

He passed through the archway of the marketplace. It did not differ from a thousand others. Stalls were scattered at will and yet there was an unspoken courtesy among the sellers. The spice stall was positioned so the prevailing breeze would brush past the back of the tent, leaving most of the merchandise unmolested. To its left, the date seller had stacked her baskets high, almost touching the spice bowls, preventing any inconsiderate buyer from passing between them and knocking her neighbor's precious powders to the ground. To its right, the baker had placed his stall right in the breeze's face, letting the breath of nature do his calling for him.

From there, fruit and vegetable stands drew a crooked path to the butcher, where carcasses of various animals hung from an overhead beam anchored by two tripods on either side of the stall. The owner was a burly man with a beard to match, wearing a blood splattered white apron, showing that his stall was clean and his produce fresh. However, his principal occupation seemed to be fly swatter, for he was ceaselessly swatting the pests trying their luck at the buffet of meat.

Something about the man drew Arent's interest. There was a no-nonsense air about him, for he batted some hopeful customers away the same as he did the flies and then accepted others with long suffering resignation or a jovial smile. An old woman, who must have fallen into the middle category, received a stiff nod but was permitted to make her selection. By the nervous tension in her shoulders and the man's deep scowl, Arent got the impression that her patronage had a short leash. She leaned forward to better study the cages at the back of the stall where the live chickens were kept and pointed to a medium-sized brown chicken. The butcher promptly opened the cage, extracted the bird, pushed it under his arm and snapped its neck before handing it to the woman as she counted out the requested number of coins on his counter. After the coins disappeared into the leather pouch tied around his waist, she too, received the fly treatment and vanished into the thickening crowd.

Arent approached the counter, and the man gave him a quick once-over before scratching the back of his neck with a raspy sound, his scowl replaced by wary caution.

"As-salamu alaykum," Arent greeted.

"Wa alaykum as-salam," the butcher returned, touching his forehead, lips, and heart in a smooth motion.

Arent made a show of looking over the hacked portions of red meats and the lengths of sausages looped wherever space permitted.

"What can I do for you, Effendi?" the butcher asked, his eyes narrowing as he once more assessed the value of the man standing on the other side of his stained and chipped wooden counter. His expensive garb was in stark contrast to the humble task of buying meat for the evening meal. "You are not here to buy meat and I have customers to serve," he said, even though there was no one waiting to be served or shooed away.

Arent nodded in understanding and dropped five silver coins on the counter, an amount that would secure him every carcass hanging before him. The butcher stared at the coins before covering them with a brown piece of waxed parchment but made no move to lay claim to the small fortune—*an honest man*, Arent thought.

"I need information." The statement merely raised the eyebrows on the brawny face. "I need to know who the biggest slave owners in town are and I don't want to advertise my ignorance," Arent continued.

"And you thought coming to me would grant you the education you seek?" the butcher asked deadpan, his irreverent tone not meant to insult but merely a habit from a life lived on a straight line.

Arent nodded. "I don't want to spend my time running from one slave owner to the next like a dog chasing a treat. You look like a man who knows his sirs from his servants; one who doesn't keep with gossip." The compliment had its intended effect and the man's demeanor warmed slightly.

"Is that your ship laying in the harbor? The one that snuck in like a ghost last eve just as the sun was setting?" the butcher asked.

"It is," Arent said.

"She's beautiful. Looks Dutch," the butcher prodded.

Again, Arent nodded while looking toward the bay, even though it couldn't be seen from where he stood, allowing a sly grin to show his satisfaction. "She used to be," he said, licked his lips and held the butcher's eyes in a firm lock.

"Congratulations," the butcher said, returning the smile, though had it not been for the crinkling of his eyes, one would have not detected the expression amongst the dense forest of hairs surrounding his mouth.

"A fine acquisition she was but a bit sluggish without an able-bodied crew to handle her. I was wondering if some fresh merchandise had come in of late, preferably European?" The smile had vanished from Arent's face and his words, and his eyes were hard now that they'd arrived at the heart of the matter. He placed another handful of coins on the counter.

"Yes, take some of the bastards off our hands," the butcher said and grunted. "Every day before sunrise and every evening before sunset, they are let out of the bagnios to roam the city for food and water. They steal like monkeys wherever they can, and we are the worst off for it. But not me," he said as he raised a wooden baton from behind his counter. "A few licks from this, and they quickly learn to scavenge elsewhere." He set the weapon down and then seemed to recall Arent's initial question.

"Ah, for what you are looking for, the best man to talk to would be the Pasha," the butcher said and pointed with his chin in the direction of the administration buildings behind the market. "But unfortunately to get to him, you need to go through his secretary." A pained expression, a sigh, and a firming of the lips followed the statement. He raised his meaty hand once more to scratch the imaginary itch brought on by his words.

"His secretary?" Arent asked.

"That is the only way," the butcher replied, shaking his head, "and a pity, that is. But you seem like a man of patience and means, and so I wish you peace in that regard."

Arent reached into his sleeve once more, but the butcher raised his hand.

"No, Effendi, I feel after the direction I pointed you in that I should be the one to pay you."

* * *

Soon after leaving the market, Arent was seated on an uncomfortable wooden chair in a large office. When he'd entered the room, he was promptly met with an outstretched hand pointing to one of four chairs neatly lined against the wall. A ten foot long, thick, and colorful rug separated him from the secretary perched behind a sturdy desk.

The wispy young man sat with his feet neatly together, knees touching, bent at a ninety-degree angle, and his back poised just so. His head was tilted ever so slightly in order to balance the delicate gold-rimmed spectacles pinched near the end of his hooked nose. With long slender fingers he traced the words on the parchment before him from right to left over several lines, then he put it aside and picked up another. The process was repeated eight more times before he decided to address the room's only other occupant.

As Arent quietly observed the secretary, the butcher's words replayed themselves in his mind—he was beginning to miss the man. Reaching inside his sleeve where his money pouch was sewn, he extracted five Venetian ducats but kept them hidden in his hand.

Arent stared at the three empty chairs next to him. The prissy little arse behind the desk was in a position of power and savoring every second.

"Do you have an appointment?"

Concealing his agitation, Arent looked at the source of the thin, tight voice.

"I wish to see the Pasha," he growled but instantly added a smile so as not to incite a startle.

"The Pasha will not attend his office this week; perhaps you'll have better luck next week," the secretary said and adjusted the spectacles which had slipped perilously close to his nostrils, thereby closing the nose slightly and making him sound more nasal than he might have preferred.

Arent adopted a thoughtful expression, but did not rush to his feet. Instead, he let the coins slip from one hand to the other like a card dealer shuffling a deck. The bright gold coins fell one on top of the other with evenly spaced crisp pings.

Heaving a deep sigh, he closed his fist around the coins and made to stand.

"Just as well. I thought you were too young to be entrusted with any responsibilities beyond reading and tallying. Alas, we must all start somewhere, and this is probably the best place for you. I bid you good day," he said with a subtle yet condescending smile.

"Perhaps if you were to state your name and your business, I can inform the Pasha of your intended visit." Against all odds, the secretary's voice had risen an octave as his eyes moved from Arent's closed hand to his face.

"No need, you seemed to be pushed to the limits of your abilities already, and I shall therefore not add to your burdens," Arent said and aimed for the door.

"Sir, please," the mouse pleaded, "my master would be very disappointed if I do not provide him with the proper information."

Arent could well understand the secretary's distress. If word were to get around that an unknown rich man was in town, one who was bestowing his benevolence indiscriminately, but who had somehow skipped the Pasha after visiting his office, the young man would be in a world of pain.

Seeming to take pity on him Arent said: "I am Shaykh Burhan, from Tunis, on the Barbary coast," he spoke in a deep, proud voice, pausing as he waited for the clerk to jot the name down on his precious piece of parchment. "I am in search of men to crew my ship back to my home. Word is your master's one of the largest slaveholders in Muscat, but the rumors must be incorrect seeing that he has employed … *you* to manage his affairs in his absence, thus leading me to believe that his affairs must be rather insubstantial."

A look of doubt and boredom now decorated Arent's face, and he let his gaze trickle down and then up the slender form of the young man who had risen to his full unimpressive height.

"A thousand apologies for having made you wait so long. My judgment has failed me, and you are correct; I am young and have much to learn. But perhaps I can be of service. If only you would be kind enough to mention my aptitude to my master, should it please you? I have a list of the names of the slaves owned by the Pasha and can certainly make recommendations as to their suitability for a life at sea, again should that please you." The little shit apparently got the run of the mouth when his nerves were rattled.

Finally, they were moving in a direction Arent could appreciate, stepping closer to the desk, he gave a slight nod to show his willingness to the proposed plan.

Soon a stack of parchment appeared on the secretary's desk and Arent felt the bile rise in his stomach as he read through lists and lists of names. The date of sale, the price, and the age of the slave accompanied each name.

"Those are dead," informed the secretary in a tone similar to what one would use when discussing the weather when Arent paused at a name that had a thin black line drawn through it.

So many names, so many pages, so many thin black lines. The secretary pulled the last three pieces from Arent's hand and placed them to the side. "Women," he explained.

Slavery was rampant everywhere, even in Europe, but to see it written out in this manner was jarring.

Arent read the pages carefully, line by line. Then his eyes stopped at the last name on the list and his heart skipped a beat: It stated that two weeks ago the Pasha bought a priest by the name of Armand. It was the same name Cornelia Stiens had given them for the priest that was taken from one of the three Dutch ships. Turning the last parchment over, he searched the back, but it was blank. Sebastiaan's name was not on the list. Unless he'd given them a false name, but Armand's entry was the last one. There were no more with the same date.

It stood to reason that Sebastiaan was in Muscat but had been sold to another. Another with considerable wealth, for Sebastiaan's skill and looks would come at a heavy price.

"There are possibly five that I would be interested in discussing with the Pasha," Arent said. "But five are not enough. Perhaps you can furnish me with the names of the other major slave owners in the city." Arent let three gold Venetian ducats drop from his fingers. "And also arrange an introduction?" He added another two.

"Oh, my lord," the young man squealed, "the names I can provide, the introductions I dare not." He seemed close to tears when Arent promptly removed the last two coins from the small tower. "However," he rushed on in a hope to have the precious two coins returned, "once a month our exalted Sultan allows for slaves to be auctioned at the palace," he pointed with an open hand to the blank wall behind him, presumably in the direction of the palace. "The most influential and wealthiest men gather there to bid against each other. And that is where you will meet the owners of these names," he said as he noted down four names in a decorative hand more suited to that of a woman.

"Shaykh Habib, Shaykh Ahmet, Shaykh Maalouf, and Shaykh Saleh. Of those, Shaykh Ahmet is the wealthiest."

Arent took the piece of parchment and tucked it inside his overcoat, dropped one more ducat on the table and turned toward the door. The secretary gasped at the four ducats and snatched them from the desk in fear that Arent might change his mind, then all but crawled on his hands and knees to the door.

"I am your servant, my lord; a thousand blessings on you and your house. May *Allah* be with you each and every day, and may He grant you a long and prosperous life." Arent resisted the urge to roll his eyes, but retracted his hand when it became apparent that the secretary was about to kiss it.

When Arent emerged from the Pasha's office, the day was well advanced. Standing atop the steps overlooking the market square, he observed the bustling activity, where the slave culture became starkly apparent. Everyone, except for the very poor, seemed to own at least one. Household slaves, dressed in colorful liveries to advertise the wealth of their masters, roamed the bazaar while others scurried back and forth, pulling carts and carrying heavy loads on their shoulders to and from the stalls. Most seemed to be of African descent, but here and there, the sharper features of the Mediterranean showed.

He had no intention to return in a week's time to meet with the Pasha; Sebastiaan's name was not on the list, rendering the point moot. Having to wait two weeks to meet the other slave owners was as much a possibility as nipples on a tortoise. He needed a different strategy. Arent walked over to the baker's stall and purchased five palm-sized shortbread cakes filled with dates and then exited the marketplace, his fare neatly wrapped in waxed parchment.

A small African boy was making his way from the river, carrying two large pails of water hung from a crude yoke across his bony shoulders. His stick-thin legs wobbled under the weight of his burden.

"Water! Fresh water," he called out in a melodic voice. He was heading for the market and Arent slowed his step, changing his direction to ensure his path crossed the boy's.

"Water, Effendi?" the boy called as he teetered his way to Arent, taking care not to spill a drop from the full pails.

A copper mug was hanging from the side of the pail. The boy unhooked it, dipped it into the cool water and handed the dripping cup to Arent with one hand while holding out the other to receive his payment. Arent stared at the slight vibration of the small, outstretched hand. Payment was not a guarantee, and this child was used to abuse. He dropped a silver shahi in the dirty hand before reaching for the cup and draining the contents. The child's large, black eyes widened at the fortune, but then he looked warily at Arent.

"You are most generous Effendi, my master will be pleased with me, but he will expect me to bring him the same tomorrow or more." The message was simple: all the money goes to his master and if he did well today, he would be expected to do so the next and, if not, he would be punished.

"Do you live with your owner?" Arent prodded. The child shook his head.

"No, I only drop the money off at the gate of his house at the end of the day," he said with a shrug of his bony shoulder.

"So, if you don't live with your owner, where do you sleep at night?" Arent asked, fearing the child would tell him he slept on the street.

"In the bagnio with the other slaves," he said, pointing toward the river.

"Close to the river?"

"Three streets over," the boy replied.

Arent nodded in understanding, then looked at the coin still lying in the middle of the outstretched hand.

"Can you hide it somewhere?" Arent asked. The child shook his head, the action laced with defeat as he kept his hand palm up toward Arent, the coin glinting in the afternoon light. Arent reached down, took it back and replaced it with one copper mangir, a fraction of the value of the previous coin, but it bought him a brilliant smile as the thin fingers closed over his earnings. Remembering the cakes in his other hand, Arent held the parcel out to the boy. At least he could give him something that had value to him and not his master. The boy took the offering and stared at Arent with uncertainty.

"Open it," Arent insisted. Careful little fingers unwrapped the contents and, seeing the five humble cakes, he dropped the water pails to the ground, sat flat on his bottom in the dirt and proceeded to devour three with minimal chewing.

"Slow down," Arent chuckled as the child looked up at him, crumbs sticking to the sides of his mouth. Then he wrapped the remaining two tightly in the piece of parchment and tucked it into the waistband of his dirty linen breeches.

"For later?" Arent asked.

"For my friend," the boy replied.

"Good lad," Arent said before taking his leave and headed toward the harbor as the child once more lifted the carrying pole over his shoulders.

Arent used the rest of the day to learn the lay of the land, get a feel for the city and discreetly start his street-by-street search. Today, he would adopt the ennui that the perception of wealth afforded him, as he strolled the streets near the harbor lined with workshops and other activities associated with shipbuilding, carefully searching every nook, corner, and workbench. He prayed that Sebastiaan was there, working on the docks and if so, he would have seen the *As-Sayf*, recognized his own ship and understood the significance of the name.

Tomorrow, Arent would hire a guide and a horse and scout the rest of the city and its outskirts. Perhaps luck would be on his side, and he might spot Sebastiaan carrying parcels from the market to some rich arsehole's home.

As the shadows stretched, so did Arent's frustration. He'd walked the entire harbor area twice, peeking into workshops, talking to craftsmen, discreetly asking after their slaves and those of others and yet there was no trace of Sebastiaan. There were many slaves, but they were all of African descent.

The hour before sunset brought a clear shift in the air. Soon, the slaves would be allowed to roam the city to steal food and water. As a result, residents rushed home to avoid becoming pickpocket victims, and stall owners gathered their goods closer. Arent was leaning against a date palm a few yards from the market entry. From his vantage point, he had a good view of many of the streets and could easily see everyone entering and exiting the bazaar. Two men approached him from behind. He could feel his nerves crackle, and then he heard their breathing—shallow and wheezing; these were no thieves, they were desperate human beings living like animals. He reached into his sleeve and withdrew a handful of copper coins.

Wordlessly, he held his hands out wide, each displaying an equal number of coins. The men approached carefully and when they were close enough to touch; they stopped. They were nothing more than walking skeletons, their skins were marred with lash marks and open sores, their hair was dirty and knotted. He looked each man in the eye and nodded. Gnarly, work-worn fingers with black, broken nails scraped the palms of his hands as they helped themselves to his generosity. And then they were gone, scurrying off and disappearing between the buildings.

Arent kept his eyes trained on the entry of the marketplace until the last of the slaves exited with the curses of the stall owners following them down the street, and still no Sebastiaan. Waiting a little longer before he too started down the street, he pondered all he had learned today. Was Sebastiaan even in the city? Or was he hidden behind the high walls of the wealthy compounds toiling away as a household slave? Was he even alive? Was his body lying in some ditch alongside all the others with thin black lines through their names? He passed buildings and streets, his eyes unseeing, his mind reeling and his heart breaking a little more with each step he took.

Ahead, a long line of slaves was lined up to enter their dormitory and Arent crossed to the other side of the street. Looking up at the high walls, the iron gate, and the armed guards, he thought *prison* was a more apt description. Unable to witness any more human suffering for the day, he dropped his gaze to his booted feet, and lengthened his stride past the line of human misery, trying to get as far from it as he could in as short a time as possible.

His chest suddenly felt tight as memories flooded his mind. He remembered how he and Sebastiaan had raced each other up the shrouds of De Coninck's ship when they were boys. He remembered the first time they got drunk together in Amsterdam. After leaving the tavern, Sebastiaan had thrown up four times before they'd stepped onto the street. When they reached the docks, he had passed out cold. By then Arent's feet were more or less following orders from upstairs and he had hoisted Sebastiaan over his shoulder and carried him up the gangway of their ship, past a disapproving De Coninck who was waiting at the top, arms folded over his chest and head shaking from side to side, past the cheering men on night duty, and all the way to their pallets where he'd dumped his friend like a sack of flour before collapsing onto his own sleeping pallet.

Arent's throat constricted at the unbidden memory. *'Where are you, brother?'*

"Arent Van Jeveren." The name scraped painfully from a throat that sounded dry and tired.

Those three words jerked Arent's feet to a halt and his mind back to the present.

He spun on his heels and stared in the direction from which the sound had come. Was it his imagination playing tricks on him? Was he hearing things? But then saw the slave at the front of the line. He was tall, dirty, thin, and covered in dust. Arent narrowed his eyes. The man was young, his skin was lighter than the others, his shoulders wide and corded with muscle. Then he noted the hair; even though it was covered in dust he could see the blond streaks peeking through—Sebastiaan.

Arent moved, and the name rose in his throat as he was about to shout it, but he caught himself in time, remembering what he looked like and where he was. Exposing Sebastiaan would be disastrous. Stupefied, he watched the guards carelessly shove the tired body through the gates; he watched as Sebastiaan stumbled and reached out his hand to stop from falling; he watched the scarred back and swollen feet disappear into the dimness beyond the ugly walls. He watched.

How was he supposed to leave? He could wait for darkness, then scale the walls. They were not that high. He could easily take out the two guards. Once inside he would cut a path through whatever obstacle presented itself, he would destroy that godforsaken place from the inside out. But instead, he turned and walked away, not realizing that his face was wet.

# Chapter 20

"**I** found him."

The simple statement knocked the breath from De Coninck. It was the news he had wanted; it was not the news he had expected.

Arent waited for the barrage of questions that were sure to follow his pronouncement, but the captain had only one: "Is he alive?"

"Yes. He's kept in one of the bagnios," Arent started as De Coninck pinned him with a hard stare. "He is …," he did not know how to describe the gut-wrenching condition his friend had been reduced to. The stinging pain in his throat was uncomfortable, and he tried to cough it away.

Turning his back and walking away from Sebastiaan this evening was the hardest thing he ever had to do. Reaching the river, he had found the crew waiting for him. He had wordlessly stepped into the small craft, and whatever had shown on his face was enough for the four men to fall silent too. No one had spoken a word until they were all gathered on deck. Some were wringing their caps in their hands, others stood with their heads bowed; they all knew that the news was bad, one way or the other. Even good news would come at a heavy price.

"Arent." The slap of De Coninck's voice snapped him back, and he blinked several times to clear his eyes. He was standing with his back to most of the crew, only the captain was close enough to see his turmoil. This report would not be given in the privacy of the stateroom. Sebastiaan was brother to them all. Even the three new lads who had joined the crew after he had left were loyal to the man they knew only from his legacy.

"He is physically …" he paused, searching for a way to put words to his memories, "they've …" he swallowed hard, remembering the state of Sebastiaan's back and feet. De Coninck had his fists planted in his sides and was leaning forward as if to draw the words from Arent's lips. "Look, he is not well, and I think we can get to him, but we need to do a bit of planning."

"Did he see you?" De Coninck asked.

"No, he didn't." Arent replied and then excused himself from the group. He needed time alone to process the things he had seen and to get his emotions under control.

* * *

The next morning, Arent was once more deposited on the riverbank. Despite De Coninck's arguments for the opposite, he again wore the disguise of a wealthy shaykh exploring a new city as his ship lay at anchor, being refit for another long and hopefully prosperous journey.

"Dressing as a commoner will allow you to crawl into places you wouldn't be able to go otherwise," De Coninck had argued.

"Yes, that is true, but I've seen him, Cap. He is working in one of the quarries. As a rich man, feigning interest in the city's projects, I can hire a guide and a horse to take me to all of them until I find the one where he is."

"Fair point," De Coninck had conceded. But it was not an easy victory for Arent.

De Coninck had wanted to storm the bagnio as soon as it was dark enough. He'd planned to take his crew, who were champing at the bit to spill blood, overrun a possibly small number of unsuspecting guards, and free Sebastiaan by force.

"There are too many unknowns, Cap," Arent had argued. "The bagnio is an old two-story bathhouse. We don't know where they keep the slaves or if it houses more guards on the upper level. The last thing we want is to storm the building in the dead of night and find ourselves outnumbered, and possibly unable to rescue Sebastiaan." De Coninck had run a frustrated hand through his hair at the logic of the words. "We will only have one shot, and if we miss, he is as good as dead."

That was the deciding factor, and De Coninck had agreed to *one* day of reconnaissance, but no more. By nightfall they would have a plan and by the next, Sebastiaan would be safely returned to them. The finality of De Coninck's ultimatum was clear. He had reached the end of his tether and there would be no more concessions after that.

*  *  *

Arent stood in the grove of date palms that flowed like a prickly blanket over a soft hill, languidly sucking on his carved clay pipe. He had a perfect view of the marketplace entry and the end of the street on which he'd seen Sebastiaan the day before. The shrill of a whistle pierced the tranquil morning twilight. A few minutes later, the laborious screeching of the bagnio's iron gate joined the four-note song of the blue-gray doves scratching and pecking beneath the palms.

A long line of ragged derelicts stumbled their way onto the streets and then broke up in pairs or by themselves. The sounds of their hobbled feet clattered through the quiet streets as they scurried away. Arent's eyes narrowed as he searched each body filing through the gate. Sebastiaan would be easy to spot for his coloring, height, and breadth, set him apart from the rest.

Arent's breathing grew shallow, his heart hammered against his breastbone, and he stifled a cough that pushed smoke through his nose. Any moment Sebastiaan would emerge from that hellhole. He watched as the last slave, the little water boy he met the day before, exited the bagnio and then the squealing gates closed again. No Sebastiaan. Straightening from his lean against the date palm, he searched the streets as far as he could see, but there was nothing. Emptying the pipe against the heel of his boot, he dropped it in his pocket and headed for the market.

A skirmish erupted near the entrance. Someone had knocked over a young man carrying a large basket of baked goods. Six slaves swarmed the scene, eagerly snatching anything their bony fingers could grasp. Curses and shouts trailed the scavengers as they scurried off, seeking a place to devour their spoils before a guard or a stronger slave took it off them.

Arent skirted the scene of the *accident.* It wasn't hard to spot the slaves in the market. One only had to listen and follow the wave of angry voices as they rose and fell. He walked through the section where the food stalls clustered together.

The slaves operated in groups or pairs, creating scenes that might have seemed comical if not for the desperation driving their actions. Some staged distractions while others pilfered from stalls, snatching as much food as they could carry off. Others traded an hour's labor for scraps before guards herded them into groups and marched them to the labor sites. One slave assisted a cloth merchant in unloading his cart, balancing bolts of fabric on one shoulder while his other hand deftly swiped fruit and bread rolls from passing stalls.

Further down the lane, a stall owner was thrashing a man with a cane. The slave was lying on his side, his arms raised to protect his head while several small oranges rolled from his hands.

Once more, the sharp shrill of a whistle sounded and the chaos subsided as the slaves were called away. The marketplace was like an estuary sucking in the incoming tide of human misery before letting it out again, and still—no Sebastiaan.

This was a problem Arent had not expected. If he couldn't find Sebastiaan, he couldn't follow him. Without following him, he'd gain no information. With no information, no rational plan could be formed. Without a plan, Captain De Coninck, in his volatile state, would likely take matters into his own hands, and such an act could cost him his life.

"Water. Fresh water," the high-pitched voice of the water boy reached him. Arent's eyes snapped up, searching for the little imp. Hurriedly, he bought a bag of dates and a few pastries before heading toward the sound.

He found the child on his way to the exit. Recognition lit in the boy's eyes as Arent paused to buy a mug of cool water.

"Meet me in the palm grove near the river when your buckets are empty," he said as he dropped a coin in the boy's hand. Emptying the mug, he handed it back and left the market.

Arent did not have to wait long before the skinny African boy made his way through the date palms, empty water buckets swaying as his knobby legs pumped up the slight incline. There was a heaviness about the child's gait today that was not there the day before, as if a spark had been snuffed out overnight. The child came to a stop just out of arm's reach from where Arent stood.

Arent held out the food, and the boy took a wary step forward to claim it.

"What is your name?" he asked.

"Jiya," the boy answered around the pastry in his mouth.

"Sit, boy," Arent said. "There is a matter I wish to discuss with you." He sank to his haunches, bringing himself almost to eye level with the child. Fear fluttered through the large black eyes and Arent gentled his voice.

"I mean you no harm, but you seem like a clever child. One of those who sees everything and knows how to keep his mouth shut."

The child did not react to the compliment, for what Arent said was the truth and he merely took it as a statement of fact. Arent noted that once again the child did not finish all the pastries but saved a few before he attacked the dates with avid fingers, wrestling the pits out and flicking them to the side.

"I am looking for a slave." The child looked up, waiting for more information. "His name is Arent. Arent Van Jeveren. Have you heard of him?" Arent watched as the child's eyes filled with tears and soon after, two thick silver tracks traced over his filthy, sunken black cheeks.

"Why?" Jiya wanted to know.

"Do you know him?" Arent asked, his voice dropping to a whisper. The boy nodded and more tears flowed.

"He is my friend," Jiya replied, snuffling loudly before swallowing the contents of his misery.

"Is he the friend you save the food for?" Arent nodded to the wrapped pastries.

"Yes," the child's voice grew in strength as if he was defying someone, breaking some rule, and would continue doing it. "He is not allowed to steal food in the mornings or the evenings, so I share mine with him."

*Jesus,* how is Sebastiaan surviving without food? Slow lethal fury ignited in Arent's gut, but he suppressed it for the moment.

"That is very generous of you, Jiya," Arent praised.

Jiya shook his head slowly. "No, we traded. I give him food and he protects me at night from the other men." The child then broke down into sobs. "But I think he might be dead now."

Icy dread snaked down Arent's spine at Jiya's words.

"What do you mean?" he asked.

"The biggest, meanest man in the bagnio came for me last night and Arent killed him. Even though he was chained to the wall, he still killed him. This morning, the guards beat him with their canes. When we left, he was not moving."

The captain was right, they should have attacked the bagnio last night. Guilt washed over Arent and threatened to rob him of his balance.

"How many … Stop crying," Arent barked at the child. "How many guards are inside the bagnio?" He asked.

"Usually ten or twelve, last night only six," Jiya replied, his sobbing muffled but not gone.

*Fuck!*

"Jiya, listen to me," Arent's voice was low and urgent. A plan was starting to take shape. With Sebastiaan beaten and broken, his master might be willing to sell him. "Who owns Arent? What is his master's name?"

"Shaykh Ahmet, but he will never sell him," Jiya said, snot running over his lip and into his mouth and before the child could lick at it, Arent offered him a linen square from his pocket.

"Why would he not sell him?"

"He paid a thousand Venetian ducats for him, but Arent insulted him in the palace. So, then Shaykh Ahmet said that he has paid for Arent's death, and he would have it. And he said that he will never sell him no matter what. Others have offered to buy him. Some say that one of the other Shaykhs has offered double what Shaykh Ahmet has paid, but still he refused to sell him. He will not sell him to you." The finality of the statement was unmistakable. Sparring with this Shaykh Ahmet would waste time they seemed to have run out of. He needed to come up with a different idea.

"Jiya," Arent said, and the child looked up. "I am going to save your friend, and you are going to help me." The child frowned.

"Effendi, why would you bother with a slave that is not yours and that might already be dead?"

"Because he is my brother," Arent said.

Shock rippled through the child's body, making his eyes stretch to resemble two black pools in his bony face. Clearly, he was trying to match the blond-haired slave to this wealthy dark man sitting before him.

"Do you want to help your friend?" Arent asked and, at the child's enthusiastic nod, he moved a little closer to the boy.

"He saved my life. I will help you," Jiya vowed.

Arent burned to promise the boy that he would rescue him as well, but he dared not make a promise he knew would probably be impossible to keep. It would be the cruelest cut if he should fail the child. Best to leave well enough alone.

"Tonight, well after dark, you tell him that his uncle has come for him. It doesn't matter if he can hear you or not. It doesn't matter if you think he is dead or not, you *tell* him. Do you hear me?" Arent pushed the words through his teeth and Jiya nodded. "And then I need you to do something for me."

* * *

After Arent's conversation with Jiya, there was no need to stay in the city any longer and instead of waiting for the crew to pick him up he hired a boat to row him back to the *As-Sayf*. Once aboard, he relayed what he'd learned together with the plan he'd put in motion. All that remained was for him to choose three men to accompany him after dark. He was about to make his selection when the captain stepped forward, with a look that dared Arent to utter so much as a breath in protest. Then Lukas, the *Annabella's* new boatswain, stepped forward less than a second later, followed by Niklas, their rake-thin and bookish navigator.

Each man on the crew was eager to be part of the rescue mission, but Niklas had beaten them all to it. De Coninck and Arent stared at him with twin looks of bewilderment, whereas Lukas just smiled at the navigator's daring.

"In case one of us needs to look smart," Niklas replied with a single shoulder shrug. Realizing too late that his words could be misread, and seeing the captain's narrow-eyed glare, he tried to smooth over his blunder.

"Well," Niklas swallowed nervously and cleared his throat. Seeing that Arent was leaning in to bear closer witness to the many different ways of digging a hole deeper, Niklas continued. "Arent said that this boy, Jiya, would call for a physician. Yes?" He looked to the others for confirmation, and Arent responded with an irritated nod.

"We will then incapacitate the physician and one of us will take his place. Correct?" Arent vigorously rubbed the crease between his eyes, stifled a groan, and nodded again.

"Well," Niklas continued, "neither of you two looks like a physician," he said, waving his hand up and down in the direction of Arent and Lukas' muscled limbs. "You are too big. And Captain, you look too much like Sebastiaan, even with your face half covered. That leaves me. I'll be the physician."

"I don't think I've ever heard you speak so many words at once," Lukas said, still smiling.

"Aye, he has a point though," Arent said. "He's got that clever, useless look about him that physicians often display when they think they know something nobody else does."

Lukas' eyes snapped to Niklas to gauge his reaction to the insult.

"What? I do," Niklas replied. Apparently, no offense was taken, as shown by the way his bony shoulders rose and dropped.

But it was Arent who put an end to the discussion.

"I don't care how useless you look or how clever you think you are. You're not coming. I need men who know how to fight; and God, in all his infinite fairness, has subtracted from your brawn and added to your brains, rendering you unsuitable for this mission."

"Then you have to make room for a fifth because I'm coming," Niklas replied with a stubbornness that appeared only during the most challenging of storms, and then he raised an ancient cudgel from his side, like a Viking about to storm a foreign beach.

"Where did you get that thing?" Arent asked as he stepped closer to get a better look at the weapon.

"It was my grandfather's." Niklas met Arent's gaze dead on.

"Give me strength," Arent muttered and shook his head in bemusement as he looked to the captain for assistance, but De Coninck seemed to have taken a keen interest in the deck planks beneath his feet.

Niklas was as ruthless and fearless as any pirate when navigating the ship, but tonight would require stealth and violence and somehow Arent couldn't bring himself to think that Niklas was the wisest choice. He decided to reason on the grounds of practicality.

"How are you going to be the physician if you can't speak the language?" Arent asked, knowing that he had effectively settled the matter.

"Oh, I can speak the language, *Bricks-for-Brains*. In fact, I speak seven languages, including Mongolian. Now put that in your ornate little pipe and smoke it," Niklas shot back in fluent Arabic.

Arent shook his head in defeated amazement.

"Fine, you can come," he said, to which Niklas drew his shoulders back and looked triumphantly at the others, a rare smile splitting his face.

* * *

Now hours later, four men crouched down, two on either side, among the clutter of the dirt street. The night was cool and quiet. It was a few hours past sunset and, with a shy moon lurking somewhere to the east, the stars alone were not enough to silhouette them against the earthen wall of the buildings behind them.

The tortured howls of two fighting cats echoed off the walls lining the street. Clumps of white hair littered their battlefield, yet the combatants focused solely on each other. Only when they noticed the men did they find common ground and flee together.

Arent and Lukas crouched behind a stack of crates. Lukas shifted, wedging himself deeper into the corner between the crates and the building while tugging his hood lower over his half-masked face.

Across the street, Captain De Coninck and Niklas' cloaked figures disappeared behind a cart that stood upright against a wall. If Arent had had his choice of troops, it would not have included these three, perhaps Lukas, but the other two were so fair in complexion and hair color that Arent feared they might glow in the dark.

Sounds of insects and the river gentling its way to the ocean floated on the night air. An owl hooted, in the distance. A child's scream signaled the first phase of their plan. The sound came from the bagnio's direction, and Arent recognized Jiya's voice. Moments later, the gates creaked, and footsteps rushed past.

"There he goes," Lukas whispered as a guard ran down the street. Somewhere further away, a dog's bark marked his progress.

Arent released a long slow breath. He had his doubts that Jiya would be up to the task, but the boy had kept his promise. Their entire mission rested upon the child's success. Arent had instructed him earlier to wait until well after dark, then raise the alarm, claiming that Sebastiaan was dying and needed a physician. Jiya was convinced that the guards would heed his pleas, for Sebastiaan's owner would be extremely upset if any of them had beaten his costly slave to death, without his permission. If Sebastiaan was to die because of the beating they'd given him, Shaykh Ahmet might request similar deaths from them in return.

"Are you sure you can pull it off?" Arent had asked the child.

"I sell dirty water in a city with a river flowing through it," Jiya had replied in a voice older than his years. "I can do it."

"The boy did it," Lukas whispered, and guilt twisted in Arent's gut at the thought of having to leave Jiya behind.

They waited for what seemed like hours, but Arent knew it was only his impatience, stretching and pulling at every second. His leg was starting to cramp, and he adjusted his position, when the captain made two sharp clicking sounds from across the street. Moments later, the faint sound of footsteps and soft grumbling drifted toward them. *Damn, that man has sharp ears.*

On the other side of the street De Coninck and Niklas readied themselves.

"Here he comes," Niklas whispered, raising his wooden club as a dim figure appeared, shuffling steadily down the center of the street. Small leather pouches hung from the figure's waistband, and thin-framed spectacles clung to his nose, marking him as the physician.

De Coninck raised a finger to his lips for silence and, with his other hand, lowered the navigator's weapon. There was no need to kill the man. De Coninck would deal with the physician, while Arent—having heard the signal—would handle anyone accompanying their quarry.

The footsteps drew closer, as did the mumbling and the scent of dried herbs. The guard must have found distractions elsewhere, as De Coninck heard only one set of footsteps. Apparently, the physician was in the habit of talking to himself, no doubt lamenting his lot in life to be roused at this ungodly hour of the night to tend a mere slave. He was going to have a hell of a lot more to lament in the morning, De Coninck thought as the footsteps shuffled past his hiding place.

In one fluid motion, De Coninck emerged from behind the cart. His silent steps closed the distance to the physician. When he was close enough to smell the sweat on the man's skin, his target spun around in a flurry of coat panels, like a startled chicken flapping to escape. De Coninck did not waste a moment and before a yelp of surprise could escape the healer, he delivered a sharp blow to the side of the physician's frail neck. The result was instant. The man's eyes rolled back in his head and his knees gave out. De Coninck clamped a hand over his mouth and wrapped an arm around his chest as Arent moved in to lift his feet, and together they hauled him to the cart's shelter.

One look at the physician's unconscious form made it clear that Niklas was the perfect choice to take his place. Both men were stripped of their attire, Niklas of his own volition and the physician with the assistance of Arent and De Coninck.

Moments later, Niklas stood before them, dressed in the physician's loose kaftan and overcoat. A visible shiver ran down the navigator's spine when Arent wrapped the few days old, oily turban around Niklas' head.

After Niklas pushed the spectacles down on his nose and wrapped the ends of the turban around his neck, he gave a brisk nod to De Coninck, and stepped from their hiding place onto the street. Soon the new physician was shuffling toward the gates, mumbling to himself as he went.

Arent took Niklas' place behind the wagon.

"He'll be fine," De Coninck whispered, sounding like he was trying to convince himself rather than Arent.

"Yeah," Arent breathed, as he wiped his sweaty palms on his thighs.

The physician was coming to, and De Coninck took Niklas' discarded cudgel and administered a single blow to the head. Not hard enough to cause actual damage, but enough to send him back into oblivion, where he would hopefully stay until they were well on their way.

* * *

The stench of human waste hit Niklas before he touched the gate to signal his arrival. He lifted his turban's edge over his mouth and nose, fumbling with his spectacles as they slipped.

"You'll get used to it," a guard said as he opened the gate just enough for Niklas' narrow frame to enter.

A few lanterns were lit across the open-air courtyard and what Niklas saw almost drove him to his knees. His step faltered, and it drew the guard's attention, but he quickly righted himself. This was what Hell looked like. Starved, hollow faces stared at him as he passed rows and rows of slaves. The guard led him to the back wall where a dark lump was lying on the bare ground. A boy was sitting cross-legged beside it. Jiya, he presumed.

Sebastiaan was laying on his side, clad only in filthy linen breeches. But it was the sight of his back that finally drove Niklas down to his knees. Fifty lashes with a cane had done a neat job of destroying every scrap of skin that once covered the proud and powerful back. There was not a single bit

250

that was undamaged. It was a bloody and bruised mess. Large dark patches marked where his blood stained the ground.

Sebastiaan was so still that Niklas feared he might already be dead. Reaching out to check for a pulse, he noticed his hand shaking enough that if the guard was paying attention, he would spot it. Relief flooded him when he found Sebastiaan's pulse, weak and uneven but present. He closed his eyes in silent prayer until his fingers grazed the warm iron band around his friend's neck. They had collared him like a dog. Though not prone to emotional outbursts, Niklas felt hatred and anger flare within him. Tracing the band, he found the chain securing Sebastiaan to the wall. All thoughts of prayer vanished in the face of his fury.

Niklas fought to control his emotions. He wanted to scream at the guard standing just feet away, his face blank with boredom. His heart was racing, and he was breathing hard through his nose. He must've bitten the inside of his mouth because the metallic taste of blood was coating his tongue. Never had a need to do another violence gripped him like it did now. The reckless impulse to right this unspeakable wrong was threatening to overcome his self-control.

"He is dead," Niklas pronounced in a voice rough with rage. The child next to him sunk to the ground and sobbed. Looking from the desolate child to the guard, he barked in as firm a voice as he could muster. "Get a stretcher and men to carry it. The body cannot remain here."

"We will move him in the morning. You can go," the guard replied and spat a shiny glob that landed near Sebastiaan's head. Niklas felt his lip curl at the disgusting sight. This was not good. If the guard turned stubborn, they were going to have a load of problems. They needed Sebastiaan outside the gates tonight, while it was still dark. Waiting for the morning would simply not do.

"In the morning?" Niklas' voice held a shrill edge that was beyond his control. "Do you know who is paying my fee?" He looked at the guard, who was busy picking his nose, and then proceeded to roll the freshly excavated content between his fingers. Niklas, who had a strong aversion to any kind of bodily excretion, could not stand the sight, but he forced himself to endure. "Shaykh Ahmet," he said and let the words hang between them for a moment. "It is also Shaykh Ahmet who had requested the slave to be returned to his compound, dead or alive. Immediately. With a full report of how this has happened," Niklas added for good measure, unsure how far this charade could stretch. At least the man had stopped probing himself, his bored expression now replaced by alarm.

The seconds burned between Niklas and the guard, but finally the man came to his senses and called another over. The pair spoke in low voices, too quiet for Niklas to hear, their postures tense and gestures sharp. Sweat ran freely down his sides, and he swallowed a nervous sigh threatening to escape. Taking slow breaths through his nose, in and out, he calmed himself. It was almost over. Arent was right; he was not made for such excursions, but Sebastiaan was his friend and brother.

One of the men called to someone on the upper floor and moments later, two young guards approached with a large wooden board. They rammed the stretcher under Sebastiaan as if scooping dirt with a spade, then gripped his shoulder and hip and roughly rolled him onto the board.

Niklas positioned himself opposite, near Sebastiaan's head, eyes fixed on his friend's face. The pain of being rolled so callously onto his back made Sebastiaan's eyes flicker, and Niklas quickly raised his hand over them as one would with a staring corpse. Then they waited, for another guard to unchain Sebastiaan from the wall.

"He's taking too long," Arent whispered to De Coninck. "Something has gone wrong."

"Give him a few more minutes," De Coninck said.

"And then what?" Arent asked.

"Then we do as we planned," De Coninck replied.

"What if he doesn't come out? What if one of them knows the physician and discovers that Niklas is not him? This was a stupid idea."

"Hush," De Coninck said. "He'll do fine."

De Coninck and Arent tensed in unison as the gates shrieked on their hinges. A short while later, three figures moved down the street. Two were carrying a stretcher bearing a body, followed by a raggedy-looking physician.

"Where are they going?" Arent whispered.

"I don't know, perhaps Shaykh Ahmet's compound is in the other direction," De Coninck replied.

"Shit, this will take us past the bagnio's gate," Arent growled.

A movement on the other side of the street caught their attention. Lukas had risen from his hiding place and was moving down the street to follow the three-man procession.

"Let's go," De Coninck said.

Lukas was flattening himself against the wall of the bagnio near the gates. His burnous was covering most of his body, and he blended perfectly with the dreary wall. Arent and De Coninck paused before stepping from the black shadow of the cart.

Lukas slowly stretched forward to peek through the narrow openings in the gate, then smoothly retracted his head, lifted his hand and signaled the all clear. Niklas and the guards neared the street's end. They couldn't let them exit it, for beyond there were no hiding places. Arent and De Coninck moved like large silent bats. Once past the gates, Lukas fell in behind them. Niklas' grumbling was significantly louder now, effectively dousing any sound that might give away their approach.

Lukas and Arent closed the last few yards in a run, with their daggers drawn. There would be no killing tonight, just a few sore heads in the morning. Arent reached the stretcher carrier at the back first and brought the handle of his dagger down on the young man's temple. The guard crumpled to the ground, dropping his side of the stretcher. His mate did not go down so easily. Feeling the stretcher dip, he glanced over his shoulder, saw Lukas closing in, and opened his mouth to scream. However, before the alarm could turn from thought to action, the unfortunate guard took a full fist to the mouth and then the side of his head met the blunt end of Lukas' dagger.

"What do we do with them?" Lukas asked, his voice muted but breathy from excitement.

They were supposed to have gone in the other direction and then the bodies would have been dragged behind the crates and the cart. Now they had very few options left.

"Drag them to the side and leave them there," De Coninck said while handing Niklas his cudgel.

De Coninck took the discarded burnous Niklas had worn earlier and draped it over his nephew's unconscious form. Emotions were colliding and wreaking havoc inside him.

"Let's go," he growled.

Arent and Lukas replaced the guards and hoisted the board smoothly before setting off at a brisk pace toward the river.

Niklas was jogging to keep up and De Coninck drew both his daggers as he took his place behind his men, covering their escape. The no deaths rule had just ended. Should any fool choose to interfere with their extraction, he would swiftly meet his end.

The skiff was completely unsuited for its purpose tonight. De Coninck cursed his lack of foresight. The damned thing was too small, for it was rocking precariously from side to side as Arent and Lukas stepped into it, balancing Sebastiaan on the stretcher and then laying him across the two benches.

For months he'd been chasing a ghost across the Indian Ocean, up the African coast and deep into the Ottoman empire, driven only by the blind need to have his flesh and blood, a man who was more son than nephew, returned to him. Never once had he considered the possibility that Sebastiaan might be dead, not once. That loss he would have felt, for it would have closed like a fist around his heart and held fast until that faithful organ stopped beating.

This afternoon, when Arent had returned with that simple plan of his, De Coninck's body had sprung into motion and had not stopped since. He could not dare stop moving, stop searching for any sign of danger, he could not yet sheath his daggers and allow himself to believe that they'd won, that they had found Sebastiaan and that he was now lying on a stretcher—breathing.

"Cap, we're good. Let's go," Arent urged in a muted voice. De Coninck felt like he was in a dense forest and if he took his eye off the way he was meant to go, he would lose his footing. He gave the palm grove and the city beyond a last, thorough hawk-like sweep before tucking the twin daggers into the small of his back and swinging his legs over the side of the rowboat.

Niklas and Lukas took the oars at the back, sitting close to the side, allowing for the stretcher to pass between them. At the front, Arent was waiting for De Coninck to take his place. His face held a brutal edge and De Coninck could read the tumultuous emotions roiling behind the young man's dark eyes.

Sebastiaan's head was resting between Arent and De Coninck and for the first time De Coninck allowed himself to look at his nephew, and the rest of the world fell away.

Sebastiaan's blond hair, dulled by dust and crusted with blood, lay still in the breeze sweeping across the river. His skin, roughened by long hours in the desert sun, stretched taut over the bones of his face. A thick, grimy beard covered his once-smooth cheeks. Yet it was still the same patrician nose, the same ears, and the same mouth and chin.

De Coninck stared at the boy beside him, seeing his golden hair glitter in the sunlight as he climbed the shrouds of the ship, running along the decks, light-footed as a thief. He could still feel the solid weight of the newborn in his arms as the babe fought for his first breath. He saw the scared, filthy little boy hiding behind his father and the large hopeful eyes that had looked up to him when he'd reached his hand out in greeting. That night was the start of De Coninck's new life, when Sebastiaan's father entrusted him to De Coninck's care and safekeeping. Sebastiaan had become the son he'd never had; he'd given meaning to his life that he'd had no right to expect.

Tears were blurring De Coninck's eyes as the emotions and memories shredded him. Unaware of the boat's movement, he reached out to touch his nephew's forehead.

And then Sebastiaan was looking at him. His green eyes staring into De Coninck's with shocking clarity, as if they'd never been closed, as if no time had passed since the last time they'd locked gazes, and a single word breathed from his lips: "Jiya."

* * *

"The city is in uproar," Arent announced as he cleared the bulwark of the *As-Sayf*, swinging the heavy brown sack from over his shoulder and carefully lowering it to the deck. "Every guard is out and about running like jackrabbits searching every nook and cranny," he said as Lukas opened the sack.

Three men were wrestling the skiff aboard while the rest of the crew climbed up and down the shrouds, securing and unfurling sails. The ship gave a sudden jerk as the last of the sails snapped out. Arent looked to the quarterdeck where De Coninck usually stood, his place now empty.

Securing the last of the lines, a sailor called out, "We're good."

Two skinny arms reached up as Arent pulled Jiya from the brown sack and held him by the upper arm as the boy swayed with the unexpected movement beneath his feet.

"Sit down, right here," Arent said and pointed to the sack from which the child had just emerged. "We are going to be busy for a while. When all is calm, I will come and get you. Do you understand?" The child sank down and crossed his thin legs beneath him.

"You'll be fine," Arent reassured him, gazing into the child's large, frightened eyes. He was anxious to get moving but patiently waited for the boy's nod before sprinting up the companionway to where Niklas deftly steered the ship toward the harbor opening.

"You cut it close," Niklas said as Arent came to stand next to him. "They're locking down the city."

"Get us out of here before they decide to lock down the harbor as well." Arent moved to stand by the railing. Shouting orders was not an option, for other vessels still surrounded them, instead the men quietly maneuvered the sails and soon they were gliding toward the twin heads guarding the harbor's mouth.

Screaming, shouting and frantic whistle blowing could be heard coming from the streets of the city behind them. Someone either had found the unconscious guards or their victims had woken up and started voicing their dismay. They should have left hours earlier under the cover of darkness, but Sebastiaan's single word had brought all their plans to a halt.

Once aboard, they'd rushed Sebastiaan to a prepared cabin. Barent had lit several lanterns and was waiting in a corner and out of the way, ready to fetch whatever was needed.

Arent and Lukas had lifted Sebastiaan from the stretcher onto the neatly made bunk bed.

"Put him on his stomach," Niklas had advised. "His back is in a bad way."

Soon after, Arent and three crewmen had returned to the riverbank, and when Jiya had emerged from the date palms ready to fill his buckets just before sunrise, Arent had called to him.

At the sound of his name the boy had whipped around. When he'd seen Arent's familiar shape, he'd abandoned his buckets and blindly run in an uncoordinated scramble of flailing limbs toward them.

"You came for me, Effendi?" the boy had asked, disbelief clearly written on his face.

"Yes, get in the boat," Arent had ordered, and the child had obeyed without a moment's hesitation.

"In the bag," Arent had said and pointed to where a large brown sack lay in the middle of the boat. "You will pretend to be a sack of dates until we reach the ship."

"I'll be the quietest sack of dates you've ever seen," Jiya had said, and disappeared into the bag with a smile that rivaled the rising sun.

Now barely an hour later the *As-Sayf* was nearing the exit to the harbor when movement on the twin peninsulas caught Arent's eyes. Two riders were lying flat over the necks of their horses as they raced toward the forts at the tips of each headland.

"We're in trouble," Niklas said as he too spotted the riders.

"Yes, I can see that," Arent growled in return. There wasn't much he could do about the riders. Hopefully, the wind would pick up and they could move a little faster.

"They are going to close the harbor," Niklas shouted.

"Don't pay it any mind, just get us out of here," Arent called back as he rushed down the companionway to the upper deck.

"Master Dekker," Arent called to the lead gunner. "Run out the guns."

The men who were not actively engaged in maneuvering the ship beat to quarters. Today, they'd blow any obstacle blocking their way out of the water. Hopefully, that wouldn't be necessary, but Captain De Coninck believed that fortune favored the prepared, and Arent echoed the sentiment.

"Sharp eyes, Master Jacob," Arent called to the lad in the crow's nest, leaning over a gleaming falconet. The sailor was still young, only just turned fourteen and new to the crew, but a better marksman Arent had yet to see.

"What am I aiming at?" the boy called down.

"Anything blocking our way out," Arent replied.

Then the water exploded on both sides of the ship. Smoke billowed from the forts, at the tips of the headlands, as they discharged their warning shots for the *As-Sayf* to not leave the harbor. Two men were screaming into the horns from both forts, their voices mingled in the wind and the snap of the sails. Arent ignored them, but the words, *turn back*, and *fired upon*, reached him clear enough.

Two galleys, aiming to block the harbor mouth, were fast approaching from opposite sides. The three ships were now on converging courses.

"There are your targets, boys," Arent called to his gunners. "But hold your fire for now." None of the gun ports were open. The demi-culverins would have to wait for another day. Today, they would rely only on the cannons on deck.

With Sebastiaan back onboard, the men brimmed with enthusiasm rivaling a New Year's celebration, but their rigorous training kept their actions calm and controlled.

"Wave at them, boys," Arent called over the deck as they drew closer to the galleys. "They're only speculating at this point. They don't know shit until they search us. So be real nice and friendly."

Another two shots rang out from the forts, and this time they were close enough to spray the deck with water.

Arent glanced over at Niklas on the quarterdeck. The *As-Sayf* was steadily aiming for the narrowing gap between the advancing galleys and the strain of wringing every knot from the breeze was pulling at Niklas' normally calm features.

Three hundred yards. The galley crews were frantically loading the cannons, perched on their bows.

"Let the top gallants fly," Arent called, and the extra sail gave them the burst of speed they needed. One hundred and fifty yards, and the first shots rang out. Their timing was slightly off, and the port side galley fired first, followed by the starboard one.

"Hold!" Arent called to the crew. The galleys had fired too early. It would take time to load the next shot.

When the next round of shots rang out, the *As-Sayf's* stern had already cleared the gap between the advancing galleys with less than fifty feet on both sides. Their wake revealed an unfortunate confluence of events, as the smoke cleared, one of the galleys was slowly sinking, leaving her sister in a desperate struggle to avoid ramming into her head on.

The cannons on the headlands were still spitting shots at regular intervals, like a jilted mistress shouting abuse at a departing lover.

Once the *As-Sayf* passed the headlands, the wind picked up and her canvases billowed out. Niklas had her at a slight angle as she leaned into the wind, racing toward the open ocean and freedom.

# Chapter 21

It was the out-of-place, sickly sweet smell of laudanum that drew Sebastiaan from the depths of his sleep. He fought the return, tried to dive down again, to stay under. Sleep was good; sleep meant no pain. But his nose pulled the other way, like a stubborn child bent on riding the herd.

Grateful to whoever had pushed him onto his stomach, he kept his eyes closed and inhaled deeply, twitching his back muscles to test the skin, assessing how badly damaged he was after the beating he'd received as punishment for killing Dario—a death he wouldn't mourn anytime soon. The skin pulled, and the pain nudged him the last few inches toward wakefulness. There was another smell lurking beneath the laudanum's reek, faint but distinct, and it plucked at his memory; sharp, necessary, *sandalwood.*

He'd wondered when he would lose his mind, smelling things that reminded him of his uncle. It was probably some poor bastard who shat his smalls in his sleep, too tired to get up and shuffle over to the Short Drop; the corner that served as the bagnio's communal chamber pot. Their lodging was not exactly equipped with necessities to promote personal hygiene. Nonetheless, he inhaled again, trying to hold on to the familiar whiff. If shit was starting to smell like sandalwood, who was he to argue?

Not only did the smell persist, but other sensations were making themselves known, such as the pillow beneath his cheek and the feel of soft sheets around his body.

Like soldiers snapping into a straight line, the points sharply arranged themselves in order. The guards would have reported his transgression to Shaykh Ahmet, along with the administered punishment and the aftermath.

Ahmet must have removed him from the bagnio while he was unconscious. Sebastiaan's reaction to his reasoning and the luxuries surrounding him, was instant and violent. His feet hit the floor before his eyes were barely open. He fought back the nausea threatening to overwhelm him. Swaying on his feet as his legs still shook, he raised his surprisingly steady hands.

"Come here, you bastard," he growled. His throat was dry, and his voice came out wrong, but it did not matter. There was sound and that was enough. "I will strangle you long and hard, so each time you swallow, you'll see my fingerprints flashing across the back of your fucking eyes."

Sebastiaan knew he'd delivered his vow in a mixture of Dutch and Arabic, but dialect aside, the sentiment remained true.

Then the floor rolled beneath him, like the deck of a ship, and he lost his already precarious balance. Thrusting his hands forward, he tried to avoid falling flat on his face. The instinctive movement tore at his back, and he shut his eyes, grunting in protest.

"That was very poetic."

The dry, amused voice came from nearby, and then strong hands gripped his shoulders, lowering him into a sitting position on the bed. Pain shot in all directions, striking the center of his chest and spreading to every joint and muscle, from his fingertips to the back of his neck. With his bare feet planted firmly on the floor, he rested his forearms on his thighs and dropped his head between his shoulders. Breathing slowly through his mouth steadied the wave of pain.

"That's it. Breathe it out."

That voice and the smell of sandalwood made Sebastiaan's head snap up. His eyes blew wide as he stared into a face he never thought he'd see again. Shooting to his feet, he sidestepped the phantom, putting distance between himself and the figure.

He was seeing things again, like he had on the galley. It was the blasted laudanum; they'd probably given him enough to tranquilize a plow horse.

Where was Jiya? Jiya would set him straight, but if he was in Ahmet's compound, then Jiya was still at the bagnio.

"Jiya," Sebastiaan croaked.

"He's here."

This was a new development. Usually, his visions were silent. This one had a voice.

Carefully, Sebastiaan allowed himself a quick study of the room he occupied. It was small with wooden paneling on the walls, a window showing a glittering ocean, a narrow cot with a matching nightstand, a desk and chair—an officer's cabin.

"Uncle?" In less than a second, those familiar hands, which had held him as a boy, pulled him from the ocean, and saved his life, closed around his shoulders again, holding him close.

De Coninck saw the confusion and disorientation fade from his nephew's expression and when he called to him, it was all he could do to not sob like an overprotective mother. He pulled the boy close, mindful not to touch his back, he held him firmly by the shoulders while Sebastiaan's body shook against his. He held him until the storm passed.

"You're safe," he whispered. They were of a similar height, but Sebastiaan's face was buried in his shoulder, and he absorbed the ragged breaths, heavy with emotion and relief, feeling the boy's sinewy arms lock around him, as if clinging to a life raft.

"I've got you," he soothed. He waited until Sebastiaan was ready to let go and then he gently lowered him to the bed again.

A rush of emotion overcame Sebastiaan, he was shaking something fierce, and he clenched his jaw to stop his teeth from rattling.

How was this possible? How did it happen? When? Thoughts and questions were racing and clashing into each other, much like a stampede of wild beasts.

Looking at his uncle, he saw him in no better shape. He should say something, but words seemed to have deserted him. He remembered that his father often resorted to discussing the weather when he found himself in a difficult situation. Sebastiaan could hardly follow suit or say anything worse.

"This is not the *Drommedaris*," Sebastiaan said as he took a better look at the rich colors surrounding him. The rug on the floor looked particularly familiar.

"No, it's the *Annabella*." A sly, relieved smile creased De Coninck's face. "She's faster," he said with a wink.

"That she is," Sebastiaan replied vacantly. Both men nodded in agreement and then took to staring at each other again.

"You need to eat," De Coninck announced abruptly, slapping his knees, finding comfort in the practical matter, and headed for the door, nearly ripping it from its hinges in his haste to see the task done.

"Barent!" he hollered. "Food! He's awake!"

Sebastiaan couldn't remember that he'd ever seen his uncle act with such a stunning lack of naval decorum. A few moments later, a cheer rocked the upper deck as the news spread.

"The crew?" Sebastiaan asked.

"All of them, except Orion. We left him with Parmar." De Coninck pulled the chair from behind the desk. They had much to talk about.

Arent and Barent arrived at the cabin door together and, for once, the cook did not bow to the first officer's orders to wait. As soon as Arent released the latch on the door, Barent shouldered his way past, using the food tray as a battering ram.

"No backslaps," De Coninck ordered, smiling as he knew their talk would have to wait until later. The cabin felt too cramped with Arent's bulk and Barent's mothering. Reaching for the door, he pulled it open and nearly tripped over Jiya, who sat in the middle of the doorway, waiting to be let in.

Jiya jumped to his feet the moment he saw De Coninck, who nodded slightly to grant him entry. The boy brushed past him, quick as a shadow. Shoving through the others, Jiya wedged himself between Sebastiaan's spread feet on the floor, crossing his legs and squirming until his back pressed against the cot. Sebastiaan's face lit up with pure joy, and he dropped a heavy hand on the small shoulder, squeezing it gently.

Looking up, Sebastiaan found his uncle standing in the doorway. He had no words. He simply stared at him, tears blurring his vision. De Coninck nodded in reply and turned toward the stateroom, giving the rest of the men time to celebrate their brother's return.

When Sebastiaan was fed and dressed to Arent and the cook's satisfaction, they led him from his cabin to greet the rest of the crew. An old habit made Sebastiaan's eyes dart to the quarterdeck railing the instant he set foot on the upper deck, finding it empty. Everything was happening so fast, and he had trouble keeping up. He constantly had to reassure himself that he was not dreaming, that this was real.

"Probably eating, washing, and napping. In that order," Arent answered the unspoken question. "He's been guarding over you for the past week, not letting any of us near, until he was sure you'd be fine."

"A week?" Sebastiaan asked.

"He kept you under so your body could heal and your mind could rest. Come on," Arent said, pointing a finger to where the crew waited, cheering loudly and punching the air with their fists.

It was an emotional affair, old friends each taking a turn to touch him in some way. The older men ruffled his hair, the younger ones punched him in the shoulder or slapped him on the chest. Lukas, in all his excitement and forgetting how fragile his friend was, fisted Sebastiaan straight into Arent, winced and pulled his head between his shoulders when Arent rewarded his exuberance with a fierce scowl. The new lads stood with caps in their hands, eager to meet the man turned legend.

Afterward, Arent walked him to the quiet quarterdeck. Sebastiaan was tired, but the thought of leaving the deck was worse than the need to sleep. The two friends didn't speak, they just stood side by side leaning their arms on the bulwark, one watching the horizon, the other tracing the trail left on the ocean as the *Annabella* cleaved her way through the blue-green waters of the Indian Ocean.

"You're not boatswain anymore?" Sebastiaan asked. It seemed like everything had changed. Life had somehow shifted itself into a new order, and he was standing on the outside looking in, like staring through a window at a family going about their business inside.

"No. First Officer. Got the promotion the day your uncle quit the VOC. Lukas is boatswain and sailmaker now." Arent spoke without lifting his eyes from the horizon, his voice was even, almost monotone—a dead giveaway of turbulence beneath the surface.

"My uncle left the VOC?" Sebastiaan asked, taken aback. Arent nodded but did not elaborate. He wasn't one for gossip and Sebastiaan knew if he wanted to know the details, he'd need to ask his uncle. "You saved my life again." It was not a question, but a statement of fact.

"It was my turn," the reply encapsulated their friendship.

"Arent—" Sebastiaan did not get to finish his thought for Arent cut him short.

"Let your uncle do the telling," he said and then turned to look at his friend, his eyes dark and alive with some dangerous emotion. "Remember this: we only helped. You saved yourself. You kept going, you stayed alive, giving us time to find you. This wasn't just us."

Sebastiaan stared at his friend for a long time. The way Arent spoke those passionate words made him think that this was not only about him. Something was eating at Arent, something deep and unspoken. Time would tell.

Once alone, Sebastiaan watched the sun dip below the horizon. He thought he would feel something, at the very least, appreciation for the moment, or the contentment that only freedom could bring, but there was nothing, just an emptiness that stretched in all directions. How many times had he watched the sun set, knowing that tomorrow would bring the same as today? The sun would continue to do so in a never-ending cycle until one day it would be the last for him. How many times had he prayed that it would be today? It was always Danielle who'd guarded that threshold, pushing him back when he came too close. Unable to face her memory now, he turned his attention to where the last rays streaked across the water.

Sebastiaan had buried everyone dear to him, everyone he loved, himself included. They would all need to be resurrected now, along with his sentiments and feelings. It wasn't as if his life lacked purpose. There was his father's business, his business now. If only he could connect his head with his body again. Perhaps some time alone was what he needed, but to his utter humiliation, he feared being by himself.

Best to let the sun set on this day. Tomorrow, he would start anew.

"Sailor's cure?" De Coninck's words drifted to him. Turning around, he found his uncle striding across the deck with two finely crafted crystal brandy snifters, amber liquid sloshing two fingers high in the round bottoms.

Sebastiaan smiled, and reached for the glass. He was dressed only in a pair of light linen trousers, leaving his feet and upper body bare, save for the bandages wrapped around his chest. Nothing better than the ocean wind to cure his wounds. Well, that was not entirely true. A dip in the ocean would be the best cure, but that would have to wait for a windless day. No need to bring the entire ship to a halt just so he could lave his battered body. The cuts on his thighs and abdomen were healing fast, more testimony to his uncle's care.

De Coninck leaned against the quarterdeck railing, swirling his brandy in lazy circles. There was so much to talk about, so much he needed to know, but he was at a loss as to how to start. He didn't want to push Sebastiaan. The boy would talk when he was ready.

The last week had been pure agony. He'd cleaned and bandaged Sebastiaan's wounds, cataloged the many new scars, watched him battle his nightmares, listened to his tortured screams, and held him when the horrors of the last few months had driven him from the bed in a delirious state. He'd slowly been weaning him off the laudanum over the past two days, and this morning, when the boy woke with clear eyes, the sun had started to shine again for the first time since he'd received the news of the attack on the *Geloof*.

"Uncle."

De Coninck turned to face his nephew.

"I …" Sebastiaan swallowed and searched for the words he wished to say. Running his hand through his hair, he stared helplessly at his uncle before dropping his gaze to his feet. *Thank you*, sounded so barren and meaningless. He looked down, hiding the tears that threatened to fall. The need to sob like a baby was more than he could bear.

"You're welcome," De Coninck replied to Sebastiaan's unspoken words, getting that insignificant hurdle out of the way.

Sebastiaan acknowledged the gesture with a wry smile.

"How did you find me?"

De Coninck told him everything, starting with the morning in Batavia when he'd received news of the pirate attack, leaving nothing out, relaying every detail until the moment he laid him on the cot in the officer's cabin.

Somewhere during the telling, they'd moved to the stateroom, where Sebastiaan sat in one of the leather chairs facing the heavily carved desk. Being with his uncle, sitting across from him, listening to his voice, reminded Sebastiaan of the night his father had left him in De Coninck's care. That night, he'd fallen asleep, clean and well-fed for the first time in months, listening to his uncle's melodic voice. The urge to close his eyes and drift off was so strong that he dropped his head forward.

It was at the mention of Cornelia Stiens' name that Sebastiaan's chin lifted from his chest. The name pulled at his memory, and then the scene unfolded like a piece of parchment. He remembered the baby girl's body flying through the black night air when Yavuz hurled her overboard. Her mother's screams and the maid's horrified expression would stay with him for as long as he drew breath. With a groan, he pinched his eyes, forcing the unpleasant images from his mind.

"I'm sorry," De Coninck said, seeing the torment on Sebastiaan's face.

"What happened to Mrs. Bouwer? Do you know?"

De Coninck shook his head before answering. "Dead, by her own hand."

Sebastiaan remained mute, but released a long, deep breath through his mouth. Better a quick death than left to slowly wither away at the hands of her slave masters. A young woman with her looks and coloring would have been passed from man to man as entertainment until she was sick with disease. Then they would have stoned or beaten her to death for her worthlessness.

* * *

A month later, Sebastiaan's body had healed, but his mind had not.

Jiya was sleeping on a pallet near the foot of Sebastiaan's bed, limbs spread out in all directions. The boy had undergone a complete transformation since their rescue. There was more flesh on his bones and his skin glowed like polished ebony. Barent made sure that every morning there was leftover bread for the boy to tuck in his pocket, which Jiya then insisted on sharing with Sebastiaan.

"You don't have to share your food with me anymore. You know that, don't you? We will never go hungry again," he'd promised him.

"I've gotten used to feeding you, Effendi," the boy said daringly, with a shrug and a sly smile.

They had adjusted to their freedom in very different ways. Jiya grew more confident by the day and Sebastiaan more quiet.

Jiya could sleep at night, snoring even. Sebastiaan could not manage two hours before his nightmares would start haunting him. Danielle screaming. Danielle calling his name so clearly that he thought she was standing next to his bed, which had him sit bolt upright last night, searching his cabin. Danielle running, her hair wild and her clothes dark with blood.

The boy seemed to find something new and interesting every day. The crew was teaching him to speak Dutch, and the lad could swear like the best of them without a hint of an accent. They were teaching him how to tar ropes, climb the shrouds, and mend the sails. Niklas had even taken a liking to the child. Jiya spent a few hours with him every day learning how to read the binnacle, hold the whipstaff so the ship stayed true and how to read the stars to steer them by night. Jiya reminded Sebastiaan of himself at that age, and the thought drained the strength from his bones.

Sebastiaan had given up on trying to live with purpose. As opposed to Jiya, he filled his days with tasks that used to bring a smile to his face and a lightness to his step, but now it simply kept his hands busy while his mind was dying.

Three weeks ago, he'd climbed to the top spar to clew the sails, remembering the awe he'd felt the first time he did it as a young boy and every time since. It had been the same as he'd remembered, the wind in his face lifting the damp hair from his sweaty skin. Up there, he had once felt free, but that feeling was gone now. It was a balancing act, his feet dancing on the swinging footrope, with the movement of the deck far below, and his torso pressed against the spar to keep him from toppling backward, leaving his hands free to work the lines. Like a tightrope artist performing high above the ground, it required some muscles to relax and others to tense until they were as hard as stone; the key was knowing when to let go and when to hold tight.

Sebastiaan's hands stilled as he stared over the ocean. It had been as good a day as any. Letting go would have been the easiest thing to do; a slight alteration to his state of being. Then he was breathing. Soon he would not be. He had been dead either way. All it required was to relax his entire body, close his eyes, and lean backward. No one was there to stop or interfere, and he gave the thought wings, letting it grow in his mind as he slowly began to relax. He waited for Danielle to appear with her withering scowl when he had approached the line between life and death, but she was not there; it was just him and the wind.

He loosened his shoulders and shifted his feet so that only his toes rested on the footrope. As soon as he raised his arms, he would fall to the deck. Would his mother and father have been glad to see him? *I have no fear for your future. You've become the man I always dreamed you would be. I love you and I am proud of you,"* his father's words, spoken moments before he'd breathed his last, blew through Sebastiaan's memory like streamers in the wind. Sebastiaan tightened his mouth, drawing a hard line across his face. He shifted his feet to secure his balance and tensed his shoulders. Irritation and anger danced in his gut. Perhaps it would be wise to leave the clewing of the sails to someone else, at least for the foreseeable future.

De Coninck had watched his nephew ascend the shrouds to the top spar, limbs moving with the fluid grace of countless climbs. Yet a chill had settled in his gut—something was wrong. He'd rushed to the deck, heart pounding. Arent, sensing it too, had broken off his talk with Niklas, eyes fixed on Sebastiaan. De Coninck held his breath, holding back the order he'd desperately wanted to shout, instead he prayed for the wind to stay down and for the ocean to remain calm.

'*Please God, don't give him an excuse. Don't take him just yet. Let him live again,*' he'd pleaded, over and over again.

When Sebastiaan's shoulders and arms finally tensed to gain a better grip, De Coninck released the breath he was holding and vowed to throttle every droplet of air from the lad the moment his feet hit the deck. Glancing over at Arent, he saw that his first officer was equally disturbed.

De Coninck had waited for Sebastiaan on deck when he stepped from the shroud, anger burning like a furnace in his eyes.

"You'll not go up there again," De Coninck said tersely and then, without another word, had turned from his nephew.

Sebastiaan hadn't seen his uncle for the rest of that day, not until evening when De Coninck had handed him a journal.

"What is this for?" Sebastiaan had asked.

"Few have gone through what you have and lived. You have a duty to record what has happened to you and others."

That was three weeks ago, and Sebastiaan had not attempted such foolishness again for De Coninck had not allowed him a moment of solitude.

Sebastiaan opened the journal and stared at the first page, blank as the day he'd received it. He reached for the quill, dipped the tip in the ink, and noted the date on the top right-hand corner. Then he watched as a large black stain spread somewhere near the middle of the page. The words were stuck in the past, hidden somewhere in the blackness of his mind, and he didn't want to retrieve them. The page was already ruined and so he wrote a single word: *Nothing,* then smiled at the irony.

* * *

Standing at the quarterdeck railing, De Coninck watched the crew. It was a windless day, affording them time to mend sails, tar ropes and patch leaks that had sprung over the last month of good sailing weather. It was still early. Lukas and Sebastiaan were swimming the length of the ship, racing to see who could win the best out of twenty lengths.

Arent had turned from the bulwark where sailors crammed side-by-side to cheer and bet on the two swimmers, claiming he was getting too old to partake in such senseless activity. Jiya was running the length of the deck, keeping pace with the two men battling in the water below. Sebastiaan was the strongest swimmer on the crew, and most placed their money on him, knowing there was no way Lukas could win. Only the inexperienced and uninformed new boys went the boatswain's way. A resounding roar of disappointment lifted from the onlookers when Sebastiaan handed the win to Lukas, leaving the three new lads to strut the deck with wide smiles and outstretched hands as they received their winnings.

By day, Sebastiaan floated about the deck like a wraith, with Jiya as his faithful shadow. Sometimes he sat with Arent, but neither man spoke. They just shared each other's company with quiet ease. In the evenings around the dining table, he ate his food without engaging in the lively conversation, smiled belatedly at jokes, and listened without hearing. De Coninck wondered if he even knew he was eating. Barent asked him once if he had enjoyed the meal and Sebastiaan replied politely that the fish was lovely; they had liver.

"He'll be alright," Arent assured him when he saw the worried look on De Coninck's face.

De Coninck favored him with a glare that immediately slapped Arent's attention back to his plate. He'd be damned if he took advice from another barely dried behind the ears stripling whose head seemed to be screwed on backward, ever since they'd left Zanzibar. De Coninck initially believed that Arent was anxious about Sebastiaan, but even after his rescue, Arent remained in a restless state.

After dinner, De Coninck summoned Sebastiaan to the stateroom, as had become his habit every night. They would go over the events of the day, Sebastiaan would update the logbook, and then he would discuss De Vries business, while Sebastiaan listened. Sebastiaan had a brilliant business mind. What he'd done in just a few short months after his father's death was remarkable. De Coninck was doing nothing more than parroting his nephew's ideas back to him, hoping to hook his interest again.

"The *Twins* will arrive soon," De Coninck said, referring to the two new ships Sebastiaan had bought shortly before he'd set sail for the Cape of Good Hope, the journey that had led to his capture. De Vries Enterprises was three ships strong now, and he knew Sebastiaan was planning on adding more. There was also the potential purchase of a diamond mine in India. The boy would be unstoppable if he could pull his head from that dark place it was currently stuck in.

De Coninck watched his nephew as he wrote in the ship's journal, the candlelight playing with his golden hair as his head moved with the task. It had been a long time since Sebastiaan had been a boy. Circumstances had thrust him straight into a hell no one could imagine or prepare him for. He'd lived it every day knowing full well he would never see the end, but lived it, nonetheless. It had hardened him, robbed him of his amiable smiles, the sparkle in his eyes, and the lightness in his step. It had robbed him of happiness and the idea that it was allowed. Where others took to vice or tried to destroy the world around them, Sebastiaan turned inward, searching for the answers inside his battered soul, demanding them from himself but coming up short. He fought a battle against overwhelming odds, but every morning he got up and continued to fight. The simple act of washing, dressing, and eating was a victory, a victory against the darkness that threatened to close in on him.

Sebastiaan's struggles reminded De Coninck of his late brother-in-law, shortly after his wife, De Coninck's sister, had died. Annabella was the light of their lives. She was like a ray of sunshine. Her hair shone like spun gold, her eyes glistened, her smile dazzled, and her son took after her in every respect.

After Annabella's death, Abel had imploded, just as his son was doing now. It had taken Abel nearly a decade to resurface, conquer his demons, and make peace with his wife's ghost. While Abel had tried to drown himself in alcohol, Sebastiaan refused to touch it. Even the casual brandy offered every night was politely accepted but left untouched. A few nights ago, Sebastiaan had flung the laudanum into the ocean with an anguished cry, believing he was alone, unaware that De Coninck watched from the shadows.

De Coninck felt a fist tighten around his heart. He could feel Sebastiaan's anguish beating like a pulse through his own veins, and he knew that he would never turn away from his nephew, but he would not wait for the rest of his life for that golden boy to return to him. He would pull him from this darkness if it was the last thing he did.

"I said, the *Twins* will arrive soon," De Coninck repeated, injecting little flecks of irritation into his voice.

"I heard you, uncle," Sebastiaan replied as their eyes locked across the desk.

"You had those ships built to your exact specifications. They've cost you a fortune. Surely you have some grand plan for them," De Coninck prodded.

"I'll think about it later," Sebastiaan said in a defeated tone, holding his uncle's stare for an uncomfortable few breaths before lowering his eyes. *He looked down*—something he was constitutionally incapable of doing since the first instant De Coninck had laid eyes on him, no matter how scared, how hungry, or how beaten he was. Backing down was a concept utterly incomprehensible to him. Even as a newborn infant, teetering on the edge of death, he'd fought for the right to live, for every single breath he'd drawn into his little lungs.

"Goddamn it Sebastiaan! Look at me! You are not a slave any longer."

At a loss for words and appalled with himself for his outburst, De Coninck slammed the ledger shut and searched for something to throw against the wall, preferably something expensive that would shatter into a million pieces.

Sebastiaan bit down on the apology that rushed to his lips. He knew he should talk to his uncle, explain, make him understand, but how the hell was he supposed to make someone understand something he himself could not fathom? How was he to explain that they'd taken something from him, that he could never get back? That galley had killed the man he used to be. He was dead inside. What was he going to do? He couldn't go to Danielle like this—an empty shell. He couldn't manage his father's empire when his heart was beating, but his soul was gone.

*'When pride comes, then comes disgrace, but with humility comes wisdom.'*

Proverbs, he thought. He'd been reading the Bible on the nights that the nightmares would not leave him be.

The only problem was that after the death of his pride, there was disgrace, yes. There was humility, yes, but the wisdom … now *that* he was still waiting for. So, he figured if God did not keep His end of the bargain, he wasn't required to do so, either. He wouldn't hand his soul to the Devil, that he'd proved in the sultan's palace and every day afterward. His soul was his to do with as he pleased, and it bloody well pleased him to let it die. It was time for his uncle to understand the ugly, disappointing truth.

"I died on that galley," Sebastiaan's voice was indifferent and cold as it filled the tense silence.

"No, you didn't," De Coninck replied without letting a breath pass between Sebastiaan's words and his. It was the first time Sebastiaan had come close to talking about what had happened to him, but if he was going to spew drivel, he might as well shut up.

Realizing that the conversation was pointless, Sebastiaan pushed from the chair, crossed the cabin and headed for the door. His uncle would not understand. Only Cornelia Stiens would. But he was afraid to talk to her, afraid of what he might say. Besides, she was too raw and too broken, so he kept his distance.

"You've not been dismissed," De Coninck growled from behind the desk.

Sebastiaan closed his eyes and prayed for deliverance. He was bone tired and wanted solitude; hell, he even looked forward to his nightmares.

"Turn around and look at me," De Coninck snapped again. "And don't slouch in my presence, boy," he added, his voice carrying the sharp edge of a deeply displeased captain. Sebastiaan had heard that tone many times aboard the *Drommedaris*, but it had always been directed at the sailors as a group, never aimed at one man alone. They dreaded the embarrassment that came with that tone, the sting of having disappointed him.

However, he was not a child any longer, nor a sailor. His uncle was pushing him toward a precipice and the need to leap, to lose control, was so strong he could taste it.

"You are not my captain," he snarled as he whipped around, taking a step toward the desk. *His* desk.

*Finally!* De Coninck thought when he saw the fuse to Sebastiaan's anger caught fire. He pushed from the desk. The boy had bulked out nicely over the last six weeks. He was even broader than before. Good food, hard work, and the hardships of his enslavement had forged a formidable man, and there was no way he was facing that beast sitting down.

Sebastiaan's eyes sparkled with temporarily suppressed menace. It was time to set that anger free. De Coninck closed the gap between them with a step he'd often used when dueling.

Sebastiaan watched his uncle rise from behind the desk. For the first time in many months, he burned for a fight. He noted that small sidestep, the one his uncle used just before he delivered a blistering jab or a corps-à-corps which was an illegal body-to-body move in fencing. Having seen that ploy a million times, he reacted and swung a lightning-fast left fist, aimed precisely at the cheekbone, while the right came up from underneath to blister and bruise the ribs, but his uncle ducked, and sidestepped at the last instant leaving Sebastiaan with only air in front of him.

Sebastiaan turned to look for his target, his fists raised and ready, expecting a blow to land squarely on his jaw at any second, but instead his uncle engulfed him in a hug that took him all the way back to his boyhood.

The fight left his body. His uncle's arms clamped around him, once more pulling him back to life. Pulling him from the darkness.

"I've got you," De Coninck said.

# Chapter 22

It was mid-April, and the weather was deceptively pleasant, but Danielle wasn't fooled. The year before, they'd arrived at the Cape of Good Hope under glorious skies, only to be battered by storm after storm weeks after setting foot on land. Good weather in April was like receiving a smile and a cuddle from a mischievous child; you're grateful for the charming behavior but damned if you trust it.

Last week had marked the first anniversary of the settlement, but the day had passed without fanfare or notice. She'd spent the day like all the others. Her mornings before sunrise were shared with Blanx. Theirs was a peculiar friendship. She was content to sit with him, just enjoying his company. It was peaceful, and that was perhaps what Blanx meant to her—peace. He asked nothing of her, not even her company, yet she felt at ease resting her head on his shoulder as they watched the ocean turn silver in anticipation of the coming day. He didn't move to touch or comfort her; he was just there. Her rock.

Danielle loathed the beach, everything about it reminded her of Sebastiaan. She saw his hair in the golden sand and the green of his eyes in the waves as they crested. The tides could wash anything away except the memory of his footprints, for she could still feel their marks in the sand, but the beach was where Blanx found his peace and so, sit she would until sunrise. Then he would shuffle off to work on Coopman's house.

Afterward, she would spend time with Maria, sewing, knitting and embroidering small clothes for the baby, who would, by the grace of God, arrive in six months. When she could stand the tediousness of the chores no longer, she would offer a hand to Mrs. Boom in the kitchen, but help was more often than not, met with a wave of her flour covered hand and an "off with you." Which was precisely what Danielle bargained on, for she had started her apothecary again and was burning to get to it.

"We should make a special luncheon, at least," Danielle had nagged Mrs. Boom.

"Whatever for?" the old cook had inquired, not averse to the notion at all, and already narrowing her eyes as she counted the loaves of bread stacked to the side of the workbench.

"To mark the anniversary of our arrival," Danielle had informed her.

"It's today?" Mrs. Boom had shrieked. "Well child, you seem to be the only one who's noticed. The governor left this morning with the Saldanhar chief to inspect the salt pan, the forest and who knows what else. The mistress is up to her elbows in preparation for the coming of the little one and Mr. Coopman, bless his heart, is trying to keep it all together. He's even settled himself in the governor's chambers."

The day came and went with no one noticing it except for her. She was becoming more and more sentimental as time went on; it was a flaw she would have to address at some point. Finding her feet after losing Sebastiaan felt like a Sisyphean task—two steps forward, then a couple back—always with the illusion that she was making headway, only to be knocked over by a smell, a word, or the way the wind blew.

There was a time when she'd isolated herself from others, but slowly she was reaching out again, trying to forge new bonds, especially with Maria and Elsje. It was a mighty effort though, for she feared that as soon as she became attached to them, something would tear them away and so her friendships were superficial at best, but the two women seemed to be blessed with patience and understanding and were not pushing her to give more; they simply accepted her as she was.

Danielle often felt a prick of guilt. She could see their need to deepen their connection to what it was before, but she preferred to be careful rather than guilt free. Best not to attach her heart, or whatever was left of it, to anyone.

Today was beautiful and Danielle was determined not to let it go to waste. Breaking from her normal routine, she left the fort early before sunrise to forage for herbs, roots and any of the multitude of medicinal plants growing in abundance in the forest. If she left the task too late, storms would destroy most of the delicate plants she needed. If she gathered them now she could have them dried, stored, and ready for winter.

Her apothecary was slowly but surely coming together. It was a hard-fought battle, but one she'd won. After she'd secured the cattle, sheep, and ostriches from the Saldanhar for her services in helping with the difficult birth of Kuhle and Xhitha's baby, Governor Van Riebeeck had finally relented to her not-so-subtle and very persistent requests. The women of the settlement were uncomfortable about taking their concerns to the fort's physician and had secretly sought her out to tend to their ailments.

After explaining the need to the governor, he'd given her permission to treat the growing female population, and Mrs. Boom had volunteered a room at her house to be used as an apothecary. The Booms' residence was a bit out of the way, but she was not about to let that small inconvenience stand in the way of her new endeavor. In truth, she was grateful to work from there and away from the fort. Of late, Mr. Coopman seemed to loom over her whenever she turned around. He was always close by, watching her, and his disapproval of her was wafting from him like an unpleasant odor. She had no idea what she'd done to offend the man, and frankly, she didn't really care. His time would be more wisely spent securing a wife, if rumors were to be believed. Aletta Verburgh seemed to be the only one, for once, who did not care for the gossip, and whenever the women discussed the handsome man's future prospects, she turned sour and pouty. Which reminded Danielle to put aside some wheat and barley seeds for the woman to urinate on later. Aletta believed she was carrying a child again, but Danielle had her doubts. For one, Aletta was still nursing her first son, and Danielle's father had always said that women find it difficult to fall pregnant whilst breastfeeding.

Danielle hadn't told anyone at the settlement that she was planning to go into the forest, but Helm had posted guards throughout the forest to patrol the area, and she'd seen one less than an hour ago. She'd waved to him, and he had responded in kind, so she was certain all would be well.

She wanted to go up the side of the mountain today. Although it was a fair distance from the settlement, she'd marked a shortcut earlier to guide her way. The mountain was no place for a woman to scamper about; the gorges were deep and cliffs sharp and high, but at the foot and a little up, the aloe vera plants grew. She only needed to cut a few leaves, which she planned to take to Mr. Boom so he could coax them into growing in his garden.

Danielle was nearing her Medusa tree. A few weeks back, she'd spotted some wormwood, but the plants were then too tender to harvest. Crouching near the patch where the plants stood proudly tall, she dropped her bags and retrieved her dagger. She'd cut as many as she dared without harming the patch when a circle of Saldanhar men stepped silently through the underbrush.

She knew the governor was presently accompanied by their chief somewhere in the wilderness and, having been to their village twice, she felt no fear or apprehension.

Rising to her full height, she tucked her dagger in her belt and waited for them to state the reason for their sudden appearance.

Danielle recognized Kuhle, and she greeted him with a smile.

"Koba is sick. She calls your name. You must come," Kuhle's words sent a chill through Danielle.

"What happened?" In reply, Kuhle's hand closed around her arm, and he pulled her with him as they moved back into the forest. Danielle lengthened her stride to keep up and stowed questions, knowing all would be revealed soon enough.

* * *

Elias Coopman watched as Elsje placed the food on the desk, the steam from the stew lazily curled its way upward. He grumbled his appreciation and focused once more on the document spread open before him.

She was talking again; Heaven only knew what about. He never listened when she started. She was as loud as her gaudy gowns, and the screech of her voice grated on his dark mood, so he did his best to ignore her.

Elias felt like a man wearing the boots of another. Everything fit, but nothing was right. He always wanted to be in control of the settlement, always wanted to sit behind this desk, in this chamber. Now, here he was, but his power would last only a few days until the governor returned and he would become the second in command, again.

It had been a month, if not more, since Miss Van Aard's return from the Saldanhar village and since then, the Saldanhar and the governor had come to an agreement. Now the settlement was trading weekly and sometimes twice a week with the tribe. The number of cattle and sheep was almost enough for the settlement to support itself. Soon they would be in a position to start their first livestock farm. The governor had already marked the best spot, and the farmer and his family were set to begin construction of their home within the next month.

Harry had disappeared and as far as Coopman knew, according to Helm and Verburgh, he'd boarded an English ship. The supposition was that the English were exploring the eastern coastline of the continent and Harry was serving as their interpreter—*God help them.* The more pressing matter was that Harry's absence left Coopman without a means to sway the Saldanhar to trade with everyone except the Dutch, and the instant that blackguard was out of the way, the settlement was thriving and the governor was becoming more beloved by the day.

All Coopman's hard work over the last year was falling apart, amounting to nothing and two people stood at the helm of the destruction: Harry with his greed and Danielle Van Aard with her interference. The latter made his stomach churn, and he put one hand to his temple to stifle the oncoming headache and the other over his chest to soothe his heart, which was speeding up like a spooked horse.

The impossible woman would be the death of him. She showed no interest in him whatsoever, no matter how much he tried to turn her head. He had thought she would notice the large house he was building and recognize the opportunities that would come with it, such as setting up her own apothecary and even a treatment room. He was sure he'd mentioned it to her once, but he was equally sure she'd not paid his words any notice. Every other unmarried woman in the settlement had visited the site, giggling behind their hands about who the lucky lady would be to live in such luxury, because no man would go through so much trouble only to end up living by himself. All except Danielle, who seemed only interested in serving Blanx his breakfast. Time was running out, for Harry would return, and Coopman would press on with his plans, but not if Danielle was free to run roughshod over the governor. He had to contain her for his plans to have any chance of success, even if it meant resorting to force. But the governor would never allow a forced marriage, and he *had* to wed her sooner rather than later.

Thoughts of Blanx, Danielle, Harry, and the pile of broken bricks and ashes that were once his carefully laid plans, drove him into a murderous rage. He wanted to break something—preferably a neck—craving the power of his hands crushing something weaker. The best he could do was let out a guttural groan and kick the leg of the sturdy desk. His reward was a creaking of the wood and a knock on the door.

"Come!" he roared, hoping it wasn't Mrs. Boom or her silly daughter coming to collect his untouched food.

A disheveled soldier burst into the room, and came to an unsteady halt, panting heavily.

Coopman could feel his brow furrowing and his fist tightening at the idiot staring at him with frantic doe-like eyes.

"What?" he barked when the man still hadn't said a word. "Surely you didn't run all that way and burst into this room just to stand there and huff at me?"

"Miss Van Aard," the man said, swallowing before continuing. He looked like he was on the brink of crying.

"What about Miss Van Aard?" A lethal calm was settling over Coopman, lending his deep voice an edge resembling a shard of ice.

"They took her." The words finally found their way out of the fool's mouth.

"Somebody took her? Who?" Coopman asked. Instinct was warning him that something significant was about to occur and he needed to keep a level head to make the most of the impending opportunity.

If that woman somehow met her end at the hands of whomever was considerate enough to take her, half of his problems would be solved.

"Tell me from the beginning," Coopman encouraged the spluttering soldier.

"I was patrolling the forest; the eastern section," the soldier said and pointed over his shoulder toward his assignment. "I saw her entering the forest earlier this morning. She was collecting plants and such, as is her habit." The man looked to Coopman as if to ask for confirmation, but Coopman gave him nothing but a blank stare, and so the man continued.

"I followed her at a discreet distance." Seeing the trench that instantly formed between Coopman's eyes at that revelation, the soldier quickly defended his actions. "Just to make sure she was safe, but then I lost sight of her. It took me a good while to find her again and when I did, I saw that she was surrounded by Saldanhar men. Then one took hold of her arm and dragged her into the forest with them. I ran after them until I reached the spot where she'd been taken from and found these." The soldier raised his hand and only then did Coopman notice the two leather satchels. "She'd left these behind. She never goes anywhere without them."

"Are you telling me she was taken against her will—abducted?" Coopman asked, as his eyes remained fixed on the two leather bags clutched in the soldier's hand.

"I think so. Why else would she leave her things?" the soldier replied. "And the speed at which they were moving made me think they didn't want to be caught."

"Where is Captain Helm? Have you told him?"

"As the captain was out on patrol, I couldn't tell him, so I thought it best to come straight to you, sir."

"You've done well," Coopman said and reached for the satchels which the soldier promptly handed over before leaving the chamber at Coopman's directive.

This was a gift beyond his wildest reckonings. He highly doubted Danielle had gone with the Saldanhars against her wishes. She would have kicked and screamed like a wildcat had that been the case. This little twist of fate could solve all his troubles. Lady Fortune was sure smiling down on her beloved son today, and he felt his mouth quirked in return.

He had to act, and he had to act fast and decisively. Governor Van Riebeeck had left him in charge of the settlement in his absence. The governor's beloved ward and settlement darling had been abducted by a group of angry natives and, praise the saints, there was even a witness to the atrocity.

He must meet this unforgivable act of violence against the settlement with force. Governor Van Riebeeck would expect him to do everything in his power to save the girl. The woman's nemophilistic tendencies had given him the miracle he'd been hoping for.

With his new plan firmly taking shape, he walked out of the governor's chamber and through the garrison's hall with long, determined strides. If Helm was still away on patrol, he would continue without him. However, he found Helm crossing the courtyard just as he descended the steps from the main building.

"Captain Helm," Coopman called. Helm must have sensed the urgency in Coopman's gait, for he stopped dead in his tracks.

"What happened?" he asked.

Coopman took a deep breath, signaling his efforts to remain calm. "Miss Van Aard has been abducted this morning by a group of Saldanhar men whilst she was foraging for medicinal plants."

Helm's face darkened at the news and at Coopman's obvious distress. He knew his friend held the young woman in high regard, and rightly so. They all did in some form, for she'd saved the settlement more than once and many of them were alive because of her healing skills, but for Coopman, Helm suspected, the connection might be more personal. It was true, Helm's own relationship with the girl was not untarnished, but he'd come to realize that the good inside her far outweighed her volatile temper.

"Tell me everything," Helm ordered.

Coopman relayed the conversation he had with the soldier, ensuring to inject a pinch of panic here and there.

Helm held his arms clutched behind his back and his head bent as he listened to the distressing retelling of the events.

"You are in command in the absence of our governor. What are your orders?" he asked.

Every VOC ship arriving from the Netherlands at the Cape had brought a steady supply of tools, seed, furniture, and horses. Many of the horses had perished during the arduous voyages but some had made it all the way to their destination and the settlement now had a stable with no less than fifteen horses.

"Ready the horses and thirteen of your best soldiers. We leave within the hour. I am bringing her back at all cost," Coopman's voice left no room for doubt, and he saw the rightness of his orders took to flame in the captain's eyes.

# Chapter 23

A young woman met Danielle outside Koba's hut, clapping her hands in greeting before placing them on both sides of Danielle's face and drawing her close so their noses could touch. She swept aside the bone hangings covering the entrance and motioned for Danielle to enter.

A drizzle had settled over the forest shortly after she'd left the settlement. Danielle was cold, her hair was wet, and her clothes clung to her body, yet the warm interior of the hut felt like home. A fire burned in the center, the crackling of the logs harmonizing with the rain outside. The smell of herbs and animal fat scented the air. Koba was lying on her *kaross* with her back to the hut's opening, facing the wall.

"Koba," Danielle breathed the name as she neared her. Koba slowly turned over and Danielle sank to her knees next to her friend. Koba's eyes were calm, and her face was serene.

"Gorab," Koba said, and the soft sound of the name as delicate as its meaning — *My flower*.

"What is the matter? Where does it hurt?" Danielle asked, searching the frail body for obvious breaks, dislocations or other damage. Not finding any, Danielle leaned closer to touch the leathery skin, but Koba gently stopped her, grasping Danielle's hand with her bony fingers. She was so fragile, and Danielle feared the merest touch could shatter her.

"A pain has been eating at me for some time now," Koba said, her voice craggy and broken and Danielle could see the life force leaving her with every word she spoke.

"Shh," Danielle soothed. "Don't speak. I will mix something for the pain. Rest a bit." Danielle had forgotten her satchels near the Medusa tree where the men had found her earlier, but she understood enough of Koba's medicines to mix a potion that would ease her discomfort.

Koba shook her head slowly, the motion barely there.

"No. The pain was everywhere this morning, but now it is gone. My spirit will soon leave as well."

"No," Danielle said. "No, we can do something. Let me do something. Do you want me to call someone?" Danielle tried to pull her hand free so she could stand up and call for the woman outside or to start on the medicine, but Koba's grasp was surprisingly strong for someone so frail.

"Daughter, listen to me," she said, with urgency. "My words are getting fewer. Don't make me say more than I need to."

"When I'm gone," Koba gave her a direct stare, and Danielle swallowed to ease her rising distress. "You will take my place."

Danielle shook her head at the impossible words. How was she supposed to take Koba's place as healer? It was wishful thinking, as impossible as walking on the moon. Koba was the heartbeat of the tribe. Everything revolved around her.

Death was hanging over the old healer. Danielle could feel its dark presence, but she refused to lie to a woman on her deathbed.

"Koba, it's not possible. I will come from time to time to tend to the sick, but I cannot take your place. Please let me call one of the women. There must be somebody else. Tell me who, please," Danielle pleaded.

A soft smile played on Koba's mouth.

"There is only one — You." And when she saw Danielle draw breath to argue, Koba said, "It is the will of the gods. We must not argue."

"How do you know?" Danielle asked, for the will of the gods had pushed her down some very rocky paths in the past and she was no longer a naïve little lamb, who blindly trusted and followed wherever those paths led.

Koba lifted the leather pouch, hung by a braided cord around her neck, over her head and handed it to Danielle

"Open it," she said.

Danielle opened the pouch and poured the contents into her hand. An assortment of small bones landed on her palm. They were all uniquely shaped and smooth from use. Some were white, and others were yellow with age.

"They are yours now," Koba said, her voice wispy as if it was already drifting away like smoke in the wind.

"What do I do with them?" Danielle asked.

"You listen," Koba replied.

"I listen? To the bones?"

"Yes," Koba sounded tired, and Danielle reached over to take hold of her hand once more.

"Take a few drops of your blood," Koba instructed. Danielle drew her dagger and pricked her palm. "Now, let it fall on the bones." Squeezing her fist, Danielle let blood drip onto the bones. "Hold them in the fire's smoke." She stepped to the fire at the hut's center, letting the smoke curl around her hand. Koba feebly patted the spot where Danielle had sat beside her.

When Danielle returned and sat down, Koba said, "Let them fall on the ground, and tell me what you see."

Danielle opened her hand and let the bones rain down on the packed dirt floor. She stared at them for a moment, then huffed a small smile, for the bones had fallen in a pattern resembling a single bird in flight.

"I see a bird, it's flying," she whispered and then looked at Koba.

The old woman was dead, her sightless eyes staring at Danielle, the soft smile still on her lips, and her limp bony hand touching Danielle's thigh.

A clap like thunder sounded from afar, but Danielle ignored it. Heedless of time, she stared into the beloved face of her friend, while silent tears rolled down her cheeks.

"Goodbye my friend," she finally whispered as she closed Koba's eyes and then placed a kiss on the wrinkled forehead. Slowly, she collected the bones and returned them to their pouch before she flicked the thong over her neck and tucked the pouch safely into the linen binding covering her breasts.

Danielle reached for another *kaross* and covered Koba's body. Somehow it felt wrong to cover her face and so she tucked the skin blanket under her chin, leaving her to her eternal, peaceful sleep.

A second clap rent the air. This time, it pierced the fog of her sadness. Instantly alert, she knew it wasn't thunder. She jerked her head to glimpse what was going on outside, but the curtain of bones obscured her view. Then came the screams.

Danielle rushed outside but froze at the doorway as women and children screamed in terror, racing past. A mother was clutching her baby on her hip with one arm while clinging to the small hand of her other child, crying and calling for the rest to keep up. Old folk were shuffling in urgency, their thin legs moving as fast as the fused joints would allow. All were heading for the shelter of the surrounding forest. Panic gripped the tribe by the throat, shattering the peace and joy Danielle knew as its heart.

The rain had stopped, but overhead the clouds still threatened, and the air was thick with the promise of more to come. A little girl slipped and fell to the muddy ground and her frantic mother grabbed her arm and dragged her away. The girl was crying and her mother spoke to her over her shoulder with words meant to soothe but they were having the opposite effect. Danielle watched as the women and children disappeared into the darkness of the forest. She noted the men were running in the opposite direction, clutching their wooden clubs and spears. They moved in a tight group, their feet sure, and their faces hardened in response to whatever was threatening their families and their homes.

Danielle didn't know how the tribe reacted when threatened by an enemy, be it human or animal, but she knew something awful was happening. Were they under attack from one of the other tribes? Less than a heartbeat later, familiar words reached her, answering her unspoken question.

"Where is she?" The angry words spoken in crisp Dutch floated to her on the breeze and Danielle's blood turned to ice. She shut her eyes and tried to listen.

A roar came from the Saldanhar men, and then another loud clap followed the shouting, but this time she recognized it as the sound of musket fire. An eerie silence followed.

Coopman's voice rang out again as he repeated the question, and Danielle could clearly hear the unyielding authority in his tone. At first, she'd doubted her ears, thinking that she was hearing things, but this time there was no mistake. How did Coopman find his way here? Then she remembered the back-and-forth trading that had been going for weeks, between the Saldanhar and the Dutch and she knew that by now the Saldanhar, and their animals had trodden a clear footpath through the forest. Even a blind man could reach the village from the fort.

By her count, three shots had already been fired. Were they warnings? How many men had Coopman brought? Had they killed someone? That final question jolted her into action.

The Saldanhars' shouts rose sharp and urgent, panic and anger threading through their tangled words. Danielle was already running toward the disturbance before her mind could weigh the wisdom of the action. Koba's hut stood near the center of the village, and she had to weave her way past many huts and abandoned, but still hissing cooking fires, to reach the edge of the large clearing. She was passing a few women and children who ran in the opposite direction; they didn't seem to pay any attention to her, and for a split of a heartbeat she wondered if she should follow them, but then decided against it.

Danielle was out of breath when she reached the edge of the village. Her chest was burning, and her legs felt shaky, but it was the macabre scene she ran into that knocked the last bit of air from her lungs. For a stunned moment, she could do nothing but stare at the spectacle before her.

A group of fifteen proud but clearly shaken Saldanhar men stood on one side, facing an almost equal number of mounted Dutch soldiers. Each soldier was armed with a rapier and musket, the latter pointing at the Saldanhars.

The smell of gunpowder and blood hung in the air, and Danielle pushed her way through the men and then came to a stop. On the ground between the Saldanhars and the mounted soldiers lay two men—dead.

Kuhle, the proud new father, the man who'd come to collect her this morning with the news of Koba's illness, was now lying motionless on his back with a neat round wound in the center of his chest. A small, jagged stream of blood was running down the left side of his body and into the mud beneath him; his surprised, sightless eyes staring coldly past her. A few feet away, another Saldanhar, a young man she recognized as one of the sentries, was lying face down with glistening red blood coating the back of his head.

Danielle's ears slammed shut and her legs gave way as she sank next to Kuhle, searching for the beat of his heart, knowing that she would find none, but unable to stop herself. She looked up at the men standing around their fallen brothers. Their lips were moving, and their eyes were angry and confused. She turned her head the other way to look at the soldiers. They appeared calm, but eager. One was trying to reload his weapon. He was young with the softness of youth still clinging to his features, and judging by the shake of his hands, had just killed his first man. Another older soldier's musket hung limp over his arm, faint smoke still swirling around it. He released a squirt of spit when he met her horrified gaze.

Through the blur of her shock, Danielle's mind raced to piece together the chaos. One of the soldiers, probably the older one, had shot the sentry first, but why? The sentry would not have attacked the soldiers. He had likely tried to flee, desperate to warn the rest of the tribe. The boy then must have shot Kuhle, whose hand was still curved around his spear and club. If he had attacked the soldiers, he would have thrown the spear. He hadn't.

Was Helm addressing the men, or her? Danielle saw his lips move, but the words were muffled. Helm? Danielle shook her head to clear her thoughts. Helm would never have ordered this. Then her eyes landed on Coopman and the cold ripple that had started at the base of her spine exploded like stars through her body. Atop his black horse, musket trained on the Saldanhar men, Coopman's flint-hard eyes gleamed. When he spoke, his voice cut through the din, sharp and clear.

"Danielle, get up," he bit the words out. "Come here."

She could see him bare his teeth as he spoke. He was visibly trying to hold on to his rage, but she feared he would fail at the slightest provocation, and yet she could not get her legs to straighten. Her hands trembled on Kuhle, searching for signs of life, but she could only shake her head at Coopman.

"Why?" Danielle screamed at Coopman, hatred ignited in her belly. She hated him, and she hated this world.

Death was everywhere. Whenever something beautiful tried to grow, death swept in and took it away. Ever since she was a child, Death had dogged her footsteps, taking and taking until she had nothing left. First her mother, then her grandmother, her father, Antoonie, Sebastiaan, Koba and now these two men. Danielle had always been afraid of death. She could sense its dark presence and it had always paralyzed her, but not anymore. No longer would she stand back and let it destroy her world.

"I will fight you, you bastard," she hissed between her teeth. She could still feel its icy, thick presence hanging like a black cloud between the two groups of men; waiting for more bloodshed, waiting to claim another innocent soul.

Coopman mistakenly took her words as meant for him, for she stared him dead in the eye when she spoke them, not seeing how she wasn't looking at him, but rather through him. He nudged his horse toward her. It was imperative he showed no outward signs of irritation, but saints above, the woman vexed him to no end.

He could see the anger rising inside her. Letting her guttural cry wash over him, he stood motionless as she closed her hand around a clump of mud, and flung it at him. The pitiful temper tantrum did nothing more than splatter against his horse's shoulder, making the animal jerk in response. Suppressing a triumphant smile, he thought it was time to throw a spark in the oil vat.

"Danielle!" he snapped, and this time the Saldanhars surrounding her responded.

Hearing the aggression in Coopman's voice, the Saldanhars moved as one, closer to where she kneeled. Danielle knew the moment they closed the protective circle around her, Coopman would fire his weapon. That thought pushed the power back into her legs and she stood up, but then slipped, and stumbled forward. The Saldanhar closest to her—she did not know his name—reached forward, closed his hand around her arm and pulled her to her feet. Another booming explosion sounded. Danielle was flung back to the ground, landing on her side in the mud, her head hitting the man beneath her on the chest.

Stunned, she looked up. White smoke surrounded Coopman's musket. It lingered in front of his face before drifting away. She looked at the man on the ground; he was alive and screaming. Coopman had shot him in the right shoulder. The wound was not fatal, but if she didn't remove the ball, he would surely die of infection.

Danielle struggled to pull the man into a sitting position.

"Danielle, move away from that man, this instant," Coopman commanded, his voice equal in volume to his musket. This time she was quicker to move, for her own rage had finally caught up to the moment.

She jumped up, flung her arms wide and inserted herself between the soldiers and the Saldanhar men.

"Stop this madness!" she screamed, but the soldiers had already selected their next targets. She stumbled to the nearest soldier, reached up and slapped the musket sideways. "Lower your weapon, you fool," she yelled, but no one seemed to pay her the slightest attention.

"Captain Helm, please," she pleaded. "Stop this madness. Order them to cease!" She did not realize she was crying, but it mattered little, for Helm's cold blue eyes were fixed on the men behind her.

"Go to Coopman. Now," he ordered without looking at her.

She ignored him and retreated to the Saldanhars at her back.

"These men are innocent," she cried at Coopman. "What has come over you?"

"They are far from innocent. These men kidnapped you. Now, for the last time. Come here!" Coopman had reached the outer limit of his patience; she could see it in the fire burning like live coals in his eyes. His body was coiled for action. He looked ready to strike, to murder, and instinct made her take a step away from him.

In an instant, his large stallion closed the short distance between them. He reached down, circled his arm around her waist like an iron band, and lifted her before slamming her down on the saddle in front of him. Ignoring the pain in her backside, she immediately tried to slide down again, but his arm was pinning her to his chest.

"I need to tend to him," she cried. "If I don't, he will die. Please. Elias, please."

A strange look flitted across his face at her use of his Christian name, but he said nothing further and turned the horse away from the bedraggled and stunned group of men, only to come to a dead stop. Later, she would think back on that moment and would remember the deathly silence that had descended upon them.

On the edge of the clearing stood Governor Van Riebeeck, the Saldanhar chief, and six of his men that had accompanied them. The governor looked like he'd seen a ghost. His face was ashen, and his eyes were wide with shock as he took in the scene before him. The chief was the first to react. Seeing his dead tribesmen, he released a cry that sounded like a wounded animal and rushed to where Kuhle lay.

Danielle felt Coopman's arms go slack and she used the moment of confusion to jump down from his horse and run back to the wounded man, still sitting where she'd left him. She had nothing to treat him with or to lessen his pain. All she could do was slow the bleeding until she could remove the ball from his shoulder. Ripping a long strip from her skirt, she folded it into a square and placed it over the wound. The man groaned as she pressed down.

"It's going to be alright," she soothed. From the pallor of his skin, she could tell he was in considerable pain. If she could get him to Koba's hut, she could treat him. Focusing on the task at hand gave her a measure of stability and she felt herself calming down enough to gain a grip on her scattered senses.

There was noise and movement all around her, but she paid it no mind. Helm was shouting at his troops to defend the governor. Coopman was shouting at her to get back on the horse. The chief was shouting, but she was not sure at whom. An amalgamation of voices erupted as the Saldanhars tried to relay the astonishing constellation of evil and horror they'd just witnessed. She picked out some of their words. "Wood. Spitting fire. Killing without moving. Evil spirits." These men could not comprehend what had happened to them or why. They had never seen a musket, let alone one in action, and now three of their tribesmen lay dead and dying at their feet because of it.

Their confusion was obvious and heartbreaking, for they did not know why the gods were punishing them. After listening to his men, the chief turned to the governor. His face was contorted with fury. The man he'd come to trust and respect had betrayed him.

"You," he barked. Unfortunately, Danielle was so engrossed in treating the wounded man that she'd not realized the chief was speaking to her. A scream tore from her as his hand unexpectedly closed around a fistful of her hair and yanked her to her feet.

"You will tell him my words," he hissed in her face, "so he will know."

She nodded; icy fear was running down her body. She'd never seen him like this. The lines in his face were stark and edged with rage. A thick vein was pulsing in the middle of his forehead, and his shoulders and neck were rigid. Danielle stared into his cold, deadly black eyes. She was terrified. It started to rain again, and this time it was as if the heavens were trying to wash this dreadful wrong from the land below.

"Tell him, he betrayed me." Water was streaming down the chief's face and bare chest. She translated. "He took me away from my people so that his men could murder mine." Danielle was openly weeping as she relayed his words to the governor. She could not look Van Riebeeck in the eye because his face closely resembled the chief's. "Tell him he is no longer a friend of the Saldanhar, but our enemy. And I shall avenge my brothers."

With the last of his words, he pushed her forward, and she fell at the governor's feet. Her hair was plastered against her face, her shirt sticking to her body, and her teeth chattering; she knew the cold wasn't the reason for her shaking.

Governor Van Riebeeck remained completely still, as if he'd been carved from wood, and she wondered if he had forgotten how to breathe. Only when the chief pulled the injured man to his feet, and the rest of his men picked up their dead and turned toward their huts, did he speak.

"Get up," the governor ordered.

Danielle's legs were shaking when Coopman lifted her back onto his horse. She did not notice how he'd gentled his touch. Her heart was breaking. How was it possible for something that was already dead and broken to still feel pain? She would never see the village again, never sit around the large fire and watch them dance, never hear the laughter of the children. She, too, was now their enemy. The loss was too much to bear, and she turned her head and wept against Coopman's shoulder.

# Chapter 24

No one spoke a word on the way back to the settlement. The rain had intensified and by the time they climbed the fort's front steps, all were soaked through.

After a quick conversation with the governor, Helm dismissed the soldiers and then joined Governor Van Riebeeck, Coopman, and Danielle in the governor's chamber.

Danielle was tired, cold, and hungry. The handful of berries she'd gathered this morning had not been enough to sustain her during this nightmare of a day. She was still reeling from how fast everything had gone from idyllic to disastrous in the span of a few hours.

This morning she'd left the settlement long before sunrise to collect herbs for her apothecary. The breeze coming over the mountain was leaden with rain, heralding the start of the winter wet. She knew she should have collected the plants sooner, but lately her days were filled to the brim and so she'd quietly slipped from the fort before anyone could stop or call her back. The forest was peaceful as it woke to the new day, and for the first time since Sebastiaan's death, Danielle dared to look to the future with something other than emptiness.

Then the Saldanhars had come for her, bringing the news of Koba. The thought of Koba brought renewed tears to her eyes, and she felt the small pouch pressing against her skin. She was grateful her friend didn't have to witness the events that had followed her passing, events Danielle still had trouble coming to terms with.

She was dizzy and unsteady on her feet, be it from exhaustion, thirst, hunger, or shock. Staring vacantly at the room and its occupants, she felt removed from it all as if she was looking at her surroundings from a great height. Her thoughts and emotions were held tight behind a high wall, blocking them from the world, and that wall was threatening to crumble. Danielle drew a breath, about to excuse herself and retreat to her room, when she heard Coopman's words.

"The soldier Helm had posted to patrol the forest witnessed Miss Van Aard being kidnapped by several Saldanhar men. They had grabbed her by the arm and dragged her into the forest before he could intervene. Instead of following, he made the wise decision to return to the settlement and raise the alarm." All three men turned to stare at her.

She heard the words spilling from Coopman's mouth but had trouble connecting them to the events of the morning. What was he talking about? Was he implying that she was kidnapped? It was preposterous, and she shook her head to set him straight, but the slight movement aggravated the dizziness and the room threatened to tilt too far.

"He went to the place from where she was taken and collected her belongings," Coopman continued, robbing her of the opportunity to speak, and then he pointed to the two leather satchels on the floor next to the desk.

So, there they were. She figured she'd left them near the Medusa tree and would have gone back to collect them. It was a good thing the soldier had found them, for they would surely have been ruined if left in the rain for a full day and night.

"She never goes anywhere without her bags and the fact that she was forced to leave them behind was further evidence to the soldier, that she was taken against her will."

Danielle moved to reach for her bags, but her legs felt oddly stiff and her feet too heavy to lift. She was in shock. All she had to do was wait it out. Soon her hands would stop shaking and heat would creep back into her fingers and toes. It would help if she could get out of her wet clothes. Her breathing and heartbeat were uneven, but she knew from past experiences those would eventually find their normal rhythm after a good rest.

Koba's death alone was enough to knock her off balance. From the first moment they'd met, there was a connection between them, a feeling of something lost for a long time, but finally found. Danielle knew Koba was old and a little unwell, but her death had come as a surprise. She was the type of person who could heal a broken heart and a broken bone with equal efficiency; she would be impossible to replace. And then there was Kuhle. The thought of the young father made Danielle's knees buckle. Her hand searched behind her where she knew the chair must be, and then she could no longer remain standing.

Helm must have seen her sway, for he reached for her and eased her down into the chair before stepping away. Coopman was still speaking, and it occurred to her she had not listened to a word he was saying.

"There were several incidents of theft over the past two weeks. Cattle and sheep had gone missing, but without hard evidence pointing to a culprit, I did not want to react. Instead, we increased the patrols around the settlement, hoping to catch the miscreants in the act."

Van Riebeeck grew angrier with each word Coopman spoke. Everything they'd worked so hard to achieve was laid to ruin. However, he refused to voice his opinion until he had a complete picture of what had transpired in his absence.

"And so, you followed with armed soldiers?" Van Riebeeck asked as he paced the room from end to end and back again.

"I did," Coopman replied, ignoring the biting tone in the governor's question. "They've become too brazen. Not to act with extreme vigilance would have been foolish. First, they'd taken livestock, but now their acts have escalated to kidnapping. It is a high offense committed against the settlement. If we were to abduct one of their women at random, would they not react with force as well?"

Van Riebeeck pinned Coopman with a hard stare and thinned lips. He was no longer pacing, but stood like a statue with his fists balled by his sides. He appeared ready to burst into flames at any moment.

"They took my ..." Coopman deliberately caught himself, "They took Danielle." He injected a little desperation dusted with feathery touches of anger and frustration into his voice.

"If they had taken your wife," he went on, and Van Riebeeck took a menacing step toward his second in command. "Would you not have wanted me to act in the same manner?"

Coopman fought to keep the smile from his face when he saw how his words pushed the governor closer to the edge of his forbearance. Governor Van Riebeeck closed his eyes momentarily and considered the scenario. He understood how much Danielle meant to Coopman, even though she didn't, and if it had been his wife in that situation, he might have reacted worse.

"Yes," he replied, his voice rasping with emotion.

Danielle inhaled to interject, but Coopman stepped closer to her and laid his hand on her shoulder. The unexpected touch made her flinch. Feeling her reaction, he removed his hand and continued.

"The soldiers were only meant to intimidate; a show of force, if you will. Nothing more," Coopman tried to placate the governor.

"Yet two men are dead, and one is badly wounded," Van Riebeeck retorted.

Coopman hesitated. He must choose his words carefully; the governor was in a belligerent state, which made him very dangerous. A tense silence stretched until Helm filled it. Coopman inwardly breathed a sigh of relief.

"I take responsibility for that, sir."

"Explain," Van Riebeeck's command sounded painfully patient.

"Governor. Please. I think —" having finally found her voice, Danielle seized the slight pause before Helm started his explanation.

"Let Captain Helm finish," Van Riebeeck said as he held his palm up to her.

"The first Saldanhar was killed by accident," Helm explained. "He emerged from the forest so silently and without warning that it startled one of my men, and he fired his weapon. I do not think he meant to kill the man, but the situation was tense, and the soldiers are not used to conflict such as this."

"What about the second?" Van Riebeeck asked.

"After firing the first shot, the men from the village came at us in a group.

They were agitated and armed, and we fired a second shot as a warning."

"Did they attack?" Van Riebeeck interrupted Helm.

"No Sir, not at first." Van Riebeeck's face darkened at the comment. "After noticing their dead tribesman, there was a moment of confusion in which Mister Coopman tried to de-escalate the situation, but when he asked for the girl to be returned to us, the Saldanhars became aggressive. One man stepped forward with his weapons raised and tried to grab the musket from Pieters, at which point the boy fired his weapon in self-defense."

Danielle listened to Helm's explanation, and with each word, her strength returned to her. By the time he finished, she was on her feet.

"Self-defense?" she spat. "Helm, were you born yesterday? Surely you must have some prior military experience to merit your position — "

Not one to suffer an insult lightly, Helm did not allow her to finish her attack.

"Miss Van Aard, I am not your enemy, though you've treated me as such on more than one occasion."

Helm did not raise his voice, but a tick had started near the top of his jaw and Danielle knew he was not as composed as he appeared.

"Yes, you are right. You are not my enemy," Danielle spoke impetuously. She was going to point out that she'd only once before treated him in an unfriendly manner but thought it best to let the matter go for now. "You just lack the aptitude to understand anything beyond what you can physically observe."

Helm had gone deathly silent. The only sign that her insult had hit its mark was the flaring of his nostrils, and the anger that flitted through his eyes like the gleam of light on a knife blade.

"Danielle, that is enough," the governor muttered between his teeth like someone displaying acute symptoms of lockjaw. "Sit down," he ordered and pointed to her freshly vacated chair. "You will not interrupt again, or I shall have you removed from this chamber and brought back in when we are done. Is that what you want?"

"No, sir," she said.

"Then sit down and hold your tongue."

"I shot the third man," Coopman said hastily. Helm would never point a finger at him. The man's loyalty was bordering on ecclesiastical. "By then, we had the situation more or less under control. It was when Miss Van Aard appeared that the mood shifted. The Saldanhar men were not keen on letting her go and were trying to form a circle around her. When one of them tried to pull her back with them, I shouted a warning. He ignored me and I shot him. However, I made certain the shot was not fatal." Coopman paused, closed his eyes, and massaged his forehead as if to erase a headache. His shoulders slumped, and he had a pained expression. "It was a most unfortunate incident, but unavoidable. If there was another way, I would have taken it. But her life was at stake, and I was not prepared to let any further harm come to her."

Danielle sat back in the chair and threw both her hands in the air. It was like listening to a fantastical story read from a book. The testimonies coming from Helm and Coopman were undiluted, homebrewed horseshit.

Van Riebeeck breathed a deep sigh and lowered himself into his chair behind his desk. He looked tired.

"Is there anything more you wish to add?" he asked as he looked from Coopman to Helm.

"No, you arrived at the scene shortly after that," Coopman concluded.

"The Saldanhar chief believes me to be his enemy. He believes that I deliberately lured him away from the village, allowing for the attack to happen." Van Riebeeck didn't speak to anyone in particular, merely voicing his troubled thoughts.

"People often accuse others of their crimes," Coopman offered sagely.

"What is your meaning?" Van Riebeeck asked, looking perplexed as he turned his attention to Coopman.

"The timing of the incident is peculiar. The Saldanhars waited until you and their chief were well away before they abducted Miss Van Aard. Could it be that the chief had planned to use Danielle as a pawn to stir trouble with the settlement?"

Words were crowding on the tip of Danielle's tongue at the outrageous statements, but she held them back.

Van Riebeeck nodded contemplatively. Then, after a long moment of silence, he looked at Danielle.

"Tell me what happened." For the first time that day there was a gentle note to his voice, and it gave her hope.

"I was not kidnapped."

"Danielle." Van Riebeeck tilted his head to his shoulder as he regarded her. "You don't have to defend the Saldanhars' actions. What's done is done. You've survived a day filled with violence you should never have been exposed to."

Shutting her eyes in frustration, Danielle shouted, "I was not kidnapped!" Her voice bounced off the walls and the stunned faces of the three men. "I was not attacked, and nobody dragged me off into the wilderness, nor did anyone try to keep me there." Her temper was now well and truly lit, and it was becoming increasingly difficult to control it.

Somewhere along her few shouted statements, Governor Van Riebeeck's gentle and understanding mood had shifted, leaving him glaring at her through slitted eyes.

"You will not raise your voice in here. Ever. Do you understand me?" Any trace of warmth or kindness evaporated from his voice like steam from a boiling pot. Danielle was too angry to respond, so she simply sat in her chair and stared at the governor's chest.

Van Riebeeck knew that waiting for an apology from the headstrong woman was an exercise in futility. She was as stubborn as he was, and he was not in the mood for a contest of wills. Better to get to the heart of the matter.

"There was a witness to the kidnapping. Captain Helm and Mister Coopman witnessed the aggression against you in the village, and yet ..." Van Riebeeck looked lost. "I don't understand. Please explain this to me. How can three people see one thing while the victim, claims another?"

She wanted to scream that she was not a victim but thought it best to start as calmly as she could at the beginning. Danielle explained how she was collecting healing plants in the forest when the Saldanhars found her with the news of Koba's illness.

"So, you left to tend to a sick woman without your bags?" The question was heavy with skepticism.

"Yes, my bags were empty except for the fresh herbs I'd cut this morning." Danielle shook her head. "I simply forgot them. I was so stunned by the news that I followed the men without a second thought."

Something shifted in the air between Danielle and Van Riebeeck, and she wondered if she'd said something to upset him. His face had grown stone cold, and his eyes bored into hers, but she wanted him to know the truth and so she continued her recount of the day. He would soon understand that Helm and Coopman made a grave mistake, borne from a mere misunderstanding.

"Koba passed away shortly after I arrived," she explained. "I was still in her hut when I heard the first shot ring out. I didn't understand at first what it was, but when the women and children started screaming and running from the village, I knew something terrible had happened." Danielle could feel her throat thicken, and she swallowed several times to regain her composure. "I heard Mister Coopman's voice, and it was the anger in it that made me run toward the disturbance." She did not dare to look at Coopman. The man disgusted her. What he'd done today was just short of murder, for the man he had shot would not survive without proper care. "When I reached the clearing by the river, I saw two men dead on the ground. Kuhle was one of them. I helped his wife with the birthing last month. He was the father of a one-month-old baby boy." She turned to Helm, who had the grace to hang his head at her words.

"He'd tried to disarm one of my soldiers," Helm retorted, the passion she'd detected earlier now gone from his face and he looked like a man who wished he could rewind time.

Danielle felt a stab of sympathy for him but quelled it as soon as it flickered to life. "I was not there when Kuhle was shot. So, I can't say if it was justified or not, but know this: these people have never seen a musket before. The deadliest weapons they have are the spears in their hands, which they have to throw to inflict damage. They do not understand that the musket can kill from a great distance with minimal movement from the man holding it. He probably thought the soldier was pointing a stick at him."

"Then his ignorance led him to his death," Coopman stated.

"It wasn't ignorance, it was innocence," Danielle protested as she stared at the governor.

"Then why did the third man try to drag you back into the village with them?" The governor asked.

"He didn't, I slipped in the mud and would have fallen had he not reached out to support me. Mister Coopman misunderstood the gesture and fired unnecessarily." This time she looked at Coopman, but immediately wished she hadn't. His eyes were gleaming in the candlelight and the look on his face made goosebumps rise on her arms. If ever the devil needed a face, he'd need not look any further. His handsome features were hard and emotionless, as if molded from iron, and his eyes shone with searing intensity.

"I think I have a clear picture of what transpired today," the governor said, and his calm words drew Danielle's attention back to him.

"Captain Helm." Van Riebeeck did not rise from his seat, but the captain of his guard snapped to attention. "Double the guards. We will meet early tomorrow morning to discuss the possibility of a Saldanhar attack. Who is your best guard?"

"Van Eck," Helm replied immediately.

"Good, send him to wait outside the door please and then you are dismissed." Helm clicked his heels and left the room with long, confident strides.

"Governor, it's been a long day and I need— ," Danielle was about to excuse herself, but the governor's gruff voice cut her short.

"No, you will stay," he said. "Mister Coopman, please take a seat." Van Riebeeck pointed to the vacant chair next to Danielle.

Coopman took the seat, leaned back, and crossed his ankle over his knee.

"Danielle," the governor addressed her. "You left the settlement this morning telling no one where you were going or for how long. Is that correct?"

Danielle frowned in confusion. "Yes, but I've done so, many times." The governor nodded.

"I am aware, and I am also to blame," he remarked, as a look of regret clouded his eyes.

"I don't understand," she said.

"You are my ward, and under my care and supervision, and I have been lax in my duties." The frown line between Danielle's eyes deepened. The conversation was veering in a direction she did not trust.

"I let you run free and wild and do as you please. Giving you too much rope and, in the end, you've hanged not just yourself, but all of us." Seeing the confusion on her face and how she struggled to object, he held a staying finger and continued. "You come and go as you please, with no regard for your safety. You say what you will, and to whom you wish, with no forethought or consideration. You act on impulse and do exactly as you please without any thought as to the consequences of your actions."

Danielle was shaken to her core by the words that seemed to flow like water from the governor's mouth. The words came so easily, as if he'd been waiting to speak them for a long time. She should say something, stand up for herself, defend her actions, and as soon as her tongue could remember its task and her mind could command it, she would.

"I am not angry with you. I am angry with myself for letting you behave in this destructive manner. You have saved this settlement more than once, and for that I owe you a debt I thought I could never repay, until now."

"What?" she breathed.

"Had you told anyone where you were going this morning, none of this would have happened. Had he known of your plans, Mister Coopman would have sent a guard with you whom you could have sent back to the settlement with the news of Koba's distress. There would have been no need to rush to the Saldanhar village to rescue you, and there would have been no deaths or misunderstandings. And we would still have the Saldanhars as our friends and trading partners." He let his words sink in. "As it stands now, we are at war with the Saldanhars, and our supply of cattle and sheep are cut off. Your actions have placed the entire settlement in jeopardy. It is not your fault," he was quick to add. "It is mine, for I've allowed you too much freedom."

To hear her actions laid out in such a harsh light robbed her of a defense.

"I never meant for this to happen," she swallowed, feeling hollow inside. She wished she could cry, or scream, or beg, but there was nothing, just this infernal emptiness that seemed to stretch from top to bottom.

"I know. You always mean well, but things have gone too far this time. You need someone to take care of you, to guide you. To keep you safe."

"What do you mean?" She pushed the emptiness to the side and stood up, instinctively taking a step toward the door.

"Please sit down," the governor ordered and waited until she was seated again before he spoke. "It is time for you to marry."

"No!" she cried.

"Yes," he said in a calming voice. "You are well past the age where most young women do."

"For the love of God!"

"Don't blaspheme," Van Riebeeck reprimanded.

"Who do you want me to marry?"

"Mister Coopman."

"What?"

"Tomorrow."

She looked from the governor to Coopman. The latter gave her a languid smile, looking utterly pleased with himself. The governor looked resigned.

"Have you both lost your minds?!" she was shouting again, but it could not be helped. "I will not!"

"Yes, you will. We will give you the night to get used to the idea and tomorrow morning at ten you will marry Mister Coopman.

"Van Eck," the governor called, and the guard opened the door.

"Take Miss Van Aard to her room and guard the door. You will be relieved in the morning."

"Sir." The guard acknowledged his orders and took Danielle by the elbow to lead her from the room.

She pulled her arm from his hand as she left, and Van Eck closed the door behind her. There were many hours between now and ten. Enough time to come up with a plan, for she would *never* marry Coopman.

# Chapter 25

Elias Coopman married Danielle Van Aard in a solemn ceremony that lasted precisely thirty minutes. Two guards stood post outside the doors of the fort's dining hall in case the bride bolted.

Danielle wore an ash gray dress, much to Elsje's horror, and with not so much as a twig in her hair for decoration. Her friend said the color drained her. Danielle did not know what that meant, but in her mind, the color fit the occasion perfectly.

Maria had come to her shortly after midnight, knowing that Danielle would be in distress and unable to sleep.

"Jan told me what happened today," she'd said as she sat down on the bed next to where Danielle was lying on her side, staring into the night.

"It is all my fault. I've destroyed everything he's worked so hard to build," Danielle said as she pushed up to sit with her back resting against the wall. Maria reached and smoothed a lock of hair away from Danielle's face, the gesture gentle and motherly.

"What's done is done. We need to move on and look to the future. Chastising yourself will fix nothing." Maria was ever practical, especially with the problems of others.

"The future? I must marry Coopman in the morning." Danielle shook her head. "I don't think I can do that." Her voice was soft, desperation wrapping around each word and filling every space between. "I hate him, Maria," she confessed.

"No, you don't," Maria replied instantly. "You're frightened and tired, but you don't hate him. It's not in you to hate, my darling." Maria gave her a pointed look. "Many women would give their two front teeth to be in your position tomorrow." There was a mischievous glint in her eyes, and Danielle knew it was a lost cause. Maria would never understand.

"Then one of them can marry him," Danielle scoffed, and wished she had something stronger to retort with.

"He doesn't want any of them. He wants you."

Danielle huffed in irritation. The man didn't want her because of some infatuation or attraction. He only wanted what he couldn't have.

There was something about Coopman that bothered her. Whenever she was near him, a spark of caution flared inside her, one she couldn't reason away. It was pointless to voice her concerns; she had no evidence on which to base her trepidation.

"Danielle," Maria's voice suddenly held a serious note. "You have to stop running."

"What do you mean?" She was too tired to argue or decipher riddles.

"Since Sebastiaan's death, you've run from one place to the next. It's time to take the next step. You cannot live your life in limbo."

"Are you telling me it's time to grow up? Time to act like the adult I am supposed to be?" Danielle asked, a melancholy smile decorating her face.

"Not in so many words, but I guess it's what it comes down to. He's a good man Danielle, you might not love him right now, but time can change that." Maria shrugged.

"Was that how it happened for you?" Danielle asked.

"No," Maria said with a soft smile. "Ours was a love match from the beginning."

Running, distractions, growing up—it mattered little, for somewhere between before and now, Danielle had made up her mind. She would marry Coopman, going against the vow she so vehemently made upon leaving the governor's chamber. She would marry him because her reckless behavior had robbed Xhitha of her husband and their son of his father. She would marry Coopman and every day for the rest of her life she would spend as penance for what she'd done—a life for a life.

"In the name of God, I, Elias Pierre Coopman, take you, Danielle Van

Aard to be my wife, to have and to hold from this day forward, for better, for worse, for richer, for poorer, in sickness and in health, to love and to cherish, until death do us part. This is my solemn vow." Coopman's rich, sonorous voice rolled through the hall. He was holding her left hand in his, and she felt a cold heaviness slide along her fourth finger. She swallowed then looked down at her hand. A simple gold band gleamed back at her.

"My mother's," he whispered, giving her fingers a gentle squeeze. His hand was warm, but his eyes were cold. Somewhere behind her, someone sniffed loudly and there was a rustle of clothing. It was her turn to recite her vows.

Her response was tentative at first, but inexorable all the same. Turning back was not an option. She might be all the things the governor had accused her of, but she was not a coward. Toward the middle of the recitation, she'd forgotten the words, and the pastor reminded her with impatient words and a disapproving frown. When she finally completed her vow, the pastor snapped his *Bible* shut and announced a somber hymn to conclude the ceremony.

There was no wedding feast. The ceremony had come as a surprise to all. Mrs. Boom had neatly burst into tears when she was told that morning and realized that she had a total of three loaves in the kitchen.

"My darling girl, this is such a joyous occasion and I have nothing prepared," she'd wailed.

Standing next to Coopman, with a flat smile slapped on her face, Danielle listened as every man and woman of the congregation stepped forward to congratulate and wish them well. Coopman thanked each in his calm, deep voice, sharing smiles, backslaps and even allowing several women to hold his hand while they pretended to include Danielle in their honeyed words. She did not care about their subtle yet inappropriate advances and wondered if she ever would.

Danielle stopped listening to the conversations and let her mind drift. Sebastiaan's green eyes flashed before her as unbidden and unexpected as a gush of rain on a sunny day. His scent filled her nose, and she drew in a sharp breath, trying to keep it in her body while searching for more. The sound must have drawn Coopman's attention, for he gave her a questioning look. She replied with a faint smile and a light shake of her head, and he turned back to his conversation.

*'I miss you so much.'*

"Did you say something?" Coopman asked. Danielle felt her eyes widen. Had she said the words out loud?

"No," she quickly answered, her voice shaking just a little. Once more he turned away from her, but this time there was a slight thinning of his lips, a telltale sign of his irritation—she'd seen it many times before.

Soon, a crowd had drawn Coopman away, and she was blessedly left on her own.

"I'm never going to see you again," Elsje said as she grabbed Danielle's hand.

"Where did you come from?  I just saw you outside, talking to Gijs," Danielle smiled as she mourned the loss of her solitude. "Of course, you'll see me again. I'm not leaving the settlement."

"Yes, but you'll be busy now with all your new responsibilities and you'll probably visit with other married women, and I'll be all alone with no one to talk to." Elsje spoke without pause, the words tumbling over each other as tears pooled in her eyes.

Danielle flung her arms around her friend and hugged her tightly.

"Oh, you silly girl. I love you with all my heart."

"I love you too. Why did you wear this ugly dress?" Elsje asked between her sobs as she noisily wiped her nose on the back of her hand.

Danielle couldn't help but laugh. "It matches my mood."

"I'm sorry for the way things turned out. I know this is not what your heart desires." Elsje was not in the habit of speaking on serious matters. Her life was filled with laughter and color and lots of noise, but when she did, everything quietened down, as if the world stood still to listen.

"You love him still?" Elsje did not have to qualify *him*.

"I always will," Danielle said, exhaling deeply, and a nervous giggle escaped her. "But we can never speak of this again," she said and gave Elsje another tight hug.

"There you are," Mrs. Boom's voice drew them apart as she and Maria made their way to where Danielle and Elsje stood. Mrs. Boom's cheeks were bright red, and Maria's eyes sparkled. They were both caught up in the excitement of the moment.

"Everyone's so happy for you both," Maria said, as she stared at the smiling faces milling about the hall and the courtyard beyond. Everyone was always happy and smiling on Sundays after the sermon. Life in the settlement was busy, and this was the only time they got to unwind and catch up on news and gossip.

"One would think that for the settlement's first wedding, he could have chosen a less serious sermon," Mrs. Boom put in, pointing her chin in the pastor's direction before turning her back on him. "Never liked the man much. He reminds me of a vulture." They all stared at her in astonishment. "What?" she asked, unperturbed. "His neck is too long; his head is too small, and his body is too big."

"Mother," Elsje reprimanded. "Lower your voice, at the very least." The light dancing in her eyes took the sting from her words, and Mrs. Boom shrugged in response.

Maria gently laid her hand on Danielle's forearm. "Dear, your husband asked that we escort you to your new home."

*Her husband,* the words slithered through her and she shivered. Danielle closed her eyes and fisted her hands, hiding her reaction from her friends. Stifling another sigh she nodded instead.

"Hendrik and Gijs took the trunk with your belongings earlier. So, you see, everything is ready and waiting for you," Mrs. Boom crooned and took a firm hold of Danielle's free hand.

"Come, my darling."

Danielle felt like a puppet with only one string and allowed the women to pull her along with them. A feeling of wanting to call something back niggled somewhere in the depths of her mind. She turned to say goodbye to Governor Van Riebeeck, but he was standing with his back to her, deep in conversation with the pastor and the bookkeeper.

Coopman's house was on the far side of the settlement. They passed the fruit orchards, then followed a well-trodden path through the wild, untamed underbrush. Heavy clouds covered the sky and Danielle hoped the rains would hold off until her friends were safely back at the fort.

The house stood proud with its freshly whitewashed walls, pitch black thatched roof and newly painted green, double front door. It was surrounded by the colors of autumn, and tall trees. Here and there she spotted the vibrant red and orange of proteas growing amidst the shrubbery. As if waiting to overrun the house, nature was held back only by the deliberate, ruthless clearing in front, a stark claim to civility. She smiled at the effort.

"It is lovely, isn't it?" Maria remarked, seeing Danielle's wistful expression. "Apparently, there is a stream nearby rumored to be the most beautiful of all. Oh, Danielle, everywhere I turn I see a scene begging to be painted."

Following in the direction of Maria's pointed finger, Danielle could hear the stream babbling its way through the trees. The house was near the edge of the forest and through the tall trees she could see the Atlantic glimmered moody and dark beneath the oppressive clouds.

"It is very isolated," Danielle replied.

"Private," Maria corrected with a secret smile.

"Well, Mistress Coopman, are you going to invite us in?" Mrs. Boom asked. Danielle stared at the older woman with a dumbfounded expression. Danielle Coopman, not De Vries. She swallowed, took the two long steps to the front door, and laid her hands on the brass door handles.

The smell of linseed oil and clay greeted her as she stepped into the dark space. Coopman designed the house in the shape of an H. They entered the large room that stretched the width of the house. To the right was the kitchen and hearth, the dining area in the center, and to the left, an empty space with an enormous fireplace, perhaps the sitting room. Tall glassless windows with dark green shutters let the midday light in. The air was strikingly still. The dense trees encircling the house shielded it from any strong gusts. Danielle could imagine the sun streaming in through those windows on a cloudless day, warming the cold stone floor.

A sturdy dining table and six chairs adorned the center of the room, standing between the front door and the hallway beyond. It begged for a vase of wildflowers, one which Danielle would fill as soon as she knew she owned one. She could see Mattheys' craftsmanship in the furniture, sturdy and functional, yet beautiful in its simplicity. Another table, more robust than the one in the dining area, was placed against the kitchen wall beneath empty shelves.

"I guess the bedroom is at the back of the house?" Elsje wondered, and Danielle could hear the astonishment in her voice.

"I guess," Danielle said, but she made no move to explore any further. The house was large, sparsely furnished, and imposing. She'd seen it a few times during construction, when she'd brought food for Blanx and Van Leyen, but she'd never paid it any attention, never thought that she would be the one living in it. It looked like it would still be here in two hundred years, and, for some reason, that thought unsettled her.

"It is unusual," Elsje noted. "Normally, the bedrooms would be at the front of the house."

"He doesn't like the smell of the hearth to infiltrate the bedclothes," Maria answered. "And so has ordered the builders to place them at the back."

Danielle wondered how it was that everybody knew so much about her new husband, and she cared so little.

"Come my dear, there is no need to be frightened," Mrs. Boom said in a tone Danielle had heard a thousand times, one that arguing against was pointless.

Two bedrooms separated by a washroom filled the back of the house, and like the rest, it was sparsely but efficiently furnished. In the bedroom on the left, a large four-poster bed dominated the room. Most people slept on straw pallets on the floor and Danielle recognized the privilege. A tall washstand filled one corner, proudly displaying her washbowl and pitcher. At the foot of the bed stood her trunk containing everything she owned.

Her friends had done so much in such a short time to make her feel at home, and she was deeply humbled by their efforts. Danielle's eyes drifted back to the bed. It was covered in crisp white sheets and a beautiful patchwork counterpane.

"Where did all of this come from?" she wondered.

"Mister Coopman is a wealthy man who did not come here with nothing. Also, he had household goods shipped from Holland with every opportunity. Jan had put the construction of the fort on hold to free Mattheys and the other carpenters to finish this house first. He owes Elias a lot," Maria replied, as she ran her hand over the colorful bedcover.

"There is fresh water in the pitcher. Do you want me to light the fire in the front-room?" Mrs. Boom asked.

"No," Danielle breathed. "No, I can do that, but thank you." She reached for the older woman's hand and gave it a firm squeeze.

"Your husband will be here soon. We shall leave you to familiarize yourself with your new home. I will send a basket of food tomorrow," Mrs. Boom said with a warm smile before she engulfed Danielle in a hug. Maria lingered a while after the Booms left.

"Danielle," she asked.

"Yes?"

"About tonight." Maria's pale skin colored violently at the thought of the impending conversation.

Danielle huffed a smile and rolled her eyes. "Please Maria, I'm a healer. There is nothing I haven't seen before, and I have delivered more babies than I care to count. I might be a virgin, but I am a long way north of uninformed."

Clearly relieved at Danielle's bold statement, Maria made to follow the other two women. "I shall come by on Tuesday," she promised.

"I would love that," Danielle replied and then listened as their footsteps echoed down the hall, followed by the closing of the front door.

And then she was alone. The house smelled new, and the air felt cold. She lowered herself carefully onto the bed. The mattress was firm but not uncomfortable. The urge to run out the backdoor in the washroom and into the forest was overwhelming, but she nipped it before it could blossom into action. She was not a coward; she would not run.

Danielle did not know how long she sat on the bed, but she didn't get up until she was certain her feet's desire for escape had well and truly died.

Evening sounds drifted through the open windows and the encroaching darkness filled the house with a grayness that frightened her. Through the windows, she saw the dark forest on all sides of the house and for the first time since coming to the Cape, it stirred a chill that made small hairs on the back of her neck rise.

With darkness creeping in, she hurried to find a candle. Near the hearth, she discovered a pile of candles and a flint box, lit one, and set it on the dining table. Turning to her first task in her new home, she closed the shutters to seal the house against the outside world, making it safe and warm. In the empty sitting room, she kindled the neatly stacked wood in the fireplace, poking and prodding until it roared to life, bathing the space in a welcoming orange glow.

The place was beautifully made she thought as she ran her hand over the smooth stone of the fireplace. Blanx and Van Leyen had laid every stone in this house. They'd built it with their bare hands and a few rudimentary tools. She would be happy here, she vowed silently. Every day Blanx and Van Leyen lived with the consequences of their actions and so would she.

Slipping her hand into her dress, she drew Sebastiaan's letter from her bodice. Yesterday's rain had drenched her shirt and turned the letter tucked within sodden, its ink bleeding into a hopeless blur of melted words. It was impossible to read, not that she needed to. Every word was carved onto the walls of her heart. She looked at the bottom of the page. His name was just a smudge, the *S* still taller than the other letters. Raising the pages to her lips, she gave it a lingering kiss, closed her eyes, and inhaled deeply. It was time. Then she tossed it in the fire and watched the sharp yellow glow as the flames consumed it.

This was the last time she would cry over Sebastiaan, she promised herself as she walked to the bedroom. In her heart, she knew tomorrow she would make the same promise and the day after that, but one day she was going to make that promise and keep it.

Placing the candle on the floor, she opened the trunk. At the top lay a crisp white nightgown with an ivory ribbon tied in a sweet bow surrounded by delicate pink flowers embroidered around the neckline. A small note fluttered to the floor as she lifted the delicate garment from the trunk.

*My Dearest Friend,*
*I've worn this only once—on my wedding night.*
*May it bring you the same happiness it has brought me.*
*All my love,*
*Maria*

Danielle quickly washed in the cold water, using the rose petal soap, and then slipped Maria's nightgown on. For once she was grateful there was no looking glass, for she did not want to see the tension she felt in her shoulders and the stiffness of her cheeks.

Combing her hair until it was free of tangles, she let it fall smoothly down her back. Then she dug through the trunk for her own blanket and her only book. She felt out of place and unsettled. The bed seemed foreign, and she didn't want to get in it. The floor was cold, and the wind was whispering through the forest, disturbing the leaves on the trees, making them rustle as if calling out to something.

She missed the fort. Even in the quiet of her little room, she knew there were others nearby, a guard patrolling the wall, Maria in her apartment, soldiers in their quarters. Here it was only her.

With the thin foot blanket wrapped tightly around her shoulders, she rushed back to the dining room, chose a chair, and positioned it near the fire. She wondered where her husband was, and at the same time was grateful that he was not home.

Looking at the book in her lap, her eyes drifted to the golden ring, still foreign to her hand as it glimmered in the firelight.

Absently she traced the embossed title on the book's cover, '*Pedanius Dioscorides' De Materia Medica*'. It was a newly translated version with beautiful watercolor images of medicinal herbs; a generous gift from a grateful ship's captain, suffering from what he thought was an incurable stomach ailment. As soon as the sun rose tomorrow morning, she would start her herb garden. The second bedroom could be used as an apothecary and treatment room for her patients, should they wish to walk the distance to her house. It was a bit out of the way, but like Maria said, wonderfully private.

The sound of hooves pounding the ground drew her from her plans. *Elias.* Her palms instantly dampened, and her breath flattened. She tried to keep reading, tried to look nonchalant, but the act took immense effort. There was no point in pretending. She was never good at it, anyway. So, she closed the book and waited for the door to open. After long, drawn-out minutes, it did. Rather, the twin panels burst inward, allowing a gust of cold wind and the dark shape of Elias Coopman to enter the warm house. He looked disheveled, his short dark hair stood on end as if the wind had swept through it and his clothes clung limply to his body like the sails of a ship caught in a storm. It must be raining again; she hadn't noticed.

Danielle felt her heart slam in her chest as it counted the seconds he stood in the door, staring at her. She shivered, without feeling cold, and yet all the heat seemed to drain from the room.

"Will you close the doors?" she asked, her voice sounding thin.

Letting his eyes travel the span of the room, he slowly turned and pushed the doors shut before sliding the cast iron lock in place.

The clicking of his boots on the stone floor and the snapping of a log in the fireplace were the only sounds she could distinguish above the pounding of her heart as he strode toward her. The tempo of her apprehension rose with every step he took.

"Do you like your new home?" he asked and lazily swiped an arm out to encompass the room and everything beyond.

She nodded, "Yes." The tension in her stomach made it difficult for the sound to form as it should, and the reply came in a tight whisper. She cleared her throat and tried again. "Yes, thank you."

He came to stand before her, causing her breath to shake through her nose. With a swift motion, he kicked her feet apart before stepping between her legs. She inhaled sharply at the callous gesture, silently raising her chin to meet his gaze, seeking comfort and assurance but finding none.

Noticing her distress, his mouth flattened into a hard smile and his eyes bored into hers with a heat and intensity enough to incinerate brimstone.

Danielle felt like a rabbit trapped in a snare.

"You frighten me," she breathed, not caring that her voice lacked power.

The smile dropped from his lips, and his face hardened. Firelight flickered in his eyes, now vacant at the edges, as he swayed slightly, leaning down toward her. He was drunk. Fear liquefied inside her before blossoming into a full wave of panic.

"Yes, sweetheart. You should be. It is time for you to start walking on eggshells." An acute sour stab of alcohol laced the breathy words, and he huffed a soundless, cynical laugh. "A novel experience to be sure, but one you will master soon enough," he said and pressed his lips to hers.

Danielle resisted his hard, passionless kiss, and held her lips tightly pressed together. Sensing her defiance, he straightened with a guttural sound and grazed his fingers along her jaw. His hand slid to the back of her head, fisting her hair and lifting her from the chair. She'd never seen him like this before; raw and dangerous. A disturbing awareness was germinating in her belly. This was his true self, a brutal savage hidden by a gossamer-thin layer of civility and self-control, polished so brightly no one could see the darkness beneath.

Fear of what was to come engulfed her, fast and heavy as mist pouring from the mountainside.

"I can't do this," she gasped. "I need time."

His hand tightened in her hair and brought her face close to his. With the other, he grabbed her jaw and tilted her head so that he could stare down into her eyes.

The smokiness evaporated from his voice when he hissed the words, "*That* you do not have. This marriage will be legal and binding. I will leave no room for an annulment. By morning you will be carrying my child. Whether or not you do so willingly is of little concern."

His words released the strength she had been searching for all day. Raising her hand, she slapped his wrist away from her face.

For the first time since entering the house, he looked pleased, almost to the point of being entertained by her show of defiance. He released her hair and, with a vicious and unexpected backhand to her cheek, he sent her stumbling backward until the back of her thighs hit the dining table. Her hands instinctively snapped behind her for purchase.

He reached her quickly, moving fast and smoothly despite his inebriated state. Bending and wrapping his arms around her legs, he lifted her clean off the floor, tossed her over his shoulder and delivered a stinging slap to her bottom.

"It is time to put this feral zeal of yours to better use," he growled and loped down the hall to the bedroom.

# Chapter 26

Danielle rose from the bed like a woman four times her age. Once standing, a dizzy spell drove her to reach for the post at the foot, and she bowed her head, waiting for her balance to restore itself. Every muscle in her body ached. She was as naked as the day she was born, and shaking, whether from cold or shock she was not entirely sure, perhaps a mixture of both.

Her steadiness returned haltingly, as if afraid of what might happen when fully regained. She opened her eyes and blinked several times to disperse the remaining black spots still floating across her vision.

The room was not completely dark; morning light was pushing through the shutters. She'd woken alone in the bed. Keeping her eyes shut and her breathing even, she'd listened for any noise coming from inside the house, but there was nothing, just birdsong piercing the silence. Elias must have left for the fort. *Thank the Lord.*

The smell of blood clung to her nose, and she knew that most came from her body. Her thighs were thickly smeared, and a thin fresh streak trickled past the inside of her right knee. She was still bleeding. Looking about, she searched for her blanket, but couldn't remember where she'd left it. Perhaps it was still in the dining room; it might as well have been on the other side of the world. She knew Maria's nightgown was somewhere amongst the tangled bundle of sheets, but he'd ripped it right down the middle, and she couldn't bear the thought of having it touch her skin again. Pity; it was so beautiful.

Danielle raised her hand to wipe the hair from her face, the other still clutching the bedpost. The strands framing her face were heavy and clumped together with the blood from her nose. There had been many blows to her face, but the one to the nose was the last she remembered. After that, she'd woken up with one hand tied to the bed. Running a finger over the bridge of her nose, she felt the slight misalignment—definitely broken. *I will not go through life with a crooked nose*, she thought, and one corner of her mouth lifted a fraction in amusement at her vanity.

It would have to be straightened, and it would have to be done right now. The longer she waited, the worse the swelling would become and the more scared she'd get. Her fingers felt thick and clumsy as she tightened them over her nose. She tried three times before gaining a secure enough grip to push the cartilage and bone quickly and firmly back into place. The pain was instant and fierce. Cold white shards shot across her face and into her forehead. Her knees caved, and she sank down to the floor. Blood poured from her face and splattered on the stone floor. Exhaling slowly through her mouth, she tried to breathe through the pain. Her lips were cold. The bedpost was like an anchor keeping her steady, and she hung on. Tears streamed down her face, but she kept the anguish at bay; if she gave in to her pain and cried, her nose would clog, making the situation much worse. Later she would have a good long cry, just not yet.

Four more deep breaths and she felt steady enough to stand again. She needed to wash. Letting go of the bed, she took the next few steps toward the stand like a young child learning to walk. The washcloth and soap were next to the bowl of water she used the evening before. Soap scum drifted like snowflakes on the cold surface.

Blood from her nose flowed into her mouth, and she spat a glob into the water bowl. More blood dripped onto her breasts and the newly crafted washstand. It's going to stain, she thought absently, but there was nothing to be done for it, except for letting it run its course.

Her teeth chattered, and she knew it was best to get the washing over and done with, starting with her thighs. She dipped the washcloth in the water, not bothering with the soap, and then slowly wiped the streaks of grime and blood from her legs, cleaning and rinsing as she went. And then at last she reached the part she tried to avoid touching or thinking about. Slowly, she spread her legs and pressed the cold, damp cloth against her swollen and abused flesh; it pulsed in gratitude. Raw primal sobs tore through her throat, the sound as foreign as the room she stood in. With one hand pushing against the washstand for support, the other pressing between her legs, she bent over and let the blood and the tears fall freely from her face.

Once she was clean, she turned to the trunk, deliberately avoiding looking at the bed. Her nose had stopped bleeding, but it was blocked and felt swollen. Time would do the rest of the healing.

She really should open the shutters, but the rain was still coming down steadily and she knew it would only push cold air into the room. Best to get dressed first. The small leather pouch Koba gifted her lay on top of her clothes, where she'd left it the night before. Careful not to touch her face, she hung the pouch around her neck. Then she reached for her old worn shift and decided not to bind her breasts; they were too bruised and sensitive to tolerate the rigid treatment. Instead, she closed her eyes and took comfort as the soft, familiar undergarment dropped the length of her body. When she reached for a shirt, her hand brushed against the solid handle of Sebastiaan's dagger, where Maria had neatly tucked it between her garments.

Danielle pulled it from the trunk. Blanx had fashioned a leather sheath with a narrow strip to tie around her waist. She usually wore it over her wide, everyday belt, but today she wanted the weapon close to her skin and so she fastened the dagger under her shift and then donned the rest of her garments: shirt, skirt, stockings and boots. Lacking the strength to wash her hair, she tied it loosely with a ribbon at the back of her neck.

With the chores of washing and dressing out of the way, she slammed the trunk shut and straightened, forgetting her rule, and stared at the bed. Even in the dim light, she could see large bloodstains marking the bedding and a part of the wall by the nightstand.

Her wedding night; a humiliating and painful, bloody mess.

This was not the time for wallowing, she chastised herself. A cup of willow bark tea would put her to rights again, after which she would return and start cleaning. Best to have it as good as new before her husband returns. She didn't want to upset him, and the way this room looked was definitely not conducive to feelings of tranquility and peace. It looked like a battleground, which was precisely what it was—a battle she'd lost.

Shuffling her way down the hall and into the kitchen, she came to stand in front of the cold hearth; looking at the neatly stacked wood and kindling, she wondered who'd done her the kindness. Lighting the fire took but a few seconds and she let the heat wash over her. The water bucket, however, was empty. She would need to fill it from the stream. At once, the common everyday task of boiling water overwhelmed her. Turning from the fire, she stumbled to the dining table.

Her lap blanket was lying in a heap on the floor. Folding it in a neat square, she placed it on the chair and gingerly sat down, releasing a groan as she lowered herself onto the softened seat. The blasted shutters were still closed, leaving the house shrouded in a bleak light that softened harsh corners and sharpened the cold. Danielle rested her arms on the table and laid her head down, but the pressure in her nose built almost immediately, so she sat up straight.

A sharp knock fell on the front door. Mutely, she stared at it. It was unlocked. She was in no shape to receive visitors and so she kept quiet hoping whoever it was would go away.

The knock persisted and then morning light flooded the dining table as the double doors were pushed wide.

Squinting, she stared at the intruder lacking the will to scowl. Danielle didn't have a looking glass, but the horror of what she looked like was reflected in Blanx's face. He stared at her with wide turbulent eyes, understanding and fury twisting his features.

Once, years ago, she and her father had arrived at the surgery door to find a woman from the brothel waiting for them on the step by the back door. Her face was bruised and swollen; her body covered in blood. Danielle had stared in open-mouthed fascination.

In a low voice, so as not to startle her, her father had asked the woman's permission to lift her from the step. The image of him simply standing there patiently waiting for consent had always stayed with her. When the woman had finally given him a nod, he'd gently lifted her in his arms and carried her inside. For the rest of that day, the door remained closed to all other patients.

Danielle knew she must look a fright. Her hair was knotted and blood clotted. Some strands were hanging loose from the binding. She'd touched the left side of her face earlier and found it numb. She suspected the swelling was hiding a cracked cheekbone. Her eyelids were thick and heavy, and the left eye felt scratchier than the right, suggesting there was bleeding around the cornea. The fractured nose would have added to the mottled array of bruises on her face, pushing dark purple half-moons beneath her eyes. It must be twice its usual width with the recent straightening as well as the initial trauma. Then there was her split and bulging upper lip. Running her tongue over the inside of her mouth, she discovered a few more cuts and a loose tooth, which hopefully would tighten over the next few days, assuming it wouldn't get dislodged again.

Danielle stared at Blanx and something unspoken passed between them—an agreement, a shared understanding.

She exhaled slowly and tried to pull her gelatinous lips into a smile, but the single tear that leaked from her eye ruined the effort.

The shackles around Blanx's ankles clicked on the stone floor as he moved to kneel by her chair. With a rough, calloused thumb, he wiped the tear away, then he reached for her hand, and placed a small packet in her palm, closing her fingers around it.

"What is this?" she asked, with a questioning frown that seemed to pull at her hairline. Blanx was already moving. Leaving her to stare at the bundle of letters in her hand. She heard him by the hearth feeding the fire, and then he picked up the empty bucket and headed for the door.

Lifting the one on top, she opened the first letter with shaky fingers and flattened it on the table. The handwriting was crisp and confident.

*March 28, A.D. 1652*

Danielle stared at the date. This letter was more than a year old, written when they were still aboard the *Drommedaris,* en route to the Cape from Holland. The next line gripped her attention and her stomach knotted firmly.

*To Captain Alain Du Bois, 34 Brouwergracht, Amsterdam, HOLLAND*
*From Elias P Coopman*

*My Dearest Brother,*

*We are still at sea. The journey is not one I would wish to repeat. It seems that every misfortune has focused its attention on us, but I am confident that we shall reach our destination soon.*

*The man you've placed on the Drommedaris to eliminate the surgeon's assistant has met his demise in an unfortunate incident involving the boatswain and another sailor. I am not entirely certain if this is a loss or a blessing. However, the problem of the assistant remains and has worsened. She has exposed you, as the surgeon's murderer to Captain De Coninck, Governor Van Riebeeck, and anyone willing to listen. The accusation carries significant weight since it became known that the surgeon was her father.*

*Governor Van Riebeeck has urged her to put her statement into a signed affidavit. I have convinced the governor to leave the matter with me since, as you are aware, my uncle on my mother's side is one of the VOC's Seventeen Lords. Unfortunately, that document was lost when an unexpected gust of wind blew it from my hands and into the ocean. I urge you to take caution until we are certain that the situation is under control.*

*In the name and memory of our father, I will do all in my power to keep you safe. My loyalty to you is unquestionable.*

*Your brother*
*E.P. Coopman*

Danielle stared at the words and the revelations they held. *'Brother.'* They were brothers. She rolled the mystery in her mind whilst staring out over the surface of the empty table. *'Our father.'* They shared a father, but not a mother. Could it be that one was illegitimate and hence the different last names, or perhaps the scoundrel had changed it? She was not sure which of the two the scoundrel was. The truth that stood like a pole above water is that her affidavit never made it to Holland. There was no justice for her father, who died at the hands of the man whose brother she wed the day before! The force of the knowledge drove her to her feet, bumping the chair backward and causing the rest of the letters to tumble to the floor.

Reaching for them, she pulled the chair back, sat down again and opened the next. Anxiety and abhorrence ran like twin horses, wrenching her mind into a frenzied spiral, scattering her thoughts into chaos.


*October 17, A.D. 1652*
  *To Captain Andrew Papley, Commander of the HMS Nicodemus*


*Dear Sir,*

*As per our previous meetings and discussions. All is now in place. The native tribes have been located and convinced that trade with the British ships is preferable to the Dutch settlement.*

*Maps are attached detailing the bays and inlets suitable to drop anchor.*


*Yours faithful*
*Thomas Bishop*

*Thomas Bishop?*
The letter was written in Elias' hand.
He used an alias.
Van Riebeeck's closest friend, confidant, second in command, was conspiring with the British against the settlement.

The thoughts hit her in single file, and she stared out the open shutters. Blanx must have opened them before he'd left to get water. The ocean was an angry slate gray with white caps chasing in all directions. Rain floated in gauzy curtains over the disturbed surface on their way to the forest, where they disappeared into the green darkness. She realized her mouth was unbecomingly hanging open and snapped it shut.

Elias, the cursed Judas! He was the reason they'd nearly starved to death, the reason for all their misfortune and suffering. Images of the night by the fire, the night the tribe welcomed Kuhle's baby, drifted through her battered mind. Harry and Elias were somehow connected. She winced at the idea. Best not to get carried away, she cautioned.

How was it that Blanx was in possession of these incriminating letters? It was a question that would remain unanswered.

She hastily unfolded the rest. There were two letters of similar content to different English ship captains and one to a Portuguese of the same rank, all signed *Thomas Bishop*. Shaking her head in disbelief, she stared at the words as they flowed across the pages.

Elias was working with Du Bois, but to what point? The question nagged. Danielle closed her eyes and tried to force a clear thought. It was like staring at the pieces of a puzzle, knowing that they were all there, but uncertain if a picture would ever emerge.

Upon opening the last letter, the pieces fell into place and the picture was revealed.

*December 25, A.D. 1652*
*To Captain Alain Du Bois, 34 Brouwergracht, Amsterdam, HOLLAND*
*From Elias P Coopman*

*My Dearest Brother,*
*Joyeux Noël. I shall not bore you with unnecessary banter, for there is much to discuss. Our plans are progressing at a steady pace, and I am pleased with the progress made thus far. The governor's popularity is steeply declining, and it would surprise me greatly if he remained in power for much longer. He is becoming increasingly desperate and irrational, and I am counting on him being overthrown or murdered soon. I am well situated to fill the role of governor, should it suddenly become vacant, at which the Cape of Good Hope will become the jewel in your empire. Our own Mecca.*
*However, and I believe this is why you came to me all those many months ago, we must prepare for the chance, slim though it might be, that our plans will not*

*succeed.*

*I have composed and attached a list of the local tribes, including their locations and numbers on whose loyalty we can count. Another list detailing the number of settlers, soldiers, workers, and the contents of the armory at the Cape of Good Hope. Also find a map marking the site for a possible second settlement should we need to land men discreetly, enough to overrun the Dutch. Everything is in place should the need for such a drastic step arise.*

*May the new year hold us firmly in its favor.*

*Your brother*

*E.P. Coopman*

Blanx did not know of the information hidden in these letters, but he knew they were important. He'd come here this morning to check on her, because she guessed he was the only other person in the settlement who knew the man behind the polished façade. Her friend had brought the letters, hoping she could use them to save herself. Had her marriage to Coopman not happened so fast it would have worked—all they needed was a day. One day for Blanx to give her the letters; one day for her to lay them before Governor Van Riebeeck. She stared sightlessly at the stack of unfolded parchments.

A shuffling of feet on the front stoop sharpened her focus. Looking up, her heart dropped as she stared into her husband's cold eyes, where he filled the entrance.

The tumult of emotions she felt at that moment must have shown on her face. Either that, or he found himself briefly stunned by the evidence of the violence he'd visited upon her the previous night. His eyes drifted over her and to the letters splayed open before her.

Last night, he had taught her what genuine fear was, and she knew it was a lesson she would not soon forget, but it paled in comparison to what she was looking at as he stood transfixed. His face was deathly pale, a demonic light had lit somewhere behind his eyes, and his body hardened like a tightly wound coil.

"Where did you get those?" he asked in a voice sounding strangled and foreign.

The urgent clanging of Blanx's shackles as he came up the two front steps made Coopman spin on his heels. The distance between the two men vanished as Blanx took one more step and swung the bucket of water at Coopman's head, leaving the contents to arch at its sudden release before falling to the stoop in a single splat.

Coopman's head flew sideways, and his body followed, landing him on his hands and knees as Blanx advanced. Coopman did not hurry to his feet, but when he did, he did so swinging, and Danielle saw the glint of a blade slashing through the air. Blanx saw it too, for he retreated in time for the knife to pass harmlessly in front of him, but the shackles around his ankles limited his range of movement and Elias advanced unencumbered. The next swing got Blanx neatly across the throat, cutting him in a nearly straight line from side to side.

The force of the strike nearly decapitated him. Blanx raised his hand, perhaps to press to the gaping wound, but made it only as far as his chest before falling to his side. Then the large man dropped to the floor like a ship with its hull ripped open would sink to the bottom of the ocean, folding in on itself as it went.

A guttural sound emerged, and Danielle did not know if it came from Blanx or Coopman, but it lifted her from the chair and propelled her toward the back door of the washroom.

She knew that if she stayed in the house, she was going to die. He was going to kill her, too. Struggling with the stiff new slide lock on the back door, she pulled twice before it gave, then cursed as she realized the door opened inward, not outward. Stepping to the side, she flung it open and ran blindly across the backyard. She heard Elias' voice and his fast-approaching footsteps as he rushed down the hall.

Danielle wasted no time or momentum turning around to see how far behind her he was. She darted through the underbrush. This part of the forest was not very dense but unfamiliar. If she were near the fort, she would have disappeared in a heartbeat. Her skirt kept snagging on thorny branches. Every so often, she had to yank it free. When it tangled itself for the third time, she ripped the buttons from their holes and left the bothersome piece of clothing flapping in the undergrowth like a downed bat.

Lighter and free of the excess fabric around her legs, she sprinted onward. It sounded like she was being chased by a rhinoceros the way Elias was pursuing her, snapping twigs and branches as he went. She heard his boots slipping a few times, followed by his angry curses, which only pushed her legs to move faster.

Elias was a man in his prime, but Danielle was much younger, knew her endurance could outlast nearly anyone. She'd done this before. The thought pushed her pain and discomfort aside and gave her strength when she remembered how she'd run from Du Bois' men the night he'd killed her father. Her speed and cunning had saved her that night, and it would do so again.

The ground was inclining, and she raised her knees to compensate for the change. Twice she tripped, almost bringing her to her knees, but she righted herself quickly and kept going. If she was struggling, so was he.

"Danielle, stop!" He was closer than she thought. The terrain was steeper, fewer plants, more boulders. She ignored the command and kept climbing, using her hands to pull herself up and over large boulders. Small pebbles crumbled beneath her boots, but she kept clawing her way forward and upward. Her breath was burning in her chest, and she could taste blood in her mouth, but she ignored that too.

"Danielle, stop this madness. I will not hurt you. Just stop and listen to me." He was out of breath and a little further behind than before. It gave her hope. The vegetation was thinning out, more suited to growing on the side of the mountain than down in the forest. The wind was also picking up in strength. She continued her climb, sprinted where the ground allowed, and climbed where it became rougher.

"I am sorry about what happened last night."

Closer again. She did not turn to see how far behind her he was, just doggedly continued on her course to get away, creating greater distance between them.

"I was drunk, and ..."

Frowning, she wondered why he didn't finish what he was about to say. Then she heard him grunt and release a vile curse. Loose gravel and small rocks tumbled down. Yes, he was struggling. Skirting a large boulder, she leaned her back against it for just a moment, trying to catch her breath, her blocked nose and throbbing head did not aid matters.

"It will never happen again. I promise," he said as he struggled for breath as well.

Damn the man! He was gaining on her. Using the cover that the large boulder gave her, she sharply changed direction and then clambered to where she could see a ledge protruding from the side of the mountain. It was a dead end to be sure, but she headed for it, regardless. She didn't have much of a choice, for turning back would lead her straight into Coopman's path and to the right the ground was steeper, with fewer boulders and more loose gravel. If she chose that route, she would be completely exposed and vulnerable to slipping. The ledge was her best option.

Coopman had grown suspiciously silent behind her, and she knew he had spotted the ledge as well. Resolutely, she made her way to the outcrop. Her fingers, raw and nails torn deep into the flesh, throbbed. She pushed the pain aside, focusing instead on each careful step. With the vertical face of the mountain pressing into her back, she shuffled along the unaccommodating, narrow ledge that led to the wider platform she'd seen earlier. A few more sideways scrapes, and she lunged onto the broad overhang.

The overhang was higher than she'd first thought, but not so much as to make her dizzy. Peeking over the side, she saw the ocean far below. Coopman's house, where it stood nestled between tall trees, with the smoke curling from the hearth, looked like it could fit in the palm of her hand. Further to the west, the round thatched roofs of the settlement's houses dotted the area beyond the white beach like moles on an old woman's body.

More small rocks and pebbles tumbled down, and she knew Coopman was close by. Searching the platform, she discovered it was indeed a dead end. The only way off it was either to jump or turn back the way she had come. She was trapped.

Danielle waited for the wave of panic to assail her, but it did not come. She felt surprisingly calm.

"I am not dying today," she spoke out loud. She had come too far, survived too much to give up now. The congruity of her situation did not escape her. This was quite literally where she would stop running.

She huffed a wry smile as Maria's words flashed through her mind. She was done running from life, from death, and from her husband. Here was where she would make her stand. This was where she would take back her life—or die trying.

With her eyes fixed on where she expected her husband to appear at any moment, she said a quick prayer.

"Thank you, father, for raising me to be strong, and thank you Sebastiaan for giving me Mary," with the last of her whispered words she reached beneath her shift and pulled Sebastiaan's dagger from its sheath. "Please God, give me strength."

Elias rounded the boulder, placing one foot on the narrow ledge and leaped onto the platform. He looked wild with fury as he pinned her with an unforgiving stare while trying to control his breathing. Her always elegant and well put-together husband looked rather unkempt. The sprint up the mountain had shattered his signature cool and composed demeanor beyond repair.

"You stupid little bitch," he hissed once his breath could support his voice. "You have nowhere to go."

Danielle moved her right hand behind her back and then retreated until she felt the cold rock pressed against her arm. She knew with absolute certainty that he did not mean for both of them to leave this mountain. She'd read his letters, knew his plans and his secrets. This was the end of the line for her. The rain had thinned to a cold mist, and the wind had stilled. There was only the two of them. No one to save her, no one to come charging to her rescue, but for once, the thought did not frighten her; instead, it gave her strength.

Elias moved toward her in slow, measured strides. His hands were empty and free of weapons. Nevertheless, the events of last night had shown her he didn't require any.

"Dear old Blanx sealed your fate when he handed you those letters."

She didn't dare take her eyes off him. She'd learned one thing: the calmer he seemed, the more dangerous he was. He was like a snake curling and writhing, lulling his victim, while readying itself to strike.

"You think you're above the law?" she challenged.

A bitter, lopsided smile tugged at his mouth. Tilting his head, he let his eyes travel the length of her body and up again.

"Danielle," her name sounded like a caress, "your naivete makes you almost endearing." The smile dropped and his eyes sharpened.

"I am not above the law. I *am* the law." He waited for his words to find their rightful place in her mind and then tightened his lips in frustration when she showed no reaction to that obvious bit of truth.

"The way I see it," he continued and closed the last few yards separating them. "You have two choices." Lifting his pointer finger to introduce the first. "You can jump of your own volition." Tilting his head slightly toward the drop behind him. "Or two," raising another finger. "I can lend a hand, so to speak. Personally, I prefer the latter, but I am a fair man and will leave the choice to you." He even accommodated her by stepping aside, opening the way for her to leap off the ledge. "But either way, it ends here. Today."

"There is a third choice," Danielle said, silently cursing herself for sounding so small.

"And what would that be, my sweetheart?" He indulged her with chilling calm.

Danielle pushed away from the clammy rock at her back, stepping toward him and using the momentum of her body to bring her arm from behind her back and in a tight, powerful thrust, she drove Sebastiaan's dagger into the soft space beneath his sternum and upward where the long blade easily cut into his heart. With a final firm angling of her wrist, she twisted the double-edged blade and watched his eyes flare with shock and disbelief.

She wanted to condemn him to hell, wanted to tell him that she did this for Blanx, wanted to promise him that if the gods were smiling on her, she would do the same to his brother but, in the end, husband and wife only stared into each other's eyes. The blood from his heart baptizing her hand as she pulled her weapon free.

A moment of fear when he remained standing gripped her and forced her to retreat. And then the world slowed. She saw a blurred movement out the corner of her eye, then heard the spear strike with a dull thud, penetrating Elias' already pierced chest, the force of it so powerful it nearly doubled his body over as it drove him over the edge.

One moment he was standing before her and the next she was looking at the sunlight streaking through a slit in the clouds above the ocean. A cool breeze lifted her hair as she slowly turned her head, retracing the spear's path.

The Saldanhar chief stood deadly still, as if he too had sprouted from the earth like the mountain itself. Danielle blinked slowly, thinking the apparition would be gone when she opened her eyes. It wasn't. Untamed relief flowed from her, taking with it her will to remain upright. Her hand opened, the dagger clattered to the ground and her body followed suit.

Kai reached her before she completely collapsed. With a firm hand around her upper arm, he held her upright, while his eyes took in every detail of her damaged face. When he felt her strength returning to her legs, he released her and bent down to pick up the dagger, which he pressed back into her hand.

"Never drop your weapon," he said and then loosened the hide mantel he wore around his shoulders and wrapped her in it.

"You move like the wind, little flower. Even *I* struggled to keep up," he said with a smile of admiration. "I was by the stream. There was blood in the air. I feared he'd killed you, but then I saw you fleeing up the mountain."

"You followed," she said, her mind struggling to bring all the ends together.

"Yes."

She wanted more, but he clearly thought his explanation satisfactory.

# Chapter 27

It was afternoon, and Van Riebeeck's belly rumbled. In anticipation of the impending food crisis, now that the settlement was not trading weekly with the Saldanhars, he had ordered the kitchen to serve only two meals per day, breakfast, and an early dinner.

More Saldanhar tribes were arriving daily at the Cape. He could see their fires dotting the mountainside at night. With Harry gone, he might have a chance of negotiating a trade agreement with a new chieftain if he could arrange a meeting. These were treacherous waters to navigate, as Van Riebeeck was unsure if Kai had persuaded the other tribes to stand against the settlement. So far, there had been no retaliation from Kai's tribe after the disastrous incident three days ago.

There were also the Watermen to the west, but they never visited the Cape if the Saldanhars were close. The Watermen were not as wealthy and strong as the Saldanhars, but if all else failed it was an avenue worth exploring.

A soft but urgent knock landed on the door, which opened upon his permission. Governor Van Riebeeck could feel his face pull at the sight of his unexpected visitor.

"Van Leyen?" he asked. He hadn't seen him in months, as the two slaves, Van Leyen and Blanx, were working on Mr. Coopman's house. The man was battered and thin with a hopelessness that hung like a low ceiling over him, forcing his shoulders to droop and his eyes to lower.

"Governor," Van Leyen spoke, and the hollow voice tugged at something deep inside the governor. "There is a matter that requires your immediate attention. Yours and Captain Helm's."

* * *

Van Riebeeck and Helm's horses walked with flicking tails and bobbing heads behind Van Leyen's shuffling feet, Fly dutifully trotting by his side, nudging his hand now and then with his long nose. The distance to Coopman's house was not so great if one attempted it on a stout horse with a brisk canter, but the shackles around Van Leyen's legs were a considerable factor in slowing the procession down.

They found Blanx lying face down on the wide stone stoop, surrounded by an impossibly large pool of blood. The dark red puddle had dried at the edges. Faint bruises showed on Blanx's pale blue-green skin where it pressed against the floor and beneath the shackles around his ankles. A water bucket lay on its side a few feet away. Fly whined and went to his fallen master, but Van Leyen called him back.

Helm was the first to dismount. "What happened here?" he asked. His eyes instantly and accusingly studied Van Leyen from the top of his head to his bare feet. The slave endured the unspoken accusation with no outward reaction.

Van Riebeeck slid from his horse. Blanx was staring right at him, with cold eyes that drew him in. The illusion was unsettling, and he stepped closer. Wanting to break the spell, he reached out his hand to lower the eyelids, but Van Leyen's soft whisper halted the movement.

"Please, sir, don't touch him. His skin and muscles have hardened."

Van Riebeeck turned toward Van Leyen, anguish and sorrow clearly written on his face. Blanx was like a brother to him.

"I am sorry, John." Van Riebeeck knew what Helm was thinking, but he could not begin to imagine that Van Leyen had a hand in this. Besides, there was not a speck of blood on him. "You knew he was here?" he asked.

Van Leyen nodded slowly.

"Blanx was set to do a few small chores here this morning," Van Leyen said, waving his hand limply in the backyard's direction. "But when he didn't return this afternoon, I came searching for him, thinking to lend a hand with whatever he was doing." Van Leyen looked at his friend, sadness, and desolation enshrouding him like a coarse winter's blanket.

"Where are Mister Coopman and his wife?" Helm asked, his voice tight with worry.

"I don't know," Van Leyen replied. "I called out, but no one answered. Went around the back, called some more, but didn't get a response. The front and back doors are open, but I did not go inside."

"Governor, I will search inside. Please wait here." Helm spoke with crisp authority and climbed the two long, wide steps stretching the length of the house leading to the front door, mindful of where he placed his feet so as not to step in the blood.

"No, we will go together." Van Riebeeck said, shrugging the woolen coat from his shoulders and carefully covered Blanx's head and upper body. He watched as the sleeves soaked and settled in the thick blood. Fear of what they might find inside whipped around him like the cold breath of a ghost and he shuddered in response.

"Come," he said, and motioned to Van Leyen to follow them.

The three men entered the large open space of the great room. A low canopy of heavy clouds obscured the late afternoon sun, leaving the room in a somber gray. Giving the area a quick glance, Helm moved down the hall to investigate the rest of the house.

Van Riebeeck stood near the dining table, a stack of letters being its only adornment. To the left, a single dining chair was left by the now cold sitting room fireplace. Only the ashes remained. He frowned at the large book lying forgotten on the floor, open and face-down, its center pages creased under its weight. In the kitchen, the embers of the burned-out hearth fire still glowed, with no evidence of cooking.

"John, find a few candles and light them, please," he ordered.

"Governor!" The panic fueling the captain's voice jolted Van Riebeeck from where he stood, and he rushed down the hall.

Van Riebeeck met his captain outside the bedroom door.

"What is it?" he demanded. Helm looked shaken. "Speak man. Tell me," Van Riebeeck snapped, his weariness and apprehension stretched to breaking point and he tried to push Helm out of the way.

"It is empty, but Governor," Helm laid an urgent hand on Van Riebeeck's forearm. "Prepare yourself."

Nothing could have prepared him for the sight that met him when he stepped into the room. Helm's two-word warning was entirely insufficient.

"I opened the shutters. Everything was so dark, I couldn't see," Helm rambled, an odd reaction for a man known for his composure and self-control.

Van Riebeeck's lips moved, but his voice did not follow, so he nodded, cleared his throat, and tried again. "A moment, if you please."

Staring gape-jawed at the scene, he faintly registered Helm's receding footsteps. His own feet felt fused to the floor as he tried to take in the scene before him. His mind could not comprehend the violence that had caused the carnage. Finally, his attention settled on a familiar object—the nightgown.

It was like the one his wife had worn on their wedding night; he could remember the small flowers around the neckline and how her fingers had nervously toyed with the embroidery. He'd told her she was the most beautiful creature he'd ever seen, and she'd said that she'd run out of pink thread so the flowers near the right shoulder were darker than the rest. They both had smiled over the silly concern.

Van Riebeeck stepped closer to kneel by the torn garment on the floor. It was cleanly ripped down the middle. The blood bespattered pink flowers and delicate light green leaves still valiantly tried to decorate the neckline. With a shaking hand he traced over the darker pink flowers near the shoulder seam and swallowed back the rising contents of his stomach. This was his wife's nightgown. She must have given it to Danielle as a wedding present. His body felt heavy when he pushed to his feet, one hand clutching the ruined garment. Instinctively, he lifted it to his nose, but stopped when he became aware of what he was doing.

There were no other pieces of clothing on the floor, only those worn by the bride. No large white shirt, no dark pants or coat. The thought seemed to scream for attention. Not understanding why it nagged at him, he pushed it aside.

Then he looked at the bed and felt the heat drain from his body, leaving him numb. He needed to sit down, but there was nowhere to sit, save sinking back to the floor, which he couldn't do for fear of not being able to rise again. The crisp white linen sheets were covered in large dark red blood stains, turning rusty brown in some places. There were splatters against the wall and a pool by the foot of the bed. It looked wet, almost as if it was more recent than the rest.

Had some evil doer overpowered the couple in their sleep? He shook his head at his reasoning. Most of the blood was isolated to one side of the bed, the same side where the blood on the wall was and the puddle on the floor. One victim, perhaps. Looking down at the limp dress in his hand—Danielle.

Van Riebeeck relaxed his lips, allowing himself to breathe through his mouth. The metallic tang in the air threatened to strangle him. This was a desecration of everything holy and beautiful. It went beyond his comprehension. Imagining his wife in a scene like this sent a sharp pain through his chest. Raising his hand, he tried to ease the stabbing sensation. The possibility that Coopman had done this to the woman he'd wanted to marry for so long was unthinkable. The man was his best friend; loyal, intelligent, and dependable, a master of his emotions and a level head in any situation. There must be another explanation. The absence of male clothing penetrated his thoughts again. Perhaps somebody had lured Coopman away; harmed him in some way, before coming here.

Van Riebeeck turned his head away from the bed and felt the bones in his neck crack with the effort. As if walking in a dream, he moved toward the washstand by the opposite wall. There was water in the bowl, but it was murky, pink-tinged with blood settled at the bottom. A stained washcloth carelessly hung over the side as if someone had slapped it there.

She'd tried to clean herself, and the miserable thought almost felled him.

"Danielle, what happened here? Where are you?" he whispered and then it all became too much. He couldn't stay in the room a moment longer. It felt like the walls were closing in and the blood was slowly creeping closer, covering his feet, his legs, creeping up his body all the way to his hands. Like a drunkard, he stumbled from the room clutching the nightgown in a death grip.

Helm and Van Leyen were waiting in the dining room. Helm was standing by the table and Van Leyen was leaning against the front door's jamb, Fly at his feet. Something in the governor's face must have made Helm reach for a chair.

"Sit down, Governor," he said, but took a step back when Van Riebeeck shook his head.

"What is that?" Van Riebeeck asked, remembering the letters he saw earlier.

"You need to sit down and read those," Helm said with palpable rage. "My guess is she did, and he found out."

"What are you talking about?" Van Riebeeck asked, his confusion hitting new heights with every passing minute. "Have you read them?"

"Yes, I have."

Van Riebeeck settled into the chair. Placing the nightgown next to the sheets of parchment, he leaned his forearms on the table and began to read. With each passing word, he could feel the pressure in his veins increase to the point where the words swam on the page and, by the third letter, he was forced to close his eyes. Regaining a sliver of control, he lifted the next letter, but his hands trembled so violently that he set it back down. Instead, he leaned forward, letting the candle's golden glow reveal the treachery, betrayal, and sickening truth behind Elias Coopman. There were some letters he had to read twice, unable to believe his eyes the first time.

Looking up, he found Helm's stare pinning him to the chair.

"Rally every soldier and settler. Search every inch of this forest and mountain. I want them found, and send four men with a stretcher for Blanx." Van Riebeeck sounded tortured as the words scraped past his lips.

Helm clicked his heels, and within two long strides, reached the front door.

"Helm," Van Riebeeck called, and Helm paused. "When you find Danielle—

" Van Riebeeck shook his head, trying to dislodge his words, and when he looked to his captain, he saw an emotion much deeper than rage flicker across his face.

"I will bring her back." A paternal tenderness cradled each of Helm's words.

"Leave Van Leyen with me," Van Riebeeck ordered.

After Helm was gone, Van Riebeeck sat for a long time, staring at the bare table before him.

"Can you read, John?" he asked the slave, still standing by the door.

"No, sir," Van Leyen replied, "but I have seen those letters before." That got the governor's attention, and he straightened from the table.

"I saw them amongst Blanx's things when we left the settlement." Embarrassment or regret at the mention of their crime made him lower his eyes.

"Go on," Van Riebeeck urged.

"I asked him about it, because like me, Blanx couldn't read either. He didn't want to talk about it." He shrugged with one shoulder. "Maybe it was just my imagination, but I got the feeling he wanted to protect me from them. Either way, after we returned, I never saw them again—didn't think about them until now."

Van Riebeeck looked long and hard into the man's guileless eyes. Eyes that carried nothing but sorrow for his dead friend.

"Is there an ax hereabouts?" Van Riebeeck asked.

"There is one in the lean-to. We used it to cut wood for the hearth and fireplaces the day before," Van Leyen said, and motioned with his chin toward the back door, taken aback by the swift change in conversation.

"Do you want me to get it for you, Governor?"

Chewing on his bottom lip in contemplation, Van Riebeeck gave an absent nod, followed by a belated, "Yes, please."

Van Riebeeck watched as Van Leyen shuffled down the hall, hearing every scrape of the shackles on the stone floor, noting the chafed skin around his ankles. He wished events would return to their normal speed. Everything was moving slowly, like oil pulsing from a bottle.

Once alone in the dining room, he dropped his head in his hands. Guilt was corroding his body from the inside out. He had failed on every account. In a moment of blind anger, he'd forced Danielle into this situation; made her marry a monster, left her unprotected and vulnerable. He had mercilessly punished Blanx and Van Leyen, trusted the wrong man and ruined the settlement's future. In a selfish instant, he wished Van Leyen would return with the ax and take his revenge by planting the blade between his shoulders.

Van Leyen placed the heavy tool against the table and Van Riebeeck winced; too honorable of a man to do such a dirty deed. Perhaps one day he might look in the looking glass and think those words of himself.

He never thought of himself as a great leader. He was only a man with a dream and a vision for a better future, but in his fervor to bring that about, he'd let go of the anchors in his life. His wife was his biggest regret. He'd let go of her steady hand to grasp the arm of a backstabbing, conniving blackguard.

"Sit down," Van Riebeeck pointed to the chair and Van Leyen hesitantly obeyed.

"I have come to realize that I have wronged you and Blanx." Van Leyen's eyes narrowed at the unexpected words. "I have treated you harshly, branded you as a traitor when the true traitor was living under my roof, sitting by my right hand and eating at my table." The governor sank to his knees before Van Leyen and spread his feet, so the chain rested limply on the stone floor, then he raised the ax and brought it down on the chain.

Van Leyen was stunned into silence by what was happening, but found his voice after the third blow.

"Governor, wait," he all but shouted.

"No," Van Riebeeck silenced him. "I am giving you your freedom. If I live to be a hundred and try every day, I still could not right the damage I've done, but by God, I am going to try." Tears were filling Van Riebeeck's eyes as he spoke the passionate words.

"I understand that," Van Leyen spoke in a voice tight with concern, lifting his hand to stay the next blow from the ax. The governor's eyes were unfocused, and his arms did not have the strength to wield the tool properly. The blade was already dancing precariously along the chain. "Let's get the blacksmith to do this." Nodding encouragingly at the governor's bewildered face. The governor was giving him his freedom, but what good would it be if he lost a foot in the process?

Dropping the tool, Van Riebeeck placed a hand on the table and hoisted himself to his feet.

"You built this house," Van Riebeeck stated. Van Leyen remained silent but nodded slowly, unsure of where the observation was leading.

"Yes?"

"I will gift it to you. The house and the land. Yours to start a new life."

"I don't want it," Van Leyen replied without hesitation. "I am grateful to you for setting me free, but all I want is to bury my friend and start anew somewhere else, not here."

* * *

It was nearing the evening of the following day, and Van Riebeeck was slowly going out of his mind. He'd spent the night explaining, talking, and then calming his wife. Maria was beyond herself with worry for Danielle and toward dawn, he'd sent for Mrs. Boom to administer a sleeping draft. He hadn't slept since the night before and was pacing the length of his study. They'd returned Blanx's body before dark and Van Leyen had dug a grave on a hill overlooking the ocean.

"We found him," Helm sounded from the open door.

Van Riebeeck came to a dead stop. His head snapped up and he stared at his captain.

"Where is he?" he hissed.

"He is dead." Helm did not look particularly remorseful. "We left him where he lay. The location is hazardous, and we cannot reach him without ropes." Seeing the frown creasing the governor's forehead, he continued. "There is an outcrop fairly high in the mountain, overlooking a gorge. We saw his body from above; a spear is protruding from his chest." Van

Riebeeck's eyebrows raced upward.

"How did you find him?"

"Harry's brother is the best tracker I know of. I asked for his help."

It was not outside the realm of possibility to think that Harry's brother might have killed him; it was hard to fathom how far and wide Coopman's influence and potential enemies stretched.

"And Danielle?" Van Riebeeck asked.

"I still have men looking for her." Helm stepped into the room and handed Van Riebeeck a heavy, dark brown skirt and a bloodied dagger.

Van Riebeeck's mouth parted and his breath ceased.

"It's Coopman's dagger," Helm said in a bleak voice. "He must've dropped it on his way up the mountain."

"Is this her blood?" Van Riebeeck asked from behind the shaking fist against his lips.

"It could be Blanx's. There is no blood on the skirt," Helm said. "We found it in the underbrush close to Coopman's house."

Sadness was rolling into Van Riebeeck's chest. It was most definitely Danielle's; she'd worn it often.

"Governor, there is also the possibility that whoever killed Coopman has killed her too. Perhaps as revenge for what happened at the Saldanhar village." Helm gave voice to the thoughts foremost in Van Riebeeck's mind, but there was another possibility: Coopman could have killed her and hid her body somewhere in the forest. If that was the case, they might never find her.

"I will talk to Kai," Van Riebeeck said. "In the morning, we will take copper and food and beg a truce."

"I don't think that is going to be possible," Helm said. "Kai's tribe is gone. They must have left recently, for the tracks are fresh. They have moved east."

The news brought relief and concern in equal measure. "At least we can strike Kai and his tribesmen from the list of possible assailants then. Did you send men after them?"

"No, the tribe can be unpredictable, and I don't want to send anyone to his death," Helm said. "Besides, I thought it would be better to focus our attention and resources on finding Miss Danielle."

***

Kai had chosen an unusual route through the forest. Sticking mainly to boulders and rocky areas, it was hard going, but he'd slowed his pace to accommodate for her condition. They had spoken little on their way to the village, but she could see his face darken each time he looked at hers, and for once she knew it wasn't because of something she did.

"Can't we walk through the forest like we normally would?" she'd questioned his decision when they'd paused by the stream for her to rest.

"The rock remembers a footprint," he'd said and pointed to his bare foot. "Come morning the dew will stick to the rock, telling anyone who wants to know that someone has walked here, but a covered foot, the rock does not remember." She didn't understand the explanation, but let it rest.

"Why were you in that part of the forest this morning?" She'd wondered about that ever since he'd appeared on the ledge.

"Maheena brought the news. She said you were forced to take a man worse than her father. An evil man. She told me where to find you."

It was clear he meant her no harm, harbored no ill feelings toward her, regardless of his rough treatment of her on the day of the killings. *The day of the killings*—it was less than a week ago, and yet it felt like it belonged to another life.

They arrived at the village to find it in a state of dismantlement. Everywhere families were stripping the skins from the wooden frames of their huts. Rolled up bundles of skins dotted the clearing like hay bales during harvesting season.

"Kai," Danielle tugged on his hand. She was still wearing his mantle and tried to hand it back to him, but he refused. "What is happening?" she asked as she took in the state of the once beautiful little village.

"We are leaving. Tonight," he said with a finality that made her gut clench.

"No," she responded pathetically. What was she to do without them? The worry came unbidden, and Danielle realized she had nowhere to go.

Returning to the settlement was not an option. She'd murdered her husband, the governor's best friend, confidant, and his second in command. It was a crime she would be harshly punished for. Governor Van Riebeeck had shown no mercy when punishing lawbreakers, and he already blamed her for the broken relationship with the Saldanhars. Coopman would have thrown those incriminating letters in the hearth. There was no way on earth he would leave the house with those still lying on the table waiting to be discovered. All she had to defend herself were the bruises on her body, and that meant nothing in the eyes of the law. She was Coopman's property, to do with as he pleased, and everyone knew that she was not the easiest person to get along with. Many would applaud his firm hand with his young wife.

"Yes, little flower. There is too much darkness here, too many things we do not understand. It is time for us to leave."

Bringing her hand to her mouth, she tried to stifle the sob that burst from her.

"You are sad to leave?" Kai asked incredulously.

Danielle was too stunned to answer immediately.

"I am leaving?"

Kai reached out his hand and pushed his fingers under the collar of her shirt. She flinched and backed away, but his fingers hooked on the cord around her neck and pulled the small pouch from under her clothing.

"You wear the bones," he said, and then he touched the skin mantle around her shoulders, "you wear the skin of the Eland bull." With those observations made, he released a loud, piercing whistle, drawing the tribe's attention from their work.

"What is happening?" Danielle asked as all the men, women, and children gathered before them, clapping their hands to the song they sang.

"They are welcoming you. You will take Koba's place. The gods spoke to her, and this is their will. We must obey their decisions." He drew her closer and matched his forearm to hers, dark brown skin against white. "Because you are so different, I think the gods will understand if you choose to go back to your people." He made it sound like the differences between them were her fault, while waiting for her to reach a decision.

"I can't go back," she spoke between her sobs.

"We know you belong with us, but you need to know it too. Koba saw you in her dreams long before you healed my leg. She'd warned me about you, told me since I was a boy that a white witch with green eyes and soft feet will follow me all my days." Danielle frowned at his words, remembering the first day she'd met him, how he'd studied her like a newly discovered insect and then allowed her to treat his wound. A wound that had left a scar he still carried.

Danielle stared at the jagged scar on his thigh. "I will go with you," she said and then she simply could not stand any longer. The weight of the last few days came crashing down on her like a falling building. Her legs folded beneath her, and she slumped to the ground. Kai reached for her, lifted her against his chest, and carried her to where Koba's hut still stood. Once inside, he laid her on Koba's *kaross*.

"I will send the other women," he said before ducking out of the entrance. Danielle was too tired and too sore to care.

They let her sleep until dark. It was only when familiar voices spoke in hushed tones that she emerged from the depths of oblivion. Xhitha and Maheena had lit the fire in the center of the hut and were stirring something in a large bowl.

"Maheena," the girl's golden face lit at the sound of Danielle's scratchy voice.

"You are awake," she said and stroked her thin fingers over the bruises on Danielle's face, her smile fading as she took in the damage done to her friend. "He was not in time," she said as she handed Danielle a small bowl of milk.

"He was," Danielle replied after emptying the bowl. She did not know how hungry she was until now. "What are you doing here?" she asked.

"I am leaving with the tribe tonight," the girl replied, her posture turning rigid with defiance.

"She is in love," Xhitha said as she came to kneel next to Danielle's *kaross* with the bowl in her lap.

"What is that?" Danielle asked, looking at the dark mud-like mixture.

"Mud," Xhitha said. "We are leaving soon. And when we do, you need to look like us. So no spying eyes can run back to tell tales." She reached over and handed Danielle a large, almost rectangular animal skin with two pointed ends. Danielle shook it open and marveled at the silky softness of the hide. She was beginning to understand what the women meant to do. Rising from the *kaross,* she unbuttoned her shirt and let it drop to the floor, then she lifted her shift over her head and discarded that as well.

Both women stared at her in shocked silence. Warriors were often bloodied and bruised, and they'd seen what a wild animal could do to the soft flesh of a human, but never had they seen a woman's body so damaged at the hands of her husband.

Danielle wanted to hide, to bow her head in shame, but the shame wasn't hers. She met each woman's gaze squarely, unflinching.

"Let's get on with it," she said, and the harsh edge to her voice snapped the others from their trance.

Maheena blinked several times to clear her eyes, then picked up Danielle's discarded clothes and threw them carelessly in the fire. Danielle tried not to look; Elsje had lovingly made every piece that was now consumed by greedy yellow flames. The clothes would soon become a small pile of soft, gray ash.

After wrapping the hide around Danielle's body and knotting the two elongated ends over her right shoulder, Xhitha tied the sides together with long, thin leather strips. Her body was modestly and effectively covered, with only the bottom half of her legs showing.

Danielle reached for her belt and dagger and fastened it around her hips. Reluctantly, she bent down to remove her beloved boots, but Xhitha stopped her.

"No. Kai said you should keep those. Your feet are too soft."

When the women emerged from the hut, the moon hung high, and the tribe stood ready to go. Maheena had woven Danielle's hair into tight braids, coating each with mud until the heavy mass rested between her shoulders. They had also smeared her face and every exposed patch of skin with the dark, clinging mixture.

Kai was most impressed with the transformation.

"Little flower, your eyes shine like the forest in your brown face. Next time we go to fight, I will take you with me. You will scare the enemy to death." His laughter rippled through the tribe and soon all joined in.

Danielle crossed her arms over her chest, the effect somewhat ruined by the heavy Eland mantle covering most of the gesture, but she narrowed her eyes and tapped her booted foot while she waited for his merriment to spend itself.

A young lad approached, leading an enormous ox. Kai draped a *kaross* over its wide back, then reached for her. Danielle retreated several steps in alarm.

"What are you doing?" she asked, fearing he was about to toss her onto the animal.

With a patient smile that creased his eyes and the sides of his face, he looked at her, then at the ox, and back at her again, confirming her fears.

"You cannot walk. Your body needs to heal first, and we need to leave now."

"I am not riding an ox," Danielle protested.

"He is very gentle, and his back is broad. He won't hurt you," he said, pointing a finger to the area below her navel. Oh, the humiliation, will it ever end? "Also, I don't want the ground to remember your footprints."

Danielle narrowed her eyes and tightened her lips before agreeing. "Fine," she said, and no sooner had the word left her mouth than she was lifted onto the broad back of the ox.

Kai spoke a few soft words to the men surrounding them and then all grew quiet and solemn as Koba's hut was set alight.

For the second time in her life, Danielle was leaving one life behind for another.

The tribe moved as a collective. Some of the older or very pregnant women rode oxen, the rest grouped together, engaging in easy banter. Babies fastened to their mother's warm backs were soon lulled to sleep, their small heads bobbing with the gentle swaying of their mothers' bodies. Their older siblings remained close, brimming with excitement. The men formed a loose circle around the group of women and children, weapons in their hands, eyes, and ears primed for danger.

Danielle's ox behaved as advertised, docile and good-natured. However, she did not know how one went about steering such a beast. Fortunately, he seemed happy to follow the rest, requiring little to no guidance from her.

As the sun rose over a new day, the group drew to a stop. It was time to eat and rest before setting out further east again. They had cleared the forest hours earlier, and the vast African landscape stretched wide and open before them.

Danielle dropped from the ox's back, misjudged the distance, hit the ground, and sank to her knees with a groan. Many hands reached for her, but it was Kai's voice that penetrated the pain.

"Stubborn woman," he roared as he made his way to her. "I will help you down. What is the point of this if you break your thin, white neck on the first day of our journey? Ha?" Every word burst from him with gusto, while his arms waved about, further demonstrating his vexation.

Rising to her full height, Danielle tipped her head back to look him in the eye. He was taller than the others, darker and more muscular, but she was not afraid of him. They stared at each other, both unwilling to back down, both enjoying the challenge. And then she laughed, not to defy or to taunt. She laughed for laughter's sake, reveling in the exhilarating rush of being alive and free.

# Epilogue



*Three months later, July 1653*

Sebastiaan prowled the dockside like a tiger in a menagerie. His ships had finally arrived last week. Now all three lay at anchor, their ropes creaking as they gently bobbed on the ripples in the Batavian harbor.

In less than a week, he would set sail for the Cape of Good Hope to collect Danielle and marry the woman once and for all. The three months at sea, after his rescue, had cured his wounds and cleansed his soul as much as it was possible. There were scars that would never heal and with those, he'd made peace.

The *Annabella*, his flagship, the *Danielle*, his heart's desire, and the *Abigaille*, named after the baby girl, who'd lost her short life at the hands of pirates, were patiently waiting for their crews to finish loading their hulls with anything a new settlement would need, from building supplies, tools, carts, blankets, silver cutlery, to flour and stockings. He was not about to arrive empty-handed.

Like the *Annabella*, the *Danielle* and the *Abigaille*, collectively known as the *Twins*, were fast and armed to the teeth. He was not taking any chances on this voyage; the three ships and their crews were a force to be reckoned with. Their guns stood proud as they lined the deck, and the *Twins* came with a special surprise. Each housed a sixteen-foot, twenty-ton cannon in her hull, ready to be hoisted to a special gun port opening just above the waterline with a compound pulley and crank system that would make Archimedes' toes curl. They fired a stone cannonball, roughly as wide as a grown man's knee is high, designed to knock over castle walls, and capable of putting a hole right through an enemy ship and the one hiding behind it.

"When is that cantankerous old devil arriving?" Arent asked as he joined

Sebastiaan on the wooden boardwalk.

"He docked early this morning. Our soon-to-be third captain is currently at the VOC office, tendering his resignation." Sebastiaan replied with a smug smile.

With his deep pockets and his uncle's wide reputation, they could crew each ship with the best in the business and be left spoiled for choice. On this voyage, Sebastiaan would captain the *Danielle*, and De Coninck the *Annabella*; only the *Abigaille* was still short a captain but if all went according to plan that vacancy would soon be filled.

"What are two soft boys like you doing playing around docks like these? Do your mothers know you're not home?" The man's voice still carried like the naval captain he used to be before the VOC poached him. He was nearing his sixties but held the vitality and vigor of one half his age. His tall frame was robust and bulky, but deep lines marred the once youthful face. Although the eyes were still sharp, they held the tinge of wisdom only afforded by age and the once bright copper red hair was now muted, shot through with strands of silver that glimmered in the sunlight.

"Captain Hooghsaet," Arent greeted him with laughter, and the two men clasped forearms in a show of brotherhood. "I was worried you got lost."

"Lost?" Hooghsaet roared with laughter, "No lad, you're confusing me with that poor woman you had warming your bed last night."

"Not bloody likely," Arent replied under his breath.

"Captain De Vries," Hooghsaet said, before he gathered Sebastiaan in a tight bear hug.

Hooghsaet released Sebastiaan but held him at arm's length while studying him with narrowed eyes. Sebastiaan returned the inquisitive stare with a hard one of his own.

"Ha!" Hooghsaet exclaimed, pleased with what he saw. "You'll do. Now, where is my ship?"

The three men walked a few yards down the docks until they reached the second of the two new ships. The *Abigaille* was sleek and beautiful, her lines clean and crisp. She was practically glowing with the morning light bouncing off her fresh paint.

"Oh, but she is a beauty," Hooghsaet crooned reverently, as he stroked the thick rope that tied her to the docks, much like one would the nose of a beloved horse.

"What about the crew?" he asked, raising his silver eyes to the busy deck.

"Worst of the worst," Arent replied. "We scraped them from the filthiest of back alleys and peeled them from the seediest of brothels."

"Oh, I like me a challenge," Hooghsaet applauded and backslapped Arent with enthusiasm. "When are we leaving?" he asked Sebastiaan.

"As soon as the loading is done. Hopefully, within the week."

"Aye lad, we'll be ready," Hooghsaet said and then marched up the gangplank without so much as a backward glance.

"You do know that loading the ships has just become a competition," Arent said as he and Sebastiaan turned toward the warehouse.

"Yes, and we've just lost."

Hooghsaet raised spirits, efficiency, and discipline wherever he set foot. If there were men at work and he happened upon them, he would make them perform better and faster no matter the task.

Arent heaved a deep sigh, shoved his hands in his pockets and said: "Brother." Sebastiaan stopped walking. He knew that tone; whatever was eating at Arent was about to breathe fresh air. "I need to beg a favor."

Sebastiaan frowned at his friend's choice of words.

"Tell me what you need and never use those words again. I owe you my life, Arent."

Arent ducked his head and looked at Sebastiaan from beneath his eyebrows.

"There is something I must do." Sebastiaan nodded, waiting for the rest to unfold. "After we've collected Danielle, I need to go to Zanzibar. There is a woman, currently a slave of Oliveira." Sebastiaan winced. He remembered the oily trader well. "Her name is Sakura."

"We will free her," Sebastiaan said, before Arent could finish. The pained expression on his friend's face was twisting his heart.

"He might sell her before I can get to her, so it could be a waste of time." Arent's shoulders dropped as he spoke his greatest fear, the one that had him tossing and turning at night.

"Then we'll find her. We will search until we find her. It's that simple."

"Thank you," Arent said. The matter aired and resolved.

"Steel yourself. Trouble is coming our way," Sebastiaan warned and pointed down the wharf to where two boys were racing toward their intended target, dodging loaded carts, double stepping around stacked goods, and pushing sailors out of the way. The chorus of grunts and threats of violence followed the two rapscallions until they came to a skidding halt before Arent and Sebastiaan.

"I win!" Orion shouted, hopping in a circle on one leg and swinging his arms.

"You cheated," Jiya protested, "and stop that. You're going to summon the rain and this place is already as wet as a baby's arse."

It had taken the two boys only a few minutes, from the moment they'd met, to decide that they were actually long-lost brothers. No matter the fact that they hailed from different parents and the one was distinctly Arabic in appearance and the other African. The two had been inseparable since.

"Cap wants to speak to you," Orion said as he took Sebastiaan's hand and began to pull him away.

"He's waiting for you on the Annabella," Jiya said, cutting Orion off before he robbed him of his share of the message.

When Sebastiaan stepped onboard his flagship, his heart beat a little deeper. She was as beautiful as the morning light.

"Lukas," he called to the boatswain. His friend greeted him with a crisp salute, followed by an obscene hand gesture. "Put these two to work before they upend the entire wharf."

Sebastiaan turned his back on the sulking boys and headed for the stateroom. Lukas was the best of babysitters. By the end of a day under his care and tutelage, the boys would still be cheerful but swaying from exhaustion. Sebastiaan rapped a crisp knock on the door and entered.

De Coninck was standing by the bank of windows, facing the door, his back turned away from the day outside.

"Uncle?" Sebastiaan asked, instantly weary, for the older man's face was devoid of any emotion—not a good sign.

De Coninck released his breath, unfolded his arms, and pushed away from the wall.

"I received a letter this morning," he said and pointed to the piece of parchment on his desk.

Sebastiaan paused, expecting more. "And?"

"It's from Governor Van Riebeeck," De Coninck said. "You need to sit down."

Sebastiaan's breath shook on the exhale. His hands felt tingly, and he curled his fingers to stop the slight tremor, but he remained standing.

"Read it," De Coninck said as he lifted the letter from where it rested on top of the journals and ledger books and held it out to Sebastiaan.

*April 30, A.D. 1653*

*To Captain Davit De Coninck, De Vries Enterprises, BATAVIA*

*From Governor Johan Van Riebeeck, Cape of Good Hope, AFRICA*

*Captain Davit De Coninck,*

*I hope this letter finds you in good health, although the circumstances surrounding it are far from ordinary. I am writing to you with great sadness to inform you of a deeply distressing matter regarding Miss Danielle Van Aard.*

*She went missing two weeks ago. After exhaustive search efforts from the entire community, we were unable to locate her. It is, therefore, with a heavy heart that I must conclude and accept that she has lost her life in the wilderness of this rugged land.*

*Yours sincerely*

*Johan A. Van Riebeeck*

Sebastiaan stared at the words. He read the letter once more before slowly closing his fist around it and crumpling it into a tight ball.

De Coninck saw his eyes glaze over and his face turn deathly pale. He'd come so far in such a short time and was nearly the man he used to be. His enslavement had robbed him of his boyish enthusiasm and had turned him into a quiet, contemplative version of his former golden, self—damaged, but unbroken. However, those few lines written in Van Riebeeck's artistic hand, held more power than all his slave masters combined. That godforsaken letter could be the final straw to shatter the man before him.

Sebastiaan stood unblinking and utterly still. De Coninck couldn't even see his chest move with his breath. He looked like he was carved from marble, with hard and unforgiving lines, but De Coninck feared he was more like a statue built of sand which would collapse into a heap with only a gentle touch or the whisper of a breeze.

"Sebastiaan?" he asked after a while.

Sebastiaan heard his name as if it was spoken from across a great distance, rolling toward him like a sandstorm across the desert; and then it hit.

"This!" he shouted, hurling the ball of parchment into the far corner of the cabin where it bounced off the wall, "This is nothing but a waste of parchment, ink and time." His anger lit like a bush fire, and he planned on letting it burn.

"He *concluded?*" his voice thundered through the room, and De Coninck took a step back. "What the hell does that mean? Who does he think he is? God?"

"Sebastiaan," De Coninck tried, but was brutally cut short.

"No. That letter means nothing. All it says is that he doesn't know where she is and that he is too stupid or inept to find her."

The inferno the letter had lit inside Sebastiaan was turning the serious but normally calm man of late into something quite the opposite. His eyes were glowing, his skin was flushed, and his muscles were tense and bulging, ready to act. The last vestiges of the slave were burning away right before De Coninck's eyes and when his nephew looked at him, his gaze held the force of a fist driving home.

"There you are. Welcome back," De Coninck said, trying to keep his emotions under control, fearing he was failing miserably. The time had come to push the lad a little further into the light, and he was just the man to do it.

De Coninck chose his next words carefully and then released them without mercy. "Regardless of the governor's lack of intellect or abilities, the possibility still exists that she might be …" He bit his tongue, even he couldn't say the words, but there was no time to ponder or search for better ones, for Sebastiaan was advancing on him like a bull in full charge.

De Coninck stepped further back, but he realized the wall was fast approaching behind him and so he swiftly grabbed the heavy chair and inserted it between them. There was the distinct possibility he'd pushed the boy too far.

"Don't you say those words," Sebastiaan warned. "I will not have it. She is not dead."

"How can you be so sure?" De Coninck asked once a healthy distance stretched between them.

Sebastiaan's shoulders lost some of the tension that had them in a vice-like grip moments earlier, and he raked a hand through his hair.

"Because *my* heart is still beating," he said, stabbing himself with a forefinger in the chest. "I am going to find her. If it takes the rest of my life, I don't care," he vowed firmly.

"You might end up chasing a ghost," De Coninck warned.

"Uncle," Sebastiaan countered, "have you ever just known that something is true, without evidence or proof?"

De Coninck didn't respond, but the answer must have shown in his unblinking eyes, for Sebastiaan's stance relaxed and the tension left his body.

"I know you understand. Because if it was not for chasing that ghost, I would not be standing here. I refuse to be jealous of the man I used to be and will not spend the rest of my life wallowing in regret." Sebastiaan made for the door but paused in the middle of the room and turned back to face his uncle.

"Light a fire under the crew's arses. Ready or not, we leave tomorrow morning. I am bringing her home."

# THE END

# Acknowledgments

First, and most importantly, I'd like to thank my readers for their support. We are all writers until someone buys our book, then we become authors. So, thank you for making me an author and allowing me to live my dream. I hope you enjoyed Danielle and Sebastiaan's journeys.

Next, I wish to thank my daughter Esti, the most talented writer I've ever known, currently working on her first five books. I can't wait to see which one is going to make it to the finish line first. Without you, I would never have been able to finish this book, nor any other. You are an absolute rock; your patience, support, and creative insights are second to none.

Thank you to my husband for your boundless love and support and for providing honest, constructive, and invaluable feedback. You are always ready to share a laugh, craft an idea or lend a very wide shoulder to cry on when the mood strikes.

Thank you, Liam, for being everything good and true that lives in the heart of all boys who grow to become breathtaking men. No matter how strong or tall you grow, never forget that you will always be my little boy, and I love you.

Louise Wesson, my editor, you are a gem! Thank you for the hard work and dedication you put into this project. I know you've spent many hours working late into the night and I appreciate it. By the way, you will note that someone had only once *"gained his feet"* in this book, everybody else merely stood up.

To Professor Adam Nichols—thank you for your support and willingness to share your bottomless wealth of knowledge about the Barbary Slave Trade. Despite being busy with your students, and without knowing me from Eve, you still took the time to answer all my questions, pointed me in the right direction and provided me with resources.

Finally, to Donna Pelot, for inspiring me to add the epilogue to this book. I had a different ending in mind, but she'd read the first book in the series and was not at all happy with the ending and so I figured, perhaps I should soften my approach to endings and end this one with *hope*.

# Interview with the Author

**Q: This book is the second book in the *Good Hope Trilogy*, but the pace feels very different from the first. Was that intentional?**

A: No. I did the research for the book and tried to keep it as true to history as I could, but then I noticed it was a touch too slow. So, I reworked it, still staying true to the story but adding little bits of spice and a lot of other things, not so nice, and from there it took on a life of its own.

Personally, I'm not a fan of slow-paced books. I want to be exhausted when I'm done with a book; emotionally, physically — like a train has hit me. I think my taste in books bled through in writing this one, especially now that I'm more comfortable with how I write, and the entire process is not so new anymore.

**Q: Van Riebeeck's journal prompted the idea for the first book. What inspired you this time?**

A: Believe it or not, but the first book only came from a handful of pages of Van Riebeeck's journal. The journal stretched over the first ten years of the settlement. Therefore, there was still a lot of information left to be uncovered.

At the same time, the settlement started at the Cape, in a different part of the world, the Barbary Slave Trade was at its peak I wanted to bring that topic to light as well. Even though it went on for over three hundred years, it's not much talked about and that motivated me to weave it into the plot.

By combining the two parallel events in one book, I hoped to honor the past and create something with depth and substance. Real and ordinary people experienced these horrors, and we should remember their suffering and sacrifice.

**Q: Does this book work as a stand-alone?**

A: Yes, it is possible to read this book as a stand-alone. However, I think reading the first book would serve it better.

**Q: What came first, the plot, or the characters?**

A: This book was very much character driven. Van Riebeeck's journal provided a lot of information but not much variety, so I relied heavily on the characters to color and guide the events.

**Q: You stated the book is inspired by true events. Which key events were real?**

A: First, the living conditions at the Cape of Good Hope were all real. In chapter one, Blanx and Van Leyen's escape, and their subsequent punishments were real. However, I did Jan Blanx a big disservice by writing him as illiterate when, in fact; I relied heavily on the journal he kept during the escape to write the scene.

Second, all the events surrounding Sebastiaan were real, only the Barbary Slave Trade happened in the Mediterranean and not so much on the east coast of Africa. The scene where the baby was tossed overboard was based on an actual event that was witnessed by a priest in Algiers where one of the captors pulled a little girl from her mother's breast and tossed her into a bush, leaving her to die. I felt it was important to mention, so I reworked it to fit my storyline. Just like Antoonie in the first book, this baby girl deserves a place in history. Unfortunately, her real name is unknown.

The scene where Van Riebeeck came dancing with the chief and his men into the fort, Maria's pregnancy, and almost all the events at the Cape with the exclusion of Coopman's scenes were real.

**Q: How do you feel about Van Riebeeck's character evolution?**

A: Van Riebeeck is such an interesting character, and I didn't have to make anything up; it's all true. I love how real he is. He is just a man who shouldered enormous responsibilities, and he was only thirty-three years old at the time. The deck was stacked against him. Getting the settlement going and viable was a near impossible task and that showed in how the governors who came after him struggled and failed. He was harsh and sometimes you truly hated him, but we must caution against judging history from a modern standpoint. He was a good and honorable man who went through challenges that would buckle most. I wanted to show him unvarnished and as true as I could, and in the end, I look back on him with pride. I think he did well. He could have done better, but that is the luxury of hindsight. He could also have done much worse.

There is one very important point that I never got the chance to raise in the book, and I'm going to take this opportunity to do so. Regardless of what the modern version of that time in history claims, Van Riebeeck was always against aggression towards the local tribes. Even though Harry and Van Riebeeck's advisors pushed for warfare against the different groups, he always advocated for peaceful negotiations, and he often had to go behind Harry's back to achieve that goal.

**Q: Which part of the book did you find the most challenging to write?**

A: All of it. This was hard. I was so intimidated by the first book, and afraid that I was a one-trick-pony, that it took me a few months to find my feet again. The weight of the topics I touched on helped. It gave me a sense of direction and purpose.

**Q: Which part of the book did you have the most fun writing?**

A: Any part with De Coninck in it — he is my little guilty pleasure!

**Q: Which of the male characters was your favorite?**

A: My favorite character in this book is Elias Coopman. I honestly don't know what that reveals about me, but he is so deviously dark and troubled. A villain that is just categorically bad, with no endearing traits, is tedious and predictable.

**Q: What about the female characters, who is your favorite?**

A: I struggled a lot to connect with Danielle in the first book. It always felt like she was standing on the outside, looking at me, waiting for me to find her. But this time, I loved how her character developed; how she found her feet, voice, and grit. Even though she went through an incredible experience in this book, she came out on the other end battered and bruised, but stronger. I feel I have a better connection with her this time around.

**Q: Do you have a message for your readers?**

A: I encourage my readers to interact with me on social media so that they know there is a real person behind this process. There is this notion amongst many authors that one should never respond to comments or reviews. I strongly disagree with that. I think it's important to have that person-to-person connection. My greatest dream has always been to create a community where we can have discussions and I can bounce ideas off and get feedback from, and somehow have my readers shape my work. I love to write with them in mind and have them be part of the process.

# Also by C.M. O'Neill

**Good Hope**

Book 1 - *Cape of Storms Trilogy*

**An exciting and gripping new historical adventure drama.**

In the shadow of 17th-century Holland's bustling harbors, where the Dutch East India Company's sails promise fortune and peril, young physician's assistant Danielle Van Aard witnesses a nightmare that shatters her world. When a ruthless captain murders her father for refusing to aid his opium smuggling empire, Danielle flees for her life—only to stow away aboard the *Drommedaris*, bound for the untamed Cape of Good Hope.

Trapped on a treacherous voyage inspired by true historical events from Governor Van Riebeeck's journals, Danielle battles fierce storms, devastating illnesses, and the suspicions of a strict captain. But amid the chaos, she finds unlikely allies: the chivalrous Sebastiaan De Vries, who risks everything to protect her, and the resilient Maria Van Riebeeck, wife of the expedition's leader. As dysentery ravages the settlers and tense encounters with local tribes test fragile alliances, Danielle's medical skills become a beacon of hope—stitching wounds, defying danger, and forging bonds that could reshape destinies.

Blending heart-pounding adventure, tender romance, and the raw grit of survival, **Good Hope** is a riveting tale of one woman's transformation from fugitive to healer in a new world. Based on real events and serving as a strong opener to a trilogy brimming with authenticity, this must-read historical fiction captures the dawn of a colony—and the unbreakable spirit that built it. **Good Hope** appeals to readers who crave epic, character-driven historical dramas with intellectual weight and emotional resonance. Perfect for fans of *The Nightingale's* emotional depth, *Outlander's* bold heroines, or *Master and Commander's* nautical thrills, **Good Hope** delivers a fresh, intense historical adventure with a powerful female lead.

Will Danielle's courage and daring forge a new destiny—or will it lead to her undoing?

**Blood of the Covenant**

Book 3 - *Cape of Storms Trilogy*

**Blood determines relation. Loyalty determines family.**

For the last 17 years, a shadow has tormented the African coast, leaving nothing but carnage and rumor in his wake.

Sebastiaan De Vries is finally ready for a quiet, uneventful life. After years of searching for the woman he lost, he returns to the Cape of Good Hope, battle-worn and empty-handed, to be closer to her memory. His newfound peace evaporates when he encounters a boy who bears his name and he is forced to reckon with fatherhood.

Thrown into a web of corruption spun by an old and vengeful enemy with a deep score to settle, Sebastiaan stands to lose the little he has gained.